Also by
Graeme Macrae Burnet

The Disappearance of Adèle Bedeau

His Bloody Project

Documents Relating to the Case of
Roderick Macrae

A NOVEL

Edited and introduced by

Graeme Macrae Burnet

CONTRABAND ⊘

Contraband is an imprint of Saraband
Published by Saraband,
Suite 202, 98 Woodlands Road,
Glasgow, G3 6HB,
Scotland
www.saraband.net

ISBN: 9781910192665
ebook: 9781910192153

Printed and bound in Great Britain by Clays Ltd, St Ives plc.

10 9 8 7 6 5 4 3 2 1

Contents

The quern performs best when
the grindstone has been pitted.

Highland proverb

Preface

I am writing this at the behest of my advocate, Mr Andrew Sinclair, who since my incarceration here in Inverness has treated me with a degree of civility I in no way deserve. My life has been short and of little consequence, and I have no wish to absolve myself of responsibility for the deeds which I have lately committed. It is thus for no other reason than to repay my advocate's kindness towards me that I commit these words to paper.

So begins the memoir of Roderick Macrae, a seventeen-year-old crofter, indicted on the charge of three brutal murders carried out in his native village of Culduie in Ross-shire on the morning of the 10th of August 1869.

It is not my intention to unduly detain the reader, but a few prefatory remarks may provide a little context to the material collected here. Those readers who prefer to proceed directly to the documents themselves are of course free to do so.

In the spring of 2014, I embarked on a project to find out a little about my grandfather, Donald 'Tramp' Macrae, who was born in 1890 in Applecross, two or three miles north of Culduie. It was in the course of my research at the Highland Archive Centre in Inverness that I came across some newspaper clippings describing the trial of Roderick Macrae, and with the assistance of Anne O'Hanlon, the archivist there, discovered the manuscript which comprises the largest part of this volume.

By any measure, Roderick Macrae's memoir is a remarkable document. It was written in the gaol at Inverness Castle approximately between the 17th of August and the 5th of September 1869, while Roderick awaited trial. It was the existence of the memoir, rather than the murders themselves, which turned the case into something of a cause célèbre. The memoir – or at least the most sensational parts of it – was later reprinted in countless chapbooks or 'penny dreadfuls' and provoked great controversy.

Many, especially among the literati of Edinburgh, doubted its authenticity. Roderick's account revived memories of the *Ossian* scandal of the late eighteenth century in which James Macpherson claimed to have discovered and translated the great epic of Gaelic poetry. *Ossian* quickly assumed the status of a classic of European literature, but was later found to have been a fake. For Campbell Balfour, writing in the *Edinburgh Review*, it was 'quite inconceivable that a semi-literate peasant could produce such a sustained and eloquent piece of writing ... The work is a hoax and those who extol this most pitiless murderer as some kind of noble savage will in time be left red-faced.'* For others, both the murders and the memoir attested to the 'terrible barbarism which continues to thrive in the northern regions of our country [and which] all the efforts of our dedicated presbytery and the great improvements† of the past decades have failed to eradicate.'‡

For yet others, however, the events described in the memoir provided evidence of the injustice of the feudal conditions under which the Highland crofter continued to toil. While taking care not to condone his actions, John Murdoch, who was later to establish the radical newspaper *The Highlander*, saw in Roderick Macrae 'a figure driven to the edge of his reason – or beyond – by the cruel system which make slaves of men who wish only to eke an honest living from a borrowed patch of land.'§

As to the authenticity of the document, it is not possible, a century and a half later, to provide a definitive answer. It is without doubt remarkable that anyone so young could produce such

---

* *Campbell Balfour, 'Our Century's Ossian',* Edinburgh Review, *October 1869, No. CCLXVI.*
† *This is a reference to the Highland Clearances.*
‡ *Editorial, the* Scotsman, *17 September 1869.*
§ *John Murdoch, 'What we might learn from this case',* Inverness Courier, *14 September 1869.*

an eloquent account. However, the idea that Roderick Macrae was a 'semi-literate peasant' is a product of the prejudice which continued to exist towards the north in the affluent cities of the Central Belt. The curriculum of the nearby Lochcarron primary school from the 1860s records that children were instructed in Latin, Greek and science. Roderick could have expected a similar education at his school in Camusterrach and his memoir attests both to this and to the fact that he was an uncommonly gifted pupil. The fact that Roderick *could* have written the memoir does not, of course, prove that he did. For this we have the evidence of the psychiatrist, James Bruce Thomson, whose own memoir attests to having seen the document in Roderick's cell. Sceptics could (and did) aver that Thomson never actually saw Roderick write anything, and it must be admitted that, were the memoir to be submitted to a modern trial, the chain of evidence could not be wholly verified. The idea that the memoir was actually written by another hand (the chief suspect being Roderick's advocate, Andrew Sinclair) cannot entirely be dismissed, but it requires the convoluted thinking of the most outré conspiracy theorist to believe this to be the case. Then there is the content of the document itself, which contains such a wealth of detail that it is scarcely plausible that it was not written by a native of Culduie. Furthermore, Roderick's account of the events leading up to the murders did, with some minor exceptions, largely tally with the evidence of other witnesses at the trial. For these reasons, and having examined the manuscript first-hand, I have no doubts as to its authenticity.

In addition to Roderick Macrae's account, this volume also includes the police statements of various residents of Culduie; the post-mortem reports on the victims; and, perhaps most fascinatingly of all, an extract from J. Bruce Thomson's memoir, *Travels in the Border-Lands of Lunacy,* in which he recounts his examination of Roderick Macrae and a visit he made to Culduie in the company of Andrew Sinclair. Thomson was the Resident Surgeon in charge of the General Prison for Scotland at Perth, where those deemed unfit to stand trial on grounds of insanity were housed. Mr Thomson put the opportunity this position afforded him to good use, publishing two influential articles – 'The Hereditary Nature of Crime' and 'The Psychology of Criminals' – in the *Journal of Mental Science*. He was well-versed in the new theory of evolution and the still nascent discipline of Criminal Anthropology, and while some of the views expressed might be unpalatable to the modern reader, it is worth bearing in mind the context in which they were written, and that they represent a genuine effort to move beyond a theological view of criminality and reach a better understanding of why certain individuals come to commit violent crimes.

Finally, I have included an account of the trial, drawn from contemporary newspaper coverage and the book *A Complete Report of the Trial of Roderick John Macrae*, published by William Kay of Edinburgh in October 1869.

It is not possible, almost a century and a half later, to know the truth of the events recounted in this volume. The accounts presented here contain various discrepancies, contradictions and omissions, but taken together they form a tapestry of one of the most fascinating cases in Scottish legal history. Naturally I have come to my own view of the case, but I shall leave it to the reader to reach his or her own conclusions.

A note on the text

As far as I have been able to ascertain, this is the first time Roderick Macrae's memoir has been published in its entirety. Despite the passage of time and the fact that for some years it was not stored with any great care, the manuscript is in remarkably good condition. It was written on loose sheets and at some later point bound with leather strings, this being evidenced by the fact that the text on the inner edge of the pages is sometimes obscured by the binding. The handwriting is admirably clear with only the most occasional crossings-out and false starts. In preparing the document for publication, I strived at all times to be true to the sense of the manuscript. At no point did I attempt to 'improve' the text or correct awkward turns of phrase or syntax. Such interventions would, I think, only serve to cast doubt on the authenticity of the work. What is presented is, as far as possible, the work of Roderick Macrae. Some of the vocabulary used may be unfamiliar to some readers, but rather than overburden the text with footnotes, I have opted to include a short glossary at the end of this section. It is also worth pointing out that throughout the memoir individuals' real names and nicknames are used interchangeably – Lachlan Mackenzie, for example, is generally referred to as Lachlan Broad. The use of nicknames remains common in the Scottish Highlands – at least among the older generation – probably as a way of distinguishing between different branches of the most widespread family names. Nicknames are commonly based on professions or eccentricities, but they can also be passed on from one generation to the next to the point where the origin of the name becomes a mystery even to its holder.

I have largely restricted my editorial interventions to matters of punctuation and paragraphing. The manuscript is written in one unbroken stream, save perhaps for moments at which Roderick took up his pen from one day to the next. I took the decision to introduce paragraphs for the sake of readability. Similarly, the text is largely unpunctuated, or eccentrically so. Thus, the majority of the punctuation is mine, but again, my guiding principle was to be true to the original. If my judgements in this seem questionable, I can only direct the reader to consult the manuscript, which remains in the archive at Inverness.

GMB, July 2015

Statements

gathered from various residents of Culduie and the surrounding area by Officer William MacLeod of Wester Ross police force, Dingwall, on the 12th and 13th of August 1869

Statement of Mrs Carmina Murchison [Carmina Smoke], resident of Culduie, 12th August 1869

I have known Roderick Macrae since he was an infant. I generally found him to be a pleasant child and later to be a courteous and obliging young man. I believe he was greatly affected by the death of his mother, who was a charming and gregarious woman. While I do not wish to speak ill of his father, John Macrae is a disagreeable person, who treated Roddy with a degree of severity I do not believe any child deserves.

On the morning of the dreadful incident, I spoke to Roddy as he passed our house. I cannot recall the precise content of our conversation, but I believe he told me that he was on his way to carry out some work on land belonging to Lachlan Mackenzie. He was carrying some tools, which I took to be for this purpose. In addition, we exchanged some remarks about the weather, it being a fine and sunny morning. Roderick appeared quite composed and betrayed no sign of fretfulness. Sometime later, I saw Roddy make his way back along the village. He was covered from head to foot in blood and I ran from the threshold of my house, thinking that some accident had befallen him. As I approached, he stopped and the tool he was carrying dropped from his hand. I asked what had happened and he replied without hesitation that he had killed Lachlan Broad. He appeared quite lucid and made no attempt to continue along the road. I called to my eldest daughter to fetch her father, who was working in the outbuilding behind our house. On seeing Roddy covered in blood, she screamed, and this brought other residents of the village to their doors and caused those at work on their crops to look up from their labour. There was very quickly a general commotion. I confess that in these moments my first instinct was to protect Roddy from the kinsmen of Lachlan Mackenzie. For this reason, when my husband arrived at the scene, I asked him to take Roddy inside our house without telling him what had occurred. Roddy was seated at our table and calmly repeated what he had done. My husband sent our daughter to fetch our neighbour, Duncan Gregor, to stand guard and then ran to Lachlan Mackenzie's house, where he discovered the tragic scene.

Statement of Mr Kenneth Murchison [Kenny Smoke], stonemason, resident of Culduie, 12th August 1869

On the morning in question I was working in my outbuilding behind my house, when I heard a general commotion from the village. I emerged from my workshop to be greeted by my eldest daughter, who was greatly distressed and unable to properly inform me of what had occurred. I ran towards the congregation of people outside our house. Amid the confusion, my wife and I took Roderick Macrae into our house, believing that he had been injured in some accident. Once inside my wife informed me of what had occurred and when I asked Roderick if this was true he repeated quite calmly that it was. I then ran to the home of Lachlan Mackenzie and found a scene too dreadful to describe. I closed the door behind me and examined the bodies for signs of life, of which there were none. Fearing a general outbreak of violence, were any of Lachlan Broad's kinsmen to lay eyes on this scene, I went outside and summoned Mr Gregor to stand guard over the property. I ran back to my own house and took Roddy from there to my outbuilding, where I barricaded him in. He did not resist. Mr Gregor was unable to prevent Lachlan Broad's kinsmen from entering the premises and seeing the bodies there. By the time I had confined Roddy, they had formed themselves into a vengeful mob, which it took some time and persuasion to subdue.

As to the general character of Roderick Macrae, there is no doubt that he was a queer boy, but whether this was by nature or had been brought on by the tribulations which his family has suffered I am not qualified to say. The evidence of his deeds, however, does not speak of a sound mind.

Statement of the Reverend James Galbraith, minister at the Church of Scotland, Camusterrach, 13th August 1869

I fear the wicked deeds lately committed in this parish only represent a bubbling to the surface of the natural state of savagism of the inhabitants of this place, a savagism that the Church has of late been successful in suppressing. The history of these parts, it has been said, is stained with black and bloody crimes, and its people exhibit a certain wildness and indulgence. Such traits cannot be bred out in a matter of generations, and while the teachings of the Presbytery are a civilising influence, it is inevitable that now and again the old instincts come to the fore.

Nonetheless, one cannot fail to be shocked on hearing of acts such as those committed in Culduie. Of all the individuals in this parish, however, one is least surprised to hear that Roderick Macrae is the perpetrator. Although this individual has attended my church since childhood, I always sensed that my sermons fell on his ears as seeds on stony ground. I must accept that his crimes represent, in some degree, a failure on my part, but sometimes one must sacrifice a lamb for the general good of the flock. There was always a wickedness, easily discernible, about that boy which I regret to say was beyond my reach.

The boy's mother, Una Macrae, was a frivolous and insincere woman. She attended church regularly, but I fear she mistook the Lord's House for a place of social gathering. I frequently heard her singing on her way to and from the kirk and, after service, she would gather within the grounds with other womenfolk and indulge in intemperate conversation and laughter. On more than one occasion I was obliged to reprimand her.

I am compelled, however, to add a word on behalf of Roderick Macrae's father. John Macrae is among the most devoted to scripture in this parish. His knowledge of the Bible is extensive and he is sincere in his observance. In common with the majority in these parts, however, even while he might parrot the words of the Gospel, I fear his understanding of them is feeble. Following the death of Mr Macrae's wife, I visited the household frequently to offer support and prayer. I observed at that time many signs about the place of adherence to superstition, such as have no place in the home of a believer. Nevertheless, while we are none of us blameless, I believe John Macrae to be a good and devout man, who did not deserve to be burdened with such noxious progeny.

Statement of Mr William Gillies, schoolmaster at Camusterrach, 13th August 1869

Roderick Macrae was among the most talented pupils I have taught since my arrival in this parish. He easily outstripped his fellows in his ability to grasp concepts in science, mathematics and language, and this he achieved without show of effort or, indeed, of any great interest. As to his character, I can offer only the most limited remarks. Certainly, he was not of a sociable nature and did not mix readily with his fellows, who, in turn, regarded him with some suspicion. For his own part, Roderick behaved with disdain towards his classmates, this at times bordering on contempt. Were I to speculate, I would say this attitude was bred by his academic superiority. That said, I always found him to be a courteous and respectful pupil, not given to unruly behaviour. As a mark of my high regard for his academic gifts, when he was sixteen years old, I called on his father to suggest that Roderick should continue his studies and might, in time, amount to something more suited to his abilities than working the land. I regret to say that my proposal received short shrift from his father, who I found to be a reticent and slow-witted individual.

I have not seen Roderick since that time. I heard some disturbing rumours about his mistreatment of a sheep under his charge, but I cannot testify as to their veracity, other than to state that I found Roderick to be a gentle lad, not given to the cruel behaviour sometimes found in boys of that age. For this reason I find it difficult to credit that he might be capable of carrying out the crimes with which he has recently been charged.

Statement of Peter Mackenzie, first cousin of Lachlan Mackenzie [Lachlan Broad], resident of Culduie, 12th August 1869

Roderick Macrae is as wicked an individual as one could ever have the misfortune to meet. Even as a small boy there was a mean spirit about him, such as one would not credit in a child. He was for many years thought to be mute and capable only of some uncanny commune with his otherworldly sister, who seemed his partner in wickedness. He was generally regarded in the parish as an imbecile, but I myself reckoned him an altogether more malicious creature, and his recent exploits have borne out this view. From an early age he was given to the spiteful mistreatment of animals and birds, and to arbitrary acts of destruction around the village. He had the Devil's own cunning. On one occasion, when he was perhaps twelve years old, a fire was set in the outbuilding of my cousin Aeneas Mackenzie, destroying a number of valuable tools and a quantity of grain. The boy had been seen in the vicinity of the building, but he denied responsibility and the Black Macrae [his father, John Macrae] swore that his son had not been out of his sight at the time in question. He thus escaped punishment, but as with many other incidents, there was no doubt that he was to blame. His father is likewise a feeble-minded individual, who conceals his idiocy behind a zealous adherence to scripture and a cringing deference to the minister.

I was not present in Culduie on the day of the murders and heard about them only on my return that evening.

Map *of Culduie and the Surrounding Area*
after Ordnance Survey Map of 1875 *by Capt. MacPherson, engraved* 1878

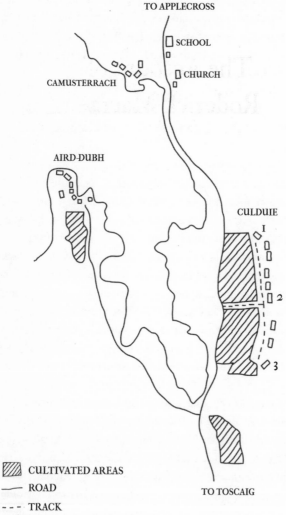

TO APPLECROSS

SCHOOL

CHURCH

CAMUSTERRACH

AIRD-DUBH

CULDUIE

1

2

3

CULTIVATED AREAS

ROAD

TRACK

1 HOUSE OF RODERICK MACRAE
2 HOUSE OF KENNETH MURCHISON
3 HOUSE OF LACHLAN MACKENZIE

TO TOSCAIG

The Account of
Roderick Macrae

I AM WRITING THIS AT THE BEHEST OF MY ADVOCATE, Mr Andrew Sinclair, who since my incarceration here in Inverness has treated me with a degree of civility I in no way deserve. My life has been short and of little consequence, and I have no wish to absolve myself of responsibility for the deeds which I have lately committed. It is thus for no other reason than to repay my advocate's kindness towards me that I commit these words to paper.

Mr Sinclair has instructed me to set out, with as much clarity as possible, the circumstances surrounding the murder of Lachlan Mackenzie and the others, and this I will do to the best of my ability, apologising in advance for the poverty of my vocabulary and rudeness of style.

I shall begin by saying that I carried out these acts with the sole purpose of delivering my father from the tribulations he has lately suffered. The cause of these tribulations was our neighbour, Lachlan Mackenzie, and it was for the betterment of my family's lot that I have removed him from this world. I should further state that since my own entry into the world, I have been nothing but a blight to my father and my departure from his household can only be a blessing to him.

My name is Roderick John Macrae. I was born in 1852 and have lived all my days in the village of Culduie in Ross-shire. My father, John Macrae, is a crofter of good standing in the parish, who does not deserve to be tarnished with the ignominy of the actions for which I alone am responsible. My mother, Una, was born in 1832 in the township of Toscaig, some two miles south of Culduie. She died in the birthing of my brother, Iain, in 1868, and it is this event which, in my mind, marks the beginning of our troubles.

* * *

Culduie is a township of nine houses, situated in the parish of Applecross. It lies half a mile or so south of Camusterrach where the church and the school in which I received my education are located. On account of the inn and the emporium in the village of Applecross, few travellers venture as far as Culduie. At the head of

Applecross Bay is the Big House, where Lord Middleton resides, and during the sporting season entertains his guests. There are no spectacles or entertainments to detain visitors in Culduie. The road past our township leads to Toscaig and to nowhere beyond, and in consequence we have little contact with the outside world.

Culduie is set back some three hundred yards from the sea and nestles at the foot of Càrn nan Uaighean. Between the village and the road is a tract of fertile ground, which is cultivated by the people. Higher into the mountains are the summer grazings and the peat bogs that supply us with our fuel. Culduie is somewhat protected from the worst of the climate by the Aird-Dubh peninsula, which projects into the sea, forming a natural harbour. The village of Aird-Dubh is poorly served with arable land and the people there are mostly concerned with fishing for their livelihoods. A certain amount of exchange of labour and goods takes place between these two communities, but, aside from such necessary contact, we keep our distance from one another. According to my father, Aird-Dubh folk are slovenly in their habits and of low morals, and he has dealings with them only on sufferance. In common with all those engaged in the fishing trade, the men are devoted to the unrestrained consumption of whisky, while their womenfolk are notoriously wanton. Having been schooled with children from this village, I can vouch for the fact that while there is little to distinguish them physically from our own people, they are devious and not to be trusted.

At the junction of the track connecting Culduie to the road is the house of Kenny Smoke, which, being the only one boasting a slate roof, is the finest in the village. The other eight houses are constructed from stones reinforced with turf and have thatch roofs. Each house has one or two glazed windows. My own family's house is the northernmost of the village and sits somewhat at an angle, so that while the other houses look out towards the bay, ours faces the village. The home of Lachlan Broad is situated at the opposite end of the track, and, after that of Kenny Smoke, is the second largest in the village. Aside from those mentioned, the houses are occupied by two further families of the clan Mackenzie; the MacBeath family; Mr and Mrs Gillanders, whose children have all gone; our neighbour Mr Gregor and his family; and Mrs Finlayson, a widow. Aside from the nine houses there are various outbuildings, many of quite rude construction, which are used for housing livestock, storing tools and such like. That is the extent of our community.

Our own house comprises two chambers. The greater part consists of the byre and, to the right of the door, our living quarters. The floor slopes downwards a little towards the sea, which prevents the dung from the animals running into our quarters. The byre is partitioned by a balustrade constructed from scraps of wood gathered from the shore. In the middle of the living area is the fire and, beyond that, the table at which we take our meals. Aside from the table, our furniture consists of two sturdy benches, my father's armchair and a large wooden dresser, which belonged to my mother's family before she was married. I sleep on a bunk with my younger brother and sister at the far end of the room. The second chamber at the back of the house is where my father and elder sister sleep; Jetta in a box-bed my father constructed for this purpose. I am envious of my sister's bed and often dreamt of lying with her there, but it is warmer in the main chamber and in the black months when the animals are indoors, I take pleasure in the soft sounds they make. We keep two milk cows and six sheep, which is what is allowed to us by the division of the common grazings.

I should state from the outset that some bad blood existed between my father and Lachlan Mackenzie long before I was born. I cannot testify to the source of this animosity, for my father has never spoken of it. Nor do I know upon whose side the fault lies; whether this enmity arose in their lifetimes, or is the product of some ancient grudge. In these parts it is not uncommon for grievances to be nursed long after their original source is forgotten. It is to my father's credit that he never endeavoured to perpetuate this feud by proselytising to myself or other members of our family.

For this reason, I believe that he must have wished for whatever grievance existed between our two families to be laid to rest.

As a small boy, I was quite terrified of Lachlan Broad and avoided venturing beyond the junction to the end of the village where the members of the clan Mackenzie are concentrated. In addition to that of Lachlan Broad, there are the families of his brother, Aeneas, and his cousin, Peter, and those three are notorious for their carousing and frequent involvement in altercations at the inn in Applecross. They are all three great powerful fellows, who take pleasure in the knowledge that people step aside to let them pass. On one occasion, when I was five or six years old, I was flying a kite my father had made me from some scraps of sackcloth. The kite plunged into some crops and I ran, quite unthinking, to retrieve it. I was on my knees trying to disentangle the string from among the corn when I felt myself gripped on the shoulder by a great hand and roughly hauled to the track. I was still clutching my kite and Lachlan Broad tore it from me and dashed it to the ground. He then hit me on the side of the head with the flat of his hand, knocking me down. I was so frightened that I lost control of my bladder, causing our neighbour a great deal of mirth. I was then picked up and dragged the length of the village, where Broad berated my father for the damage I had done to his crops. The commotion brought my mother to the door and at this point Broad released me from his grip and I scuttled into the house like a scared dog and cowered in the byre. Later that evening, Lachlan Broad returned to our house and demanded five shillings in compensation for the portion of his crops I had destroyed. I hid in the back chamber with my ear to the door. My mother refused, arguing that if any damage had been done to his crops, it had been caused by him dragging me through his rig. Broad then took his complaint to the constable, who dismissed it. One morning, some days later, my father found that a great portion of our crops had been trampled underfoot overnight. It was not known who carried out this destruction, but no one doubted that it was Lachlan Broad and his kinsmen.

As I grew older, I never entered the lower end of the village without an accompanying sense of foreboding, and this feeling has never left me.

* * *

My father was born in Culduie and lived as a boy in the house in which we now dwell. I know little of his childhood, only that he attended school rarely, and there were hardships such as my generation has not known. I have never seen my father do more than sign his name and, although he insists he can write, a pen sits awkwardly in his fist. He has, in any case, little need for writing. There is nothing he requires to commit to paper. My father is wont to remind us of our good fortune in being brought up in the current times with the luxuries of tea, sugar and other shop-bought goods.

My mother's father was a carpenter who built furniture for merchants in Kyle of Lochalsh and Skye, and sailed his wares round the coast. For some years my father had a third share in a fishing vessel, which anchored in Toscaig. The other parties in this concern were his own brother, Iain, and my mother's brother, whose name was also Iain. The boat was named *The Gannet*, but was always referred to as 'The Two Iains', which irked my father as he was the eldest of the three and, by virtue of this, thought himself head of the enterprise. As a girl, my mother liked to go to the pier to greet The Two Iains. It was assumed that she went to welcome her brother, but her real purpose was to watch my father as he stepped from the boat, his foremost foot hovering above the water as he waited for the swell to propel the vessel to the quay. He would then secure the rope to a bollard and heave the boat to the wall, all this accomplished as if he was quite unaware of being observed. My father was not a handsome man, but the unhurried manner in which he went about the business of tethering the boat drew my mother's admiration. There was something, she liked to tell us, in his flickering dark eyes which set a quickening in her throat. If my father was nearby, he would tell my mother to stop her tittle-tattle, but he did so in a tone which betrayed that he took pleasure in hearing it.

Our mother was the great beauty of the parish and could have had her pick of the young men. In consequence, my father was far too bashful to ever address a word to her. One evening towards the end of the herring season of 1850, a storm broke and the little vessel was smashed against rocks some miles south of the harbour. My father swam to safety but the two Iains were lost. Father never spoke of this incident, but he never again set foot on a boat, nor would he allow his offspring to do so. To those ignorant of this episode in his past, he must have seemed to have an irrational fear of the sea. It is due to this incident that it came to be regarded in these parts as inauspicious to venture into an enterprise with one's namesake. Even my father, who scorns superstition, avoids doing business with anyone who shares his name.

At the gathering following my uncle's funeral, my father approached my mother to offer his condolences. She looked so forlorn that he told her he would gladly take her brother's place in the coffin. These were the first words he had ever addressed to her. My mother replied that she was glad it was he who had survived, and that she had prayed forgiveness for her wicked thoughts. They were married three months later.

My sister Jetta was born within a year of my parents' marriage and I followed from my mother's womb as swiftly as nature allows. This proximity in years bred a closeness between my sister and I which could scarcely have been greater had we been *bona fide* twins. Yet in outward appearance we could hardly have been more different. Jetta had my mother's long slender face and broad mouth. Her eyes, like my mother's, were blue and oval and her hair as yellow as sand. When my sister reached womanhood, folk were wont to comment that when she looked at Jetta, my mother must think she was gazing upon her fetch. For my part, I inherited my father's heavy brow, thick black hair and small dark eyes. We are, moreover, similar in build, being of shorter than average stature, and barrel-chested with wide shoulders.

Likewise in temperament we mirrored our parents, Jetta being quite gay and gregarious, while I was said to be a taciturn and gloomy boy. In addition to her likeness to my mother in appearance and character, Jetta shared with her a great sensitivity to the Other World. Whether she had been born with this gift or had learned it from some secret teachings of my mother I cannot say, but both were prone to visions and were greatly concerned with omens and charms. On the morning of her brother's death, my mother saw an empty place on the bench where he should have been sitting at his breakfast. Fearing that his porridge would grow cold, she went outside and called him. When he did not answer, she went back inside and saw him at his place at the table, shrouded in a pale grey winding sheet. When she asked where he had been he replied that he had been nowhere other than the bench. She begged him not to go to sea that day, but he laughed at her suggestion and, knowing that providence could not be bargained with, she said nothing more about it. Mother often told us this story, but only outwith my father's hearing as he did not believe in such uncanny happenings and did not approve of her speaking of such things.

My mother's daily life was governed by rituals and charms intended to ward off ill fortune and unchancy beings. The doorways and windows of our house were festooned with sprigs of rowan and juniper, and concealed within her hair, so that my father could not see it, she wore a plait of coloured yarns.

During the black months, from the age of eight or so, I attended school at Camusterrach. I walked there each morning hand in hand with Jetta. Our first teacher was Miss Galbraith, who was the daughter of the minister. She was young and slender and wore long skirts and a white chemise with a ruff at her neck, secured at the throat by a brooch depicting a woman's profile. She wore an apron tied around her waist, which she used to clean her hands after she had been writing on the blackboard. Her neck was very long and when she was thinking she would cast her eyes upwards and tip her head to the side so that it made a curve like the handle of a cas chrom. She wore her hair secured on top of her head with pins. While we were at our lessons, she would let her hair down and hold the pins in her mouth while she fastened it back up. She did this three or four times a day and I took pleasure in secretly observing her. Miss Galbraith was kind and spoke in a soft voice. When the older boys did not behave, she had great trouble quietening them and only succeeded in doing so by threatening to fetch her father.

Jetta and I were quite inseparable. Miss Galbraith often commented that I would climb inside the pocket of my sister's apron if I could. For the first few years I spoke very infrequently. If Miss Galbraith or one of my classmates addressed me, Jetta would answer on my behalf. What was remarkable was the accuracy with which she expressed my thoughts. Miss Galbraith indulged this habit and would often ask Jetta, 'Does Roddy know the answer?' This closeness between us isolated us from our peers. I cannot speak for Jetta, but I felt no desire to befriend any of the other children and they showed no desire to befriend me.

Sometimes our classmates would gather round us in the playground and chant:

Here stand the Black Macraes, the dirty Black Macraes.
Here stand the Black Macraes, the filthy Black Macraes.

The 'Black Macraes' was the nickname given to my father's family, on account, he claimed, of their swarthy colouring. Father greatly disliked this designation and refused to answer if someone addressed him in this way. Nevertheless, he was known to everyone as the Black Macrae and it was a source of amusement in the village that, given my mother's flaxen hair, she came to be known as Una Black.

I too disliked this name and felt it to be a particular injustice that it was attached to my sister. If our classmates' chants were not interrupted by the end of the break, I would strike out at whoever was in front of me, an act which only served to increase the glee of our tormentors. I would be pushed to the ground and accept the kicks and blows of the other boys, happy to have diverted attention from Jetta.

Roddy Black, Roddy Black, the imbecile is on his back!

Strangely, it pleased me to be the centre of attention in this way. I understood that I was different from my peers and I cultivated the very characteristics which set me apart from them. During breaks, in order to free Jetta from the taunts, I detached myself from her and stood or crouched in a corner of the playground. I observed the other boys, buzzing round like flies, chasing balls or fighting with each other. The girls too engaged in games, but these seemed less violent and stupid than those of the boys. Neither did they have such a mania to commence them as soon as they spilled onto the playground or continue after Miss Galbraith rang the bell to end the break. At times, the girls were quite calm and gathered in a sheltered corner to do nothing more than converse in hushed voices. Sometimes, I sought out their company, but was invariably shunned. In the classroom I inwardly mocked my fellows as they thrust their arms into the air to provide the teacher with the answer to the most obvious questions or struggled to read the simplest sentences. As we grew older, my knowledge began to surpass that of my sister. One day, during a lesson in geography, Miss Galbraith asked if anyone could tell her the name for the two halves of the earth. When nobody answered, she turned to Jetta: 'Perhaps Roddy knows the answer.' Jetta looked at me and then replied, 'I'm sorry. Roddy does not know and nor do I.' Miss Galbraith looked disappointed and turned to write the word on the board. Without thinking I stood up from my chair and shouted, 'Hemisphere!' to the laughter of my classmates. Miss Galbraith turned round and I repeated the word as I resumed my seat. The teacher nodded and complimented me on my answer. From that day Jetta ceased to speak for me, and being reluctant to do so for myself, I became quite cut off.

Miss Galbraith married a man who had come to Lord Middleton's estate for the shooting, and left Camusterrach to live in Edinburgh. I liked Miss Galbraith a great deal and was sorry when she left. After that came Mr Gillies. He was a young man, tall and thin, with wispy, fair hair. He was not at all like the men from these parts, who are mostly short and stocky with thick black hair. He was clean-shaven and wore oval spectacles. Mr Gillies was a very educated man, who had studied in the city of Glasgow. As well as reading, writing and calculation, he gave us lessons in science and history, and sometimes in the afternoon, he would tell us stories about the monsters and gods of Greek mythology. Each of the gods had a name and some were married and had children who were also gods. One day I asked Mr Gillies how there could be more than one God and he said that the Greek gods were not gods like our God. They were just immortal beings. Mythology was a word which meant that something was not really true; they were just stories to be enjoyed.

My father did not like Mr Gillies. He was too clever for his own good and teaching children was not proper work for a man. It is true that I cannot imagine Mr Gillies cutting peats or wielding a flaughter, but the schoolmaster and I had a special understanding. He called on me only when none of my fellows could furnish him with an answer, knowing quite well that if I chose not to put up my hand it was not because I did not know the answer but because I did not wish to appear cleverer than my peers. Mr Gillies often set me different tasks from the other pupils and I responded by making special efforts to please him. One afternoon at the end of lessons, he asked me to stay behind. I remained in my place at the back of the classroom while the others made their rowdy exit. Then he beckoned me to his desk. I could not think of anything I had done wrong, but there was no other reason to be singled out in this way. Perhaps I was to be blamed for something I had not done. I resolved to deny nothing and accept whatever punishment was due to me.

Mr Gillies put down his pen and asked me what my plans were. It was not a question which a person from our parts would ask. Making plans was an offence against providence. I said nothing. Mr Gillies took off his little glasses.

'What I mean,' he said, 'is what do you intend to do when you finish school?'

'Only what is meant for me,' I said.

Mr Gillies frowned. 'And what do you think is meant for you?'

'I cannot say,' I replied.

'Roddy, despite your best efforts to conceal them, God has granted you some uncommon gifts. It would be sinful not to make use of them.'

I was surprised to hear Mr Gillies couch his argument in these terms as he was not generally given to religious talk. As I made no reply, he took a more direct approach.

'Have you thought of continuing your education? I have no doubt that you have the necessary ability to become a teacher or a minister or anything you choose.'

Of course, I had considered no such thing, and said so.

'Perhaps you should discuss it with your parents,' he said. 'You may tell them that I believe you have the necessary potential.'

'But I am required for the croft,' I said.

Mr Gillies let out a long sigh. He appeared to be about to say something more, but he thought better of it, and I felt that I had disappointed him. As I walked home, I thought over what he had said. I cannot deny I was gratified that the schoolmaster had spoken to me in this way and for the duration of the walk between Camusterrach and Culduie I imagined myself in a fine drawing room of Edinburgh or Glasgow, clad in the clothes of a gentleman, conversing on weighty matters. Nonetheless, Mr Gillies was mistaken in supposing that such a thing was possible for a son of Culduie.

* * *

Mr Sinclair has asked that I set out what he calls the 'chain of events' which led to the killing of Lachlan Broad. I have thought carefully about what the first link in this chain might be. One might say that it began with my own birth or even further back when my parents met and married, or with the sinking of The Two Iains, which brought

them together. However, while it is true that if any of these events
had not occurred, Lachlan Broad would be alive today – or would at
least not have died by my hand – it is still possible to conceive that
things might have taken a different course. Had I followed Mr Gillies'
advice, for example, I might have been gone from Culduie before
the events to be recounted here came to pass. I have thus tried to
identify the point at which Lachlan Broad's death became inevitable;
that is, the point at which I can conceive of no other outcome. This
moment arrived, I believe, with the death of my mother some eighteen months ago. This was the well-spring from which everything else
has followed. It is thus not to rouse the pity of the reader that I now
describe this event. I have no wish nor use for anyone's pity.

My mother was a lively and good-natured person who did her
best to foster a cheerful atmosphere in our household. Her daily
chores were accompanied with singing and when some ill or hurt
befell one of the children, she did her best to make light of it, so
that we did not dwell upon it. People often called at our house
and were always welcomed with a strupach. If our neighbours
were congregated round the table, my father would be hospitable
enough, but he rarely joined them, preferring to remain standing, before announcing to them that, even if they did not, he
had work to do; a remark which invariably had the effect of pre-
cipitating the dissolution of the gathering. It is a mystery why
my mother married someone as disagreeable as my father, as she
could have had her pick of the men of the parish. Nevertheless,
owing to her efforts, we must, at that time, have loosely resembled a happy family.

It was something of a surprise to my father when my mother
fell pregnant for the fourth time. She was then thirty-five years old
and two years had elapsed since the birth of the twins. I recall quite
clearly the evening on which her labour commenced. The night was
quite wild and as my mother was clearing away the crockery from
our evening meal, a pool of liquid appeared at her feet and she
indicated to my father that it was time. The midwife, who resided
in Applecross, was sent for, and I was dispatched to Kenny Smoke's

house along with the twins. Jetta remained to assist with the birth. Before I left the house, she called me into the back chamber to kiss my mother. Mother gripped my hand and told me that I was to be a good boy and look after my siblings. Jetta's face had a grey pallor about it and her eyes were clouded with fear. In hindsight, I believe they both had a portent that we were to be visited by death that night, but I have never broached this with Jetta.

I did not sleep one moment that night, although I lay on the mattress that was provided for me with my eyes closed. In the morning Carmina Smoke informed me amid much weeping that my mother had passed away during the night due to some complication in the birth. The infant survived and was sent to my mother's family in Toscaig to be nursed by her sister. I have never met this brother of mine and I have no wish to do so. There was a general outpouring of grief in our village, my mother's presence having been akin to the sunlight that nurtures the crops.

This event brought about a great number of changes to our family. Chief among these was the general air of gloom which descended on our household and hung there like the reek. My father was the least changed of us, largely because he had never been much given to joviality. If we had once enjoyed some moments of collective amusement, it was always his laughter that died away first. He would cast his eyes downward as though this moment of pleasure shamed him. Now, however, his face acquired an unalterable bleakness, as if fixed by a change in the wind. I do not wish to portray my father as callous or unfeeling, nor do I doubt that his wife's death grievously affected him. It is rather that he was better adapted to unhappiness, and that to no longer feel obliged to feign pleasure in this world came as a relief to him.

In the weeks and months after the funeral, Reverend Galbraith was a frequent visitor to our home. The minister is an impressive figure, invariably attired in a black frock coat and a white shirt fastened at the collar, but without a neck-tie or cravat. His white hair is kept closely cropped and his whiskers grow densely on his cheeks, but are likewise neatly trimmed. He has small dark eyes, which folk frequently remark seem to have the power to penetrate one's mind. I myself avoided his gaze, but do not doubt that he could discern the wicked thoughts I often entertained. He speaks in a sonorous, rhythmical voice and although his sermons were frequently beyond my understanding, they were not unpleasant to hear.

At the service to mark my mother's funeral, he discoursed at length on the theme of torment. Man, he said, was not only guilty of sin, but was a slave to sin. We had given ourselves in service to Satan and wore the chains of sin around our necks. Mr Galbraith asked that we look around us at the world and its numberless miseries. 'What means,' he asked, 'the sickness and discontentment, the poverty and the pain of death we witness every day?' The answer, he said, was that these iniquities were all the fruits of our sin. Man alone is powerless to throw off his yoke of sin. For this reason we require a redeemer: a deliverer without whom we will all perish.

After my mother was committed to the earth we formed a solemn procession over the moors. The day, as is often the way in these parts, was entirely grey. The sky, the mountains of Raasay and the water of the Sound offered only the smallest variations on this hue. My father shed no tears either during the sermon or afterwards. His face adopted the obdurate cast from which it would henceforth rarely deviate. I have no doubt that he took Mr Galbraith's words greatly to heart. For my own part, I was quite certain that it was not for my father's sins that our mother had been taken, but for my own. I reflected on Mr Galbraith's sermon and resolved there and then with the grey sod beneath my feet that, when the opportunity came, I would become my father's redeemer and deliver him from the wretched state to which my sinfulness had reduced him.

Some months later, Mr Galbraith received my father as an elder in the church, this on account of my father's acceptance that his sufferings were just recompense for the sinful nature of his life. My father's suffering was instructive to the congregation and it benefitted them to see him prominently exhibited in the church. I believe that Mr Galbraith was quite glad of my mother's death, as it bore witness to the doctrine he professed.

The twins cried constantly for their mother and when I think of that time it is to the accompaniment of their unremitting wailing. On account of the disparity in our ages, I had never felt anything other than indifference towards my younger siblings, but they now aroused positive enmity in me. If one was quiet for a moment, the other would commence to weep, thus setting off the other. My father had no tolerance for the infants' lamentations and sought to silence them through blows that served only to renew their bawling. I well remember them clinging to one another on their mattress, a look of terror on their faces as my father made his way across the chamber to administer a beating. I left it to Jetta to intervene and had she not been there to do so, I could quite imagine my father doing the poor wretches to death. It was suggested that the twins should also be sent to Toscaig, but my father would not hear of it, insisting that Jetta was old enough to play mother to them.

My dear sister Jetta was as greatly transformed as if her fetch had overnight taken her place. The gay and charming girl was replaced by a morose, brooding figure, hunched over at the shoulders and clad, at my father's insistence, in widow's black. Jetta was obliged to assume the role of mother and wife, preparing the meals and serving my father as our mother had previously done. It was at this time that Father decreed that Jetta should sleep in the back chamber with him as she was now a woman and merited a degree of privacy from her siblings. In general, however, Father disdained her, as if, in her resemblance to his wife, it pained him to look upon her.

As the most cheerful among us Jetta must have felt the general despondency which pervaded our household most keenly. I do not know if she had fore-knowledge of my mother's death, for she has never spoken to me of it, but rather than abandon the rituals and paraphernalia which had done nothing to ward off this ill fortune, she clung all the more fervently to them. I saw no efficacy in such things, but understood that Jetta was privy to intimations from the Other World to which I was insensible. In a similar way, my father turned more fervently to the reading of scripture and away from the modest pleasures he had previously allowed himself, as if he believed that God was punishing him for the infrequent dram he had taken. For my part, my mother's death demonstrated nothing more than the absurdity of their respective creeds.

As the weeks passed, none of us wished to be the first to leaven the atmosphere with some mischief or a few lines of a song, and the more time elapsed, the more fixed we became in our gloomy ways.

* * *

My mother died in the month of April and some weeks later I was alone on the shieling, charged with keeping watch over the sheep and cattle grazing there. The afternoon was very warm. The sky was clear and the hills across the Sound were various hues of purple. The air was so still that it was possible to hear the lapping of the sea and the occasional cry of children playing far below in the village. The animals which I had been charged to watch were rendered slothful by the heat and did not stray far from one hour to the next. The stirks lazily flicked at horseflies with their tails.

I was lying back in the heather, watching the slow progress of the clouds across the sky. I was glad to be away from the croft and from my father, whom I had left leaning on the handle of his cas chrom, puffing on his pipe. I pictured my mother next to him, bent over the ground, thinning weeds from the crops, singing to herself as she always did, her hair falling over her face. It was some moments before I realised that she was not there, and was instead beneath the earth of the burial ground in Camusterrach. I had often come across the carcasses of animals, and I wondered whether the process of decomposition had already taken hold of her body. I felt quite keenly then the reality that I would never see her again and closed my eyes to prevent myself from weeping. I tried to concentrate my thoughts on the sounds of rustling grass and the bleating of the sheep, but I was unable to banish the image of my mother's decaying body. An insect landed on my face and this had the effect of rousing me from my thoughts. I waved it away with my hand and raised myself onto my elbows, blinking in the sunlight. The hornet then landed on my forearm. I did not draw my arm away, but slowly raised it to the level of my eyes, so that the tiny creature loomed larger than the cattle in the distance. Mr Gillies had, once, with the aid of a diagram drawn on the blackboard, taught us the names for the parts of insects, and these pleasing words I now recited: thorax, spiracle, funiculus, ovipositor, mandible. The hornet negotiated the dark hairs on my arm, as though uncertain of the terrain upon which it had alighted. It was with the detachment of a scientist that I watched the creature halt and bring its gaster down on my skin. I instinctively slapped my hand down upon it and brushed the little corpse from my arm. The insect's tail had left a tiny barb in my skin and the area around quickly swelled into a pink bleb.

I decided to climb to the waterfall further up the Càrn to bathe my sting, now and again casting a glance over my shoulder to check on the livestock. The waterfall was among a cluster of birch, with a deep pool at its well. It was cool among the trees. The rocks were worn smooth by the centuries' passage of water. I cupped my hands into the pool to take a drink, then splashed water over my face and head. I took off my clothes and stepped into the water. I closed my eyes and let myself float on my back. Light flickered orange through my eyelids. I listened to the roar of water on water and felt that when I emerged Culduie, Aird-Dubh and everything else would be gone, and I would be entirely alone in the world. I wished only that when I opened my eyes Jetta would be standing on a rock, stepping out of her clothes and joining me in the pool. I opened my eyes and watched the droplets of water fly up like sparks from a fire. I would have happily remained there for the rest of the afternoon, but I was conscious of my duty to the livestock. I allowed the sun to dry my skin, before dressing and setting off down the hillside.

As the roar of the water subsided, I heard the sound of a sheep. Sheep are naturally in the habit of conversing among themselves, but this was the pained bleating of a single animal, akin to that of a ewe that has lost her lamb. I stood on a hummock and surveyed the hillside, but I could not see the animal in question. A hundred yards or so up a steep incline, the hillside yielded to a boggy plateau, invisible from below, where our peat is cut. I clambered towards it, the bleating growing ever more intense. When I emerged over the ridge, I found a distressed ram, lying on its side, half submerged in the mire. Even in summer the bog remained gluey and treacherous. Older folk in the village were wont to warn children that if they strayed into the bog they would be sucked into the bowels of the earth where they would be devoured by trolls. As a child I had accepted this as fact and although I no longer believed in trolls, I remained wary of the bog. The animal flailed its free limbs uselessly, succeeding only in working itself further into the slough. As I neared the stricken beast, keeping to the heathery outcrops upon which it was safe to stand, I whispered soothing sounds in an attempt to calm it. The sheep turned in my direction, like a sick old woman too weak to raise her head from the pillow. I felt no pity for the beast, only a kind of loathing for its stupidity. A large crow landed on a nearby hummock and studied us with interest. I assessed my possible courses of action. The first of these was to return to the village to fetch a rope and someone to assist me in pulling the beast from the quagmire. I dismissed this idea as, even if the sheep had not been drowned by the time I returned, the crow and his brethren would certainly have set about it. This course of action would also entail disclosing that the ram had strayed into the bog while under my supervision, an eventuality I preferred to avoid. There was thus no alternative to rescuing the sheep unaided.

Without further delay, I knelt on the edge of the bog and, spreading my weight as widely as possible, reached out towards the sheep's haunch. The mud smelt sour. Clouds of flies flew up in a haze from the fetid surface water. I managed to grasp the sheep's hoof, but not firmly enough to gain proper purchase. I tested the ground between us and tentatively manoeuvred myself onto my backside, mud seeping into my breeches. The crow observed my progress with interest. I was now able to take hold of the curled horn on the beast's head. I levered myself backwards and heaved, feeling the muscles at the back of my thighs tauten. The sheep kicked its legs with renewed vigour and emitted a fearful bleating. Then the bog gave a slabbery belch and released its grip on the animal. I collapsed backwards onto the heather, spattered in black mud. In my relief, I laughed out loud. The freed beast struggled in vain to get to its feet and I saw that the hind leg which had been submerged in the bog was dislocated and protruding from the ram's body at a wholly unnatural angle. The animal collapsed onto its side, its uninjured legs scrabbling in the air. Its bleating continued unabated. The crow emitted a sharp caw, as if in mockery of my efforts. I formed a handful of mud into a ball and threw it in the direction of the evil bird, but it merely watched it plop into the bog, before fixing me again with a haughty stare. I had no choice but to swiftly deliver the sheep from its suffering. It may be a simple matter for a gentleman to dispatch a deer or a grouse by squeezing the trigger of a gun, but to do to death an animal with one's own hands or with a manual tool, no matter how well adapted to the purpose, is an entirely different matter. I have always shrunk from killing so much as a hen, and do not understand why educated men regard the killing of living creatures as sport. Nevertheless, in these circumstances, it was my duty to end the life of the stricken beast. I considered straddling it and by gripping the horns, twisting back its head to break its neck, but I did not know whether I would have the strength for such an act. I then spied a peat iron protruding from the opposite side of the bog. I fetched the tool and used it, on my return, to shoo away the crow, which flapped a few feet into the air before hopping back to its former vantage point.

'Are you quite comfortable?' I asked.

The crow replied with a cackle that I should hasten to the job in hand as he was impatient for his repast.

The head of the iron had a good heft. The sheep looked at me. I scanned the hillside, but there was no one to be seen. Without further delay, I raised the iron above my head and brought it down with as much force as I could muster. The beast must have moved or I may have misjudged the trajectory as my blow only succeeded in catching the beast on the snout, the blade of the iron splintering the bone. The animal snorted, choking on blood and bone, and made renewed and pitiful efforts to get to its feet. I took aim for a second time and brought the iron down on the top of the beast's head with such force that my feet left the ground. Blood sprayed into the air, spattering my face. The iron was embedded in the sheep's skull and it took a considerable effort to extricate it. This done I turned away and brought up the contents of my stomach, steadying myself on the handle of the tool. By the time I recovered myself the crow had taken up residence of the dead beast's skull and was making short work of its eyes. Two of his fellows had joined him and were strutting around making a methodical inspection of the carcass.

The marking on the fleece revealed to whom the sheep belonged, and it was with a strong sense of dread that I returned to the village.

That same evening a meeting was held at the home of Kenneth Murchison. Mr Murchison was known to everyone as Kenny Smoke, on account of the fact that he was never seen without a pipe between his lips. He was a burly man, who had to stoop to pass through a door. He had a wide handsome face with a black moustache as thick as a broom-head. He had a bellowing voice and addressed women in a loud cheerful way, just as if he was speaking to a man. I never saw my mother so lively as when Kenny Smoke called. He was a great teller of tales and was able to recite long passages of poetry from memory, and during the black months it was in his house that the people gathered for a ceilidh. As a boy I was enthralled by his stories of ghosts and unchancy beings. My father was wary of Kenny Smoke, as he was of all men whose minds he said were filled with worldly things.

His wife, Carmina, was a striking woman, with fine features, large dark eyes and a slender figure. Her father was a merchant in Kyle of Lochalsh and Kenny Smoke had met her at market there. It was unheard of for such a woman to marry into a village like Culduie, and it was often said (although I did not understand what was meant by it) that Kenny Smoke must have been endowed with a great gift in order to tempt her from such a metropolis.

The Smokes had six daughters, which was regarded as a great misfortune. A succession of old crones of the parish had offered remedies for this affliction, but Kenny Smoke turned them all away, proclaiming that any one of his daughters was worth ten of another man's sons. The Smokes' house was large and spacious. There was a chimney at the gable end and Kenny Smoke had constructed a large hearth, around which were arranged a number of upholstered chairs. A range of fine crockery was displayed on a dresser, built by a carpenter in Kyle and transported to Culduie by boat. Kenny Smoke and his wife slept in a chamber at the back of the house and there was a separate chamber for their daughters. After his marriage, Kenny Smoke had rented extra land and built a byre for his cattle, saying that he would not have any of his girls living under the same roof as livestock. He always referred to his wife as one of his girls, and on summer evenings they could often be seen walking hand-in-hand to the point at Aird-Dubh. If my father saw them he would mutter that, 'She has to hold his hand to stop him doing the Devil's work.'

In the middle of the living quarters was a long table at which the Smokes took their meals. Around this table were assembled myself and my father; Lachlan Broad, who was the owner of the sheep I had killed; and his brother, Aeneas. Kenny Smoke himself sat at the head of the table. There was nothing of the convivial atmosphere that usually attended gatherings in the Smoke household. Lachlan Broad had refused Kenny Smoke's offer of a dram and sat quite erect with his hands clasped on the table in front of him, the right enclosing the fist of his left, gripping and ungripping it as if his hands were a beating heart. His gaze was directed at the dresser behind my father and I. Broad, it should be said, was a most impressive specimen of the human race. He stood six feet tall, with wide shoulders and great meaty hands. He had been known to carry the carcass of a stag, which two men might struggle to lift, the length of the village. His narrow eyes were pale blue and his great heavy head was topped with thick yellow hair, which grew to his shoulders, this colouring on account, it was said, of some Norse blood on his mother's side of the family. He never appeared to feel the cold and even in the black months strode around in an open chemise. As if he were not unmistake-able enough, he habitually wore a yellow neckerchief, tied at his throat. His brother was of smaller stature, plump with a ruddy complexion and small bird-like eyes. He had little to say for himself, but habitually brayed like a tinker's ass at whatever remark his kinsman made. Aeneas sat at his brother's shoulder, his left ankle resting on his right knee, and was absorbed in the business of cleaning the muck from his boot with a pocketknife.

Kenny Smoke puffed quietly on his pipe and constantly smoothed the whiskers of his great moustache with his thumb and middle finger. My father, whose pipe remained in his pocket, held his cap in both hands in his lap and stared at the table in front of him. We were awaiting the arrival of Calum Finlayson, a boatman from Camusterrach, who at that time held the position of constable to the parish.* It remained bright and sunny outside, which only served to emphasise the sombre atmosphere in the house. Presently, Mr Finlayson made his appearance and greeted the company in a cheerful manner. Kenny Smoke stood up and shook his hand heartily and made some enquiries about the wellbeing of his family. The constable accepted the offer of a cup of tea and Carmina Smoke was summoned. She busied herself preparing the tea and setting out a cup and saucer in front of each of us, even though it was

---

* *The village or parish constable was an official elected by members of the community to serve as a go-between between the factor and the people. It was his role to enforce the crofters' terms of tenancy and to settle disputes. The factor, in turn, was the steward or agent charged with the running of the estate on behalf of the laird. The factor was, generally speaking, an unpopular and feared figure.*

only Mr Finlayson who was wanting it. Lachlan Broad observed her intensely, as if appraising a piece of livestock at market.

When the tea had been poured and Carmina Smoke had retired to the back chamber, Calum Finlayson opened the proceedings.

'Let us see whether we cannot settle this matter amicably, gentlemen,' he said.

Kenny Smoke nodded earnestly and said, 'Indeed.'

Lachlan Broad exhaled noisily through his nose, and his brother emitted his braying laugh. Calum Finlayson ignored this rude sound and, in a gentle tone, requested that I relate as precisely as possible what had occurred that afternoon. I felt quite anxious in front of the assembled men, but told the story to the best of my ability, omitting only the interlude at the waterfall, which could reasonably be construed as a neglect of my duty to keep watch over the livestock. I included the detail of being stung by the hornet, calculating that it might be thought that it was this that had distracted me when the ram had wandered off. I also stated that when I found the sheep, its eyes had already been put out, this in order to stress the suffering of the beast and my lack of choice in acting as I did.

When I had finished, Mr Finlayson thanked me for my account. I had kept my eyes all this time on the table in front of me, but thinking that this might be the end of the ordeal I now raised them. Lachlan Broad shifted his weight in his seat and gave a dismissive snort through his nose. He leaned forward as if intending to speak, but Mr Finlayson raised a finger in his direction to silence him.

'Was it not your duty, Roddy,' he asked, 'to keep watch over the animals for the duration of the afternoon?'

'It was,' I replied.

'And did you keep watch?'

'I did, Mr Finlayson.' I was suddenly afraid that someone might have seen me make my way towards the waterfall and was about to be brought forth to contradict my story.

'So how can it be,' asked Mr Finlayson, his tone still placid, 'that the sheep was able to wander off into the bog?'

'I cannot say,' I replied.

'Perhaps your attention wandered,' he said.

'If the sheep strayed while I was guarding it, then my attention must have wandered,' I said. I was relieved that there did not
appear to be any witness to appear against me. 'I wish to say that
I am sorry for the suffering of the sheep and I am willing to do
what is required to compensate Mr Mackenzie for its loss.'

Mr Finlayson nodded as if he was pleased by my remark. Kenny
Smoke took his pipe from his mouth and said, 'We all know that
it's not possible to keep track of fifty sheep on a hillside. The boy
has said he's sorry, should we not leave it at that?'

Lachlan Broad turned his gaze upon him. 'I note that it is not
your sheep that has been bludgeoned to death, Mr Murchison,
and while we all appreciate your hospitality, I do not see that your
opinion has any bearing on this matter.' His brother sniggered and
shifted his weight on his seat.

Mr Finlayson raised his hand to quell any further discussion
and addressed his comments to Lachlan Broad. 'Nevertheless, Mr
Murchison is quite right to state that it is no easy task to keep track
of the livestock and if a mistake has been made then it was an
honest mistake and no malice has been intended.'

'There is malice in abundance in that boy,' said Broad, directing
a thick finger at me.

Mr Finlayson stated that we were not there to make insulting
remarks, but that if Mr Mackenzie now wished to put some questions to me, he was free to do so.

Broad satisfied himself by muttering something about the
impossibility of getting a word of truth out of me.

Mr Finlayson allowed a few moments of silence to settle on the
room and then stated that if everyone was satisfied with what they
had heard, it fell to him to determine on the matter. 'I propose,'
he said, 'that for the loss of the ram, John Macrae pay thirty-five
shillings in compensation to Lachlan Mackenzie, that being the
price at market for such a beast.'

'And what about the winter feed and labour I have incurred in
rearing the animal?' said Broad.

Calum Finlayson appeared to give this question due consideration. 'Had you sold the beast at market, these costs would not have been restored to you. Furthermore, in addition to the thirty-five shillings, you also have the fleece and flesh of the animal.'

'Aye, what's left of them after the crows had set about it,' said Broad.

Mr Finlayson ignored this remark and turned to my father to ask if his determination was acceptable. My father indicated with a brief nod that it was.

'It seems to me,' persisted Lachlan Broad, 'that you are letting the boy off scot-free. Surely there should be some additional punishment.'

'What would you suggest?' said the constable. 'A public flogging?'

I had already received, in front of my siblings, a most thorough beating from my father, but I did not think it was my place to divulge this. Nor did my father see fit to mention it.

'I can think of worse ideas,' said Broad, fixing his gaze on me. 'Perhaps we might beat some truth out of the runt.'

'Aye, beat some truth out the runt,' repeated Aeneas Mackenzie.

Calum Finlayson stood up and leant across the table towards the two men. 'I did not come here to listen to foul language and insults,' he said. 'The boy has owned up to his deed and should be commended for doing so. I have proposed a settlement in your favour. If it is not acceptable, I suggest that you take the matter to the police.'

Lachlan Broad glowered at him. The suggestion was quite impractical as such an action would involve a journey of seventy miles to Dingwall, and, moreover, any failure to accept the adjudication of the constable would be poorly received in the community. 'Perhaps the factor would be interested in hearing about what has occurred.'

'I can assure you,' said Mr Finlayson, 'that the factor has more important matters to concern himself with than the loss of a sheep. As Mr Macrae has accepted my proposal I suggest you do the same.'

Lachlan Broad indicated with a gesture of his hand that he

accepted the judgement. My father, who had barely spoken during the proceedings, then raised a craggy finger. The constable asked him if there was something he wished to say.

'The matter of payment,' said my father.

'Yes?' said Mr Finlayson.

With some difficulty my father explained that while he accepted the settlement, he did not, at that time, have thirty-five shillings, nor anything like it.

This caused Lachlan Broad and his brother great mirth. 'I am sorry to hear that, John Black,' he said. 'Perhaps I could take that gloomy daughter of yours instead. I'm sure I could put a smile on her face.'

'We could both put a smile on her gloomy face,' put in Aeneas Mackenzie, with a stupid giggle.

Kenny Smoke rose from his seat and leaned across the table. 'I will not have such talk in my house, Lachlan Broad.'

'Perhaps you would rather I had one of your daughters,' said Broad. 'The eldest is quite ripe now.'

Kenny Smoke became quite red in the face and I was sure he was about to fly at him, but Calum Finlayson rose from his seat and placed a hand on his chest.

Lachlan Broad broke into a laugh, his arms folded across his chest. Kenny Smoke remained standing for some moments, glaring at Broad, who smirked back at him. My father stared at the table in front of him. Under the table I could see his hand worrying at the coarse cloth of his breeches.

Eventually, Kenny Smoke resumed his seat and Mr Finlayson, no doubt anxious to bring the proceedings to a close, continued, 'Given Mr Macrae's circumstances, I propose that the sum agreed be paid at a rate of one shilling per week until it is settled.'

Lachlan Broad shrugged his shoulders. 'So be it,' he said in a mocking tone, 'I would not wish to be the cause of any hardship to my poor neighbour here.'

And in this way the discussions were concluded. Lachlan Broad pushed back his chair and slapped his brother twice on the thigh to indicate that they were leaving. When they were gone Kenny Smoke let go a long breath and uttered an oath which does not bear repeating here. Mr Finlayson told me that I had conducted myself well. Kenny Smoke went to the dresser and fetched a bottle of whisky and four glasses, which he placed on the table between us. I was gratified that he had included a glass for me, but, before the whisky could be poured, my father stood up and thanked Mr Finlayson for the fairness of his ruling, though I could not help but think that he would have happily agreed to Lachlan Broad's proposal to have me flogged. Kenny Smoke begged him to share a dram, but he refused. Father then prodded me on the arm and we left. I feared a second beating when we got home, but I was merely deprived of my supper. I lay on my bunk picturing Kenny Smoke and Calum Finlayson drinking whisky and laughing about the incident while my father nursed his pipe in the gathering gloom.

* * *

My cell here in Inverness is five paces long and two wide. Two planks fastened to the wall and covered with straw serve as a bed. There are two pails in the corner, one in which I perform my ablutions, the other for my bodily functions. An unglazed window, the size of a man's hand, sits high in the wall opposite the door. The walls are thick, and only by standing with my back pressed to the door am I able to see a small rectangle of sky. The purpose of the window is, I imagine, less to afford the occupant of the cell a view than to allow a little air to circulate. Nevertheless, in the absence of other diversions, it is surprising how much entertainment can be gleaned from watching the slow alterations in a small patch of sky.

My gaoler is a great brute of a fellow, so wide he has to turn sideways to enter my cell. He wears a leather waistcoat, a filthy chemise hanging outside his breeches and heavy boots which clatter noisily as he makes his way up and down the flagstones of the passage outside. He keeps his breeches tied around his ankles with string. This puzzles me as I have seen no mice or other vermin here, but I have not asked him the reason for it. Nor have I asked his name.

The gaoler treats me with neither kindness nor contempt. In the morning he brings me a piece of bread and some water and, if my pail is full, he removes it. In the first few days I made some attempts to converse with him, but he did not respond. When the table and chair at which I am writing this document were brought to me, he made no comment. He is not a mute, however, as I have sometimes heard him conversing in the passage. I suppose I am a matter of no concern to him and no different from the occupants of the other cells along the passage. There is, in any case, little to talk about here. After he has left, I hear him performing the same duties in the remaining cells. I have not seen anything of my fellow inmates and nor do I have any wish to, as I have no desire to fraternise with criminals. At night, men often cry out in the coarsest terms or hammer on the doors of their cells with their fists, activities which only serve to set the other men shouting for quiet. These periods of uproar last for some time, before all of a sudden the clamour subsides and there are only the faint sounds of the night outside.

Every second day I am taken from my cell and allowed to stretch my legs in a cobbled enclosure. On the first occasion I was unsure of what to do there. On account of the height of the walls, no sunlight reaches the ground and the cobbles are slimy and overgrown with moss. I observed that around the edges of the yard, a path had been worn and so I took to pacing around the perimeter. The gaoler remains all the time at the entrance, but I do not have the impression that he is observing me. I feel some pity towards him. His life here appears no more pleasant than mine and long after I have left this place he will remain. The distance around the yard is twenty-eight paces, and I generally complete around sixty circuits in the time allowed to me. This is roughly the distance between Culduie and Camusterrach and I try to imagine that this is where I am walking.

Later in the day I am brought a bowl of soup with a piece of bread or a bannock. The majority of my time is passed in the production of this document. I cannot see that what I am writing here will be of interest to anyone, but I am glad to have some activity with which to occupy myself.

In the first days of my incarceration, I had little time to accustom myself to my new surroundings, inundated as I was by numerous visits from officers of the law. I was frequently taken to a room in another part of the gaol in order that I might be interrogated about my deeds. The same questions were put to me on so many occasions, so that I no longer had to think about my responses. I frequently had the impression that it would please my interlocutors if I were to invent some other version of events or to attempt in some way to absolve myself of responsibility for what I have done, but I did not do so. I have been treated courteously by everyone and would have liked to repay their kindness, but I could see no purpose in lying. Often, when I had repeated my story for the third or fourth time, those present would exchange glances as if I had amused them in some way, or was a mystery to them. However, having reflected on this, I imagine that such gentlemen are more accustomed to dealing with criminals who are disinclined to admit their guilt. Eventually, I told my story in the presence of a writer, and after numerous cautions that I was not obliged to do so, signed my name to a statement.

Now, aside from my visits from my advocate, Mr Sinclair, I have little human contact. This morning, however, I was interrupted in my labours by a visit from the prison doctor. He was a genial man with ruddy cheeks and unruly whiskers. He introduced himself as Dr Munro and informed me that he was required to ascertain the state of my health. I told him that I was quite well, but he nevertheless asked me to remove my shirt and conducted a thorough examination. As he busied himself around me, I could smell his breath, which had the sweet stench of fresh manure, and I was relieved when he completed his examination and retreated from me. He then put a series of questions to me regarding my crimes and I gave my customary responses. Now and again he took a pewter flask from the inside pocket of his coat and swigged from it. He noted my answers in a little book and did not seem in the least perturbed by anything I told him. When he had concluded

his questions he folded his arms and regarded me with some interest. He asked me if I was sorry for what I had done. I told him I
was not and, in any case, it mattered little whether I was sorry or
not, what was done could not be undone.

'That is quite true,' he said. After some moments he added,
'You are quite the curiosity, Roderick Macrae.'

I replied that I was not a curiosity to myself, and that he was
likely as much of a curiosity to me as I was to him. At this he
laughed jovially to himself and not for the first time I was surprised by the affable way I was treated, as if I was guilty of no
more than the theft of a pat of butter.

* * *

Towards the end of the yellow months, Mr Gillies paid a visit to
my father. It was early evening and Jetta was clearing away the
bowls from our evening meal. My father was taken aback by the
arrival of the schoolmaster, who appeared in the doorway, still
holding the reins of his garron. I was sent outside to tether the
pony and, having done so, I remained by him a few minutes, stroking his neck and murmuring in his ear. When I went inside, Mr
Gillies was sitting on the bench at the table and Jetta was preparing him a cup of tea. A bannock had been set on a plate in front
of him. My father stood awkwardly in the middle of the room,
fidgeting with his pipe, unwilling to sit in the presence of his better. Mr Gillies was making various enquiries of Jetta and telling my
father what a pleasure it had been to teach her. When he saw me in
the doorway, he said in a jovial manner, 'Here's the boy!'

He then asked my father if he would not sit down, and my
father took his place at the head of the table.

'I have noted that since our term has resumed, Roddy has not
returned to school.'

My father puffed steadily on his pipe. 'He is not a child,' he said.

'That is quite true and as such he is no longer required to attend
school,' said Mr Gillies. 'However, perhaps Roddy has told you of
the conversation he and I had at the end of the last school term?'

My father replied that I had not told him of any conversation. Mr Gillies then looked towards me and invited me to join them at the table.

When I had sat down, he continued. 'Our discussion concerned your son's future, that is, with regard to his continuing education. Did he not mention this to you?'

'He did not,' said my father.

Mr Gillies then looked at me and furrowed his brow. 'Well,' he said in a breezy tone, 'your son has shown considerable potential in his school work, potential which in my view it would be shameful to squander.'

My father glared at me as though I had committed some misdemeanour or was guilty of conspiring with the schoolmaster behind his back.

'Squandered?' he repeated, as if the word was entirely alien to him.

Mr Gillies looked around our dim abode, quite aware of the trap which my father had set for him. He took a sip of his tea before answering.

'I mean simply that were he to continue his education, he might, in the future, have a greater number of paths from which to choose.'

'What sort of paths?' My father knew very well what sort of paths Mr Gillies meant. I have no doubt he was vaguely aware of my achievements in the classroom, but he had never shown any interest in them or offered me any praise.

'I have no doubt that Roddy could aspire to become a ...' – here, he cast his eyes towards the roof-trees as if he was contemplating the question for the first time – '... to become a minister or a schoolmaster. Or anything he wished.'

'To become someone like yourself?' said my father, rudely.

'All I mean, Mr Macrae, is that certain options would be open to him.'

My father shifted his weight on the bench. 'You mean that he might become something better than a crofter,' he said.

'I would not say better, Mr Macrae, but different certainly. I put this to you only to be assured that you are aware of the opportunities afforded to your son.'

'We have no use for opportunities here,' said my father. 'The boy is required to work on the croft and earn money for his family through his labour.'

Mr Gillies responded by saying that perhaps it might be useful to ask what I would like to do. At this my father got to his feet.

'We shall do no such thing,' he said.

Mr Gillies did not rise from his seat. 'If it is a question of money,' he said, 'certain arrangements can be made.'

'We have no call for your charity here, Mr Schoolmaster.'

Mr Gillies opened his mouth to speak, but then thought better of it. He nodded, as if to accept that the matter was closed, and stood up. He stepped towards my father and offered him his hand, which was refused.

'I did not intend to give offence, Mr Macrae.'

My father made no answer and Mr Gillies, having bid good evening to myself and Jetta, who for the duration of the conversation had occupied herself with the washing of our bowls, took his leave.

I accompanied him outside on the pretext of assisting him with his pony. I wished him to know that I was grateful for his visit, but had I been asked I would have agreed with my father that I was now required to work for the family and that such things were not meant for the likes of us. In any case, none of the boys of my age in the parish attended school and I would have felt foolish sitting among the children. Nor did I wish to become a man like Mr Gillies with his weak features and pink, flabby hands. He thanked me for untethering his pony and told me that should I wish to return to school I would be very welcome and that arrangements could be made to pay the fees. I am sure that he did not expect to see me again and in this he was correct. I watched him climb onto his pony and ride slowly out of the village. His legs reached almost to the ground, so that he cut a quite comic figure. The garron plodded along with the characteristic gait of the Highland pony, as if expecting at any moment to strike its head on a low beam.

My father's plans for me to contribute to the income of the household proved futile. Soon after the conversation with Mr Gillies he secured a position for me for the duration of the stalking season. I was to report at first light to the ghillie's lodge and this I did. The ghillie was a tall man with narrow eyes and a thick, wiry beard, speckled with grey. He was wearing tweed breeches with thick woollen stockings and stout brogues. His waistcoat was unbuttoned and he held a pipe with an S-shaped stem in his left hand. He asked my name and I replied that I was Roderick Macrae of Culduie. He looked me up and down and told me to wait in the courtyard at the back of the Big House.

I continued through the grounds feeling, despite the sanction of the ghillie, like a trespasser, but no one challenged me. The courtyard was accessed through a stone archway to the right of the main entrance. I found myself in a cobbled yard with stables along one side and, on the other, windows looking into the kitchens of the house. I did not wish to press my nose against the glass, but there appeared to be a great deal of activity within. I leaned against the wall to the right of the kitchen door and did my best to look as if I belonged there. I could hear the horses shifting and whinnying in their stalls. I imagined them to be great thoroughbreds and I longed to enter the stables and look at them, but did not do so for fear of being reprimanded. Presently another boy, a little older than myself, arrived. He did not speak, but stared at me quite openly. He leaned against the wall of the stable, placing the sole of his right boot against it so that it formed a triangle. This attitude made him appear quite at ease in his surroundings, so I mimicked it. After some minutes, the boy took a small pipe from the pocket of his jacket. He made a thorough examination of it, before putting the stem in his mouth and chomping noisily on it. There was no tobacco in the bowl, or if there was, he had made no attempt to light it. Nevertheless, I took this display as confirmation of his worldliness and was suitably impressed. Later, when the march through the glen brought us to talking, he explained that there was no need to light a pipe to glean the benefits of tobacco. As long as the pipe had been previously used, all that was required was to suck vigorously on it.

Some time later two men arrived and went into the stables, where I could hear them readying the horses. When the ponies were led out I was disappointed to see that they were not stallions, but the same stocky garrons with heavy low heads that were kept in the villages. At the same time various supplies and tackle were brought out from the kitchens and set down on the cobbles. The boy with the pipe and I were instructed to load up the first pony. The second was left unburdened, so that it might convey any game from the mountain. With the preparations made, a stout woman in a pinafore and apron emerged from the kitchen with a tray of four cups of tea. This was Lachlan Broad's wife, Mimi, who worked for Lord Middleton during the yellow months. She bid me good morning in a manner which suggested she was not surprised to see me there. I did not normally drink tea as my father thinks it fit only for womenfolk, but not wishing to set myself apart from the group I took the cup offered to me. And indeed, the communal imbibing seemed to beget a sense of fellowship between the four of us. The tea was sweetened with sugar and less unpleasant than I expected. As we drank one of the men addressed me for the first time.

'So you are the Black Macrae's boy?'

I replied that I was the son of John Macrae of Culduie and the two men exchanged a look, the meaning of which was mysterious to me. I was taken aback that these two strangers knew my father's name and appeared to pass judgement on me due to some idea they had about him.

Mimi Broad returned to collect our cups and asked if I had brought something to eat as we were to be the full day in the hills. Jetta had given me two potatoes, and she nodded in a way that suggested I had done well to be thus prepared. The ponies were led across the cobbles to the front of the house where we awaited the stalking party. One of the men pointed out a large wooden coffer, which I was to carry. It was three feet wide and two deep and fastened at diagonally opposite corners with a heavy leather strap the width of a man's hand. There was a good weight in it and one of the hands had to lift it over my head and secure the strap over my shoulder. He then told me that it was important not to bump the box or let it tilt to one side as the contents could be broken. I did not ask what was inside, but I felt that I had been entrusted with a task of great importance and resolved to carry it out well. By the time the ghillie joined us, the strap had already begun to cause me some discomfort, but I did my best to conceal it. The ghillie made a cursory inspection of the ponies and made one or two remarks to the men. A gun rested in the crook of his arm. A few minutes later, four gentlemen emerged from the entrance to the house, all dressed in tweeds and holding guns in the same manner as the ghillie. The men were not at all like the natives of these parts. They were tall and straight-backed with fair hair and pink complexions, like that of my erstwhile schoolmaster. The ghillie shook hands with the eldest of the men, whom I took to be Lord Middleton. He then greeted the other men in turn and declared that it was a fine morning and that he was confident they would return with a stag from the mountain. He then addressed them in general terms about what would occur that day and gave out one or two instructions regarding the manner in which to handle their firearms and behave on the mountain. The gentlemen listened attentively and I was greatly impressed for, despite his fine clothes, the ghillie was a Highlander, here addressing his betters with no hint of deference. At the end of his little speech, Lord Middleton clapped the ghillie on the shoulder and, turning to his companions, said, 'Fear not, his bark is worse than his bite.' This caused great amusement among the party, except for the ghillie himself, who took a silver watch from the pocket of his waistcoat and declared that it was time they were starting out. We then set off towards the glen, the ghillie and Lord Middleton at the head, followed by the three gentlemen, then the stablemen leading the two garrons, with we two boys bringing up the rear. The morning was warm and overcast. It was not long before the coffer began to knock painfully against the back of my knees. My companion, who was carrying a similar, though clearly lighter box, showed me how to walk with my shoulders back and my hands resting on the sides to prevent it from bumping. This exchange broke the ice between us and he told me that his name was Archibald Ross and he was the eldest of six siblings. I told him that my mother had lately died during the birth of my youngest brother and this had caused our family a good deal of hardship. Archibald Ross replied that for folk like us there was no other ship than the hard ship. I was greatly impressed with this reply and thought my new friend the cleverest person I had ever met.

When we left the track which led through the middle of the glen and started up the hillside, it became impossible to prevent my coffer from swinging this way and that and I became resigned to damaging the contents and incurring the wrath of the ghillie. Archibald Ross maintained a constant monologue, talking in an entertaining manner about his siblings and neighbours in Applecross. He told me quite openly that his father thought the people from the Point to be lazy and inferior beings, especially those from Aird-Dubh, who he regarded as dirty and mendacious. He was at pains to stress that he did not share his father's view, but I nevertheless reminded him that I was from Culduie and not Aird-Dubh.

As soon as he was old enough and had saved enough for the passage, Archibald intended to emigrate to Canada. There, he told me, young men like us could prosper. Great tracts of fertile land awaited us and within a year one could make more money than our fathers would in a lifetime of scratching a living from their crofts. A cousin of his who had left with nothing but a bag of sowens, now lived in a house twice as grand as Lord Middleton's. He proposed that we should go together to make our fortunes and I was much excited by the idea. Archibald then told me in a conspiratorial tone that if I made myself particularly useful to the gentlemen, they might at the end of the day slip me a penny or even a shilling. The prospect of such earnings redoubled my resolve to ignore the pain that the coffer was causing me.

After perhaps two hours we reached a plateau overlooking the glen and stopped. I had never had cause to wander this far into the mountains and we were afforded a great vista over the bay of Applecross towards the mountains of Raasay and Skye. The stablemen retrieved two large rugs from the first of the ponies and laid them on the ground. My coffer was lifted from me and from it were taken items of crockery, glasses and bottles of wine. On the ashets were placed an array of cold meats, vegetables, condiments and breads. The gentlemen declared themselves impressed with the spread and commenced eating without the saying of grace. The two hands, having laid out the meal, loitered by the garrons. I sat on a hummock and slowly ate the first of my potatoes. I was tempted to eat the second, but, knowing I was to be a long time on the mountain, resolved to keep it for later. Archibald sat nearby and chewed slowly on a bannock he had taken from the pocket of his jacket. He offered me a piece, which I refused as I did not wish to share my potato. The ghillie ate with the gentlemen, but did not join in their conversation. Nor did he accept the offer of a glass of wine. The gentlemen quaffed freely and competed with one another in ever more elaborate descriptions of the scene before their eyes. One of the gentlemen rubbed his temples and made a joke about having taken too great an advantage of Lord Middleton's hospitality the previous night. His companion raised his glass and declared, 'The hair of the dog!' – a statement which mystified me. Lord Middleton took one small glass of wine and spoke in a low voice to the ghillie. The ghillie made a remark to the effect that the gentlemen would not be shooting many stags after quaffing so much wine and, although he said it in a jocular fashion, I understood that it was meant quite seriously and he did not approve of the gentlemen's behaviour. The gentlemen appeared oblivious to the ghillie's displeasure, however, and emptied three bottles between them.

When the men had declared themselves sated, the crockery and foodstuffs were packed away and I was informed, to my relief,

that there was no need for me to carry the coffer further as I
could retrieve it on our return journey. I was thus in good spirits
as we resumed our trek and this increased when one of the hands,
wishing to fill his pipe, asked me to lead his garron. I took great
pride in this elevation of my duties, and felt that it signified my
acceptance by the men. We took a turn to the south between two
peaks and I imagined our party as explorers venturing into undis-
covered lands. Lord Middleton's guests were in high spirits and
conversed loudly with one another. The ghillie was obliged to tell
them to keep their voices down or there would be no sport that
day. I was taken aback to see the ghillie address the gentlemen in
this curt fashion, but Lord Middleton did not appear in the least
affronted. The gentlemen looked quite shame-faced and continued in silence. The ghillie now took the lead and every hundred
yards or so, he directed us to halt by stretching the palm of his
hand from his side. We stood, barely taking a breath, as he scanned
the mountainside and seemed to be smelling the air, before wordlessly directing us to proceed this way or that with a further gesture of his hand. After an hour or so, we came to a ridge and the
ghillie instructed us to keep our heads down. I lay on my belly in
the heather. The mood of our party was now quite sombre. Below
us a herd of thirty or forty deer grazed. The hinds all faced in one
direction, their heads lowered to the sod, moving slowly forward
like a group of women sowing crops. We were close enough to see
the unhurried rotation of their jaws. At the head of the group was
a stag with antlers like a pair of craggy hands held towards the sky.
The beasts were quite unaware of our presence.

The ghillie silently indicated to one of the stalkers to come forward. This gentleman silently, and with some competence, loaded
his weapon and directed it towards the stag, resting his head on
the butt. It was a moment of great solemnity. I was close enough
to the gentleman to see his finger move towards the trigger. I
looked again to the stag and felt it a terrible shame that it should
die in order that this man might mount its head on the wall of his
parlour. The gentleman's finger curled around the trigger. Without

any forethought, I leapt suddenly to my feet and bounded over the ridge, flapping my arms like a great bird and crowing like a cock. The deer below took flight and the gentleman loosed his shot into the air. The ghillie leapt forward, grabbed me by the arm and threw me roughly to the ground. I was, at that moment, as shocked as he by my actions and immediately regretted them. The ghillie uttered a series of crude oaths and, fearing that he would set about me with the butt of his weapon, I covered my head with my arms. He did not do so, however, and I was left prostrate in the heather feeling dreadfully foolish. The two hands laughed heartily, but were silenced by a stern look from the ghillie. Lord Middleton's face had turned quite purple, whether from the effects of the mountain air or from rage, I could not say. The three gentlemen stared at me in astonishment. I fancied that the ghillie might send me running down the glen so that the guests might take shots at me in lieu of the sport I had disrupted. Nothing of that nature occurred, however. Lord Middleton stepped forward and asked the ghillie my name.

'He is Roderick Macrae, son of John Macrae of Culduie,' he replied.

Lord Middleton nodded and said, 'See that he is not employed on the estate again.'

He then turned and apologised to his guests. Had I been given the opportunity I would have done the same, but I was sent off the mountain and reminded to collect my coffer and return it to the kitchens. I struggled to my feet, grateful to Lord Middleton for the leniency of my punishment. As I departed the group, Archibald Ross averted his gaze, not wishing to associate himself with such an imbecile.

When I returned that evening I said nothing about the incident on the mountain. The following morning I left with my two potatoes in my pocket as if nothing untoward had occurred and spent the day loitering among the lochans on the Càrn. When I returned in the evening my father had heard word of my misdemeanour and I received a deserved and thorough beating.

* * *

Some time after the incident with the sheep, a rumour arose that Lachlan Broad had paid a visit to the factor. The provenance of the rumour was unclear. A number of inhabitants of Applecross claimed to have seen Broad walking in the direction of the factor's house, but this in itself could hardly be said to constitute proof. It was unheard of for a person to visit the factor of their own volition, but had he been summoned, the notice would have been served through the constable, and Calum Finlayson had served no such notice. My father muttered darkly that the most likely source of the rumour was Lachlan Broad himself. In any case, through force of repetition the story came to be accepted as fact.

What is certain is that shortly after this alleged visit, Calum Finlayson was himself summoned to see the factor. Mr Finlayson's tenure as constable was due to end in a matter of months and, somewhat exceptionally, he had succeeded to see out his term in this unwanted role without estranging himself from his neighbours. As the factor's factotum, the constable is in an unenviable position. If he fails to enforce the regulations, he invites the wrath of the factor, while if he implements the terms of tenancy too vigorously he alienates himself from the community. Mr Finlayson had succeeded in avoiding the latter situation by choosing to quietly draw attention to any transgressions over a strupach, rather than hastening to the factor at the first opportunity. Similarly, where possible, he had encouraged tenants to resolve disputes between themselves and, when required to arbitrate, he was generally thought to have done so in an even-handed manner. The great majority of the community wished him to continue in the position, but accepted that it was a measure of his good character that he had no wish to do so.

After his audience with the factor, Calum Finlayson made it known he had been informed that he had not been pursuing his role with sufficient vigour. Whether this had been brought to the factor's attention by Lachlan Broad was a matter of speculation, but the consequence was that for the remainder of his term he would be obliged to enforce the regulations with greater stringency. In order to compel him to do so, the factor had ordered that he must raise a certain amount in fines in his remaining months in office. Were this sum not achieved, the constable would be obliged to pay the shortfall from his own pocket. Mr Finlayson was greatly distressed by the situation.

A meeting attended by the great majority of inhabitants of our townships was held at Kenny Smoke's house. It was decided that in order to spare Mr Finlayson from the obligation to levy the necessary fines on his neighbours, the regulations would be adhered to as scrupulously as possible. It was further decided that in order to raise the sum required by the factor, those families in a position to do so would contribute five shillings to a general fund. Those that were less well off could contribute according to their means. After the meeting, despite the resentment at being forced, as Kenny Smoke put it, to line the factor's pockets, the people were in high spirits and there was singing and much drinking of whisky.

Lachlan Broad and his kinsmen were not present at the meeting and later refused to contribute to the fund. My father did not approve of the scheme on the grounds that it involved deception and defiance of the powers-that-be. Nevertheless, he contributed a shilling as a mark of the esteem in which he held Calum Finlayson. As no one wanted a black mark against their name for having transgressed the regulations, it was agreed the fines would be recorded as having been levied equally against the families of the parish. In this way, no family or individual could be singled out for further sanction. As the summer wore on, despite the hardship caused by the unnecessary expenditure, the scheme became a source of some amusement. Fines were levied for ever more frivolous transgressions. My father's contribution was recorded as a penalty for allowing his cock to crow during the hours of darkness. Kenny Smoke was fined for failing to enquire after the health of the factor, and Maggie Blind, a widow from Camusterrach, for setting out to walk to church with her left foot. When the time came for Mr Finlayson to hand over the funds, the factor must have suspected that all was not as it seemed, but he could scarcely accuse his constable of failing to execute his duties zealously. The people were generally highly delighted with the success of the scheme, seeing it as a small victory over the authorities. My father, however, was of the opinion that the people should not be so pleased to be handing over their money to the factor, and I shared this view.

Towards the end of the summer, Lachlan Broad made it known that he intended to put himself forward for the soon-to-be vacant role of constable. It was unheard of for anyone to volunteer for this thankless position. Even those who might enjoy the authority the role bestowed knew better than to admit it. It was widely held that Lachlan Broad would relish the exercise of power over his neighbours and, for this reason, an alternative candidate was covertly sought. My father, though not well-liked, was respected in the community, and one evening a number of men, Kenny Smoke among them, visited our house to persuade him to allow himself to be put forward. My father asked each of the men in turn why, if they felt it was so important to oppose Lachlan Broad, they did not do so themselves. Each of the men had their own excuses for not doing so and by the time the last of them had spoken, my father had no need to declare his refusal. The fact was that the meeting between Lachlan Broad and the factor, whether real or imagined, had led to the perception that he was the factor's man, and for no other reason than this, no one wished to put himself up against him. In the end the only person who could be persuaded to stand was Murdo Cock, an imbecile who lived in a hut in Aird-Dubh and was said to survive on a diet of sowens and limpets.

The vote was held at the manse in Camusterrach. On the appointed evening the men of the three villages filed in, their caps stuffed in the pockets of their jackets or clasped in front of them. Reverend Galbraith greeted each of the men as they entered, making general enquiries after their families and remarking on any recent absences from the kirk. The atmosphere was subdued. The factor stood flanked by the two candidates and briefly addressed the assembled company. He thanked them for their attendance and reminded them of the importance of the role of the constable in the happy management of the estate. He commended neither man, noting only their public-spiritedness in standing and expressing his confidence that the men would choose the most able candidate. Reverend Galbraith then took the opportunity to lead the men in prayer. When it came to the vote, not one man raised their hand to oppose Lachlan Broad.

Broad was not long in exercising his new powers. One evening shortly after his appointment, he paid a visit to our house. Jetta was just after putting away the crockery from our meal and had taken up her knitting. Father was in his chair by the window. I had remained at the table. It was still light and I had been staring out of the open door for some minutes, watching Lachlan Broad and his brother approach. It was only when they had passed our neighbour's house that I realised they intended to call on us and by that time it was too late to alert my father to their imminent arrival. Broad's large frame filled the doorway. He did not utter any greeting and I believe it was the alteration in the light which led my father to look up from his book. At this point, the new constable bid us good evening. My father stood up, but made no pretence of welcoming him. Aeneas Mackenzie remained outside, with his arms folded as if to stand guard against any intruders. Lachlan Broad took one or two steps inside the house and announced that, in his recently acquired capacity, he was visiting all the households under his jurisdiction.

My father said in a sly tone, 'So we are now under your jurisdiction, are we?'

Lachlan Broad replied, 'You are under the jurisdiction of the laird, and since his factor is entrusted with the management of the estate and I am now the representative of the factor in these townships, then, yes, you are under my jurisdiction.'

He then gestured towards the table with his right hand and said, 'Am I not to be welcomed into your house?'

My father indicated that he should take a seat and instructed

Jetta to take her knitting elsewhere, but he did not offer Broad a refreshment as he would to another visitor. Lachlan Broad watched Jetta withdraw to the back chamber before taking a seat on the bench and bidding me good evening. I returned his greeting in as civil a manner as I could muster, as had I said what was truthfully in my mind, he would surely have levied a fine against us.

When my father had taken his place at the head of the table, Lachlan Broad began by stating that he was gratified to have gained the support of the community in securing the position of constable. He then discoursed at some length on the responsibility of individuals to comply with the terms of their tenancies. The regulations, he said, did not exist for the amusement or profit of the laird, they were for the benefit of everyone in the community. 'If there were no regulations,' he said, 'we would be living in a state of anarchy, would we not?'

As he spoke he drummed the middle three fingers of his right hand on the table, so that they made a sound like the distant galloping of a pony. His fingers were thick and chafed, the nails chipped and ingrained with dirt. Throughout his speech, his gaze remained fixed somewhere between the top of the dresser and the roof-trees as if he was addressing a parish meeting. He paused for a few moments as if to give my father an opportunity to respond, but when he did not do so, he continued.

He was of the opinion that, of late, our community had brought shame upon itself through its lack of adherence to the regulations, and by the laxity with which they had been enforced. We had been behaving, he said, like schoolchildren when the teacher's back is turned, and had been indulged in this by an authority who, in wishing too much to be liked, had ill-served his community. However, he took his election as constable as a sign that the people wished to mend their ways. He was thus taking the opportunity to remind all tenants of their responsibilities under the terms of their leases. If things did not change for the better, measures would have to be taken. He was silent for a few moments before adding, as if as an afterthought, that he spoke with the full authority of the factor.

My father's expression had not altered since the beginning of Broad's speech. But he now took his pipe from his mouth and set about refilling it from his pouch. This done, he lit it and took a few slow puffs.

'You have no call to remind me of my responsibilities, Lachlan Mackenzie. I have never transgressed any regulations and have never had a black mark placed against my name.'

'I regret to say, Mr Macrae, that your response only confirms the state of anarchy into which we have lately fallen, such that we have so disregarded the regulations we no longer know when we are breaking them.' He then added, 'In any case, it is not for you or anyone else to know whether there are black marks against their name.'

My father puffed steadily on his pipe. It was rarely possible to know what he was thinking, but at that moment I sensed from a certain hardness in his eyes that he was displeased. Lachlan Broad's fingers ceased their drumming and he placed his left hand, which until then had been resting on his lap, flat on the table. I interpreted this action as a sign that he meant to stand up and take his leave, but he did not do so. Instead, it transpired that his remarks up to that point had been a mere preface to the real purpose of his visit.

'Aside from these generalities,' he said, 'there is an additional matter which concerns your household in particular.'

His fingers resumed their drumming. I assumed he was about to re-open the matter of the killing of the sheep and use his newly acquired powers to increase the fine against my father, or at least demand its immediate payment. But in this I was mistaken.

'It has been decided,' he continued, 'that the extent of your croft should be reduced.'

My father's expression did not alter.

'Since your wife's death, your household has decreased in number and, assuming you have no plans to re-marry, this reduction must be permanent. Your allocation of land is therefore to be reduced by one fifth. There are other larger families whose crofts are smaller than yours and the land will be allocated to one of those.'

'You mean to yourself,' said my father.

Lachlan Broad tutted softly and shook his head as if he was offended by the suggestion. 'Certainly not to myself, Mr Macrae. That would be an abuse of my office. The land will be allocated to an appropriate family.'

'None of my neighbours will accept it,' said my father.

Lachlan Broad pursed his lips. 'We shall see,' he said. 'It would be in no one's interest for the land to lie fallow.'

'My father and grandfather worked this land before me.'

'Yes,' said Broad, 'but it did not belong to them and it does not belong to you. It belongs to the laird and it is at his discretion that you have the privilege of working it.'

'What about the rent?'

I inwardly cursed my father, as his question clearly signified his intention to yield on the matter of the reduction of the croft. If my mother had been alive, she would have immediately ejected Lachlan Broad from the house with an earful of insults, but my father was not made of such stuff.

'What about the rent?' said Broad.

'If the extent of the croft is to be reduced, then so, surely, should the rent,' said my father.

The constable gave a little laugh through his nose, to indicate the absurdity of the idea.

'Your rent, I believe, has been in arrears for some years,' he said. 'If I might offer you some advice, I would not provoke the powers-that-be by asking for a reduction.'

My father stood up and, placing his knuckles on the table, leaned towards Lachlan Broad.

'I shall seek an appointment with the factor to discuss this matter,' he said.

Broad remained seated and spread his hands out in front of him. 'You are quite free to do so,' he said, 'but I can assure you I speak with the factor's authority. I'm sure you do not wish to gain a reputation as one of those who seeks to agitate against the smooth running of the estate, the management of which, I remind you, is carried out for the benefit of the community rather than any individual. As you have yourself stated, you do not wish to have any more black marks placed against your name.'

At this point Lachlan Broad stood up and said in a matter-of-fact way, 'The re-allocation will take place in spring so that you will have the opportunity to take this year's crops from the land. You may decide yourself which portion of land you wish to give up and tell me in due course.'

He then informed us that in future we should address him as Constable Mackenzie or simply as Constable, this in order that we should not forget that he was acting in an official capacity.

My father did not seek a meeting with the factor and in spring the portion of the croft furthest from the house was given to our neighbour, Duncan Gregor, who lived with his elderly mother, wife and four children. Mr Gregor called on my father to assure him that he had never sought to obtain this portion of his croft and had no wish to profit at my father's expense. He proposed that the two families work the piece of land in common and share the harvest between them. My father refused this generous offer, saying that he had no wish to cultivate land that was not his to work and that, in any case, Mr Gregor's needs were greater than his. Mr Gregor spent some time putting various arguments to my father, but he would not be moved. Nor would he accept any other compensation for his loss.

* * *

The nature of Lachlan Broad's regime quickly became clear. In previous years, whoever held the post of constable had done so reluctantly and only performed their duties when pressed to do so. Lachlan Broad, however, threw himself into the role with the fervour of a fox in a hen house. He strutted round the villages under his jurisdiction, notebook in hand and a pencil behind his ear, most often accompanied by his imbecilic brother, cousin or both. The upkeep of crofts and the condition of the paths, ditches and tracks were all subjected to his scrutiny. Nor did he confine his inspections to communal areas. He thought nothing of marching unannounced into his neighbours' houses and scribbling notes in his little book, the contents of which he would not divulge to anyone. These notes did not result in immediate fines. People knew only that the constable had taken note of something and that it might be used against them at some time in the future. Consequently, Lachlan Broad found people acquiescent when asked to work on his croft or carry out other tasks from which his self-imposed duties kept him.

Lachlan Broad decreed that the roads and tracks connecting our houses and villages had been allowed to fall into an unacceptable state of disrepair. A general programme of works was drawn up and the able-bodied men of the parish were mandated to give ten days' labour at a time dictated by the constable. Those bold enough to question this obligation to provide their labour free of charge were informed that they were required by the terms of their tenancy to keep the communal roads and tracks properly drained and in good repair. It was thus a matter of leniency that villagers were merely being asked to carry out responsibilities they had previously ignored, rather than being fined for their neglect. Despite the grumblings about the high-handed nature of Lachlan Broad's methods, it was widely accepted that the improvements he instituted were for the general good.

In maintaining his good name, the constable was assisted by the large number of his kinsmen who resided in the villages under his authority. Like those of other clans, Mackenzies were naturally inclined to spring to the defence of one of their own and it became commonplace, or at least it was believed to be commonplace, for disparaging remarks about Broad to be reported back to him. People thus saw the wisdom of keeping their thoughts about the constable to themselves.

One evening my father was taking the air on the bench outside our house. Kenny Smoke joined him and the two men sat in silence for some minutes sucking on their pipes. Lachlan Broad was making his way along the track which led from the road to the village, making some minute inspection of the ditches. Kenny

Smoke took his pipe from his mouth, leaned in towards my father and muttered, 'Lachlan Broad is a great arse, but there is no denying the improvement in the upkeep of the place.'

My father did not reply. He did not approve of language of this nature.

Lachlan Broad's influence extended into every aspect of village life. The end of the black months is, in these parts, signified by the cutting and drying of the peats, which takes place as soon as the weather permits. This is a task performed by the village as a single entity, as it makes no sense for families to cut peat only for themselves. It is arduous work, but generally takes place in a good-natured atmosphere, with singing and communal refreshments. This year, however, despite the fact that the peat-cutting had been successfully accomplished since time immemorial, the constable took it upon himself to oversee the process. Work rotas were drawn up and deputies (invariably one of Broad's own kinsmen) appointed to oversee the work in each of the villages under his jurisdiction. These deputies did no work themselves, but spent the day prowling around the bogs, barking orders at the cutters and determining at what time refreshments would be taken. This caused a great deal of resentment, as it appeared that labour which villagers had previously undertaken of their own volition, was now being carried out only at the behest of the authorities. There was thus none of the singing and good humour that normally accompanied this work. I was subject to special scrutiny, as, since the incident with the sheep, it was said that I could not be trusted with a peat iron. I was thus forced to work at some distance from the others and if I paused so much as to mop my brow, Aeneas Mackenzie would bellow at me to stop idling. I confess that I would have happily taken my tool to his skull, but not wishing to bring any more trouble to my father I worked as hard as I could, returning each evening from the mountain with arms and calves aching from my exertions.

One morning, some days into the cutting of the peats, I realised that I had forgotten the bannocks which Jetta had set out for

me. Without a word to my fellows, who were resting around the
edges of the bog, I set off down the hillside. It was a warm, sunny
day and the morning's work had raised a sweat on my back. As I
strode down the hillside I thought I might take a few moments'
rest on the bench outside our house with a cup of milk. The village was quiet. Most of the menfolk were on the mountain and
the women were likely occupied with their own household chores.
My father, who by that time lacked the strength for a full day at
the peats, was labouring at the foot of the croft with his cas chrom
and, observing his feeble efforts, I reflected that when the cutting
of the peats was done, it would be my next task to properly break
the ground of what was left of our land.

I stood for a moment at the threshold of the house. After the
bright sunshine, my eyes took some time to adjust to the gloom
inside. A faint glow emanated from the smouldering fire and a
thin shaft of light penetrated the window. I was taken aback to see
a figure standing with his back to the door at the end of our table.
My surprise increased when I discerned from his proportions and
from the yellow neckerchief around his neck that it was Lachlan
Broad. He appeared to be struggling to shift the table, his hands
gripping the sides and his legs and body straining against it. This
puzzled me as I could think of no reason for the constable to
be attempting to move our furniture; and moreover, our table is
not of such weighty construction that a man of Lachlan Broad's
stature would struggle to lift it. I was about to announce my presence when I saw two legs projecting from either side of Lachlan
Broad's hips. These legs were suspended in the air, slightly bent
at the knee, roughly parallel to the earthen floor of the house. I
could tell by the black boots on their feet that they belonged to
my sister. I then discerned midway along the table, a second pair
of hands, exerting a firm grip on the rim. I stood silently at the
door and watched for some minutes as Lachlan Broad continued to strain with increasing intensity at the table. He commenced
to make some animalistic noises and then, all of a sudden, quit
without having moved the furniture more than a few inches. He

stepped back from the table and turned towards the window. I saw his member protruding from his breeches, greatly engorged and rigid as a broom handle. He took it in his hand and pushed it into his trousers. He was breathing heavily from his exertions and there was sweat on his forehead. I had made no sound, but he turned his head towards me, as if he had all along been aware of my presence. He bid me good morning, as though there was nothing unusual in his presence in our house. He then untied his neckerchief and used it to mop his brow and neck, before unhurriedly smoothing back the hair from his face. He glanced down at Jetta, whose hands had now released their grip on the table, and walked towards me. I stood aside to allow him to pass.

He paused at the doorway and said, 'Should you not be at the peats, boy?'

I have always disliked being called 'boy', as this is how my father addresses me when he is displeased, and I blurted out, 'I am not your boy, Mr Mackenzie.'

I immediately regretted this outburst, thinking he would inform my father that I had spoken disrespectfully to him and fine us a shilling. But instead he clasped the back of my head and pushed his face close to mine and said, 'When you're older you'll realise that a man has to satisfy his needs somewhere. Especially now that your dear mother is no longer with us.' Then he laughed raucously and left. I watched him stride along the village, twirling his neckerchief in his right hand, and felt a dreadful loathing for him.

Jetta remained on the table, her own chest rising and falling, and my eyes were drawn to the dark region between her parted thighs. Without raising her back from the table-top, she pushed down the skirts and petticoats which were rucked around her waist. Then she pulled herself into a sitting position and sat there for some minutes, her feet dangling above the floor. Her face was flushed and there were beads of perspiration on her brow. I did not know what to say, so I said nothing. Eventually she stood up and smoothed down her clothing. She asked me what I was doing there and I told her that I had forgotten my bannocks. She fetched them from the dresser and brought them to where I stood by the door. Her cheeks were glowing as if she had been running or dancing. She told me to say nothing to Father about what I had seen. I nodded and asked if there was a cup of milk for me.

I took my bannocks and sat down on the bench outside the house. Jetta brought me a cup of milk and went back inside without a word. My father had his back to the house and did not look up. I watched him as he struggled with the plough, his foot frequently slipping off the peg. He worked methodically, but with little impact on the ground. I cannot say whether he had seen Lachlan Broad entering or leaving our house. Certainly for the few minutes that I watched him, he did not once look up from his labour.

When I returned to the peat-bog, Aeneas Mackenzie called me to him and told me that he would be reporting my absence from the mountain to his brother. I replied that there was no need as I had already seen him and I heard no more about the matter.

*   *   *

It was around this time that I made the acquaintance of Flora Mackenzie, the eldest daughter of Lachlan Broad. We had attended school together, but my unsociable nature in those days meant that to all intents and purposes we were now meeting for the first time. She was a year or so younger than me, and on account of this and the bad blood between our families, we had had little contact. At school Flora sat at the front of the classroom and, although I was unable to see her face, I imagined it to be a picture of rapt attention. She was always first to volunteer to clean the blackboard for Mr Gillies and was inordinately proud of herself when he granted her this privilege. If I had any impression of her at that time, it was of a silly girl, over-anxious to please those in authority.

One afternoon, I had been put to work breaking ground on Lachlan Broad's croft. Flora was sweeping outside the house and attending to her infant brother, Donald. Although I had my back to her, I became aware that she was observing me. I continued my labour for some minutes, all the time conscious of her eyes upon me. I paused and turned towards where she was standing. She was leaning on the handle of her broom and made no attempt to conceal that she had been watching me. I leant on the handle of my flaughter, imitating her stance, and stared back at her. We remained there for some moments, as if engaged in a game. Then she shrugged her shoulders and went inside as if she had suddenly remembered some pressing task there. Some time later, she emerged from the house and brought me a cup of milk.

'I thought you might be thirsty,' she said, handing it to me.

I took it from her and drained it at a single draught.

'Thank you,' I said. I wiped my mouth with the back of my hand. She took the cup from me and went back to the house, her hips swinging as she clambered over the furrows.

One evening some days later, I was coming out of the outbuilding behind our house. I had pulled the wooden door over and was winding the rope around the rotting jamb, when I became aware of the presence of another person. I completed the task of fastening the rope as if I did not know that anyone was there. I cannot say why I engaged in this small pretence, except perhaps that I did not wish the person to think that I had been engaged in any secret activity. I must have assumed it to be Jetta, although there was no reason for her to have been silently watching me. I knew it was not my father because, after supper, he had already taken his seat by the window and once there he rarely moved until he retired to bed. Certainly it was not Flora Broad I expected to see standing by the quoin of the Gregor's house. My expression must have betrayed my surprise, because she giggled and put her hand to her mouth, as if it had all along been her plan to startle me and she was pleased with the success of her enterprise.

I did not know what to say, so I just looked at her. Flora had changed markedly since our schooldays. Her features had become less childish, her nose and mouth somewhat larger. Her hair was tied up in the way that the womenfolk wore it, rather than in girlish pigtails. Her figure had grown fuller and her bosom now filled out the bodice of her dress pleasingly. Her skirt reached within

an inch or two of her ankles and the frilled border of her petticoats was visible beneath the hem of this garment. On her feet
she wore a pair of neat black boots. I wondered if they had been
bought with the shillings we were paying to her father in compensation for the sheep. She studied me with her head on one side, as
if I was a curiosity in a travelling show.

Flora bid me good evening and asked what I had been doing. I
replied that it was no business of hers what I was doing, and that
I might ask her the same question. She said that if I would not
tell her what I had been doing in the barn, I must have been up
to some mischief. She then added that her father said I was a bad
lot and had told her to keep away from me. I was not surprised
to hear Lachlan Broad's low opinion of me, but it struck me that
Flora's motive was less to cause offence than to convey that in
seeking me out she was defying her father's wishes.

'And what would your father say if he knew you were talking
to me now?' I said.

Flora shrugged her shoulders and widened her eyes as if it was
a matter of no consequence to her.

'If I was your father, I would give you a sound thrashing,' I said.

'Perhaps he would give you the thrashing instead,' she replied.

'I have no doubt it would give him great pleasure to do so.'

Flora giggled, as if the prospect of seeing me beaten amused
her. She then asked me for a second time what I had been doing
in the barn. Feeling now that there was some bond between us, I
told her I had been tending a fledgling which, two or three days
before, I had found in the grass at the very spot where she was
now standing. I pointed to a nest in the gable of the house above
her head from which the little bird had fallen.

'Why did you not put it back in the nest?' she asked.

I did not know how to answer this question as had I merely
wanted to save the little bird; this would indeed have been the simplest course of action. The truth was that I often nursed injured
birds or animals, but I did so in secret as my father would regard
my hobby as a waste of time, or, worse, as a defiance of God's

will. In any case, more often than not my charges died. Two years previously, however, I had reared a fledgling I found while bringing peats from the hillside. As it grew feathers I realised it was a crow and I named him Blackie. One evening when I went to the barn to feed my charge, he was gone and I assumed he had grown strong enough to make his own way in the world. I do not know whether these birds remain in the vicinity of their birth, but whenever I saw a crow strutting over the stubble of a croft or perched on the dyke by the Toscaig road, I wondered if it was Blackie and if there was some glint of recognition in his eye.

In these parts, crows are an unwelcome sight as they are thought to be an augury of ill fortune. The folk of Aird-Dubh, being mostly concerned with fishing, are particularly ill-disposed to these birds and the sight of a crow perched on one of their vessels causes great consternation among them. I have witnessed fishermen hurling sizeable rocks at an offending bird with no regard to the damage they might cause the boat, as if in repelling the symbol they will avert the misfortune it portends. Yet I have never known a native of Aird-Dubh, or elsewhere for that matter, to alter their course of action when thus alerted to danger. The outlook in these parts is that if one is to be visited by misfortune, there is nothing that can be done to avoid it. If a crew of men were to abort their fishing trip, it might be that one of them would later that day be struck on the head by a falling roof-tree in his house. It is not possible to know in advance what form the misfortune will take and it is thus futile to do anything other than what one intended in the first place. All of which renders the action of hurling missiles at the harbinger yet more mystifying. Crows are, moreover, very numerous in these parts and one might spend a good portion of each day attempting to ward them off. It seems to me that if a person is struck by misfortune, it is quite probable that he will be able to think back and remember that a crow was perched that morning on his gable, but this does not make it reasonable to believe there is any connection between the two events.

I asked Flora if she would like to see the injured bird and she replied that she would. I cast my eyes around to convey that what we were about to do was a secret to which she alone was privy. I then unfastened the rope and Flora followed me inside. I pulled the door to behind us. The only light came through the gaps in the slats of the walls and from a small window high in the gable. I had an impulse to take Flora by the hand to lead her to the rafter where I had hidden my charge, but I did not do so. Instead we stood close together, allowing our eyes to become accustomed to the murk. I could hear the soft sound of Flora's breathing. I led the way to the corner and drew up the milking stool which I stood on to tend my charge. I indicated that Flora should stand on it in order to view the little bird. She drew closer and held out her hand to steady herself as she stepped onto the stool. She raised herself onto the toes of her little boots, which were laced neatly around her ankles. Her fingers lingered in mine for a moment before she placed both her hands on the rafter. I had built a makeshift nest from twigs and grass and lined it with feathers from the hens. In addition there were some strips of cloth which I had placed over the little bird to mimic the warmth of its mother. Flora gave a little sigh as she saw the fledgling's head protruding from the bundle of rags and she remained there for some minutes, even though it was sleeping and not much to look at.

'What do you feed it?' she asked in a whisper.

'Insects,' I replied. 'And worms from the croft.'

She held her hand out behind her, so that I could support her as she stepped off the stool. Then she made her way back towards the door. I put the stool in the opposite corner of the barn so that my father would not see it and wonder why it was under the rafter. I would have liked to stay longer in the barn with her, but I could not think of any pretext for doing so. I pushed the door open and stuck out my head out to check that there was no one to see us, before ushering Flora out.

'Thank you for showing me,' she said.

'I'm glad to have shown you,' I replied.

She took a step away from me. 'I had better be away. Father will be wondering where I have got to.'

'You will be in for a good thrashing.'

'If I tell him where I've been, it will be you that gets the thrashing,' she said with a little smile.

Then she disappeared round the corner of the house. I secured the rope around the jamb for a second time and went to the front of the house. I sat down on the bench and watched Flora make her way along the village. She had a way of walking as if her body was singing a song. It was by that time getting dark and the reek hung low over the water. A little later, Jetta came out of the house and sat down next to me with her knitting. I listened to the pleasing clack of her needles in the still air and I asked what she was knitting. She ignored my question and asked me instead who I had been talking to in the barn. I felt my cheeks turn red and answered, 'To no one.'

She laid her knitting on her lap and looked at me with a serious expression.

'Now, Roddy,' she said, 'You know very well that you were talking to someone and you know very well that I know you were talking to someone.'

'Then you must know to whom I was talking,' I said.

'But I would like you to tell me.'

I glanced towards the door of the house, and then said quietly, 'To Flora Broad.'

'Flora Broad!' exclaimed Jetta as if this came as a great revelation to her. 'Pretty little Flora Broad!'

I shushed her. 'Father will hear you,' I said.

'So now you are running after Flora Broad,' she continued. 'Is Jetta not enough for you any longer?'

'I am not running after her,' I said.

'But you must have noticed what a pretty thing she is and how nicely she now fills out her dresses.'

'I have noticed no such thing,' I said, my cheeks reddening for the second time.

Jetta laughed. I was glad of it, for she had not been much given to laughter these recent months. Then her face darkened in the way that it always did when she had an augury of some ill fortune.

'Poor Roddy,' she said, 'I know you do not mean any harm, but I am obliged to tell you that no good will come of this and you must stay away from Flora Broad.'

I cast my eyes downwards, dismayed that she had so swiftly chosen to alter the mood between us. I did not doubt that her advice was based on some intimation from the Other World, but I could do nothing to alter the course of what was to occur, and nor at that point did I wish to.

* * *

Some days later, my father and I rose early to catch the low tide. It was a damp, still morning. The reek from the houses clung to the ground like a shroud. Dew lay thick on the broken ground of the croft. It was our intention that morning to gather the sea-ware which, along with the winter's dung from the livestock, would nourish our crops. We made our way to the waterline, frequently slipping on the slimy rocks. My father was stiff with rheumatics, so it fell to me to cut the sea-ware from rocks and I set about this task. It was arduous work. The blade of my croman was blunt and each fistful of sea-ware I hacked from the rocks required considerable effort. My father leaned on his pitchfork, watching me work, passing frequent comments about how I should alter my grip on my tool or straighten my back while I worked. I made no response to his advice. After I had gathered a sizeable pile, Father began the task of shifting it above the high-tide line. He lost half of his cargo from the tines of his fork on each journey but did not trouble to stop and retrieve it. On more than one occasion, he completely lost his footing, sending the entire forkful flying into the air and himself into a bony heap on the rocks. Despite the waste of our labours, I could not help laughing when this occurred. My father resembled an upturned crab, limbs struggling uselessly in the air, until he managed to right himself.

Nevertheless, as the morning wore on we found some kind of rhythm. As the tide turned I worked continually further up the shore, so that my father's journeys became ever shorter. Father

even set to singing a little to himself. It was a weird kind of singing, more spoken than musical and comprehensible to no one but
himself, but it was a singing all the same, and I was glad to hear it.
By midday, we had gathered a pile four feet high, enough to cover
half of our land. From there it could be transported to the croft
by hurlie, a straightforward task. Father sat down on a rock next
to our heap and took his pipe from the jacket of his pocket and
lit it. This I took to signify the end of our morning's work. We sat
in silence for some minutes, feeling some communal satisfaction
in what we had achieved. Father then instructed me to go to the
house and bring some milk and bannocks.

As I made my way back down the rig I saw the figures of
Lachlan Broad and his brother walking along the road towards
where my father was sitting. They stopped and bid my father good
day to which he made no response, or at least I did not hear him
do so. He had his back to me and I could see a thin wisp of smoke
rise from his pipe. As there was no wind, it lingered around his
cap as the reek had earlier hung around the houses. I feared that
Lachlan Broad was going to make a complaint about my association with his daughter, and hastened towards them as if this would
deter him. I handed my father his cup of milk.

'I see you are gathering the sea-ware,' Lachlan Broad was saying.

My father did not say anything.

'For what purpose, may I enquire?'

'Now, for what purpose would I be gathering sea-ware?' my
father responded. He kept his eyes fixed straight ahead towards
the bay. A seal put his head above the water and observed the
scene for a few moments before silently arcing back under the
surface.

Lachlan Broad made a gesture with his hand that seemed to
suggest that there might be many reasons one might gather sea-
ware. He waited some time before continuing.

'Are you not going to answer my question?'

'I know of only one reason for gathering sea-ware,' my father
replied. 'As such, I see no purpose in answering your question.'

The constable turned to his brother with an air of bewilderment, as if he could not understand why my father was behaving so obstructively. Aeneas Mackenzie bleated like a sheep.

'Since you oblige me to guess,' he continued, 'can I assume that you are gathering the sea-ware for the purpose of spreading it on your land?'

'You are very astute, Constable,' said my father, with a special emphasis on this last word.

Lachlan Broad now pursed his lips and nodded slowly, as if this answer troubled him.

'You are aware, are you not,' he said, 'that the fruits of the shore, including its sea-ware, are the property of the laird?'

My father took his pipe from his mouth, but did not say anything. Lachlan Broad pressed his point.

'Are you aware of this, Mr Macrae?'

My father took up his milk and drank it at one draught. The cream formed a yellow caterpillar on his moustaches which remained there for the remainder of the conversation.

'And what would the laird want with a few forkfuls of sea-ware?' he said. He kept his gaze all the time directed at the horizon.

Lachlan Broad shook his head, as if my father had misunderstood him, or rather as if the fault was his own for not making clear his meaning.

'It is not that the laird might have use for the sea-ware, my point is merely that the sea-ware is the property of the laird.' He paused for a moment. 'I'm sure I do not need to instruct a devout man like yourself that it is not for one man to be taking what belongs to another.'

Father's eyes darted towards him.

'As you well know, Lachlan Broad, the people have always taken sea-ware for their land, yourself and your father included.'

'That is quite true, but it is only through the beneficence of the laird that we have done so. It is quite contrary to the terms of your tenancy to make use of the fruits of the land or shore without first having sought permission to do so.'

My father stood up from the rock he had been sitting on and took a step towards Broad.

'Can I assume no such permission has been sought?' asked the constable.

My father was a good six inches shorter than Broad, but he thrust his chin towards his face in a forceful fashion. His chest was only inches from Broad's. Aeneas Mackenzie took a step closer to his brother's shoulder and emitted a stupid snigger. I had no doubt that he would gladly lay my father on the rocks if he made any further advance.

Lachlan Broad appearing quite unperturbed by the proximity of my father.

'Mr Macrae,' he said, 'when I became constable to these villages, I stated that observance of the regulations which govern our existence had fallen into a neglect which shamed us all. And since, if memory serves, you did not oppose my election, I must assume you are of the same opinion.'

'I know nothing of these regulations with which you are so besotted,' said my father.

Broad chuckled to himself. 'I think we are all aware of the regulations. It does not become you to feign ignorance of them.'

My father inhaled sharply through his nose. His pipe was gripped so tightly in his fist that his knuckles had turned white.

'I regret that you have wasted a morning's labour,' said Broad, 'but I must ask you to return this sea-ware from whence it came.'

'I shall do no such thing,' said my father.

Lachlan Broad exhaled slowly and made a clicking sound with his tongue.

'As your village constable I would advise you to do as I suggest. I am giving you the opportunity to rectify this transgression without levying a fine, which I know you can ill afford to pay. And I am quite sure you would prefer to resolve this matter without the involvement of the factor.'

He took a step back from my father, then gave him a pat on the shoulder and said, 'I shall leave it to you. I have no doubt you will make the correct decision.'

Then he made a sign to his brother and the two of them made their way back to the village. My father snapped his pipe in two, then cast the pieces on the shore and crushed them under the heel of his boot. Then he told me to return the sea-ware to the shore, and strode off back towards the house.

That same evening, Lachlan Broad paid a visit to our house. My father was sitting in his chair gazing out of the window and must have seen him approach, but when Broad stepped over the threshold, he lowered his eyes to the book on his lap and pretended to be unaware of his presence. Jetta looked up from her chores and upon seeing him her eyes widened and she inhaled sharply, her lips parted. Lachlan Broad looked at her intently, but did not greet her. He then knocked on the door jamb to gain my father's attention and asked if he might have a few words with him. My father returned his gaze to his book and affected to finish the passage he was reading. He then stood up and took a few paces towards Broad.

'No doubt if I were to refuse you entry to my house,' he said, 'you would point out that it is not my house at all, but the property of the laird, and as such I have no right to impede you.'

Lachlan Broad laughed heartily as if my father had made an amusing joke. 'I'm sure we have not yet reached the point where we would refuse each other the hospitality of our homes.'

He then slapped him on the arm as if they were the best of friends and, keeping his hand about my father's shoulder, steered him towards the table. 'I would be loath to think that our conversation this morning might tarnish our good relations.'

To this my father made no reply, but he did not resist Broad's manoeuvre. The two men sat down at the table – my father at the head, Broad on the bench with his back to the door, so that his face was lit only by the orange glow of the fire. He appeared eager for the atmosphere to be convivial. I was standing with my back to the dresser. He enquired after my health and, not wishing to displease him, I replied that I was quite well. He asked me if I was not going to join them at the table. I looked to my father and, as he did not object, I did so. Broad then gestured towards the swee and in an excessively jovial manner said, 'Jetta, is there not a strupach to greet the weary traveller?'

Jetta looked to my father, who made no sign one way or the other. She thus took it upon herself to prepare tea, and while she did so Broad directed a number of questions towards her, all in a most affable tone. Jetta replied politely, but with a minimal expenditure of words and without once raising her eyes to him. I noticed, however, that her cheeks were quite crimson as she placed the cup before our visitor. She then, at my father's behest, retired to the back chamber. Broad took a sip of his tea and let out an appreciative sigh, as if he had indeed travelled a great distance to reach us.

'John,' he began, leaning forward, 'I fear the incident on the shore might have provoked some ill feeling in you. I thus thought it wise to apprise you of my view of this morning's occurrence, so that you might understand that I had no alternative to acting as I did.'

As my father made no response, he continued, 'I only ask that you consider the consequences of allowing you to gather the sea-ware.'

'Families have gathered sea-ware since time immemorial,' said my father, 'and I recall no consequences, as you call them.'

'That is of course true,' said Broad, 'but perhaps I have not expressed myself clearly. It is not, in itself, the gathering of the sea-ware which is at issue. The issue is the absence of the proper authority to do so. Had I allowed you to continue with your harvesting this morning, would that not have been taken – by individuals less scrupulous than yourself – as an indication that it was acceptable to gather sea-ware as and when people wished? I could hardly have allowed you to continue and then tomorrow ask Mr Gregor to desist. He would quite rightly object that I had allowed you to gather sea-ware, so why should he not do the same? The regulations, I'm sure you would agree, must apply equally to all.'

Here he spread his great hands in front of him as if to suggest that what he had said was irrefutable.

'Now, while I appreciate the inconvenience of returning the sea-ware to the shore, I am sure that you can see that had I not acted as I did, I would have been sanctioning all such unauthorised gathering of sea-ware. As you rightly point out, such gathering has long taken place unchecked, but while you might think there are no consequences to this, I would contend that the consequence is the general flouting of the regulations of which we have all been guilty. As I was elected to the position of constable with the express purpose of restoring order, had I overlooked this morning's transgression, I would make a mockery of my regime.'

He paused for a sip of tea and placed the cup delicately back on the saucer. My father's eyes followed the motion of his hand. A period of silence ensued, which it was clear that my father was not going to break. Lachlan Broad turned to me and said, 'Your father is a man of principle, Roddy. I fear I have not convinced him of my good intentions.'

I did not reply, but cast my eyes to the table to avoid his gaze. He then addressed my father again, his tone now betraying a sense of exasperation.

'Perhaps you feel that my application of the regulations is fanatical, or that I obtain some personal gratification from the exercise of these powers. I can assure you that nothing could be further from the truth. It is quite true that, in itself, the gathering of sea-ware is a trifling matter, but if it is permissible to take sea-ware from the shore, would the people not be correct in concluding that it is also permissible to take fish from the rivers or deer from the hillside?'

'I do not see that the two things are comparable,' said my father.

'But they are,' said Broad, wagging his forefinger to emphasise the point. 'I would not assume to instruct a devout man like yourself on matters of theology, but the Eighth Commandment does not, I believe, make any distinction between the theft of a large item and a small one.'

'Do you accuse me of stealing?' said my father quietly.

'I accuse you of nothing,' said Broad, with a wave of his hand, 'but it is difficult to see how the taking of something which does not belong to you could be otherwise construed.'

My father considered this for a few moments before stating that if Broad had said his piece, there was no reason for him to remain any longer.

The constable did not stir from the bench. He drank the last of his tea and ran the back of his hand over his mouth. His fingers remained at his face for some moments, smoothing his moustache.

'I did not come here to make accusations, John,' he said. 'If I have expressed myself clumsily, forgive me. I have come, on the contrary, in a spirit of reconciliation. Under normal circumstances the fine for this morning's transgression would be ten shillings. However, in light of the fact that, as you rightly point out, sea-ware has been taken from the shore since time immemorial and that, when I drew attention to your error, you returned the sea-ware to the shore, I am prepared to waive the penalty on this occasion.'

If Lachlan Broad thought that my father might thank him for this act of charity, he was mistaken.

'I would rather pay the ten shillings than be in your debt.'

Lachlan Broad nodded. 'I respect that, but as there is no ten shillings to pay, you need not count this as a favour for which you should feel indebted.'

He drummed his fingers once on the table as if to indicate the satisfactory conclusion of the matter. He appeared to be about to take his leave, but then paused as if another thought had suddenly struck him.

'Of course,' he said, 'your need for sea-ware remains.'

'I have no wish to take that which does not belong to me,' said my father.

'As I have been trying to explain,' said Broad, 'it is not a question of taking what does not belong to you, it is merely a matter of following the proper procedures.'

'I have heard quite enough about procedures and regulations these last months.'

'That's as may be, but the procedures exist and they must be followed. In this case, all that is required is that you make an application to the factor that you wish to collect sea-ware from the shore for the purpose of spreading on your croft. Such an application may be made through the factor's representative.'

'You mean to yourself,' said my father.

Broad indicated with a slight nod of his head that this was indeed the case.

'Given the understanding we have reached this evening,' he said, 'I can see no reason not to accept an oral application and I can assure you that such an application would be looked on favourably.'

My father's thin lips twitched, but he said nothing. After some moments a plump hen appeared, silhouetted in the doorway, and thrust its head over the threshold as if it was looking for its companions. Its left leg was suspended in the air, curled underneath its breast like a withered hand. Then, not finding what it was looking for, it retreated and disappeared from view. Lachlan Broad shrugged and said, 'I take it then that you wish to make no such application.'

He then bid us good evening in a manner suggesting we had just spent a convivial hour in each other's company, and took his leave. I have no doubt that he felt greatly pleased with himself and I felt at that moment a terrible hatred of him. He was for sure a clever fellow and my slow-witted father was no match for him.

Father remained at the table and spent the rest of the evening staring blankly towards the empty byre. There being nothing to say about what had passed, I took myself outside and sat on the bench there. The hen that had lately appeared at the door was now pecking at the dirt between the houses. Some minutes later, Lachlan Broad emerged from Mr Gregor's house and without looking in my direction set off along the village, calling next at the house of Kenny Smoke.

The following morning at low tide there was a general gathering of sea-ware from the shore and by evening it had been spread on all the crofts, save our own. My father passed no comment on the proceedings and went about his business as if nothing was amiss. Some days later I heard him remark to Kenny Smoke as they shared a pipe on the bench outside our house that there was no way of knowing whether sea-ware brought any benefit to the crops. It was merely something that the people did out of habit, because their fathers and grandfathers had done so before them. Kenny Smoke replied that the same could be said of many of our practices.

* * *

Mr Sinclair calls on me here quite frequently and I have come to enjoy his visits. The first time he entered my cell I offered him my bed to sit on, but he looked at it with some disdain and remained standing with his back to the door. He suggested that I make myself comfortable, but I thought it improper to sit in the presence of my superior, so I stood in the corner beneath the high window. He was dressed in a tweed suit and brown leather brogues quite ill-suited to his dismal surroundings. His complexion was fresh and his hands pink and soft. I would estimate him to be around forty years old.* He spoke in the measured, elegant manner of a gentleman.

Mr Sinclair informed me that he had been appointed as my advocate and that it was his duty to represent me to the best of his ability. He then told me that he was very pleased to make my acquaintance, and the idea that a gentleman would address a wretch like myself in such a manner struck me as so comical that I began to laugh quite uncontrollably. He waited for me to recover my composure, then informed me that anything I told him was confidential, before explaining the meaning of the word 'confidential' in the manner of a schoolmaster addressing a backward pupil.

---

* *Andrew Sinclair was sixty-two years old at the time.*

I told him that there was no need for him to explain the meaning of this or any other word and, furthermore, that I had no need of his services. He replied that if I wished to have another advocate, it could easily be arranged. However, it was not the identity of my advocate which was at issue, I explained, rather that I did not require the services of any advocate, as I had no intention of denying the charges against me. Mr Sinclair looked at me for some moments with a serious expression. He told me that he understood my position, but the law required that I be represented in court.

'I have no interest in what the law requires,' I replied. 'The law is nothing to me.'

I do not know what possessed me to speak to him in this ill-mannered way, other than a dislike of being told what was or was not required of me. In addition, I felt a degree of mortification at being in the presence of a gentleman while the contents of my bowels lay in a pail by my feet, and I heartily wished him to leave me alone.

Mr Sinclair drew his lips together and nodded slowly.

'Nevertheless,' he said, 'it is my duty to advise you that to dispense with counsel would be quite contrary to your interests.'

He sat down on my bunk and adopted a more conversational tone. He explained that I would be doing him a service if I would be so good as to allow him to put a few questions to me. Feeling somewhat repentant, I indicated that I had no objection and he seemed pleased. The gentleman had treated me with unwarranted courtesy and I had no reason to cause him any trouble.

Mr Sinclair then proceeded to ask me some general questions about my family and the circumstances of my life, quite as if we were two equals getting to know one another. I answered his questions truthfully, but without elaboration, as I could not see that the particulars of my life in Culduie could be of interest to him or anyone else. Nonetheless, Mr Sinclair had a gentle, pleasing manner and I began to warm to his company. If nothing else, our dialogue served to break the monotony of the day. The longer we talked the stranger it seemed that he should converse with me as if the circumstances were quite normal; rather than the fact that he, a gentleman, was engaging in discussion with an uneducated murderer. I wondered if perhaps he had not been informed of my crimes; or if I was not in prison at all, but in an asylum and Mr Sinclair was one of my fellow inmates. However, as the general part of our conversation reached its conclusion, Mr Sinclair came to the point of his visit.

'Now, Roderick,' he said, 'some days ago a dreadful crime was committed in your village.'

'Yes,' I replied, not wishing him to continue. 'I killed Lachlan Broad.'

'And the others?'

'Them too,' I said.

Mr Sinclair nodded slowly. 'You are not saying this in order to take the blame for another person?' he asked.

'No,' I said.

'And did you act alone in this enterprise?'

'Yes,' I said, 'I acted entirely alone and as I have no intention of denying anything, I have no need of the services of an advocate. I do not repent my actions and whatever happens now is a matter of indifference to me.'

Mr Sinclair gazed at me for some moments after my little speech. I did not know what was in his mind, for I have not been much in the company of the educated classes and their manners are quite different from my own people.

Eventually he said that he appreciated my candour and asked my permission to visit again the following day. I said that he was welcome to visit whenever he wished as I had enjoyed talking to him. He replied that he had enjoyed talking to me too. Then he struck the door twice with the flat of his hand and the gaoler, who must have been waiting outside all along, turned the key in the lock and let him out.

Mr Sinclair has indeed continued to visit and I admit that I have come to look forward to his company and regret my rudeness to him on that first day. It is a mark of his superior breeding that he has been prepared to overlook my ill manners. As my cell has now been furnished, at Mr Sinclair's insistence, with a table and chair for me to write at, our time together has become a little more comfortable. Mr Sinclair sits on the rickety chair by the desk while I sit on the bunk or on the floor beneath the window. My advocate's eyes often wander towards the pages I am writing. It was on his second or third visit that he suggested I make a record of the events leading up to my crimes and he seems pleased that I have taken to the task wholeheartedly. One afternoon, as he ran his thumb through my pages, he told me that he was curious to know what was contained in them. I am discomfited by the idea of an educated man perusing my crude text, but I told him I was only writing it because he had asked me to do so and he was welcome to take away the pages whenever he wished. He replied that he preferred to wait until I had finished and that it was important for me to continue as if I was writing neither for him nor for any other audience.

Mr Sinclair seems to me to be a man of great patience. He begins each day by asking me the same questions regarding my general comfort and whether my meals are adequate. He has said several times that it would be possible for a meal to be brought to me from a local inn, but I reply that I am quite accustomed to plain fare and there is no need to go to any inconvenience on my behalf. This morning, however, our conversation took a quite different turn. Mr Sinclair has, in general, avoided discussion of the details of the murders themselves. Today, however, he pressed me on the issue of what was in my mind at the time I committed them. I replied that my only thought was to deliver my father from the injustices visited upon him by Lachlan Mackenzie. Mr Sinclair probed at this point for some time, re-phrasing his questions over and over until I felt that he was trying to catch me out, but he did not succeed in doing so.

Mr Sinclair then asked what I would think if he proposed that at trial we entered a plea of not guilty. I replied that it was an absurd idea as it was quite clear that I was guilty and had never made any attempt to conceal the fact. Mr Sinclair then explained to me that in the eyes of the law, in order for a crime to be committed there must be both a physical act and a mental act. It was clear, he said, that in this case there was a physical act, but whether there was a mental act – an evil intention, he called it – was a matter which concerned the contents of my mind. I listened courteously to Mr Sinclair's earnest summary, feeling increasingly that it was sometimes the case that in his mania to employ his great cleverness he quite disregarded the most obvious facts. However, I responded only that I did not see how anything he had said had any bearing on the present case.

Mr Sinclair then adopted a tone which suggested that he did not wish to injure my feelings. 'What if it was suggested that what you believe to have been in your mind at that time was not what was actually in your mind?' he said.

I laughed quite rudely at this silliness. 'If something else was in my mind, then I would surely have known it,' I said. 'Otherwise it could not have been in my mind.'

Mr Sinclair smiled at my response and tipped his head to one side as if to concede the point. He told me that I was a very clever young man. I confess I was flattered by this pronouncement and I blush at recording it here.

He continued, 'Do you think it is possible, Roddy, for a madman to think that he is of sound mind?'

This proposition initially seemed equally as absurd as his previous statement, but then I thought of Murdo Cock, the imbecile of Aird-Dubh, who was often known to sleep in his hen house and crow like a rooster. Would he, if asked, answer that he was insane? I realised that Mr Sinclair, in his delicate manner, was suggesting that I, in my own way, was like Murdo Cock. I took some moments to respond, realising that I might indeed appear the maniac if I answered intemperately.

'I can assure you,' I said in a measured tone, 'that I am fully in possession of my faculties.'

'It is precisely the fact that you believe that to be true which suggests the opposite,' he replied. I must have seemed quite

offended by this statement, as he then added, 'You must understand, Roderick, that it is my duty to examine all possible avenues
for your defence.'

'But I have no wish to defend myself,' I blurted out, immediately regretting the rudeness of my interruption.

Mr Sinclair nodded briefly and stood up. He looked a little sad
and I felt that I hurt his feelings and wished to make amends.

'All the same,' he said, 'I wonder if you might consent to
being examined by a gentleman who is most eager to make your
acquaintance.'

I was struck once again by the absurdity of the situation in
which, by virtue of making a murderer of myself, gentlemen now
sought out my company, but I replied simply that I would be
happy to meet whomsoever he pleased.

'Good,' he said, and with that he made his usual sign for the
gaoler to release him.

* * *

A few days after the sea-ware incident I met Flora Broad for a
second time. I was sitting on the dyke that separates the crofting
land from the road, teasing some crows by means of a mouse tied
to a length of string. My back was to the village so I was unaware
of Flora approaching. She must have seen that I was engaged in
a game of some kind because when she appeared beside me she
asked what I was playing. I felt ashamed to be engaged in such a
childish pursuit so I let the string drop from my fingers and said
that I was not doing anything.

'It seems that you are always busy doing nothing,' she replied.
'The Devil will find work for your idle hands.'

'And what work would that be?' I said.

Flora shrugged her shoulders and cast her eyes skywards.
She sat down next to me on the dyke. She was carrying a basket
covered with a checked cloth, and this she set on her lap. Her
skirts brushed against my leg. A few moments later the string I
had dropped snaked its way through the grass and a crow hopped

away with the prize between its beak.

'Are you not afraid your father might see us?' I asked.

'It is you that should be afraid,' she said, 'as it is not me that will receive the thrashing.'

Nevertheless, she glanced over her shoulder towards her house.

'I am taking these eggs to Mrs MacLeod in Aird-Dubh,' she said, lifting the cloth to show me the contents of the basket. The Broad Mackenzies kept a fearful number of hens, so many that they were able to supply eggs to the inn at Applecross. Mrs MacLeod was an ancient widow known as the Onion on account of the great number of layers of clothing she wore. It was said that since her husband died she had not once cast off a garment.

Flora asked if I would like to accompany her and I said that I would be glad to. She walked so slowly that I had to pause every few yards to let her catch up. When we reached the junction of the road to Aird-Dubh, Flora asked if I would carry her basket. I took it from her and from that point she walked a little faster, as if it had been the weight of the eggs which had been slowing her down.

'How is the patient?' she asked.

I had that morning found the fledgling dead on the floor of the barn beneath the rafter. Flora looked quite sad and said that she was sorry to hear this news.

'It is one of these things God sends to try us,' she said in a sing-song voice.

I looked at her sideways. It was an oft-expressed sentiment in our parts.

'I cannot imagine that God has no greater concerns than trying us,' I said.

Flora looked at me quite earnestly.

'Then why do such things happen?' she said.

'What things?' I said.

'Bad things.'

'The minister would say that it is to punish us for wickedness,' I said.

'And what would you say?' she asked.

I hesitated a moment and then said, 'I would say that they happen for no reason.'

Flora did not appear unduly disturbed by my answer and I took encouragement from this. 'I do not see that God is much concerned with me, or with any of us for that matter,' I went on.

Flora told me that I should not say such things, but I did not feel that she disagreed with me, only that it was wrong to utter such thoughts.

'Maybe God is just a story like the ones Mr Gillies used to tell us in school,' I said, glancing at Flora out of the corner of my eye. The breeze blew a wisp of hair across her forehead and she raised her hand to her face to arrange it behind her ear. She looked straight ahead and we continued our walk in silence.

When we reached Aird-Dubh, Flora took the basket from me and put her head inside the door of the Onion's house. A bent old woman appeared at the threshold. Her neck was so twisted she had to turn her head to the side, like a hen, to squint up at our faces. It was a warm evening and there was a good fire roaring in the house, but she wore a thick overcoat buttoned up to her neck and tied for good measure around her midriff with a length of string. She seemed pleased to see Flora and invited her into the house. Flora said she had brought some eggs and handed her the basket.

'And who is this you have with you?' she said.

'It's John Black's boy,' Flora said.

'And does he have a name?' Her voice was harsh as a gull's.

'It's Roddy,' said Flora.

The Onion peered at me for some moments and then told me she was sorry for my mother's passing, even though it had been over a year. She took the basket from Flora and disappeared into the smoky gloom of the house. Flora quietly hummed a song to herself while we waited, and I was reminded of my mother singing in the fields. The old woman returned with the empty basket and thanked Flora for the eggs.

On the way back to Culduie, I offered to once again carry the basket, but Flora explained that it had not been that the basket was burdensome, only that she wished to have me carry it for her. In any case, relieved of the eggs, our conversation was freer. Flora made some disparaging remarks about how Mrs MacLeod smelt and I told her that my father did not like the inhabitants of Aird-Dubh because they were filthy and ate limpets. Flora laughed gaily at this. When her laughter subsided she said, 'Sometimes I think your father does not like anyone.'

'He doesn't,' I replied.

I then bent over and mimicked my father hobbling along with his stick. 'Be sure your sins will find you out,' I muttered, wagging a crooked finger in Flora's face. 'You're on the path to the eternal bonfire, young lady!'

Flora stopped in the road, putting her free hand to her mouth to cover her laughter. Then I straightened up, suddenly ashamed to have ridiculed my father in this way.

'Do it again,' she said, but I felt foolish and continued along the road.

When we reached the junction where we had met, in order that we might not be seen I told Flora I would continue along the road. She did not protest. We stood looking at each other for a few moments. Then she said that we might see each other again some other evening and turned and walked up the track, swinging her empty basket in her hand. I made my way along the road and climbed the dyke at the foot of our croft, feeling quite light, as if I had, all of a sudden, been unburdened of a basket of peats. As I made my way through our sickly crops I saw Jetta hurrying along the track from the direction of Lachlan Broad's house, a scarf pulled over her hair and hunched over like a widow. I could not think what business might have taken her to the lower end of the village and waited outside the house for her, but she scurried past me without a glance.

Father was in his chair by the window smoking his evening pipe. I fully expected him to question me about my whereabouts and he duly did so. His chair was angled somewhat away from the window, so that the squib of light from the portal illuminated his text. As he could easily have seen us part at the junction, I told him straightaway that I had been to Aird-Dubh with Flora Broad to deliver some eggs. My father asked who the eggs were for. I could not see what difference it made who the eggs were for, but I told him that too. He made no reaction to my answers, which convinced me that he already knew perfectly well where I had been, and had only enquired to see whether I would tell the truth. He took a couple of pulls on his pipe. Jetta had taken up her knitting and pretended to be oblivious to our dialogue.

I felt aggrieved that I should be questioned this way, particularly as Jetta had received no similar interrogation. My father took his pipe from his mouth and said that he did not wish me to associate with Flora Broad or any other members of her family. I was not in the habit of answering back to my father, but on this occasion I did so. Flora, I told him, had not caused him any injury and she had been grateful to me for carrying her basket. I did not expect my father to engage in a discussion with me and nor did he. Instead, he reminded me that I was not too old for a thrashing. I cast my eyes towards the floor in a semblance of contrition, but I had no intention of obeying his decree. This was far from the first occasion that I felt my father to be overly strict towards myself or my siblings, but it was the first time I resolved to defy him. With the benefit of hindsight, however, I am forced to admit that it would have been prudent to heed his advice.

I went outside and sat on the bench, hoping that my sister would join me, but she did not do so. The following morning, when Father was out of the house, I asked Jetta where she had been the previous evening. She replied without looking up from her chores that she had been visiting Carmina Smoke. I knew that this was not true, as she had come from beyond the Smoke's house, but I did not say so. Instead I asked if Kenny Smoke had been home. Jetta stopped what she was doing and fixed me with a serious stare.

'I already have one father,' she said. 'I do not need another.

There are some things which do not concern you, Roddy.' She then handed me a bannock and ordered me out from under her feet. I felt quite sad as I had never known Jetta to keep a secret from me, although had she been in the habit of doing so, I would hardly have known about it. Perhaps she kept all sorts of secrets from me.

I did not see Flora Broad for some days after this. I was occupied labouring on Lachlan Broad's schemes and in the evenings Father invented tasks for me to do when there were none. I do not know whether this was intended as punishment or merely a measure to keep me from seeing Flora. In any case, it achieved its purpose. When my father had finally done with me, I sat three evenings on the dyke, hoping that Flora would pass by on some errand, or on seeing me there invent some pretext for doing so. But she did not come and I confess that despite the small amount of time we had passed together, I found myself yearning for her company.

It was around this time that I took to travelling abroad at night. Sleep no longer came easily to me and even when I drifted off I was awoken by the slightest stirring of the twins or of an animal outside. In the quiet of the night, all sorts of visions summon themselves from the embers of the fire or the lowing of a stirk. I sometimes fancied that I saw figures rising from the smoke, or heard some voice outside whispering to me, and I would lie on my bunk in a state of fearfulness, awaiting the arrival of some horror. I thus took to forsaking my bed and wandering the hills. I imagined myself as one of my own visions, a shape half-seen in the murk, glimpsed from the corner of one's eye before being dismissed as a fancy. My habit was to disappear between the gables of houses, climb some distance onto the Càrn and gaze down upon the township. In the yellow months, the nights here are never properly dark. The world appears instead as if all colour has been drained from it, and when the moon is high, everything is silver, as if rendered in the etching of a book. If I found myself close to the windows of my neighbours, I would gaze enviously at the slumbering bodies. My object in these excursions was only to empty my mind of uninvited thoughts, and this I achieved by roaming the hills to the point of exhaustion. Not wishing anyone to know of my nocturnal activities, I always returned before my father or sister rose in the morning and would spend the ensuing day in a state of light-headedness. I once or twice fell asleep where I was working, causing Jetta to think I had fainted and come running to my aid.

I determined to use one such nocturnal jaunt to establish whether Flora had returned to the Big House. While I longed to see her, I hoped that she was once again in Lord Middleton's employ, and was thus not avoiding my company of her own volition. On this particular night the moon was obscured by clouds and emitted only the weakest glow. I made my way between the outbuildings and climbed some way up the Càrn. The nature of my mission made me all the more anxious to remain unobserved. I placed my feet soundlessly on the ground and kept my back stooped until I was out of sight of the village. I then traversed the hillside until I was beyond the point where the Broads' house lay. I had never once encountered any more than a sheep on my excursions, but now the blood coursed in my temples. Even in daylight, I dreaded setting foot on Lachlan Broad's property, but to do so under the cover of darkness was an altogether more forbidding prospect. If discovered, I could hardly state the motive for my presence there. Ever since I was a child I have found it hard to dissemble. Once when I was five or six years old, I was sent to the barn to fetch the eggs. I neglected to take the bowl we used for this purpose and rather than retrace my steps to the house, I decided that there was no need of it. I collected the eggs and as I left the barn with them piled in my hands, a bird flew up, startling me and causing me to drop my load. I stared at the mess of albumen and yolk on the ground and immediately the thought came to me to claim that I disturbed a tinker stealing our eggs. When my mother came to look for me, however, I merely burst into tears and told her I had dropped the eggs because I had forgotten to bring the bowl. She took pity on me, wiped away my tears and told me there was no harm in it, there would be more eggs tomorrow. Later when we sat down for our meal, she told my father that there had been no eggs that day and winked at me. I could not, however, count on Lachlan Broad similarly taking pity on me if he were to disturb me lurking behind his house in the dead of night.

Nevertheless, having set my course, I felt compelled to see it to its conclusion. As I made my way down the hillside I struck upon an idea. I had heard tales of those who rise unconscious from their sleep and move about the world as if they are fully awake. Yet, when addressed, they are quite unseeing, as though there is another reality before their eyes. These are the somnambulists and I resolved that, were I to be apprehended, this would be my defence: I would be a somnambulist. In this spirit I approached the dwelling quite unguarded. I was not familiar with the layout of the house, but as there were two small windows in the rear wall, I supposed that these must be the sleeping quarters. To my surprise there was a faint glow in the second of the windows, and I pictured Flora there in her nightclothes, waiting for me by candlelight.

I pressed myself against the wall and inched silently towards the first window. The stones were mossy and damp against my palms. I hesitated, then, holding my breath, slowly moved my head towards the glass. The chamber was in darkness. After some moments I discerned a bed and the dark outlines of bodies wreathed in blankets. Nothing stirred. At the foot of the bed was a cot, and I could see the yellow hair of Flora's infant brother. My breath condensed on the glass. I took three sideward steps towards the second chamber. Abandoning all caution I stepped in front of the window. A candle was flickering and, in a heavy chair, swathed in blankets, sat not Flora, but an ancient woman, Lachlan Broad's invalid mother who had not set foot outside the house for years. Her eyes were open and directed towards the casement, but she did not appear to register my presence. She seemed quite dead and the sight of her set my scalp tingling. To her right was a small bed, empty, and this I thought might be Flora's. I watched the crone for a few moments, until I saw the faint rise and fall of her blankets. Then she blinked slowly, as if regaining her sight, and a bony finger emerged from beneath the covers and pointed towards me. Her lips moved soundlessly. I turned and bolted back up the hillside. Somewhere a dog set to barking and I imagined Lachlan Broad stirring from his sleep and blundering out of bed to investigate the disturbance. I threw myself into the damp grass behind a hummock of heather and lay there awhile, waiting for my breath to come back to me. No one stirred in the houses below and I returned home undetected. I spent what remained of the night lying awake on my bunk, thinking of Flora's empty bed, and feeling quite pleased with the success of my enterprise.

* * *

Our crops grew poorly that summer. I cannot say if this was for the want of sea-ware on our land or due to some other cause. My father had taken the view that we would have a poor harvest and so tended the croft less diligently than usual. When Kenny Smoke commented on the weeds growing in our furrows, Father shrugged and said, 'What's the use? The land is exhausted.'

It seemed to me that it was not the land that was exhausted, but my father. I spent many days working on Lachlan Broad's projects. There were first the days that I was myself obliged to give. Then, as my father's state of health meant that he could not usefully be employed in heavy labour, I worked in his stead. In addition to this, I sometimes laboured for half a shilling a day in lieu of others who were busy with more profitable occupations. I turned over everything I earned to my father and was glad to contribute something to the family's income. Nevertheless, labouring for Lachlan Broad was an irksome business. There was rarely a moment when the constable or his brother were not strutting about like great roosters, ensuring that none of us paused to take breath or wipe the sweat from our brows. Even when Broad was absent we worked relentlessly, fearful that he would suddenly appear and order us to give another day's labour for our idleness. This constant toil meant that I had little time to tend our own crops and, as a consequence, there would be less to eat in the black months.

One evening Lachlan Broad paid us a visit to inform us that it had come to his attention that our croft had fallen into a state of neglect. It had become a favourite expression of his to say that such and such a thing had 'come to his attention'. It perpetuated the notion that whatever anyone did or said would be noted and reported back to him, a notion which ensured a high degree of compliance with whatever decrees he issued. It also led people to look askance at their neighbours and treat them with a degree of suspicion hitherto unknown in our parts. On this occasion, Broad fined my father ten shillings and reminded him that the proper upkeep of the croft was a condition of his tenancy and that if he could not meet his obligations, the factor would have no choice but to review his tenure. In order to raise the funds to pay this fine, I was obliged to labour further on the roads and by-ways and as a consequence the croft fell into an ever more shameful state.

A few days after this latest visit from the constable, my father remained seated after Jetta had cleared the table. I had the impression that he had some announcement to make and I was not mistaken. After filling his pipe and lighting it he informed us that he intended to seek an interview with the factor. I asked him for what purpose. My father ignored my question and stated that he wished me to accompany him, as I was an intelligent boy and would not be bamboozled by the factor's words. I was discomfited at this admission of my father's limitations and protested that he was the equal of the factor, or anyone else for that matter. My father shook his head and said, 'We both know that that is not true, Roderick.' He then said that he intended to go to Applecross in two days' time and that if I had agreed to labour for Lachlan Broad I should find someone to work in my place or make my excuses in advance. He then got up and took his place in his chair by the window.

From the outset, I felt that no good could come from my father's plan. No one from our parish had ever sought a meeting with the factor, and when individuals were summoned to see him, they did so with great trepidation. Father may have reckoned that our lot could hardly be worsened, but I did not doubt that when his visit was brought to Lachlan Broad's attention, he would not hesitate to avenge himself in some way.

Father and I set out for Applecross early in the morning. Lachlan Broad, it transpired, had gone to Kyle of Lochalsh on some business or other and I realised that my father must have chosen this day for our visit with this in mind. The day brought the great contrasts in weather to which we are accustomed in our parts. By the time we reached Camusterrach, a squall had soaked us, before the skies abruptly cleared and the sun began to dry our clothes. As we approached Applecross, however, the skies darkened again and the rain began to fall in large, weighty drops. My father did not react to these changes in the weather. Indeed, I could not say with any certainty that he even noticed. He continued at a steady pace, his arms rigid by his sides, his eyes fixed on the road a few yards ahead. We did not discuss our forthcoming business, so that I still had no real conception of what my father intended to say to the factor or what role he wished me to play. I secretly hoped that the factor would not be at home, or would refuse to receive us, and we could return without having further provoked the powers that be.

The factor's home was to the rear of the Big House. We took a circuitous route around the grounds, my father no doubt wishing to avoid being challenged for trespassing on the laird's property. When we reached the grey stone two-storey house, my father tapped the brass knocker with a timidity that did not augur well for our interview. Presently a housekeeper appeared. She looked at us as if we were tinkers and asked what we wanted. My father removed his cap, even though the woman was a servant and no better than he, and replied that his name was John Macrae of Culduie and that he wished to speak with the factor. The housekeeper then asked if we had an appointment. She was a scrawny woman, with a pinched mouth and long nose, who clearly believed that her employment in the factor's house made her the better of

a crofter. My father replied that we did not. The woman closed
the door without a word and left us standing on the threshold.
As it was still raining we huddled in the small vestibule. It is difficult to say how long we remained there. Certainly enough time
elapsed for my hopes to rise that the factor was not at home. I was
about to express this thought to my father when the door opened
again and we were invited inside. The servant showed us into a
wood-panelled study and told us to wait. A fire was roaring in the
hearth, but neither of us dared to stand near it to dry our clothes.
Instead we stood in the centre of the floor where our presence
would give least offence. On the walls either side of the fireplace
were paintings of distinguished gentlemen, dressed in fine clothes.
I recognised Lord Middleton in one, sitting in an armchair with a
gundog at his feet. In front of us was a large desk of heavy dark
wood. Arranged on the surface were some writing implements
and a number of thick leather-bound ledgers. The wall to our left
was entirely lined with shelves of books.

The factor arrived and, to my surprise, greeted my father with
some warmth. My father made a cringing bow before him, twisting his cap nervously in his hands. I stood for some moments
at his shoulder, trying to appear at ease, my own cap clasped in
front of me. The factor was shorter than I remembered, but had
a pleasant, open face, with dense whiskers growing on his cheeks.
The hair on the top of his head was sparse, but what was there
was wiry and unkempt, unlike that of the other educated men I
had met.

'And who might this be?' he asked, gesticulating towards me.

My father told him and he looked curiously at me for some
moments as if he had heard something about me, which I sincerely hoped he had not. The factor took a seat behind his desk
and looked at my father, expecting him to explain the reason for
his visit. As my father did not do so, the factor then turned his
gaze to me. I could not speak on my father's behalf, however,
as he had not advised me of what he wished to say. Some more
moments of silence ensued. From the corner of my eye, I saw my

father glance towards the factor from beneath his brow.

'Mr Macrae,' the factor began, his tone still jovial, 'I trust you have not walked all the way from Culduie to partake of the warmth of my fire.' He laughed a little at his own joke, before continuing, 'Much as I enjoy parlour games, I cannot guess what mission brings you here, so I must oblige you to state your business.'

My father glanced at me. I thought that he had lost his nerve, or did not understand what was being asked of him, but after clearing his throat he said in a low voice, 'Perhaps you have heard something of the troubles we have been having in Culduie?'

'Troubles?' said the factor. 'I have not heard of any troubles. What troubles?'

'Various troubles, sir.'

'I have heard of no troubles. On the contrary, I hear only good reports of the improvements taking place in your township. Have you spoken to your constable of these "troubles"?' He pronounced this last word with a peculiar emphasis, as if it belonged to a foreign language.

'I have not.'

The factor furrowed his brow and look askance at my father.

'If you are experiencing difficulties, you must speak to Mr Mackenzie. I cannot imagine that he would not feel slighted to know that you had come to me without first seeking his assistance. It is the role of the constable to address any problems you might have. I cannot be concerned with the minutiae of ...' He let his words trail off with a dismissive gesture of his hand.

My father said nothing. The factor drummed his fingers on the table.

'So?'

My father raised his eyes a little from his feet.

'I have not spoken to Mr Mackenzie about these troubles because Mr Mackenzie is the source of the troubles.'

At this the factor burst into laughter which did not strike me as genuine, but rather as a way of conveying the absurdity of my father's words. When he allowed his laughter to subside, he let out a great sigh.

'Would you care to elaborate?' he said.

My father, to my surprise, was not entirely cowed by the factor's laughter. 'It is true that relations between myself and Mr Mackenzie are strained, but I would not presume to involve you in such things.'

'I should think not, Mr Macrae. It is my understanding that Mr Mackenzie is carrying out his duties with a dedication that has been sorely lacking in recent years. And since, if I recall correctly, he was elected unanimously, I can only assume that he is doing so with the support of your community. If some private differences exist between yourself and the constable, then ...' He threw up his hands and let out a loud puff of air.

'Of course,' said my father.

'So if you have not come to vent some personal grievance, I suggest you tell me why you are here.' The factor's jovial manner had given way to impatience.

Father twisted his cap in his hands and then, as if realising that this action did not contribute to a favourable impression, abruptly ceased and placed his hands at his sides.

'I wish to see the regulations,' he said.

The factor looked at him curiously for a few moments, and then turned his gaze towards me, as if I might be able to explain my father's words.

'You wish to see the regulations?' he repeated slowly, his hand stroking his whiskers.

'Yes,' said my father.

'Of which regulations do you speak?'

'The regulations under which we exist,' he said.

The factor shook his head curtly. 'Forgive me, Mr Macrae, I'm not sure I follow.'

My father was now quite confused. Clearly he had not expected to meet with any such obfuscation and naturally he assumed the fault was his for not expressing himself with sufficient clarity.

'My father,' I said, 'is referring to the regulations under which our tenancies are governed.'

The factor looked at me with a serious expression. 'I see,' he said. 'And why, may I ask, do you wish to see these "regulations", as you call them?'

He looked then from myself to my father and I had the impression that he was amusing himself at our expense.

'So that I might know when we are transgressing them,' my father ventured eventually.

The factor nodded. 'But why?'

'So that we might avoid any black marks against our names or penalties for breaking them,' said my father.

At this the factor leaned back in his chair and tutted loudly.

'So, if I understand you correctly,' he said, clasping his hands under his chin, 'you wish to consult the regulations in order that you might break them with impunity?'

My father's eyes were downcast and I had the impression that they were becoming quite watery. I cursed him for placing himself in this situation.

'Mr Macrae, I applaud your audacity,' said the factor, spreading his hands.

'What my father wishes to express,' I said, 'is not that he seeks to disobey the regulations, rather that by properly familiarising himself with them, he might avoid breaking them.'

'It seems to me,' persisted the factor, 'that a person wishing to consult the regulations could only wish to do so in order to test the limits of the misdemeanours he might commit.'

My father was by this time quite lost and to bring an end to his distress, I told the factor that our visit had been misguided and we would not trouble him any further. The factor however waved away my attempts to bring the interview to an end.

'No, no, no,' he said, 'that will not do at all. You have come here, first of all, making accusations against your village constable, and, secondly, with the stated aim of seeking to avoid punishment for breaking the regulations. You cannot expect me to let matters rest at that.'

The factor, seeing that my father was incapable of further discourse, now addressed himself entirely to me. He pulled his chair closer to his desk, selected one of the ledgers and opened it. He turned a few pages and then ran his finger down a column. After reading a few lines, he returned his gaze to me.

'Tell me, Roderick Macrae,' he said, 'what are your ambitions in life?'

I replied that my only ambition was to help my father on the croft and to take care of my siblings.

'Very commendable,' he said. 'Too many of your people have ideas above their station these days. Nevertheless, you must have thought about leaving this place. Are you not minded to seek your fortune elsewhere? An intelligent young man like yourself must see that there is no future for you here.'

'I do not wish my future to be anywhere other than Culduie,' I said.

'But what if there is no future?'

I did not know how to respond to this.

'I will tell one you thing quite frankly, Roderick,' he said, 'There is no future here for agitators or criminals.'

'I am neither of these things,' I replied, 'and nor is my father.'

The factor then looked meaningfully down at the ledger in front of him and tipped his head to one side. Then he loudly closed the book.

'Your rent is in arrears,' he said.

'In common with all our neighbours,' I replied.

'Yes,' said the factor, 'but your neighbours have not presented themselves here as if they are somehow the injured party. It is only due to the lenience of the estate that you remain on the land at all.'

I took this warning to imply that the ordeal was over and nudged my father, who had been standing those last few minutes as if in a trance. The factor stood up.

I turned to go, but my father stood his ground.

'Am I to understand then that we may not see the regulations?' he said.

The factor seemed amused rather than angered by my father's question. He had taken three or four paces from behind his great desk, so that he now stood only a few feet from us.

'These regulations that you speak of have been followed since time immemorial,' he said. 'No one has ever felt the need to "see" them, as you put it.'

'Nevertheless …' said my father. He raised his head and looked the factor in the eye.

The factor shook his head and gave a little laugh through his nose.

'I'm afraid you are labouring under a misapprehension, Mr Macrae,' he said. 'If you do not take the crops from your neighbour's land, it is not because a regulation forbids it. You do not steal his crops, because it would be wrong to do so. The reason you may not "see" the regulations is because there are no regulations, at least not in the way you seem to think. You might as well ask to see the air we breathe. Of course, there are regulations, but you cannot see them. The regulations exist because we all accept that they exist and without them there would be anarchy. It is for the village constable to interpret these regulations and to enforce them at his discretion.'

He then waved us towards the door with a dismissive wave of his hand. I suddenly felt that since my father had brought us here, there was no sense in leaving without properly expressing our grievances.

'If I may return to the troubles my father spoke of,' I said. 'What my father truly wishes to convey is that, through his enforcement of these regulations, Lachlan Broad has waged a campaign of harassment against our family.'

The factor looked at me with an expression of incredulity. 'A campaign of harassment?' he repeated, appearing rather pleased by the phrase. He took a few steps back and leaned against the desk. 'That is a most serious allegation, young man, a most serious allegation indeed. Those in power cannot be permitted to abuse their office, can they? Nor, of course, can individuals be permitted to make unsubstantiated claims about their superiors. You had better, therefore, tell me what this "campaign of harassment" has consisted of.'

I felt encouraged by the factor's words and believe I took an involuntary step towards his desk. I then related, at some length, how Lachlan Broad had at the first opportunity reduced the extent of our land, had later denied us sea-ware to fertilise our crops which were now failing, and had then fined us for the poor upkeep of our croft.

The factor listened intently, his eyes all the time upon me. 'Is there anything else?' he said.

I wished to tell him also of the general atmosphere of oppression under which we lived, but I could think of no means of expressing this. Nor did I think it prudent to describe the incident I had witnessed with my sister, if for no other reason than it remained a secret from my father.

The factor looked disappointed when I had nothing more to add. 'And this you describe as a "campaign of harassment"?' he said.

'Yes, sir,' I replied.

'So your true objective in coming here is to slander, for whatever private motives, an official who, from what you describe, is doing nothing more than performing his duties conscientiously. I shall indeed make note of what you have said and when I next meet with Mr Mackenzie, I shall offer him my congratulations on the manner in which he has conducted himself.'

I felt a dreadful sinking in my stomach, but I saw nothing to gain by protesting.

The factor then addressed my father. 'I hope you will not see fit to call on me in this manner again. I remind you that your tenancy continues at Lord Middleton's discretion. And at the discretion of his deputies.'

He then shook his head and waved us out of the study.

My father did not speak on the way home, nor did his expression betray his thoughts. The rain had ceased. That evening I stayed about the house, awaiting the arrival of Lachlan Broad, but

he did not appear. Nor did he come on any of the subsequent evenings and I concluded that he was leaving us to stew on whatever
retribution was to be loosed upon us. A few days later, I was working in the ditches beside the road to Aird-Dubh when Lachlan
Broad passed by. He stopped and watched me work for some
minutes, but said nothing before going on his way. Following our
interview, I had imagined the factor taking the first opportunity to
report what had occurred to his constable, but when it appeared
he had not done so, I realised that to these important men our
actions were of simply no consequence.

* * *

Some days later, after supper, I stepped out of the house for no
other reason than to escape the black atmosphere. My father's
mood at that particular time was so dark that it cast a pall over the
entire household. I had not seen Jetta smile for days or weeks and
she seemed to daily shrink further within herself, so that she carried herself with the bearing of an old crone. If the infants played
at all, they did so silently and in ways mysterious to all but themselves. When Jetta addressed them, it was in a whisper, calculated
not to remind my father of their existence. I myself, due to my
longing to see Flora Broad, had been labouring under a cloak of
despondency, which only augmented the general gloom.

On stepping out of the house, however, my mood immediately
brightened. Flora was sitting on the dyke at the junction of the
Toscaig road. I was tempted to break into a run, but a moment
of circumspection led me to forsake the track through the village
and instead make my way down through the rig, before climbing
the dyke and joining the road some two or three hundred yards
from where Flora sat. I affected a manner intended to suggest
to anyone who might be observing that I was merely wandering
neither here nor there with no particular destination in mind. In
this way I imagined that when I encountered Flora our meeting
would appear to be a matter of chance. Flora never once looked
up as I approached and seemed to be occupied with something on

her lap. As I drew nearer, I was struck by the delicacy of her features. Coils of hair blew unnoticed around her face in the breeze. I stopped a few paces away, but Flora was quite absorbed, or pretending to be so, in the methodical destruction of a dandelion, the yellow petals of which littered her skirts.

I greeted her and she looked up from her activity.

'Hello, Roddy,' she said.

I was to unable to engage in any prevarication. 'I have been looking out for you these last days,' I said. 'And was sorry not to have seen you.'

'Is that so?' she said.

A faint smile played on her lips and she cast her eyes down towards the petals on her skirt as if my statement had pleased her.

'I have been working at the Big House,' she said.

I was pleased that Flora saw fit to furnish me with this explanation for her absence.

I nodded and stepped a little closer to her.

'Where are you going?' she asked.

'I am not going anywhere,' I said.

'Then it is a fortunate thing that you happened to be passing on your way to nowhere when I was sitting here.'

'Yes,' I said. 'A very fortunate thing.'

'Perhaps I could walk to nowhere with you,' she said.

She pushed herself off the dyke, brushing the petals from her clothing. We walked a little way in silence and, without discussion, took the turning to Aird-Dubh. It pleased me that this custom seemed to have been established between us, as if we were a long-married couple. The breeze dropped and the water of the Sound was entirely still. We walked in such close proximity that it was not necessary to raise our voices above a whisper, and I had the feeling that we were proceeding through a world which had for the moment set down its tools to take pause. If I could by some magical means suddenly transport myself to the house, Jetta and my father would be quite frozen in their activity and the infants' play would be all suspended.

After some time, I asked Flora what she had been doing at the Big House. She described how, on account of a large shooting party, extra hands had been needed in the kitchen and to serve at the banquets. She described the dishes of meats, vegetables and sweets which were brought to the guests, and the great quantities of wine that were imbibed at the table. It was, she said, a most wondrous sight. She then described the fine dresses of the ladies, who were one more beautiful than the next. There was a most handsome gentleman with flowing dark hair to whom all the ladies cast their eyes and who seemed the leader in toasting the hospitality of Lord Middleton. It had been a splendid week, said Flora, and she had earned two shillings for her labour. Then, feeling that there should be no secrets between us, I told Flora of my short-lived employment in the service of Lord Middleton. She did not laugh, but looked at me quite gravely and said, 'That was not a very clever thing to do, Roddy.'

'It was not,' I replied, 'for my father gave me the soundest thrashing I have ever had.'

Again Flora did not seem to find this amusing and I was dismayed that she seemed to frown on my behaviour. I told her that I only acted as I had because I did not wish to see a fine stag destroyed for the amusement of the gentry. Flora then said that the deer were on the mountain for the sport of the gentlemen and that Lord Middleton's livelihood depended on such pursuits. I replied that Lord Middleton's livelihood was no concern of mine. Flora retorted that it should be my concern as it was the estate that provided the people with employment.

'Without the beneficence of Lord Middleton,' she said, 'we would all be scratching a living from the land.'

Her reply made me feel quite foolish and, not wishing to sour the atmosphere between us, I said no more on the subject. We continued in silence to Aird-Dubh and I felt that the closeness between us had dissipated a little. We strolled through the scruffy jumble of houses and outbuildings of the village. The Onion was seated on a bench outside her house, sucking noisily on a small pipe. Flora paused and bid her good evening.

'Have you no eggs for me?' said the old woman.

Flora shook her head and said she was sorry but she did not. She then enquired about the state of the old woman's health. Mrs MacLeod ignored her question, instead, taking her pipe from her mouth turned her gaze upon me, her flabby lips all the while making a sound like the slapping of the sea against a rock.

'And this is the Black Macrae's boy?' she asked.

'Yes,' said Flora.

The crone continued to eye me disapprovingly.

'Has the Devil got your tongue, Roddy Black?' she asked eventually.

I could think of no sensible answer to this question, so I merely stared back at her. She stuck her pipe back in her mouth and sucked noisily on it. It was not lit.

'I have lately seen your sister,' she said.

I could think of no reason for my sister to have been to Aird-Dubh and said as much.

'Well, she has been here. Or her fetch has. A pretty girl, very much like her mother.' These last words were spoken in a sly tone, and if her intention was to rile me, I confess she succeeded. Had Flora not been by my side, I would have told her that she was a wicked old hag, but I held my tongue.

'And you are very much like your father,' she said.

'You do not know my father,' I replied.

'I know him well enough,' she said. 'Tight as a knot of wood.' Then she started cackling to herself. Not wishing to hear any more I moved away and Flora followed me, having first bid the crone good evening.

'Tell your sister, I hope she finds her condition improved,' she called after us.

I pretended I had not heard, but when we were some distance away, Flora asked what she had meant. I replied that she was nothing but a mad old woman and she should pay no heed to her.

We passed Murdo Cock's hut and the sound of our footsteps brought him to his door. He stared at us as we passed, his mouth twitching so that the single tooth in his head was prominently displayed. Then he made a sound like a gull and disappeared back inside, like an animal down its burrow. Flora gave a little shiver. I drew closer to her and allowed the back of my hand to graze against her sleeve, hoping that she would hold it, but she did not do so and I withdrew to my former distance. We found ourselves at the point and sat down on the rocks there. A number of boats pitched gently on the swell. I told Flora the story of my father's fishing vessel and about the incident in which the two Iains were drowned. I described how my mother would go to the pier in Toscaig to watch my father bring in the boat. I cannot say why I related this, except perhaps that I thought to rouse her pity, so that she might like me better. When I had finished, she said that it was a very sad story, and I regretted telling it.

In order to break the silence which grew between us, I asked if she soon would be working again at the Big House.

'If I am required and if I acquitted myself well,' she replied. I then remembered the girl I had observed at school, forever anxious to please Mr Gillies, and I felt that she had perhaps not changed so much after all. She then told me that the following year, when she was sixteen, she was to be sent into service at a merchant's in Glasgow. Her mother had secured a position through the housekeeper at the Big House. Flora asked me if I had ever been to Glasgow and I said that, on account of my father's fear of water, I had never been so far as Kyle of Lochalsh. She told me a great many tales of the grand streets, emporiums and townhouses in the city. She asked whether I did not plan to leave Culduie, and I told her that my father needed me for the croft and, in any case, I did not wish to go anywhere, for Culduie was where I was from and where I wished to spend my days. Flora expressed the opinion that there was a great deal more to the world than Culduie and that I must surely want to see a little of it. I did not reply, for since I had made her acquaintance I had wanted nothing more than what was on my doorstep. Flora told me how she hoped that when she was in Glasgow she would catch the eye of a fine young man who might make her his wife. I replied that I was sure that there were plenty of young men in Culduie who would wish to do the same.

Flora looked at me with an earnest, puzzled expression. 'You do not mean yourself, do you?' she said.

I looked away from her, out towards the sea.

'If you did not mean yourself, who did you mean?' she persisted in a playful tone.

I turned to face her. Then without thinking I thrust my face towards hers and for a moment my lips brushed her cheek. Flora drew away and got to her feet.

'Roddy Black!' she said. Then she giggled stupidly and I laughed as well, to show that I had only acted in jest.

After a few moments, she sat down beside me. We neither of us said anything. I wanted nothing more than to run off and burst into tears.

Flora pushed me playfully on the arm and said that I was just a silly boy who knew nothing of the world. There were in any case, even in Culduie, Kenny Smoke's six daughters who I might run after. I did not say what was on my mind, as I had no wish to expose myself to further ridicule.

As we walked back to Culduie, the knowledge that Flora meant to leave Culduie weighed heavily upon me. I realised that, quite unbidden, I had conceived of a future in which she and I would be together. I cannot say when these thoughts came first to my mind, but certainly before our meeting in the barn I had never once entertained the notion of taking a wife. My life up to that point had been with father and Jetta, and until I met Flora I had never wanted for any other company. I cursed myself for having harboured such thoughts. I saw that to Flora I was nothing more than an amusing distraction who she would forget the moment she set foot in the city.

Flora must have seen that I was downcast, for she attempted to make conversation about trivial matters and nudged me playfully with her shoulder, but I pushed my hands deeper into the pockets of my breeches and made no response.

* * *

None of us were in the proper humour for the summer Gathering
when it arrived, but Jetta had knitted a great number of shawls to
sell at market, so there was no question of not attending. Father
declined to accompany us, satisfying himself with a muttered
warning that I should keep myself out of trouble. I assured him I
had no intention of getting into any trouble, and his absence did
something to lighten our mood as we set off.

Jetta's goods were piled into a hurlie and the twins, to their
delight, were set on top of these. The road was thronging with
similar parties and there was singing and a general air of festivity.
Jetta joined in the singing for the sake of the infants, and, to an
onlooker, we must have loosely resembled a happy family. For
my part, I remained burdened by melancholy feelings about Flora
Broad, but I resolved for the sake of my siblings to put these to
one side. As we approached Camusterrach we passed the Onion,
moving at such a slow pace that I remarked she must have left
home two days before. Jetta quickened her pace as we passed her,
then pinched her nose and pulled a face. The twins laughed and
mimicked her gesture. Further on, we fell in with the Smokes. Jetta
conversed in hushed tones with their eldest daughter. Carmina
Smoke enquired after my father and I told her that he had stayed
behind to tend the croft. She looked at me in a sceptical manner,
but did not say anything more. For the remainder of the journey I
dawdled at the back of the party, not speaking to anyone.

The road between the shore and the row of cottages which
constituted the village of Applecross was crammed with trestle
tables displaying cheeses, wood carvings, pipes, gimcracks and
items of clothing. Jetta found a place towards the end of the
village and arranged her wares on the cart, before taking a seat
on the low shore wall. The twins played at her feet. I loitered
awhile before wandering back along the village. The entire parish seemed to have packed into the narrow road. The womenfolk
were dressed in their finest clothes. The girls' hair was arranged
prettily and adorned with flowers. I wondered if I might see Flora

Broad, but was sure she would take no interest in me. Crofting folk mingled with guests from the Big House, who conversed in loud voices and pointed rudely at the goods on display.

I fell in behind two well-dressed gentlemen and eavesdropped on their conversation. The first declared in a loud voice, 'It is easy to forget that such primitives still exist in our country.' His companion nodded solemnly and wondered aloud whether more might be done for us. The first gentleman then expressed the view that it was difficult to assist people who were so incapable of doing anything for themselves. They then paused to drink from a flask and watch a knot of girls pass by. I did not wait to hear what remarks they passed and continued along the street.

I spotted Archibald Ross leaning at the threshold of the inn. He was dressed in a fine tweed outfit with brown brogues and breeches tucked into his stockings. I stood and stared at him for a few moments. He looked every inch the young gentlemen from a shooting party. Although I was standing only a few yards from him, he did not appear to recognise me. I recalled that almost a year had passed since we had met and took a step or two closer to him. He had a pipe in his right hand, which I saw was now filled and alight. I thought perhaps that following my exploit on the hillside he would not wish to associate with me, but a look of recognition crossed his face and he thrust out his hand and exclaimed, 'Roddy, old chap!' We shook hands warmly. I was gratified that he seemed to bear no ill feelings towards me.

'I thought you might be in Canada by now,' I said.

'Canada?' he said.

'With your cousin.'

He made a flamboyant gesture with his pipe. 'There's nothing for us in Canada these days. Things are worse there than they are here. Besides, I'm now with the ghillie.'

I nodded and told him that he looked very well in his outfit. He waved his pipe ostentatiously to dismiss my comment, before returning it to his mouth and puffing heartily on it. I dearly wished at that moment to have a pipe of my own. Then he took me by the arm and steered me inside the inn. I glanced over my shoulder, fearful that one of our neighbours might see me. I had never before set foot in the inn. My father considered it a den of iniquity and regularly declared that those who frequented it were on the path to the eternal bonfire. Inside, a great deal of men in their shirtsleeves were crammed together, bellowing cheerfully in one another's faces. Archibald manoeuvred us through the throng to a tiny table in the corner, upon which two stone tankards of ale were presently set by a sturdy woman in a checked dress. Archibald grabbed one of the vessels and, clanking it noisily against the second, declared, 'Here's to the health of them that like us.'

I picked up my tankard, which so surprised me by its weight that I almost dropped it, and repeated his toast. Then we drank. The ale tasted quite foul and I would have spat it on the floor had I been on my own. Archibald took a second long swallow and prodded me in the ribs with his elbow to do the same.

'First rate to see you, old boy,' he declared. 'You're quite the character, are you not?'

I was so delighted to be in the company of such a fine fellow as Archibald Ross that I raised my tankard to my lips and emptied half its contents into my gullet. I wondered what my father would think to see me in such a place, but by the time the ale reached my stomach, I no longer cared. Two burly men, standing to our left with their arms around each other's shoulders were singing heartily:

> *When we were in the Coille Mhùiridh*
> *It was not then Lowlanders who woke us,*
> *But the lowing deer calves and roaring stags*
> *And the cuckoo in spring making music.*

Before long the entire company joined in the song. Archibald got to his feet and tunelessly bellowed out the words:

> *My country is the beautiful one,*
> *The bright country hospitable and broad,*

Deer found in the mouth of every pass,
The buck and doe, the grouse and salmon.

At this point the two swaying men to my left landed in my lap, spilling the remains of my ale. Archibald roughly shoved them off and called to the landlady for two more. The song petered out in a melee of tangled bodies and laughter. Two more tankards were duly delivered and Archibald resumed his seat looking greatly pleased with himself.

'Well, Mr Macrae, here's to us and them that like us!'

'To them that like us!' I repeated.

This second ale tasted a good deal better than the previous one and I concluded that the first must have been off. Archibald then explained to me how, at the end of last year's season, the ghillie had offered to make him his apprentice and he was now living in quarters behind the Big House. He was making a shilling a day and more if he ran errands for Lord Middleton's guests. These seemed great riches to me and I told him so.

'I would enquire if there might be a position for you,' he said, 'but I fear you are not well remembered by the ghillie.' He then flailed his arms and squawked noisily in imitation of my performance on the mountain, laughing uproariously. Archibald must have seen that I looked crestfallen, for he immediately stifled his guffaws and enquired about my plans for the future. I told him that I was labouring on the roads and on my father's croft and was content to be doing so. Archibald adopted a serious expression and asked if this was the limit of my ambition. Not wishing to disappoint him I told him that this arrangement was merely for the short term, and once I had saved sufficient money I intended to seek my fortune in Glasgow. Archibald nodded approvingly at this untruth.

'I hear there are great opportunities there for a man of ambition,' he said.

I agreed, thankful that he did not question me further, and he shouted for more ale. We were now in high spirits and he told me a number of tales about the gentlemen who visited the estate, mimicking their habits and manner of speech to great effect. The ghillie, he told me, was not half so fearsome as he first appeared and often invited Archibald into his lodge of an evening where they would sit at the hearth smoking their pipes and recalling the day's events. When there was no shooting party, the ghillie instructed Archibald in the art of stalking, so that he could now tell by inspecting blades of broken grass, or disturbances in the heather invisible to the untutored eye, whether deer were nearby and in which direction they were travelling. Archibald boasted that he now knew the hills and glens better than the inside of his own home and I confess I felt quite envious of his new station in life. He set to refilling his pipe and enquired why I did not have one of my own. I replied that I was saving all my money for my journey to Glasgow and did not wish to squander it on tobacco. Archibald opined that such habits would make me a wealthy man. For a moment I pictured myself as a rich merchant, seated by the hearth of a grand townhouse with Flora at her sewing by my side.

I do not know how long we remained at the inn or how many tankards of ale we drank, but at a certain point the rabble streamed out into the street. The time for the great event of the day, the shinty match between the parishes of Applecross and the Point, was approaching. Archibald settled our account, which was fortuitous as I had no money of my own. He waved away my thanks, insisting that having invited me to share a drink, he would be a blackguard if he allowed me to pay.

I found myself swaying from the effects of the ale, but felt no shame in my condition. I ambled along the street, buffeted by the crowd and drawing disdainful looks from passersby. Archibald draped his arm over my shoulders and together we doffed our caps at all and sundry and thought ourselves the most delightful fellows. Toward the end of the road we reached the spot where Jetta had set out her goods. She looked quite aghast at my state of inebriation.

'I hope, for your sake, that Father does not hear of your condition,' she said in a low voice.

I ignored her remark and, with a gesture towards my companion, said, 'May I present my friend, Mr Archibald Ross.'

Archibald made an elaborate bow. 'Delighted to make your acquaintance, Miss Macrae,' he said. 'There can be no fairer maiden in the parish.' He then took hold of her hand, which she had not proffered, and kissed it. Jetta stared at him with astonishment, wondering, no doubt, how her brother could have come to make the acquaintance of such a charming fellow. Archibald stepped back to inspect Jetta's wares. He assumed the air of a connoisseur, gently running items between his fingers and muttering appreciatively. Jetta seemed pleased by this attention and told us that not ten minutes before she had sold a shawl to a lady from the Big House for a shilling.

'A shilling!' said Archibald. 'You are underselling your fine work, my dear.'

He then declared that he would buy the shawl he was holding for his mother and gave my sister two shillings for it. Jetta was greatly pleased and thanked him profusely. As Archibald was making his way from the stall, she gave me a shilling and whispered not to say a word to Father about her sales. I put the coin in my pocket and pursued Archibald into the crowd, pleased that I would later be able to invite him to the inn to drink more ale. We made our way beyond the village towards the Big House where the match was to take place.

'Your sister is quite striking, but she dresses like an old crone,' Archibald told me in an affable tone. 'She will never find a husband attired in such unflattering garb. If a fellow sees a girl swathed in sackcloth, he has every right to assume there is good reason to conceal what lies underneath, ha ha.'

He made his familiar flourish with his pipe, which I now understood was intended to signify that whatever statement he had made was indisputable. I had to admit that there was some truth in his words and that if I looked upon Jetta with a dispassionate eye, she cut a less than appealing figure. As if to underline the point, there were in the vicinity any number of attractive girls bedecked

in pretty dresses, their hair pleasingly pinned up, so that it was possible to see the smooth, pale skin of their necks.

Archibald then took the shawl he had bought, bundled it up
and stuffed it into a bush. I was quite horrified and asked what he
meant by such an act. Archibald shrugged and looked at me with
a grin on his face.

'Old chap, I would not give my dog such a rag to sleep upon. I
only purchased it so that your sister might have a little money to
buy herself some less dreary attire.'

I thought of the many hours that my sister had laboured to
produce the shawl and felt quite wounded by my friend's callous-
ness. Thinking that Jetta might later see her work discarded in the
bush, I ran back and retrieved it. It was snagged in thorns and I
took some time to unpick it from the branches. The shawl was
ruined but I folded it as carefully as I could and stuffed it inside
my jacket. Archibald watched me with amusement.

'What are you going to do with it now?' he said when I caught
up with him. 'It's quite destroyed.'

I was not inclined to answer. We continued in silence for some
minutes. The shinty match, arranged at the behest of the laird,
was to take place on a pitch that had been marked out in sawdust in front of the Big House. Spectators had begun to gather
around the markings. After some minutes my ill feelings towards
Archibald subsided. He must have sensed this as he set to talking
again in a confidential tone.

'I, myself, do not intend to seek a wife for some years. Why
would young men like us restrict ourselves to one dish when there
are so many to try?' he said, glancing towards a group of girls. 'If
you sister spends her money wisely, I would consider taking her
for a turn round the back of the inn. After the two shillings I gave
her, she will no doubt feel somewhat obliged to me.'

He prodded me in the ribs with his elbow, and, having only
the vaguest idea what he meant, I nodded in agreement. Lord
Middleton's guests sat on chairs which had been set out on the far
side of the field. As this area was clearly for the gentry, the villagers

spread themselves around the three remaining sides. A marquee had been erected and, as the game had not yet commenced, most of the men-folk loitered by its entrance. Archibald steered me into the tent, where he purchased two measures of whisky. We toasted and drank them down and by the time the spirit reached my stomach I had quite forgotten the incident with the shawl. The teams trotted onto the pitch and we took our place among the crowd, which had by now pressed itself so closely around the pitch that there was little need for the sawdust lines. There was a great deal of shouting from all sides.

Naturally, Lachlan Broad took the leading role in the team from the Point, roughly slapping his team-mates around the shoulders to rouse their passion. He cut an imposing figure as he marched towards the centre of the pitch, chest thrust out, his caman resting on his shoulder like an axe. The remainder of our team, Kenny Smoke excepted, was a sorry and bedraggled crew, most of whom looked as if they heartily wished to be elsewhere. Since I was a boy, I have greatly disliked all games and shinty strikes me as a particularly violent and farcical spectacle. At school I would loiter at the side of the pitch and run in the opposite direction if the leather came towards me. Despite the lack of able-bodied young men from our parish, such was my ineptitude that I had never been enlisted to take part in the match.

The game began in a clatter of sticks in the centre of the field. Two men immediately collapsed and were carried off, while the game thundered around them. Lachlan Broad got hold of the leather in the midfield and gave it a mighty whack towards the Applecross goal. He then strode across the turf to berate Dunkie Gregor, who was barely twelve years old, for not collecting his pass. In the meantime the leather was launched back upfield and, amid much cracking of sticks and bones, was fired through the goalposts. Lachlan Broad, to the laughter of the crowd, shoved Dunkie Gregor to the ground and ran back to chastise the rest of his team. The Applecross players celebrated their goal by swigging from a wooden quaich of whisky behind the goal. The longer the match went on the more it descended into violence, and the more vehemently the crowd exhorted their side to assault their opponents. The gentlemen seated on the far side of the field appeared to find the spectacle enormously amusing and cheered on the combatants with gusto. Archibald too applauded each new assault with increasing fervour. The crowd reached its peak of delight when an old woman took a caman hard on the side of her head and sank unconscious to the ground. In the end, the leather was quite forgotten and, with the crowd forming a close circle in the centre of the pitch, the teams took to battering each other around the head and legs with their sticks. And then, quite without warning, the battle subsided and the two teams were each acclaimed the winner by their supporters. The bloodied players were carried off at shoulder-height, passing vessels of whisky amongst them. Archibald and I followed in their wake, my friend enthusing about acts of particular brutality. A quaich was shoved into our hands and we drank deeply. The crowd now swirled around me and I proposed to Archibald that we return to the inn to take some more ale. He insisted that we stay awhile at the marquee as all the village girls were there and we might, he said, try our luck with them.

Having pushed our way into the tent and purchased more ale, Archibald took to appraising the girls who stood around the perimeter of the heaving scrum of men, leaning close to each other to whisper in each others' ears, faces aglow from the excitement of the spectacle. It was at this point that I spotted Flora Broad lingering at the edge of the shinty field. She was in the company of a tall girl I did not know and appeared deep in conversation with two young gentlemen. I noted with displeasure the way in which her face was eagerly thrust upwards towards these suitors. The fingers of her right hand continually toyed with a strand of her hair, which was prettily arranged for the occasion. As I was not anxious to renew our acquaintance, I attempted to draw Archibald further into the crowd, but he had set off towards a group of girls and, as they were in the opposite direction to Flora, I gladly followed at his heels. I had some difficulty placing one foot in front of the other and by the time I caught up, Archibald was presenting himself in charming fashion to the three young women, all of whom were adorned in embroidered white dresses. He then introduced me in most complimentary terms. I removed my cap and made a bow of sorts, managing only to make the girls snigger.

'And why did you not take part in the match?' the tallest of the girls asked.

Archibald waved his pipe. 'We are the sort of chaps who prefer to best our opponents with wit rather than clubs,' he declared.

He nudged me in the ribs, no doubt wishing me to confirm his statement by way of some clever remark, but I could muster no more than a stupid grin. Archibald was not discouraged, however, and took to informing the girls that I would soon be making a great fortune as a merchant in Glasgow.

'But is this not the Black Macrae's boy?' the tall girl asked, pointing an accusing finger in my direction.

'It is true, he is of the Black Macraes, but I would put it to you that we are none of us slaves to the reputations our forefathers have earned us,' said Archibald grandly.

I felt the need to contribute something to the discourse, but only succeeded in waving my fingers in the air and swaying towards the girls, so that Archibald had to catch me by the elbow to prevent me falling among them.

He then asked the girls whether they might care to take a turn around the grounds of the estate with us, since, he said, it was difficult to converse among the great mass of inebriates. The girls demurred and with a brief bow, Archibald led me away by the arm. He did not seem in the least cowed by this rebuff, insisting instead that I only required some more ale to loosen my tongue and counter the effects of the whisky we had drunk. Back in the marquee and with tankards of ale to hand, I told Archibald that I had no interest in these girls as my heart was set on another. Archibald asked who this girl was and I told him something of what had occurred between myself and Flora Broad. When I had finished, Archibald sucked for some moments on his pipe as if giving serious thought to my situation. He then clutched my lapel and drew me close towards him.

'If I might offer you some advice,' he began, 'would it not be better that when you depart for Glasgow, you do so unfettered by any attachments to this place? You will soon forget this girl when you are surrounded by the riches the city has to offer.'

I told him I could not forget her and nor did I wish to.

Archibald nodded slowly. Then as if coming to a sudden decision, he thrust his pipe in the air and declared, 'In that case you must make your feelings known to her.'

I then told him of our exchange at the point in Aird-Dubh, omitting the most humiliating details.

'If your feelings are as profound as you suggest,' said Archibald, his arm now clasped around my shoulder, 'you must make some declaration to her. At least then you will properly know where you stand. In any case, you should not be so easily discouraged. It is quite customary for a girl to spurn a chap's advances, but such refusals are not to be taken seriously. Indeed, it should be taken as a measure of her esteem for you that she did not submit at the first opportunity. She is merely testing your resolve. You have seen a cock in the henhouse, I'm sure. He must make a display of his tail feathers. A young woman is just like a chicken, she has to be wooed. You must strut a little for her, Roderick.'

He then imitated a cock, flapping his elbows like wings and throwing his head back to crow. Some of the men around us stopped drinking to stare at him. When he had concluded his display, he wagged a finger at me. 'Do you wish to be a cock or a cuckold?' he declared, evidently proud of his maxim.

I then explained that even if my feelings were reciprocated, a great deal of bad blood existed between our families and that her father would never consent to our being together.

'It seems to me,' said Archibald, 'that you have erected so many obstacles in your mind that you have quite defeated yourself before you have even begun.' He then prodded me roughly on the forehead and told me that I should make less use of what was between my ears and more of what was between my legs. At that precise moment, I saw over Archibald's shoulder that Flora had abandoned her admirers and was walking arm in arm with her friend around the perimeter of the now deserted shinty field. I made no response to my companion's advice and he must have noticed the momentary dwam that came over me.

'I discern from the colour in your cheeks that you have spied the maiden in question,' he said, pointing the stem of his pipe in the direction of the two figures. 'Let us resolve this question once and for all.'

I had no desire to resolve any questions and greatly regretted having disclosed my thoughts about Flora in the first place, but Archibald had already set off, his arm clamped firmly around my shoulders. As we approached the two figures, I protested that I did not think that I was in any condition to properly converse.

Archibald waved away my objections. 'Nonsense,' he declared. 'Your situation has arisen precisely because you have failed to express yourself. If your tongue is now loosened by ale, all the better.'

We cut across the centre of the field, so that by the time Flora and her companion rounded the corner of the pitch, it appeared that we were meeting them quite by chance. They were so engrossed in conversation that they did not notice us until we were only a few yards away. It was by that time quite impossible, short of running away, to avert our meeting. Archibald began loudly discoursing about the grandeur of the landscape and our small place within it, and affected great surprise when we almost collided with our prey.

'Hello, Roddy,' said Flora.

She did not seem in the least disconcerted by our appearance and I felt all of a sudden that perhaps all was not lost between us, and that seeing me in the company of such a fine fellow as Archibald Ross, she might revise her opinion of me.

Archibald feigned surprise that Flora and I knew each other and prevailed upon me to introduce him. I did so, and Flora then introduced her friend as Ishbel Farquhar. Archibald made the same low bow as he had to my sister and declared that, had he known that such pretty flowers grew in Culduie, he would have long ago taken up residence there. The two girls looked at each other and communicated some secret thought with their eyes. Archibald then asked if we might accompany the girls on their turn around the grounds and they made no objection. Archibald, having explained his position with the ghillie, pointed out some features of the house and described in entertaining terms some aspects of the life that went on there. Flora then volunteered that during the summer months her mother worked in the kitchens and that she had herself been employed there. It irked me that Flora thus connected herself to the life that Archibald led. The two of them fell to discussing various members of the household, and Flora was greatly amused by the descriptions and anecdotes which my friend related. Ishbel and I followed in silence and the more Flora tittered at Archibald's conversation, the blacker my mood became. As we reached the outermost limit of the field, Archibald broke off from what he was saying and suggested we continue towards the burn, which, he declared, was most picturesque at this time of year. Our companions agreed and we continued past some outhouses towards the woods which grew around the river. Archibald then asked how long Flora and I had known each other. Flora replied that we had been neighbours all our lives, but, as I had always been such a solitary boy, it was only in these last few months that she had come to know me. Archibald replied to the effect that I was quite a character and while many young men were happiest listening to the sound of their own voices, I was an altogether more thoughtful individual. He then expressed the opinion that it was a pity that Flora and I would not have the opportunity to become better acquainted on account of my imminent departure for Glasgow. Flora conveyed some surprise at this remark.

'But what of your father's croft?' she said.

'I have lately had a change of heart,' I muttered.

Flora looked askance at me. 'And what do you intend to do in Glasgow?'

Archibald answered on my behalf: 'There is no end to the opportunities there for an enterprising young fellow like Roddy.'

At this Flora and Ishbel glanced at each other and began to laugh. We reached the stone bridge that traverses the burn. The sunlight filtered through the canopy of trees and sparkled on the water. We came to a natural pause and stood the four of us on the path looking at one another for some moments. Then quite suddenly Archibald took Ishbel by the arm and led her onto the bridge, saying that there was something he would like to show her. They leant over the water, their bodies quite close together and Archibald pointed to something in the river and spoke in hushed tones to her. Flora and I stood looking at each other. I felt most ill at ease and conscious of my state of inebriation. Over Flora's shoulder I saw Archibald look towards me and with a movement of his head spurred me to action.

I asked Flora if she would like to walk a little farther with me. She did not object and we set off along the path by the burn. After some yards, I could not resist the temptation to look over my shoulder at Archibald, who was by that time leaning in so close to Ishbel that his lips might have been touching her neck. Flora too glanced over her shoulder, as if she did not wish to be out of sight of her friend. Although we had been alone together before there was now a tension between us which had not previously existed. I expected Flora to make some remark or other, but she did not do so, and, as I could think of nothing to say, the silence thickened between us. The path was narrow and we were obliged to walk so close together that Flora's sleeve brushed my arm. Remembering Archibald's advice, I told Flora that her dress was very becoming. Presently the path reached a dip which was thick with mud. Flora took the opportunity to propose that we turn back.

I suggested instead that we might sit down for a moment. There was a large rock by the burn and this we used as a bench.

Not wishing to let the silence grow between us again, I told Flora that Archibald and I had earlier visited the inn and shared some tankards of ale.

'I can see that you have been drinking,' said Flora, 'and I can only imagine what your father will do when he finds out.'

I responded by saying that my father need never know and, in any case, it was worth it to spend some time in the company of such a fine fellow as Archibald.

Flora then said that she did not like him and that she did not think he was a suitable friend for me. I was quite offended on my friend's behalf, but I did not say so and we once again lapsed into silence. Perhaps Flora sensed that she had hurt my feelings, for it was she who spoke next.

'So you have had a change of heart?' she said, referring to our earlier conversation. 'I thought you were quite married to Culduie.'

Perhaps it was her use of the word 'married' that loosened my tongue, but I then embarked quite spontaneously on a declaration of my feelings.

'It is not Culduie to which I wish to be married, but you,' I said. 'I would go to Glasgow or to Canada or anywhere to be with you.'

Flora looked quite taken aback. The colour had risen to my cheeks and I immediately regretted my outburst.

'Roddy,' she said, 'I am quite sure that when you are older you will find a wife, but it will not be me.'

I felt tears spring to my eyes and in order that Flora would not see them, I took her by the shoulders and buried my head into her hair. For a moment I felt the skin of Flora's neck against my lips and inhaled her smell. I felt a great coursing in my groin. Flora pushed her elbow into my chest and shoved me from her with some violence. She then slapped me hard across the face and, in my shock, I slipped from the rock and landed on my backside in the moss. Flora got to her feet and ran off through the trees. I lay there for some time with my hand to my cheek. Eventually I sat upright and wiped the tears from my face with the sleeve of my shirt, before retracing my steps along the path. Archibald was waiting for me by the bridge, smoking his pipe. To my relief, Flora and Ishbel had gone.

I felt terribly downhearted by what had occurred, but Archibald seemed to find it very amusing. As we made our way back towards the village he recounted the incident over and over again, with ever more elaborate embellishments, so that I greatly regretted confiding in him. I kept my eyes fixed on the road beneath our feet. Flora was right, I was no more than a silly boy. Archibald must have seen that I was downcast, for he ceased his bantering and put his arm around my shoulder.

'Come on, old chap,' he said. 'All the better for you to strike out for Glasgow unencumbered.'

I was in no mood to listen to his commiserations, not only because his words seemed quite hollow, but also because I felt he had played a quite deliberate role in my rejection. I tried to shrug off his arm, but he kept me in a firm grip. Tears stung my eyes. Archibald came to a sudden halt and we stood face to face. I turned my head away, expecting him to mock me, but he did not do so, instead, making a series of apologies for his insensitivity towards what he called my 'finer feelings'. I felt somewhat appeased and wiped the tears from my face with the back of my hand.

'What you need, my friend,' he said, slapping me on the shoulder, 'is a good jug of ale.'

I forced a smile and we set off again towards the inn. I took the shilling Jetta had given me from my pocket and showed it to him.

'We shall get as drunk as lords,' Archibald declared.

The inn was even more crammed with bodies than before, but Archibald navigated the throng with ease, dragging me behind him by the sleeve of my jacket. A fiddler and accordionist were playing reels in the corner. Before long we were settled at a table with tankards in our hands and I felt considerably cheered.

'To them that like us!' Archibald cried.

All the men around us raised their tankards and repeated Archibald's toast and I felt proud to be in the company of such a fellow. I regretted telling him that I would be leaving for Glasgow, as I wished to remain friends with him and meet him every evening at the inn to quaff great quantities of ale. We were soon singing and swilling our beer with gusto. I had no idea of the price of a pint of ale or whether my shilling would meet the cost, but I was quite indifferent to such considerations. Archibald climbed onto a chair and led the company in a song and was roundly cheered. Tankards appeared in our hands with great frequency and I felt a surge of fellow-feeling towards my compatriots. The incident with Flora and the miseries of my family were quite forgotten. I had discovered the union of men. In order to express my high spirits, I climbed onto a table and poured a tankard of ale over my head. I then began to jig to the fiddler's tune, hoisting my hands above my head and spinning like a top. The men below stamped and beat time on the tables until I lost my footing and crashed to the floor. I picked myself up to great cheers and continued my jig. It was at that moment that I saw Lachlan Broad standing before me with several of his kinsmen. I felt suddenly foolish and ceased my capering. The stamping which had accompanied me petered out. Voices called upon me to continue, but I had no wish to make a further spectacle of myself. My shirt was soaked through with ale and my hair was plastered to my head.

Lachlan Broad took a single step across the floor towards me.

'Come on, Roddy Black, do not stop on my account.'

He called to the musicians to strike up a tune. The men around me were clapping for me to begin, but I remained fixed to the spot. Lachlan Broad took a pot of ale from one of his kinsmen and, to great applause, threw it over my face.

'A dance, boy!' he bellowed. Aeneas Mackenzie stamped a rhythm on the floor behind him, snorting like a pig. Lachlan Broad whipped the crowd into a greater frenzy with his arms.

I flew across the room at him. He met me with an outstretched palm and pushed me back across the floor. I landed on my behind in a tangle of legs. Arms dragged me to my feet and propelled me back towards Broad. This time he met me full in the face with his fist. I sank to the floor, then got up and swung my fists wildly at him. There were roars of approval and much laughter. The constable caught me a blow in the midriff and as I crumpled towards him he brought his boot up between my legs. The wind was all knocked out of me and I lay on the floor struggling for breath. Archibald came to my side, but Lachlan Broad shoved him roughly away. Then he knelt beside me and whispered in my ear, 'I'll have your old man off his croft by the year's end, you filthy Erse shite.'

Then he dragged me to my feet and, gripping me by the lapels, threw me violently across the room. I landed on my back on a table, sending ale flying every which way. I was hauled to my feet and expected Broad to come at me again, but he had had his sport and turned back to his huddle of kinsmen, who raised a loud toast to the Mackenzie clan and drained their tankards.

I awoke the following morning in a ditch by the road, not far outside Applecross. My clothes were soaked and there was a painful throbbing in my temples. I lay there awhile, but could remember nothing more of the evening than what I have already related. A crow observed me from the verge.

'What are you after?' I said.

'I was thinking I might make a breakfast of your eyes,' he replied.

'I'm sorry to disappoint you,' I said.

I crawled out of the ditch onto the road and got to my feet. The crow followed my progress attentively, as if not yet convinced he would not have his feast. I swung my boot at him and he flapped a foot or two into the air before settling on his former spot. It must have been very early in the morning, for the dew clung thickly to the grass and there was not a sound in the air. I set off towards Culduie. I felt quite indifferent to the reception I would receive on my return. The morning was not cold, but on account of my wet clothing I shivered all over. As the events of the previous day came back to mind I felt dreadfully ashamed and resolved to accept any punishment from my father without complaint. I did not see a soul on the road and as I approached Culduie no one was yet at work on their land. I thought perhaps that my father might still be a-bed and I could return to the house undetected, but this was not to be the case. As I made my way along the road at the foot of the crofts I felt something beneath my arm, I opened my jacket and found Jetta's shawl still lodged there. It was nothing but a sodden mass of fibre. I stepped onto the shore and looking around to check that there was no one observing me I threw it in the sea. It unravelled in the water and snagged among the tentacles of sea-ware that rode the swell.

My father was at his breakfast when I stepped over the threshold. He neither looked in my direction nor said a word. There being nothing else for me to do, I lay down on my bunk and remained there the entire day.

* * *

This morning, after his usual enquiries regarding my wellbeing, Mr Sinclair asked whether I might be willing to meet a gentleman whom, he said, had travelled some distance to see me.

'Have my crimes so elevated me,' I asked, 'that gentlemen now seek out my company?'

Mr Sinclair smiled thinly at my remark and informed me that it might benefit me to receive this gentleman. I naturally agreed, in the first place, as I did not wish to displease my advocate, but also as it is hardly the right of a prisoner to choose his guests. Mr Sinclair seemed pleased by my decision and went out into the passage where the visitor must have been waiting. The two men entered together and as neither wished to take the seat at my writing table, we all three remained standing, myself beneath the high window, Mr Sinclair by the table and the gentleman at the foot of my plank bed to the right of the door. Mr Sinclair introduced the visitor as Mr Thomson and explained that he was a most eminent practitioner in his field, although I do not believe he specified what field this was. I confess I found this gentleman's countenance quite repellent and he must have felt similarly, for he gazed upon me with an expression of unveiled repugnance. He was a tall man – he had to stoop to pass through the door – with sharp features and small, blue eyes. He was dressed in a black suit with a white shirt fastened so tightly round his neck that folds of slack skin spilled over his collar. He was hatless and his hair was wispy and grey and no longer grew on the uppermost parts of his skull. He kept his hands clasped over his chest, the middle finger of his right constantly worrying a thick ring set with a green stone on the fourth finger of his left.

He then addressed Mr Sinclair. 'He is certainly of the low physical type one would expect. Do you find him generally alert when you visit? Does he sleep a great deal?'

Mr Sinclair appeared uncomfortable to be questioned this way. 'I find him extremely alert and to the best of my recollection I have never found him asleep.'

The visitor made a little clicking sound with his tongue. 'He is likely disturbed by the grating of the key in the lock.'

He took two tentative paces towards me as though he was afraid I might spring at him. He stooped his head and spent some minutes running his eyes over my face and the rest of my person. I stood quite still, believing that there must be some reason beyond my grasp for his rude behaviour. Nevertheless, I felt like a piece of livestock. At length, he drew away and retreated in the direction of the writing table. He tapped the fingers of his left hand on the sheets stacked there.

'And these are the pages you say he has been composing?'

'Indeed,' said Mr Sinclair. 'He has been working tirelessly on them.'

Mr Thomson gave a little snort through his nose. 'I very much doubt that we will find anything of interest contained there. I suspect, Mr Sinclair, that you are guilty of some naivety in your approach to your client, but I suppose that speaks well of you.'

He then flicked through a few of the pages. I had a strong urge to step across the room and snatch them from him, as I had no wish for him to read the words I had written and believed that were he to do so, it would be for the sole purpose of scoffing at my ill-composed sentences. I did not do so, however, as I did not wish to confirm the negative impression the gentleman seemed to have formed of me.

He then pressed the tips of his fingers of his two hands together and asked my advocate if he might leave the two of us alone for a few minutes. Mr Sinclair assented and made to quit the room. Mr Thomson arrested him with a motion of his hand.

'Do you believe the prisoner to be a danger to your person?' he said in a low voice.

Mr Sinclair smiled at this and replied that he did not. Nevertheless, Mr Thomson called the gaoler and kept him stationed by the door. He then quite slowly and deliberately pulled back the chair from my writing table and sat down, placing one foot on the plank bed and leaning his elbow on his knee.

'Now, Roderick,' he began, 'it seems you have made an excellent job of drawing the wool over Mr Sinclair's eyes.'

I did not say anything because his statement did not appear to require an answer.

'I am sorry to say, however, that I am of quite different stock from your learned advocate. I have examined hundreds, thousands of your type and I'm afraid that I see you for exactly what you are. I'm afraid you will have a good deal more difficulty hoodwinking me.'

I felt quite affronted to hear Mr Thomson abuse Mr Sinclair in this way, but I did not think it prudent to enter into debate with him.

'Nevertheless,' he continued, 'as I have travelled some distance to examine you, we should get down to business.'

The gentleman got to his feet and carried out a minute examination of my person, all the time making notes in a little book he must have brought for this purpose, and now and again muttering to himself as he went about his task. No animal at market has ever been subjected to such an intimate inspection, but I submitted to his various proddings and instructions without demur.

His examination complete, he resumed his seat, again resting his foot on my bunk. 'I now propose to put some questions to you, which I would be obliged if you could answer as fully as you are capable,' he said. 'Mr Sinclair has assured me that you have a good grasp of language and are able to express yourself quite lucidly, so let's see, shall we?'

I found my gaze wandering to the gaoler, who was stationed behind Mr Thomson and showed no sign of following the gentleman's conversation. His eyes were directed towards the small window high on the wall above me and I reflected again that it must be quite as unpleasant for him to be confined within these walls as it was for me. My eyes wandered towards the window and after some time I became aware that I had not been following the questions which Mr Thomson had put to me. I returned my gaze to him. He had taken his foot from my bed and was sitting stiffly as if his back was giving him trouble. He fell silent and then stood up. The gaoler stood aside and Mr Thomson left without bidding me good day. The gaoler closed the door and turned the key in the lock. I felt then that I might perhaps have treated the gentleman with some discourtesy. I did not regret doing so for his sake, as I had not taken to him from the outset, but I felt that Mr Sinclair might be disappointed in me and for that I felt some remorse.

* * *

My father did not speak to me for several days after the Gathering. I do not know if he had heard about my antics at the inn, but in our community few events go unnoticed or unremarked upon. Jetta, too, addressed me only when necessary, and when she did it was in a curt tone to which I was not accustomed. Whether this was due to her disapproval of my behaviour or on account of some troubles of her own I cannot say. Our meals were eaten in silence and the atmosphere in the house was blacker than ever. There was a general sense of dread, as if we were all aware that events were soon to draw to their conclusion.

I nightly expected the appearance of Lachlan Broad at our threshold, but he did not come. However, the knowledge that our visit to the factor and my foolish advances towards his daughter would not go unanswered weighed heavily on me. It is not the blow that causes greatest distress, but the anticipation of it, and I existed at this time in a state of anxiety which increased with each passing day. I was not called upon to work on any of Lachlan Broad's schemes, and neither he nor any of his kinsmen so much as ventured beyond the junction of the village. I was quite certain that what was in store for us was not the raising of some petty fine, but the culmination of the constable's campaign against us.

I passed as little time as possible in the house. The days I spent pulling weeds and attempting to improve the prospects for our harvest, but I did so half-heartedly and if I downed tools and wandered off, my father did not question or chastise me. In the evenings I took myself into the hills and sat looking down on Culduie. Viewed from far above, the township seemed no more than a child's toy. The people and livestock were no larger than specks of ash and it was difficult to credit that anything which occurred there was of any consequence. I thought of what lay beyond the mountains, of the great cities to the south, and, to the west, the vast Atlantic with its promise of Canada. I found myself wondering if I might after all make a new life for myself. In one thing Flora was quite correct – there was nothing for any of us in Culduie. Why then should I stay? All that was required was to set out one morning and never return. This was, at first, no more than an idle thought, but in the hours I spent on the Càrn it began to take hold of me. I was not yet a prisoner. There were no walls to prevent me from striking out. I need only set one foot in front of the other. First to Camusterrach, then on to Applecross and then over the Pass to the metropolis of Jeantown.* From there, I might catch a boat or simply continue walking. I would bid no farewells. Nor would I formulate any plan, for beyond the Pass I knew nothing of the world. Over a period of days, this idea thickened within me until it had assumed the proportions of an irresistible force.

And so it happened that on a perfectly ordinary morning, I left the house and made my way down through the rig, clambered over the dyke and set off. I did not acknowledge to myself that I was leaving.

---

* *Jeantown is the former name of the village of Lochcarron.*

I told myself I was merely setting off towards Camusterrach. From there I might continue or turn back. I had taken no possessions or even food, for to do so would be to admit to myself what I was doing. I said nothing to Jetta and I did not allow myself to think, as I watched her stirring porridge at the swee, that I would never see her again. As I reached the brow of the hill which would take Culduie out of view, I resisted the urge to look back. In order to empty my mind, I counted my steps aloud and in this way I walked the mile to Camusterrach. There I passed Reverend Galbraith on the road. He did not greet me and I wondered if, later, when I had not returned, he would recall seeing me.

At the outset I ambled along unhurriedly, but as I left Camusterrach behind, my pace increased. As the distance between Culduie and myself grew, I experienced a feeling of lightness. When I reached Applecross, I realised I had been running, and so as not to draw attention to myself I slowed to a walk. My progress along the village was observed by a few crones stationed on benches outside their houses. Then, as I neared the inn, I spotted Archibald Ross on the road ahead, in conversation with a thickly bearded man I recognised as the blacksmith. A dog circled at their feet. Not wishing to meet my friend, I stepped into the gap between two houses. After a few moments, I craned my head around the quoin. Archibald was now approaching, the dog at his heels. There was no escape to the rear of the house, so rather than be discovered lurking between the houses, I stepped out, adjusting my breeches as if I had been relieving myself. Archibald did not seem the least taken aback to see me appear in this way.

'Well, the pugilist returns! That was a fearful beating you took,' he said, laughing. 'But no disgrace in it. The fellow was twice your size.'

I did not say anything.

'What business brings you to Applecross?'

I told him that I was on an errand for my father.

'An errand?' he repeated. 'What kind of errand?'

'A family matter,' I said.

'I see,' he replied gravely. 'And you do not trust your friend with the particulars? Well, never mind. I am sure you will not refuse me the pleasure of your company for a glass of ale.' He jerked his thumb in the direction of the inn.

I knew very well that if I entered the inn my resolve would swiftly dissipate and excused myself from Archibald's invitation.

'I cannot believe,' he protested, 'that your errand can be so pressing that you would leave an old friend high and dry.'

'I must go to Jeantown,' I said.

'But that is eighteen miles away,' Archibald exclaimed. 'You cannot think to walk that distance over the Pass.'

'I intend to spend the night there,' I said.

'But you must get there first.' He pondered my dilemma for a moment and then, taking me by the elbow, led me along the village. 'We will fetch you a garron,' he said, excited by his plan. 'You can ride to Jeantown and bring it back on your return. You come back tomorrow?'

I nodded dumbly.

'All the better!' he said.

'But I have no money to pay for a garron,' I said.

He waved away my protests.

'Leave it to Archibald Ross,' he said. 'I have no doubt you will find some way to re-pay me in the future.'

He was then struck by the idea that the following evening, once I had returned the pony, we could take some ale in the inn.

'Then perhaps you will feel able to tell me about your mysterious errand,' he said.

I had no choice but to accompany Archibald to the courtyard behind the Big House where I had first made his acquaintance. He strutted across the cobbles with impressive assurance and put his head inside the stable door. Presently a hand appeared beneath the stone archway.

'Have a pony saddled for Mr Macrae here,' Archibald said without explanation.

The hand, who was perhaps fifty years old, looked askance

at me, but he did not demur. As we waited in the courtyard, Archibald filled his pipe and lit it. His dog sat at his feet and gazed at him with great devotion. It struck me that Flora might currently be employed in the kitchens, so I leaned against the wall to conceal myself from the window. Archibald instructed me to make sure the pony was properly fed and watered before my return journey. After some minutes the hand led out an ancient piebald garron. Archibald slapped it roughly on the haunch and invited me to mount it, which I did with some difficulty. Any pleasure I might have felt (for there was nothing I had ever wished for more than to ride a pony) was entirely spoiled by the situation I found myself in. Archibald walked me to the front of the Big House and sent me on my way with another hearty smack to the pony's rear and a declaration that we would drink the inn dry the following night.

The garron plodded forward at no more than walking pace. I tried digging my heels into its sides as I had seen other riders do, but it refused to quicken its tempo. No matter, as we trekked back towards the village I assessed the courses of action open to me. My first thought was simply to tether the garron at the junction which led to the Pass and continue on foot. An abandoned pony would quickly garner attention, however, and I imagined a party being quickly assembled to apprehend me. I had to remind myself that I was not a fugitive. Was I not free to go wheresoever I pleased? I was not in breach of any law or regulation, and if I wished to ride to Jeantown on a pony loaned by a friend, it was no concern of the powers-that-be or anyone else. Indeed, to Lachlan Broad my exile would no doubt be a matter of satisfaction. Even to my father it would likely be a blessing. My existence had not prevented any of the tribulations which had befallen us. In truth, it had been my own actions and foolishness which had brought about a great deal of our troubles and my continued presence in Culduie would do nothing to avert whatever ills were to come. It was with these thoughts that I continued on horseback beyond the junction and began the slow ascent to the Pass.

It became apparent, too, that Archibald Ross was quite correct. To walk the eighteen miles over the Pass would have been quite impractical, not only because of the distance involved, but also because on foot I would have cut a far more conspicuous figure. Riding a pony, even one as ancient and lame as mine, bestowed a certain authority. Those individuals I passed on the road simply bid me good morning or even touched their caps to me. No one (as I had imagined they would) interrogated me about my destination or accused me of stealing my mount. I began to feel as I ascended higher into the mountains that Archibald's intervention had been a matter of great providence; that this was, after all, what was intended for me. As the road became more deserted, I allowed myself to contemplate what might lie in store beyond Jeantown. No doubt, as Archibald had said, there were no end of opportunities in the cities to the south. I might establish myself in some employment there and in so doing prove myself of far greater worth to my family than had I stayed to await our fate. I might even be able to send home funds to raise my family out of their abject state. In time, perhaps Jetta could join me and we could live in comfort and happiness. Such thoughts, however, did not detain me for long.

Towards the head of the Pass, the air grew frigid. The wind buffeted tussocks of brown grass by the roadside. The garron's head dropped lower and his pace grew heavier. I dismounted by a burn to allow him to drink a little. I was by this time cold and hungry and cursed myself for not filling my pockets with bannocks before I left the house. I pulled my cap low over my eyes and continued on foot, leading the garron by the reins. It took some hours to reach the head of the Pass. I sat down on a boulder and gazed out at the grey vista before me. The road twisted downwards through a craggy glen. Beyond that was a stretch of water. I do not know what I had expected to find, but the scene before me filled me with a kind of dread. I realised that I had no idea where I was going or, if I ever reached Jeantown, I had no real idea of what I would do there. Certainly the shilling in my pocket would not take me very far. Perhaps I could find some outbuilding to sleep in and some scraps of food to eat, but this prospect did not fill me with joy. No matter how wretched my life in Culduie, I had no wish to live like a mendicant. I thought then of Jetta, who would certainly have missed me by now, and I imagined how unhappy my desertion would make her. And I felt keenly how contemptible it was to have thought to leave. Like a tethered dog, I had reached the limits of my territory. I climbed onto the garron and dug my heels into his flanks, but the exhausted beast refused to move. I dismounted and with some effort coaxed him to follow me back down the Pass. It was late in the afternoon before we reached Applecross.

Not wishing to meet Archibald Ross, I approached the Big House with even greater trepidation than usual. In order to placate him I had concocted a story that the fellow I was to see in Jeantown had in fact met me on the road, thus allowing me to return that same day. It mattered little to me whether Archibald would believe such a preposterous tale, but in any case, he did not appear. The sound of the garron's hooves on the cobbles brought the hand from the stables. He took the reins from me without a word and I thanked him for the use of the pony.

I felt terribly weary as I approached Culduie, both from the exertions of the day and from the certainty that there was now no escape from whatever providence had in store. Set against this, whatever my father had to say about my absence was a matter of indifference to me. I wanted nothing other to lay down on my bunk and sleep. As I stepped over the threshold, I was surprised to see a black-clad figure seated at the table with his back to the door. I recognised him by his close cropped hair as Reverend Galbraith. My father was at the head of the table. Jetta was loitering by the dresser like a dark ghost. Even in the dim light, her face was pale. I assumed that the minister had come to report his sighting of me in Camusterrach that morning, but this was not the case. On the table was a sheet of parchment, folded in thirds and bearing a broken wax seal.

The minister instructed me to sit and then said, 'Your father has today received this letter.'

He reached across the table and pushed it towards me with his fingertips. His knuckles were gnarled and swollen. I took up the paper and unfolded it. As the light was insufficient to read, I took the letter to the fire. It was written in an elegant hand and headed with the words, underlined, 'Notice of Eviction'. I do not recall the precise wording of the letter, but it first named my father ('the tenant') and specified the extent of the croft, house and outbuildings. It then stated that the factor, through the authority vested in him by the laird, hereby gave notice for the tenant to quit the said property by the 30th day in September 1869, this date being determined to permit the tenant time to lift the crops from the ground. There followed a list of grounds for eviction: failure to maintain the croft to a proper standard; failure to properly maintain houses and outbuildings; appropriation of the property of the laird; agitation against the office of the village constable; and arrears of rent and fines imposed. Various sums were then enumerated, the total far exceeding the value of all our livestock and worldly goods. It was signed and dated by the factor.

I returned to the table and laid down the letter. My father's gaze remained fixed in front of him.

'I have explained the contents of the letter to your father,' said the minister, addressing me. 'I am dumbfounded that he has allowed his affairs to fall into such disarray that these measures have been necessitated.'

'Necessitated?' I repeated.

The minister looked at me with a thin smile on his lips. 'We are all responsible for the management of our affairs. The laird cannot be expected to permit tenants to exploit his land free of charge, nor to do so with such disregard for the terms of tenancy.' He then shook his head and made a soft tutting sound behind his teeth.

I could not help but feel that he took some pleasure in our situation and saw no purpose in appealing to him to intervene on our behalf. He then stated that he had not seen my sister or I in church these last few months.

'Perhaps if you had paid more attention to your spiritual welfare,' he said, 'you would not have found yourself in such circumstances.'

'I see no relation between the two things,' I said.

'That is precisely my point,' said the minister. 'You are a great discredit to your father.'

He then informed us that he would make what enquiries he could about finding alternative accommodation. My father thanked him and he took his leave. When he was gone my father snatched the letter from the table and tore it into pieces. He pounded his fists on the table, making the scraps of paper leap into the air. I watched him as I might have watched a wounded animal struggle in a trap. The twins were woken on their bunk and Jetta went to comfort them. Father then stood up and advanced upon Jetta. He gripped her by the back of the neck, dragged her to the table and set her roughly on the bench next to me. The twins toddled after her, wailing horribly.

'It is your wickedness that has brought us to this,' he said quietly.

Jetta bowed her head and clasped her hands in her lap, twisting a plait of coloured threads between her fingers.

'That is not so,' she replied.

I did not think it wise to contradict my father when he was in such a humour, but Jetta appeared quite steadfast.

Father then got to his feet and with surprising speed, gripped Jetta roughly by the hair at the back of her head. He pulled her face close to his own.

'You think by swaddling yourself like an old woman you can conceal your condition from me? I am not blind.'

Jetta shook her head as vigorously as his grip would allow.

'You are a whore.'

He then brought my sister's head down towards the table and struck it repeatedly against the surface. Jetta did not cry out. I grabbed his wrist and tried to loosen his grasp, but his fingers were tightly entwined in her hair. As I struggled with him, Jetta was buffeted between us like a fishing vessel on the swell.

'I want to know who is responsible,' he hissed.

Jetta kept her lips firmly closed. Her eyes streamed with tears. I implored him to let her go. Despite my efforts he then thrust Jetta's head against the table with such force that his feet left the ground.

'Who is responsible?' he snarled, gobbets of spit flying from his mouth. Blood seeped into the surface of the table. Jetta indicated by a movement of her head that she would not answer. I feared for her life and blurted out, 'It is Lachlan Broad's doing.'

My father stared at me wildly, his little eyes darting to and fro, and I took advantage of the moment to throw myself across the table at him. I wrenched his grip from Jetta's head, tearing out a great clump of her hair. The three of us fell together to the floor. I wrestled myself on top of him. He struggled half-heartedly for some moments, and as I lay with my arms around him, I realised he was no more than a skinful of bones. There was no strength in him and what fight he had was soon spent. Jetta ran from the house. The twins howled like dogs. Father lay on his back while I righted the table, which had been overturned in the scuffle. I picked up various items which had been strewn on the floor and set them in their proper places. Father struggled to his feet and wearily brushed the stoor from his clothing. Then he sat down in his chair and sank his head in his hands. I went out to look for Jetta.

I found her in the barn. She was sitting on the milking stool I had lately used to reach the rafter where I had built my fledgling's nest. The hair on the left side of her head was matted with blood, her left eye bloodied and swollen. She was twisting a length of rope on her lap. She looked up when I entered, her engorged eye twitching.

'Hello, Roddy,' she said sadly.

'Hello,' I said. I could think of nothing else to say, so I went and stood by her. She put her hand to her scalp and touched it gently with the tips of her fingers. Then she examined the blood on her hand, as if it was not her own. I knelt on the floor beside her. She turned her head towards me, the movement causing her to wince.

'Our lot in this life is not a happy one, is it, Roddy?' she said.

'It is not.'

'I fear that Father will not have me back under his roof.'

'We shall none of us be under this roof for long,' I said.

She nodded slowly.

'Shall you go to Toscaig?' I asked.

'I fear that in my current condition I would not be welcome there,' she said.

'Then what?'

She formed her lips into a sad smile and shook her head to indicate that she had no answer to this question. I saw for the first time that her nose was entirely flattened against her face. It pained me to see her so ruined.

'It is all over for me,' she said. 'My concern is for you. You should leave this place. You must see that there is nothing here for you.'

I said nothing of my hapless excursion to the Pass, as the thought of my flight shamed me.

'What about Father?' I said.

'Our father is never more happy than when he is suffering,' she said. 'You must not tether yourself to his mast.'

'And the twins?'

A large tear rolled down the uninjured side of Jetta's face. 'They will be taken care of,' she said.

'It is Lachlan Broad that should be taken care of,' I said.

'This is not Lachlan Broad's doing,' said Jetta, moving her hand to her broken face.

'It is all Lachlan Broad's doing,' I replied. 'I should like to be revenged on him.' These were, for the time being, empty words, spoken in bravado. I had not thought, until that moment, of retribution and had no notion of how such a thing might be accomplished.

Jetta shook her head vigorously.

'You must not say such things, Roddy. If you understood more about the world, you would see that Lachlan Broad is not responsible. It is providence that has brought us to this point. It is no more Lachlan Broad's doing than yours or mine or Father's.'

'What if I had not killed the sheep, or if mother had not died or if the Two Iains had not sunk?' I objected.

'But all these things did occur.'

'If Lachlan Broad did not exist ...' I began, with no idea of where that thought would take me.

'But he does exist, and he no more chose to be brought into this world than you or I.'

'Then neither will he choose the method of his leaving,' I said.

Jetta let forth a long sigh. 'Nothing you can do will alter anything, Roddy. In any case, you need not concern yourself with Lachlan Broad.' She lowered her voice to a whisper. 'He is not long for this world.'

I drew my head away from her, so as to properly see her face. She gestured with her fingers for me to come closer.

'I have twice seen the winding sheet about him.'

I struggled for some moments to grasp the implications of my sister's statement, and when I did so I was gripped by a feeling of elation, thinking that the departure of Lachlan Broad from this world would release us from our troubles. I expressed this thought to Jetta.

She chided me for taking pleasure in an event which would make a widow of his wife and orphans of his children. I retorted that I would rather be an orphan than be raised the offspring of Lachlan Broad.

'Such sentiments ill become you,' said Jetta. 'Nothing that happens to Lachlan Broad can undo my condition. Nor can it revoke the factor's letter.'

I stood up, refusing to believe her, and paced around the barn in a state of agitation. I demanded more details about her vision and the imminence of Lachlan Broad's demise, but she refused to elaborate. The constable's fate was of no relevance to our situation.

Jetta suddenly looked terribly weary. She closed her eyes and let her head drop forward. I knelt down in front of her and clasped the back of her head in my hand. I did not have access to the contents of her mind, but I had a strong presentiment of what she meant to do and could see no alternative for her. She squeezed my hand in hers. Then she opened her eyes and told me to leave her. Tears ran down my cheeks. I bid her goodnight and left her there on the milking stool. I pulled the door fast behind me, tethering the rope on the rotting jamb. And in this way I took my leave of her.

Having no desire to return to the house, I made my way down through the croft towards the shore. The evening was calm and the sky above the islands had taken on the rosy hue of late evening. At this time of year in our part of the world the hours of darkness are short, so much so that I have heard that visitors are often disturbed in their sleep. I watched a heron for some minutes stand stock-still on the shore, before silently taking to the air with the lack of grace peculiar to that species. It flew low across the bay and settled on the point at Aird-Dubh. I set to thinking about what Jetta had told me. She was not in the habit of sharing her visions with me, but I had often seen a shadow cross her face and knew that in these moments she was experiencing some silent commune with the Other World. To some degree, Jetta had never fully dwelt in Culduie, but flitted between the two worlds. If she was now to depart, it would be a smaller death than for those of us who inhabit only the physical world.

It was as I sat by the shore watching the slow movement of the tide, that I first thought to kill Lachlan Broad. I dismissed the notion, or attempted to do so, but it was dogged and the more I tried to set my mind to other things the more it took hold of me. The knowledge that Lachlan Broad was soon to die loosened the ordinary provisos. If providence had decreed that he was not long for this world, of what importance was the method of his leaving? That he might die by my hand seemed so just as to be irresistible. The idea excited me. I would become the redeemer that Reverend Galbraith had spoken of at my mother's funeral. And this in the knowledge that while I might be the instrument of Lachlan Broad's demise, I would only be hastening what was, in any case, due.

Jetta's vision of the winding sheet spoke nothing about the manner of Lachlan Broad's death, or if it had she had not told me of it. One would struggle to think of an individual in our parish who was in such rude health and less likely to be stricken by some sudden ailment. Nor was it easy to imagine how he might meet with some fatal misfortune. Was it, thus, possible that Lachlan Broad was not merely destined to meet his end, but that this end lay in my hands? The thought weighed heavily on me and by the time I roused myself the sun had sunk below the horizon and what passed for darkness at that time of year embraced me.

When I returned to the house, Father had taken himself to bed. The twins were sleeping soundly on their bunk and I envied their tranquillity. I slept only fitfully that night, waking frequently, and each time I did so the thoughts kindled by Jetta's vision burned in my mind. I longed to douse them with sleep, but the gathering light of the morning prevented me from doing so.

* * *

I left the house before my father emerged from his chamber. On account of the events of the previous evening, I feared that he would not be in good humour, and after his treatment of my sister I had no wish to converse with him. I took two bannocks to the foot of the croft and ate them slowly. The rig was overgrown with weeds and, compared to those of our neighbours, was a shameful sight. The air was exceptionally still and wisps of cloud hung low over the water like strands of wool. I could see no other living soul and the only sounds were the calls of the birds and the distant noises of the livestock from the grazings.

I had hoped that just as one emerges from a dream, the notion to murder Lachlan Broad might have melted away, but if anything it had thickened inside me. Nonetheless, at this point, it remained no more than an idle speculation upon which I had no intention of acting. If I contemplated killing Lachlan Broad, it was in the spirit of a mathematician approaching a problem in algebra. My schoolmaster, Mr Gillies, had once explained how in order to solve a problem a scientist must proceed, first, by advancing a hypothesis and, then, by testing it through observation or experiment. It was in this manner that I moved forward.

Certainly, the killing of a large, powerful man like Lachlan Broad would be no simple matter. When I enumerated the various means by which one might do a man to death, each presented its own difficulties. One might, for example, kill a man with an axe blow to the head, but this would necessitate lying in wait in some concealed place in the hope that he might happen to pass by. One might stab a man with a blade, but I could not be confident of getting close enough to Lachlan Broad, or having sufficient strength to administer a wound severe enough to do more than merely injure him. A man could be killed by means of a firearm. This had the advantage that it could be carried out at distance, but even if I were able to acquire such a weapon – from the Big House, for example – I had no knowledge of how to load or discharge a gun. It might be possible to poison my victim, but this would entail consulting one of the old crones of the parish who had knowledge of such things, and then finding some way of administering the toxin. In contemplating these latter methods, I realised that they failed a test of which I had, until that point, been unaware. My objective was not merely to remove Lachlan Broad from this world, something which was, in any case, to occur without any intervention on my part. Rather, at the moment of his death, it was necessary that he was cognisant of the fact that it was I, Roderick Macrae, who was ending his life, and that I was doing so in just payment for the tribulations he had caused my family.

My father emerged from the house. I do not know how long I had been lost in my thoughts. I found a croman at my feet and began to turn over the weeds growing in the furrows. My father made his way down the rig to where I was working and asked what I was doing. His face was haggard and grey, and I fancied his gait more bent than usual. I replied that we still had a crop to lift, and if we did not properly tend the croft, there would not be enough food to see even the twins through the winter. Father muttered something to the effect that if God wished to provide for us, He would do so, but he said it without conviction and left me to my labour without further comment. I am quite certain we were both aware that there would not be any lifting of crops that year.

Our neighbours were by this time emerging from their homes and setting about the daily round. The morning must have appeared entirely commonplace and, were it not for what was soon to occur, they would likely have had difficulty recalling it or distinguishing it from any other morning. Indeed in every aspect, aside from the dark thoughts that had taken up residence in my mind, the day was entirely unremarkable. But it struck me, as I gazed around our scattering of houses, that the removal of Lachlan Broad would lift a burden which had long weighed heavily on our township.

I got up from my knees and wandered back towards the house. My previous thoughts about the means of killing Lachlan Broad had been no more than procrastination. It mattered not what was in my mind or what I planned to do. If fate dictated that Lachlan Broad was to die by my hand, then it would be so. The success or otherwise of my enterprise was outwith my control. In this spirit, I determined that if I were to kill Lachlan Broad, I must first proceed to his house. It would, furthermore, be necessary to go armed with some weapon with which I might accomplish the task. What better than the croman which providence had just then placed in my hand? As I reached the top of the croft, I came upon a flaughter leaning against the gable and this I also took up. I then set off along the village. I told myself that I was not on my way to murder Lachlan Broad, but merely to discover what would happen if I paid a visit to his house thus armed.

I proceeded along the track at a normal pace. Carmina Smoke emerged from her house and greeted me. As I did not wish to raise her suspicions, I paused and returned her greeting. She saw the flaughter in my hand and asked me if it was not a little late in the year to be breaking ground. I told her without thinking that I was going to clear some land behind Lachlan Broad's house where a dyke was to be built. The ease with which this lie came to my lips led me to believe that my project was destined for success. Carmina Smoke said that she had heard nothing about a new dyke, but she did not question me further. I bid her good morning and continued along the village. I sensed that she was watching me, but I did not look round, for fear of appearing furtive. I spoke to no one else as I made my way past the remaining houses. I felt something of the old anxiety I always experienced when encroaching on Mackenzie territory. The incident with the kite flitted through my mind and my heart began to beat more rapidly. I paused outside the Broads' house and leant on the handle of my flaughter, as though taking stock of the work ahead of me, which in a sense I was. A crow settled on the gable of the house. Little Donnie Broad was playing in the dirt some yards from the threshold. He squinted up at me and I greeted him in a normal manner. He then returned to whatever harmless game he was playing. I looked back along the township. Carmina Smoke had disappeared. A number of villagers were bent over their crops, all oblivious to the events which were about to occur. A thin wisp of smoke rose from the Broads' chimney. I stepped past Donnie Broad into the doorway.

Inside, the house was dim and it took some moments for my eyes to adjust to the gloom. The sun cast a rectangle of light on the earthen floor and my legs were silhouetted within it. Flora was at the table scrubbing potatoes and placing them in a pot of water. When I stepped inside the house she looked up from her work. She seemed startled to see me and asked what I was doing there. There was a light sweat on her brow and she raised her right hand to push away a strand of hair which had fallen over her face. I could think of no errand that would have brought me there, nor of any reason to lie, so I replied that I had come to kill her father. She put down the potato she had been scrubbing and said that that was not a very funny thing to say. I could, I suppose, have pretended it was a prank, but I did not do so, and from that moment my course was set. Instead I asked where her father was. Flora's eyes widened and she let out several short breaths. I took a few steps into the chamber. She moved to the far end of the table that now stood between us. She told me I should leave before her father returned or I would get myself into terrible trouble. I replied that I was already in terrible trouble, all of it brought on by her father. Flora said that I was frightening her. I said I was sorry, but that even if I wished things to be otherwise, they could not be so.

Then quite suddenly Flora darted to her left and ran towards the door. As she passed the end of the table, I swung my flaughter and caught her around the knees with it. She crumpled to the floor like a puppet whose strings had been cut. The blow must have struck her dumb for she did not cry out or make any noise other than a soft sobbing. I laid down my tools and bent down next to her. I lifted up her skirts and saw that her knee was collapsed at a quite unnatural angle. Flora's eyes darted wildly around, like an animal in a snare. I stroked her hair for a moment to calm her, then, as I did not wish her to suffer, I took up my flaughter and planted my feet on either side of her hips. I raised the tool above my head and, remembering the sheep at the peat bog, took careful aim. Flora made no attempt to move and I brought the back of the blade firmly down on her skull. The weight carried the tool clean through the bone as if it was no thicker than an eggshell. Flora's limbs twitched for some moments before she came to rest and I was glad not to be obliged to administer any further blows.

I stepped back from the body and surveyed it for some moments. Flora's skirts were disarrayed around her legs. Her arms were by her sides and were it not for the fact that her skull was broken open, it might have appeared that she been struck down by a bolt of lightning. As her body was not illuminated by the light from the window, anyone entering the house might stumble over it. To avoid this eventuality, I leaned my flaughter against the wall and carried her to the table where she had lately been at her potato peeling. She was not heavy, but as I lifted her a good deal of matter spilled from the back of her skull onto the floor. I laid her on her back with her legs hanging from the end of the table, upsetting the pot in which she had been placing the potatoes. The water ran off and formed a puddle on the floor. I collected the potatoes and placed them back in the pot. I retrieved the flaughter from the wall and with my croman still in my hand, stepped into the darkness on the far side of the door in order to obscure myself.

After some minutes, Donnie Broad appeared at the threshold. He called his sister's name, but, of course, received no reply. He stepped into the chamber and saw Flora's legs dangling from the end of the table. He started to toddle towards her, but as he did so he slipped in some of the matter from her skull and fell face-first onto the floor. He began to cry. I stepped forward and hit him on the side of the head with my flaughter. I did not mean the little boy any harm, but I could not permit him to raise the alarm. I did not know then if I had killed or merely stunned him, for I had not hit him with any great force, but he lay quite still and after some time I concluded that he must be dead. I left him lying where he had fallen and stepped back into the shadows.

I do not know how much time passed while I remained there. The rectangle of sunlight on the floor slowly lengthened, as if its corner was being tugged by an invisible thread. I began to grow anxious. I would have been saddened to have killed Flora and the boy for no purpose.

Presently, I heard a dog bark close to the house and this proved an augury of Lachlan Broad's arrival. He appeared at the threshold, his great frame entirely blocking out the patch of sunlight which had been creeping across the floor. I do not know if he stopped because of the dimness of the room or because he saw the bodies before him. As he had his back to the light, I could not discern the expression on his face. In any case, after a few moments he took three or four steps towards where his son lay in the dirt. He knelt down and turned over the body and seeing that the boy was dead, looked wildly about the chamber. I remained in the shadows, not daring to draw breath. He then rose and moved towards the table where Flora's body lay. Seeing that she too had taken her leave of this world, he put his fist to his mouth and emitted a stifled cry, somewhat akin to an animal being slaughtered. He steadied himself with both hands, knuckles down to the table, his feet planted apart. A great sob racked his body, but then he mastered himself and pushed away from the table. He turned and took two or three steps towards the door. At this point I stepped from the gloom and he came to a halt. We stood no more than three paces apart. I was struck by the size of him and had grave misgivings about my ability to dispatch him as I had the others. He seemed to take some time to register who was standing before him. Then he drew himself up to his full height and said in a calm voice, 'Is this your doing, Roddy Black?'

I replied that it was and that I had come to deliver him from this world in repayment for the suffering he had caused my father. He did not say anything further. He took a step forward and lunged towards me. Without thinking, I planted my right foot behind me and thrust forward my flaughter. The blade caught Lachlan Broad in the ribs, but his weight carried him forward and we both crashed to the floor. I kept hold of my tools and, swinging my croman with my right hand, caught him on the temple with the flat of the blade. He raised his hand to where I had struck him, then stood up and let out a great roar. I feared that I had done no more than enrage him and would not have the strength to overpower him. I scrambled backwards across the floor and got to my feet. Lachlan Broad looked about him, perhaps hoping to find some weapon to hand. I ran at him, swinging my flaughter. This time, however, he anticipated my blow and raised his arm to parry it. He grabbed the shaft below the blade and wrenched it from my grip. He stared at me wildly for a few moments. A thin stream of blood seeped from the wound on his temple. He held the flaughter in his two meaty fists, the blade pointing towards me, then sprang forward. I stepped to the side and his momentum carried him past me. He turned clumsily, perhaps dazed by the blow I had earlier struck. I now had my back to the door and was aware that I could flee, but if I did not do so, it was because I did not wish to depart without achieving my objective.

Lachlan Broad made a second charge towards me. I recalled the day when I was a small boy that Kenny Smoke's bullock had run amok in the village and it had taken six men to subdue it. As Broad swung the flaughter, I stepped inside its trajectory and, reaching my left hand onto his shoulder, landed a blow with my croman on the back of his head. The blade did not penetrate the skull, but the impact was enough to bring him to his knees. He dropped the tool and remained, stunned, on all fours. I stepped behind him and stood astride his body, as if straddling a garron. I raised my croman and, keen to conclude the business without further delay, brought it down with both hands. The blow knocked him flat to the floor, but it did not penetrate the bone, and I was struck by the resilience of the human body. He lay face down on the earth, his eyes wide, chest pumping like a landed fish. I now had time to properly measure my stroke and when I next brought down my weapon, the blade properly entered his skull with an unpleasant sound like a boot being sucked into a peat-bog. It was with some effort that I extracted the blade from his head. His hands were twitching by the side of his body, but whether he still had a breath in him I could not say. Nevertheless, I administered a final blow with the heel of the croman, this time entirely destroying the integrity of his cranium.

I then stood away from the body and surveyed my handiwork. The blood was pumping in my temples and I was quite dazed, but I felt some satisfaction in the successful execution of my project. To an outside observer, the scene in the house must have looked quite dreadful, and I confess that I had to avert my eyes from the sight of the dead infant.

It was then that I noticed old Mrs Mackenzie, seated in an upholstered chair in the murk at the back of the chamber. She was perfectly still and I wondered if she too had taken her leave of the world. Her face wore no particular expression and I wondered

if she was gone in the head or not cognisant of her surroundings. I had heard many tales of old folk who habitually cried out
for people long dead, or became lost a few yards from their own
door. I approached her, the croman still in my right hand. Her
eyes were watery and flitted rapidly to and fro, perhaps distressed
by the scene which she had just then witnessed. I held my left
hand in front of her face and moved it from side to side, but she
made no reaction. There was no reason to do her any harm. Aside
from bringing Lachlan Broad into this world, she had caused me
no injury. She was no more responsible for the actions of her son
than my father was for mine. I had accomplished what I set out
to do and, as I had no intention of denying responsibility for any
of it, her killing would have served no purpose. In any case, to do
to death a helpless old woman would be a pitiless thing, and I had
not the stomach for it.

Glossary

ashet a large serving dish

bannock an oatcake

the black months winter

byre a cowshed

caman a shinty stick

Càrn nan Uaighean translates as 'heap of tombstones'

cas chrom a long-handled foot plough

ceilidh a gathering with singing and story-telling

croman a hand-tool for breaking ground, like a single-sided pickaxe or mattock

dwam a stupor

Erse Irish

fetch a double or doppelgänger

flaughter a spade with a pointed triangular blade

garron a Highland pony

ghillie a man who leads shooting and fishing expeditions

gimcrack a cheap ornament or knick-knack

hurlie a hand-cart

laird lord

quaich a traditional shallow drinking vessel

quern a stone hand-mill for grinding corn or other grains

quoin the external corner of a building

reek smoke

rig a strip of land

roof-tree a beam

sea-ware seaweed

shieling pasture land

shinty a violent form of hockey still played in the Scottish Highlands

sowens a kind of gruel, made from husks of grain

stirk a heifer

stoor dust or dirt

strupach a pot of tea, a brew

swee a chain from which a pot is suspended over a fire

unchancy supernatural

winding sheet a shroud

the yellow months summer

Medical Reports

re. the victims, carried out by Charles MacLennan, M.D., resident of Jeantown, and J.D. Gilchrist, surgeon, of Kyle of Lochalsh

Applecross, August 12th 1869

At the request of William Shaw esq., sheriff, and John Adam esq., Procurator Fiscal, we this day examined the body of Lachlan Mackenzie, crofter and village constable of Culduie, Ross-shire, aged thirty-eight years. The body was shewn to us in the outbuilding of a neighbour, Mr Kenneth Murchison, to which, on the evidence of Mr Murchison, it had been removed shortly after its discovery. The body was laid out on a table and covered with sackcloth.

The face of the victim was greatly discoloured and covered with much blood in a hardened state. The right side of the face, from the cheekbone to the temple, was entirely collapsed and the nose broken. The back of the skull was entirely collapsed and incomplete and much of the cerebral matter was missing. We were informed by Mr Murchison that fragments of the skull and cerebral matter had been retrieved from the floor of the house in which death had occurred and placed in a bowl. This bowl we examined and found to contain fragments of bone consistent with those missing from the skull. The external ear on the right side was almost entirely torn off. On the remaining parts of the skull, fragments of shattered bone had been forced into the cerebral tissue. It is our opinion that these injuries must have been caused by blows from a heavy blunt object or tool wielded with great force.

There was much bruising to the chest, in particular to the left side of the sternum. A wound six inches across had penetrated the skin between the lower ribs and of these we found two to be broken. The internal organs were intact. This wound we judged to have been caused by a wide, blunt blade, consistent with the flaughter which had been retrieved from the scene, and which was shewn to us.

On the outer part of the right forearm was a large bruise six inches below the elbow. The palms of both hands bore a number of minor lacerations and were penetrated by a number of splinters of wood. The fourth finger of the left hand was broken.

On no other part of the body was to be seen any appearance of injury.

We are decidedly of the opinion that the blow or blows delivered to the back of the skull were sufficient to cause instantaneous death and were the cause of death.

> Attested upon soul and conscience,
> *Charles MacLennan, M.D.*
> *J.D. Gilchrist*

* * *

Applecross, August 12th 1869

At the request of William Shaw esq., sheriff, and John Adam esq., Procurator Fiscal, we this day examined the body of Flora Mackenzie, aged fifteen years, daughter of Lachlan Mackenzie, and resident of Culduie, Ross-shire. The body was shewn to us in the outbuilding of Mr Kenneth Murchison, to which it had been removed from the place of death. The body was laid out on a stretcher and covered with funeral cloths.

The back of the skull was entirely caved in and fragments of bone had deeply penetrated the soft tissue. The hair was matted with a great deal of hardened blood. The features of the face were intact and it is our opinion that the damage to the skull was caused by a single blow of a heavy object or tool wielded with great force.

We observed a number of lacerations and bruising to the pubic region. The soft outer parts had been quite pulverised and the pubic bone was broken on the left side.

The left leg was fractured at the knee and the outer part of the knee severely bruised. This injury we judged to have been caused by a heavy blow, from an object consistent with the flaughter shewn to us, and would have rendered the victim unable to walk.

On no other part of the body was to be seen any appearance of injury.

We are decidedly of the opinion that the blow to the back of the skull was the cause of death, though whether instantaneous or not we could not say.

> Attested upon soul and conscience,
> *Charles MacLennan, M.D.*
> *J.D. Gilchrist*

* * *

Applecross, August 12th 1869

At the request of William Shaw esq., sheriff, and John Adam esq., Procurator Fiscal, we this day examined the body of Donald Mackenzie, aged three years, son of Lachlan Mackenzie, and resident of Culduie, Ross-shire. The body was shewn to us in the outbuilding of Mr Kenneth Murchison, to which it had been removed from the place of death. The body was laid out on a cot and covered with funeral cloths.

A large bruise, from the front temple to the ear, was observed on the skull. The skull had in these parts collapsed inwards, though the bone had not fragmented. The skin was broken around the borders of the bruised area and some blood had seeped out and hardened.

On no other part of the body was to be seen any appearance of injury.

The injury to the skull was most likely caused by a blow from a heavy blunt object consistent with the flaughter shewn to us, though not wielded with such force as with the injuries noted to Lachlan Mackenzie and Flora Mackenzie. However, such an injury might also have been caused by a heavy fall on a hard surface. We are decidedly of the opinion that this injury was the cause of death, but as to the agency of this injury we can only conjecture.

> *Attested upon soul and conscience,*
> *Charles MacLennan, M.D.*
> *J.D. Gilchrist*

TRAVELS
in the
BORDER-LANDS
of
LUNACY

by J. Bruce Thomson

*James Bruce Thomson (1810–1873) was Resident
Surgeon at the General Prison for Scotland in Perth.
In this capacity he examined around 6,000 prisoners
and was an acknowledged authority in the then
nascent discipline of Criminal Anthropology. In 1870,
he published two influential articles, 'The Psychology
of Criminals: A Study' and 'The Hereditary Nature
of Crime', in The Journal of Mental Science. His
memoir Travels in the Border-Lands of Lunacy was
published posthumously in 1874.*

I ARRIVED IN INVERNESS ON THE 23RD DAY OF AUGUST 1869, and spent the night at an inn where I was met by Mr Andrew Sinclair, advocate to a young crofter accused of murdering three of his neighbours. Mr Sinclair had written to me expressing his desire to have my opinion, as the country's pre-eminent authority on such matters, as to the sanity or otherwise of his client. We are none of us entirely immune to such appeals to our vanity and, as the case had several interesting features, not least the alleged intelligence of the perpetrator, I consented and travelled from Perth as soon as my duties permitted.

From the beginning I found Mr Sinclair not to be a man of the highest calibre, which was hardly unexpected given the limited opportunities for educated discourse in a backwater such as Inverness. He was entirely unversed in current thinking in the field of Criminal Anthropology and I spent much of the evening outlining to him some of my continental colleagues' recent innovations in this discipline. Naturally, he was anxious to discuss his client, but I bound him to silence, wishing to reach my own conclusions unencumbered by prejudicial thoughts, no matter how ill informed.

The following morning I accompanied Mr Sinclair to Inverness gaol to inspect the prisoner, and I again directed the advocate not to speak of his client before I had the opportunity to examine him. Mr Sinclair preceded me into the cell, in order, he said, to ascertain whether his client was willing to receive me. I found this a most irregular occurrence as I have never before heard of a prisoner being consulted about who may or may not enter his cell, but I attributed it to the advocate's lack of experience in dealing with cases of this nature. Mr Sinclair remained some minutes inside the cell before informing the gaoler that I might be admitted. From the first instance, I found the relations between advocate and client to be quite unorthodox. They conversed together, not as a professional man and a criminal, but rather in the manner of two acquaintances somehow in cahoots. Nevertheless, the dialogue between them provided me with an opportunity to observe the prisoner before commencing my examination proper.

My initial impression of R—— M—— was not entirely negative. In his general bearing, he was certainly of low physical stock, but he was not as repellent in his features as the majority of the criminal class, perhaps on account of not breathing the rank air of his urban brethren. His complexion, however, was pallid, and his eyes, while alert, were close-set and capped by thick eyebrows. His beard grew sparsely, although this may have been due to his relative youth, rather than any hereditary deficiency. In his discourse with Mr Sinclair, he appeared quite lucid, but I noted that the advocate's questions were frequently of a leading nature, requiring the prisoner only to offer confirmation of what had been suggested to him.

I dismissed the advocate and in the presence of the gaoler directed the prisoner to remove his clothes. This he did without protest. He stood before me quite without shame, and I commenced a detailed examination of his person. He stood 5 feet 4½ inches tall, and was of smaller than average build. His chest was disproportionately protruding – what in layman's terms would be called 'pigeon-chested' – and his arms longer than average. The upper- and forearms were well developed, no doubt as a result of his life of physical labour. The hands were large and calloused, with exceptionally long fingers, but there was no evidence of webbing or other abnormalities. His torso was hirsute from the nipples to the pubis, but he was quite hairless on the back and shoulders. His penis was large, though within the normal range of dimensions, and the testicles properly descended. His legs were scrawny, and when asked to walk the length of the cell (admittedly not a great distance) his gait appeared somewhat rolling or lopsided, suggesting an asymmetry in his bearing. This may have been due to some injury sustained at an earlier time, but when asked, the prisoner was unable to furnish me with any explanation.

I carried out a detailed inspection of the subject's cranium and physiognomy. The forehead and brow were large and heavy, while the skull was flat on top and markedly obtruding to the back. On the whole, the cranium was quite mis-shapen and not dissimilar to many of those I had examined in my capacity as prison surgeon.

The ears were considerably larger than average, with large, flattened lobes.*

As to the visage: the eyes, as already noted, were small and deep-set, but alert and darting. The nose was protuberant, though admirably straight; the lips thin and pale. Likewise, the cheekbones were high and prominent as, it has recently been pointed out, is often the case among the criminal breed. The teeth were quite healthy and the canines not preternaturally developed.

R—— M—— thus shared a certain number of traits with the inmates of the General Prison (these being chiefly, the misshapen cranium, unappealing facial features, pigeon chest, elongated arms and ears). In other respects, however, he was a healthy and well-developed specimen of the human race and if one were to observe him in his natural environment, one would not instinctively mark him out as a member of the criminal class. From this point of view, he formed an interesting subject and one which I was curious to study further.

I allowed the prisoner to dress and put a few simple questions to him. He was entirely unresponsive. He appeared at times not to have heard my questions, or pretended not to have done so. I suspect he was well aware of what was being asked, but refused to answer, for motives of his own. Such a strategy did, however, suggest that the subject was not an outright imbecile and was capable of some reasoning, flawed or otherwise. Nevertheless, I saw no purpose in prolonging my enquiries in the face of this stubborn attitude, and had the gaoler release me from the cell.

Mr Sinclair was waiting outside and questioned me impatiently as soon as I emerged. His manner was less that of a professional man than of a nervous parent eager for information about his child's health. As we advanced along the passage I outlined my findings to him.

As a point of interest for the future development of Criminal Anthropology, it might prove to be of great value for a study to be made of analogous structures in the physiology of criminals who have had no contact through interbreeding. [Footnote in original.]

'But as to his state of mind?' he asked.

I was aware that the advocate was anxious for me to pronounce on this question, so that he might offer a plea of insanity
to the court, thus saving his client from the gallows, and perhaps
not incidentally garnering a good deal of renown for himself.
Nevertheless, at this point, I refused to venture an opinion.

I explained that as a man of science, I could not be guided by
speculation or conjecture. What matters, I told him, are facts –
facts and instances!

'Your client exhibits a number of the physiological characteristics of the criminal class with which my work has acquainted me.
However, while he might share some of their features, without
acquainting myself with the stock from which he has issued, I
cannot venture an opinion as to whether he has acquired these
traits through heredity. If one's cup of water is foul, one must
first ascertain if the well is poisoned. If we find that the well is
indeed polluted, it may have some bearing on whether or not he is
responsible for his deeds.'

We had reached the end of the evil-smelling passage along
which we had been walking and paused in our conversation while
the gates were opened for us. Mr Sinclair, cowed by the superiority
of my knowledge and intellect, assumed a more deferential manner. We continued in silence to the outer gate and, once released,
breathed deeply of the warm summer air.

We then, at my suggestion, proceeded to the inn as I wished
to put some questions to the advocate. When we were settled at a
table with some refreshments, Mr Sinclair asked what I proposed
to do. I told him we would revisit the gaol the following day in
order for me to continue my examination of the prisoner.

'Then,' I said, 'we must check the well.'

Mr Sinclair did not grasp my meaning.

'We must,' I explained, 'pay a visit to whatever God-forsaken
shanty the wretch has sprung from.'

'I see,' said the advocate, in a tone suggesting that the prospect
of such an expedition did not greatly appeal to him.

'What,' I enquired, 'do you know of your client's background?'

Mr Sinclair took a long swallow of ale, no doubt gratified to be asked to furnish me with some information.

'His father is a tenant farmer – a crofter – of good character. His mother was a respectable woman who died in child-bed a year or so hence. There are, or were, three siblings, an elder sister and much younger twins.'

'"Were", you say?'

'The sister was found hanged in an outbuilding on the evening of the murders.'

I paused for a moment in my questioning. This information was certainly pertinent to my investigation.

'And was this sister of sound mind prior to this event?' I asked.

'I cannot say,' he replied. 'In the confusion following the murders, her absence was not noticed for some time. A search was made and she was found, as I say, in the barn. The coroner was unable to establish a precise time of death.'

I nodded slowly. The existence of a suicide did not speak well of the family's psychological constitution. Furthermore, in our day and age, for a woman to die in child-bed is likely indicative of some congenital weakness. In short, the picture emerging was not of a robust and healthy tribe.

'And of the younger siblings?'

'I know nothing,' replied the advocate, slowly shaking his head. 'They are no more than infants.'

'And what evidence do you have of the father's good character?'

'Only what I have learned from my conversations with R——.'

'My point precisely,' I replied. 'I am sure you would agree that we cannot accept the words of a devious and violent individual like your client. We must attempt to establish the truth about his background in an objective manner. Facts and instances, Mr Sinclair! It is to these we must attend.'

He protested that he had not found his client to be in the least bit devious, but I waved away his objections.

'We shall depart for this Culduie the day after tomorrow. I shall leave the arrangements to you.'

Mr Sinclair asked if he might dine with me that night, but, knowing that we would be passing a great deal of time in each other's company in the following days, I refused. I sent word to the prison in Perth that I would be absent for some days and wrote to my wife informing her of the same. I then perused a dossier of witness statements and medical reports, which Mr Sinclair had provided, and compiled my notes of the day's events. I took my evening meal in my chamber, not wishing to associate with the habitués of the public rooms, who recalled all too keenly of the inmates of my own institution. The meal was quite adequate and I drank enough wine to counteract the effects of the uncomfortable mattress and the sounds of carousing from below.

The following day I instructed Mr Sinclair to have a hearty meal and bottle of wine delivered to the prisoner from a local inn. The advocate informed me that he had often proposed to have meals brought to his client, but these offers had, on every occasion, been refused. This was not, I advised him, because the prisoner did not want the meal; it was because he did not wish to place himself in his advocate's debt. Acts of honest kindness are so alien to members of the criminal classes that they are invariably met with suspicion. However, my own proposal, I am compelled to admit, was not made out of kindness. It has been well established that hunger can induce in a prisoner a state of restiveness, irritability or even aggression. When I arrived, I wished R—— M—— to be in a state of indolence induced by the rich food he had consumed, and thus be in a frame of mind more conducive to interrogation. The meal was to be delivered at noon and I arranged to meet Mr Sinclair at the gaol at one o'clock, by which time I calculated that the victuals would have taken proper effect.

I arrived at the gaol somewhat earlier than I had stated, as I wanted first of all to put some questions to the gaoler. This I wished to do outwith the presence of my legal associate, as, in my not inconsiderable experience, those tasked with such menial labour tend to form an allegiance with the first educated man they encounter, in much the same way as an orphaned lamb attaches itself to the first hand that feeds it.

The gaoler closely conformed to the low physical type one routinely finds employed in the prisons and asylums of our land. He was of average height, but broadly built with powerful shoulders and forearms. His complexion was florid and scrofulous; his cranium somewhat mis-shapen, with large protruding ears. His hair was dark and wiry and grew low on his forehead. Likewise, his whiskers grew densely on his cheeks. His visage bore the singularly stupid and insensate look prevalent among those on the opposite side of the cell door, and I would have been not at all surprised to have encountered him there. He was, *sans doute*, entirely suited to his vocation, but in my present mission I was not looking to him for wit or intellect; he had a pair of eyes in his head, and it was these of which I wished to make use.

The gaoler showed no surprise when I indicated that I did not wish to enter the prisoner's cell immediately. This class of being exists almost entirely in the present; they think little of the past nor project their thoughts into the future, and are thus incapable of being surprised by anything. They are similarly incapable of experiencing boredom and are accordingly well suited to undemanding and repetitive labour. I led the brute to the end of the passage in order that we would not be overheard by the subject of our conversation. I first ascertained that R—— M—— had been under the gaoler's watch since his arrival; and that he was responsible for bringing the prisoner his meals, removing his faecal matter and periodically observing him through the aperture in the door. The gaoler answered my queries with difficulty and I had often to re-phrase them to make myself understood.

I then put a series of questions regarding the prisoner's behaviour and I here recount the substance of his responses:

The prisoner did not sleep excessively and was at all times alert and aware of his surroundings. He ate with good appetite and had made no plaint about the quality or quantity of his food.

Likewise, he had not protested about excessive cold or heat in his cell, nor had he requested extra blankets or other items. He had never enquired about the wellbeing of his family or expressed any curiosity about the outside world. In short, no meaningful discourse had passed between the two men. R—— M—— was at all times permitted by daylight occupied with the preparation of the papers on his table, but the gaoler had expressed no interest in their contents. The prisoner had not once been seen or heard raving, or calling out as if in thrall to some hallucination. At night he slept soundly and did not appear disturbed by bad dreams or night visions.

At the end of our intercourse, I pressed a shilling onto the palm of the warden's hand. He gazed stupidly at it for a few moments before pushing it wordlessly into the pocket of his greasy waistcoat. At this moment, Mr Sinclair arrived and appeared quite astonished to find me in congress with the brutish gaoler. Clearly, it had not occurred to him to thus make use of the individual – however limited in intellect – in closest proximity to the prisoner. No doubt, in common with the majority of his brethren in the legal profession, he preferred supposition and conjecture to evidence. I saw no reason to furnish him with an explanation for my actions and he did not have the temerity to question me.

When we entered the cell, R—— M—— was standing with his back to the wall opposite the door and I suspected that, despite my precautions, the discussion in the passage had alerted him to our presence. As Mr Sinclair had established some bond with the prisoner I allowed him to enter the cell ahead of me and kept my counsel while he engaged in some ludicrous pleasantries. I noted at once that the tray of food which I had requested from the inn had been placed on the floor, next to the writing table. A bowl which appeared to have contained a broth of some kind was empty, but a plate of mutton and potatoes was untouched. Likewise, the bottle of wine remained uncorked.

I asked R—— M—— in a friendly manner why he had not finished such a hearty meal and he replied that he was not accustomed to rich foods and had eaten an adequate sufficiency. He then added that if I was hungry I was welcome to what was left, an offer I politely declined. Mr Sinclair explained that I wished to put some questions to him and that it would benefit him greatly if he were to answer them fully and truthfully. R——— M——— replied that he could see no benefit to himself, but if it pleased Mr Sinclair he would answer any question put to him. I sat down on the chair next to the writing table and asked the prisoner to take a seat on his bunk, which he did. Mr Sinclair stood with his back to the door, his hands clasped over his abdomen.

The evidence I had so far gathered – that is, from my physical examination and from my conversation with the gaoler – was not sufficient to draw any conclusions regarding the sanity or otherwise of the accused, nor about his moral responsibility for the crimes he had committed. On a large number of points, he corresponded to the dreary procession of imbeciles who daily passed through my care, but on others, such as his general alertness and ability to apply himself to a task, he did not. I did not for a moment believe that the pages with which he appeared to have been so diligently occupied would contain anything other than gibberish and ravings, but the fact that he had thus applied himself was in itself noteworthy. In my long experience with the criminal classes I have never encountered a single individual capable of any aesthetic appreciation, far less of the production of any literary of artistic work. The literary ambitions of the average prisoner do not extend beyond scratching some vulgar phrases on the wall of his cell. A man of science must, of necessity, keep abreast of the theories and precedents of his chosen field, but he must not allow these theories to blind himself to the evidence of his own eyes, or to dismiss what does not accord with his expectations as aberrant or insignificant. However new and startling any evidence might be, it must be received honestly. As Mr Virchow has stated, 'We must take things as they really are, and not as we wish them to be.'*

---

* *Rudolf Virchow (1821–1902) was a German scientist known as 'the father of modern pathology'.*

It was quite clear that R—— M—— was not a raving maniac, the madman of popular imagination, but as has been well-established by Mr Prichard[*] and others, there exists another category of lunacy: that of *moral insanity*, whereby the grossest perversions of the natural impulses, affections and habits can exist with no concomitant disorder of the intellect or reasoning faculties. Certainly, from what I had thus far observed, R—— M—— exhibited some degree of intelligence, an intelligence which in all probability could only be harnessed to deception or evil ends, but which nevertheless set him apart from the degenerate prototype. It was, therefore, with the intention of exploring the extent of the prisoner's reasoning faculties that I set about my interrogation.

In order to foster the illusion that we were merely two men engaging in conversation, I did not take any contemporaneous notes and this account is based on the record I compiled from memory upon returning to the inn.

I began by telling R—— M—— that I was curious about the literary project upon which he had embarked. He replied that he was only writing the pages because Mr Sinclair had instructed him to do so. I retorted that that did not seem an adequate explanation for the dedication which he had shown towards the task. At this, the prisoner gestured around the cell and replied, 'As you can see, sir, there is little else with which to amuse myself here.'

'So it amuses you to write these pages?' said I.

To this he made no response. He sat quite erect on the bench, his gaze directed at the wall in front of him, rather than at his interlocutor. I then told him I wished to ask some questions about the deeds which had brought him to this place. His little eyes flickered momentarily towards me, but other than that there was no alteration in his bearing.

'I understand from Mr Sinclair that you do not deny responsibility for these crimes,' I said.

'I do not,' he replied. His eyes remained firmly fixed on the wall

---

[*] *James Cowles Prichard, Treatise on Insanity and Other Disorders Affecting the Mind (1835).*

in front of him.

'May I ask,' I said, 'what led you to commit such violent acts?'

'I wished to deliver my father from the tribulations which he had lately suffered.'

'And what was the nature of these tribulations?'

R—— M—— then described a series of trivial disputes which had occurred over a period of months between his father and the deceased.

'And you felt justified, in view of these incidents, in doing Mr Mackenzie to death?'

'I could see no other course of action open to me,' said R—— M——.

'Might you not have sought out some authority in your community to act as an intermediary in these matters?'

'Mr Mackenzie was the authority in our community.'

'You seem to be an intelligent young man,' I said. 'Could you not have sought to resolve these disagreements through reasoning with Mr Mackenzie?'

R—— M—— smiled at this suggestion.

'Did you make any attempt to reason with Mr Mackenzie?'

'I did not.'

'Why not?'

'If you had had the opportunity to meet Mr Mackenzie, you would not ask such a question.'

'Did you carry out the killing of Mr Mackenzie at the behest of your father?' I asked.

R—— M—— shook his head wearily.

'Did you discuss your plan with any other person?'

'I would not say that I had a plan,' he responded.

'But you proceeded to Mr Mackenzie's house armed with weapons. You must have had it in your mind to do some harm to him.'

'I did.'

'Then that surely constitutes a plan, does it not?' I spoke these words in an affable tone, as if we were merely engaged in a friendly discussion of a matter of mutual interest. I did not wish to set the prisoner against me by seeming to attempt to wrong-foot him.

'I went to Mr Mackenzie's house with the intention of killing him, but I would not say that I had a plan.'

I feigned some bemusement at the minute distinction he was making, and asked if he could explain what he meant.

'I simply mean that while I had the intention' – he gave this last word a special emphasis, as if it was he, rather than I, who was conversing with his inferior – 'to do him harm, I had not formulated a plan as such. I went to Mr Mackenzie's house thus armed only to discover what would happen if I did so.'

'So, you believe then that you are not wholly responsible for Mr Mackenzie's death – that it was, to some degree, a matter of chance.'

'You might as well say that everything that happens is a matter of chance,' said the prisoner.

'But was it happenstance that put a croman in your hand and led you to enter Mr Mackenzie's house?'

'It was a matter of chance that I happened to have a croman in my hand before I set off.'

'And this second weapon –'

'The flaughter,' Mr Sinclair interjected.

'It was not,' I continued, 'chance that put the flaughter in your hand.'

R—— M—— replied in a bored tone, 'The flaughter was propped against the gable of our house.'

'Nevertheless,' I insisted, 'you took it up. It was not chance that put it in your hand. '

'No.'

'Because you planned to kill Mr Mackenzie.'

'It is true that I wanted Mr Mackenzie to die by my hand. If you wish to call that a plan, you are free to do so. I merely wished to give my undertaking every chance of success.'

I nodded sagely at this parody of logic. 'And were you pleased by this success?'

'I was not displeased,' said R—— M——.

'But you cannot be pleased to be incarcerated in this cell.'

'That is a matter of no consequence,' he declared.

'You understand that your actions and your statements about them will likely lead you to the gallows?'

To this, R—— M—— made no response. Whether his diffident attitude was feigned or was the product of some misplaced bravado, I could not say. Nor could I say at this point whether the matter-of-fact answers he had given were entirely ingenuous, or due to some ploy to seem quite out of his mind; that he calculated that by admitting so openly to such brutal acts, he would be pronounced not to be in possession of his reason.

I then turned to the other victims of R—— M——'s assault.

'You have stated that you wished to murder Mr Mackenzie and I understand that in your own mind you were justified in doing so, but to kill a young girl and an infant is a quite different matter. Did you also bear some grievance against Flora or Donald Mackenzie?'

'I did not.'

'Then to do them to death is quite monstrous,' I said.

'I acted only out of necessity,' he replied.

'Out of necessity?' I repeated. 'Would it not have been possible for a powerful young man like yourself to restrain a young girl and a small boy?'

'With the benefit of hindsight it might seem so. Perhaps if I had had a plan, as you call it, that might have been possible. As it was, this was merely the way it transpired.'

'So, in order to carry out your goal of killing Mr Mackenzie, you were willing to murder two individuals who, in even your own eyes, were entirely blameless.'

'It was not my intention to kill them,' he replied, 'but I had no choice in the matter.'

'You acted only out of necessity?'

The prisoner shrugged his shoulders as if he was growing weary of humouring me. 'If you wish to put it that way, then, yes, I killed them out of necessity.'

At this point I took from my satchel the medical reports, quite ably compiled by a local practitioner, detailing the injuries sustained by the victims. I then read to the prisoner a paragraph detailing injuries to Flora Mackenzie too obscene to relate in these pages. 'What is described here seems to greatly exceed the demands of necessity,' I said.

R—— M—— had thus far sat quite motionless on his bunk, his gazed fixed on the cell wall. On hearing this account of the wounds he had inflicted, however, his eyes darted rapidly to and fro, and his hands, which until then had rested on his lap, began to worry at the material of his breeches.

'Can you explain why you felt the necessity to inflict such injuries?' I asked, maintaining an even and affable tone.

The colour rose to the prisoner's cheeks. It is often the case that even inmates who are capable of exercising control over their verbal statements are unable to suppress the physical manifestations of anxiety. R—— M—— cast his eyes about the cell, as though searching for an answer to my question.

'I do not recall inflicting such injuries,' he replied after some moments and in a quieter voice than that with which he had previously spoken.

'But you must have inflicted them,' I said.

'Yes, I must have,' he said.

I did not feel the necessity to press the prisoner further on this point, having already achieved my purpose in thus confronting him. I returned the papers to my satchel and stood up to indicate that the interview was at an end. Mr Sinclair pushed himself from the wall against which he had been leaning and stood to attention. I indicated that we were ready to leave and he had us released from the cell. I instructed the gaoler to remove the tray of food brought from the inn and was quite sure that he would have no compunction about helping himself to the remains.

* * *

Mr Sinclair and I arrived in Applecross on the evening of the 26th of August after an arduous journey. The inn where we were to stay the night was commendably clean with white-washed walls, simple furniture and a good fire burning in the hearth. We received a hospitable welcome and were served a meal of mutton stew by a well-proportioned girl with a healthy complexion. The local men were generally swarthy and of low stature, but were otherwise robust and did not display any apparent congenital deformities. They conversed in the barbaric tongue of the region, so I cannot attest to the content of their discussions, but despite the large quantities of ale they imbibed, their behaviour was not dissolute; nor did there appear to be any prostitutes on the premises. Our presence did not seem to warrant any special attention and when I questioned our hostess about this, she replied that on account of the great number of people who came to the Big House for the shooting, it was not in the least unusual for gentlemen to stop at the inn. I retired at the earliest opportunity, leaving my Mr Sinclair to his convivial surroundings, and slept soundly.

We rose early and were served a breakfast of blood pudding and eggs accompanied by a tankard of ale, which my companion drank with enthusiasm. There being no jig to convey us from Applecross, two ponies were provided and we set off for Culduie. The morning was bright and the air crisp and fresh. The village of Applecross was most pleasingly situated on the shore of a sheltered bay and the houses there, though primitive, were soundly built. Despite the early hour, a number of crones were seated on benches outside their houses, a good proportion of them, I would estimate, well into their eighth decade. Some of them puffed on small pipes, while others occupied themselves with knitting. All of them eyed us with curiosity, but none greeted us.

After a mile or so we passed through the village of Camusterrach, a ramshackle collection of huts arranged around a simple harbour. This village boasted a church of rudimentary construction, a fine stone manse and a school, and these latter buildings lent the place a little propriety. Certainly, neither Applecross nor Camusterrach

– primitive as they were – prepared us for the wretched collection of hovels that comprised the domicile of R—— M——. The short ride between Camusterrach and Culduie afforded, it must be said, a magnificent vista of the isles of Raasay and Skye. The strait that separated these islands from the mainland sparkled agreeably in the sunlight. The contrast when we turned into the track which led to Culduie could not have been greater, and I can only imagine that the unfortunate natives of this place must daily avert their eyes from the beauty before them, so as not to be reminded of the squalor in which they dwell. The majority of houses, if they can be termed as such, were of such rude construction that one would have taken them for byres or pig-sties. They were built from a clutter of stones and turf, and topped with rough thatch, which despite the warmth of the day reeked with peat smoke, so that it appeared that each of the houses was gently smouldering. As we made our way along the track, a man at work on his crops paused and stared openly at us. He was a squat figure, thickly bearded, and quite repellent in his visage. Only the house at the junction of the village boasted a slate roof and looked fit for human habitation. It was here that we stopped to ask directions to the house of Mr M—, the father of the accused. We were greeted at the door, to my great surprise, by a most handsome woman, who, before we had the opportunity to state the reason for our visit, invited us into her home. I admit that I was curious to observe at first hand the living conditions of these people and I was pleasantly surprised by the interior of the house. Although the floor consisted of no more than earth, it was freshly swept and there was a general atmosphere of good hygiene. There were a number of items of crude but serviceable furniture and we were invited to sit in two armchairs arranged by the hearth. Mr Sinclair began to explain that there was no need for us to sit as we had only called to ask directions to the home of the M— family, but I quieted him and said that we would be pleased to accept our hostess's hospitality for a few minutes. As we had travelled a great distance to learn something of the community that had spawned R—— M——, it would be negligent not to take advantage of any opportunities to do so. The study of the criminal class should not focus exclusively on heredity, but must as well pay heed to the conditions in which the degenerate individual exists. Heredity cannot, in itself, account for the perpetration of a crime. The foul air of the slum, hunger and a general milieu of immorality must also be admitted as factors in the manufacture of the criminal. Numerous studies have been made of degenerate offspring who, having been removed from the squalid haunts of their parents, have been brought up to lead, within the limitations of their intellect, quite productive lives.

I was thus pleased to have this chance to learn a little about the well from which R—— M—— had issued. Once we had introduced ourselves, Mrs Murchison called two of her daughters to serve us tea and sat with us by the fire. Excepting her plain clothes, I would not have been ashamed to present Mrs Murchison in a drawing room in Perth. She had fine features and intelligent brown eyes. She bore herself with a dignity that suggested she was not unaccustomed to conversing with educated men. Her daughters, whom I judged to be around twelve and thirteen years old, moved with a similar grace and were pleasingly proportioned, both in body and countenance. Mrs Murchison explained that her husband, a stone mason, was that day away from home. I enquired how she had met him and she explained that they had become acquainted in the nearby town of Kyle of Lochalsh, where her father was a merchant of good standing. Mr Murchison had thus avoided the great folly of the coastal tribes of Scotland, who through incessant intermarriage to those in closest proximity, perpetuate their physical peculiarities and deficiencies. The tea was served in china cups, along with scones spread with butter. I complimented Mrs Murchison on her well-bred children. She replied that she had four further daughters and I offered my condolences on her misfortune not to have been blessed with a son.

I then explained the nature of our mission in Culduie and asked her opinion of the accused. Mrs Murchison avoided my question, instead remarking on the tragic nature of the recent crimes and the effect it had had on their little community.

I noted her use of the word 'tragic', and asked why she characterised the events in this way.

'I cannot see how else one might describe such events.'

'I was only curious,' I replied, 'as to why you might term such deeds as "tragic", rather than, say, evil or wicked.'

Mrs Murchison then glanced at both of us, as if seeking assurance that she might speak openly with us.

'If you wish to have my opinion, Mr Thomson,' she said, 'I believe there is far too much talk of wickedness in these parts. The way some people talk, one would think that we existed in a state of perpetual debauchery.'

'I can see that that would indeed be an erroneous view,' I said, casting my hand about the room. 'Nonetheless, one must endeavour to find some way to account for the actions of your neighbour.'

At this point, Mrs Murchison sent her two daughters from the house, telling them to busy themselves with their chores. She then replied that it was not for her to venture an opinion, but she could only imagine that when he had perpetrated his terrible crimes, R—— M—— could not have been in his right mind. She then begged our pardon for offering an opinion in the company of two gentlemen who must know a great deal more about the workings of the mind than she.

I waved away her protestations and told her that although I had made a study of a great many criminals, I was a man of science and as such valued evidence over generalisations and speculation. It was precisely because I wished to know the views of those acquainted with the accused that I was here.

'I have no doubt you will find no shortage of people eager to offer an ill opinion of him,' she said, 'but I never knew him to wilfully harm another person.'

'You would not have thought him capable of committing such acts?'

'I would not have thought any man capable of committing such acts, Mr Thomson,' she replied.

I then asked her if she knew of any cause for R—— M—— to act as he had. She seemed reluctant to answer this question.

'Certainly there had been some disputes between Mr Mackenzie and Mr M——,' she said eventually.

'And who, in your opinion, was at fault in these disputes?'

'I do not believe it is for me to say,' she replied.

'Perhaps you do not wish to speak ill of the dead,' I said.

Mrs Murchison looked at me for some moments. She truly was a quite striking creature.

'I can say in all certitude that Flora and Donald Mackenzie were not at fault,' she said eventually, before commencing to weep.

I apologised for upsetting her. She took a linen handkerchief from inside her sleeve and dabbed her eyes in perfect imitation of a woman of good breeding. I construed from the concealment of this handkerchief on her person that she was presently frequently given to such outbursts of emotion. When she had taken posses- sion of herself, I asked what she could tell me of the character of R—— M——. She looked at me for some moments with her pleasing brown eyes.

'He was generally of good character,' she said vaguely.

'Generally?'

'Yes.'

'But not always?' I persisted.

'All boys of R——'s age are sometimes given to mischief, are they not?'

'No doubt,' I said. 'But to what kind of mischief do you refer?'

Mrs Murchison gave no reply and I was struck by her strange reluctance to speak ill of a person who had committed such mon- strous deeds. I thus thought it better to make my questions more specific.

'Was he given to stealing?'

Mrs Murchison laughed off this suggestion.

'Did you ever know him to commit acts of cruelty to animals or small children?'

Mrs Murchison did not laugh at this proposition, but she

answered in the negative.

'Did you ever hear of him raving or labouring under some hallucination or fantasy?'

'I would not say that I saw him raving,' she replied, 'but, on occasion, when walking through the village or working in the fields he might mutter to himself.'

'Were these mutterings audible?'

Mrs Murchison shook her head. 'He would be tight-lipped,' – she here imitated what she meant with a twitching of her mouth – 'as if he did not want to be overheard. If you approached him, or he saw that he was being watched, he would cease.'

'So he must have been conscious of what he was doing,' I said more to myself than to the company. 'Did you ever speak to any other person about this tendency of R———'s?'

'My husband also noticed it and remarked on it to me.'

'And what was the substance of these remarks?'

'No more than to state what he had observed. We did not think it a matter of any consequence.'

'Nevertheless, it was unusual enough to be worthy of comment.'

'Clearly,' said Mrs Murchison. She took a sip of the tea that she was holding daintily in her lap. 'You must understand, Mr Thomson, the great unhappiness which has afflicted R———. Since the death of his mother, his whole family laboured under a cloak of grief which was painful to observe and quite immune to the good offices of their neighbours.'

'So you believe that the death of Mrs M——— wrought some change of character in her son?'

'In the whole family,' she said.

I nodded.

'You should also know that John M——— is a severe man, who ...' – she now lowered her voice and cast her eyes towards the floor as if she was ashamed of what she was about to say – '... who did not show a great deal of affection to his children.'

She then added that she did not wish to speak ill of a neighbour and I assured her of my discretion.

'You have been of great assistance,' I told her. 'As I have said, our motives in making these investigations are entirely professional.' I paused for a moment before continuing. 'As you are clearly a woman of some education, might I make one further enquiry, an enquiry of a somewhat delicate nature?'

Mrs Murchison indicated that I could.

'Forgive me,' I said, 'but did you ever know R—— M—— to commit any indecent acts?'

A little colour rose to the woman's cheeks, which she attempted to conceal by touching her hand to her face. My suspicion on seeing this was less that she was discomfited by what I alluded to, but rather that I had struck upon something she might have preferred not to discuss. She at first attempted to deflect my query by asking what kind of acts I meant.

'It is clear,' I said, 'that if the answer to my question was in the negative, you would have no need to ask for such clarification. I ask you to remember that I am a man of science and set aside your natural reticence.'

Mrs Murchison set down her teacup and looked around to confirm that her daughters were not present. When she spoke, she kept her eyes all the time trained on the dirt floor between us.

'Our daughters – the eldest is fifteen – sleep in a chamber at the back of the house.' She here indicated a doorway which presumably led to this room. 'On a number of occasions, my husband surprised R— outside the window.'

'At night?' I said.

'At night or early in the morning.'

'He was observing your daughters?'

'Yes.'

'If you will excuse my indelicacy, did your husband find the boy in a state of arousal?'

The colour now rose more vividly to the good lady's cheeks.

'He was engaged in onanistic activity?'

Mrs Murchison nodded faintly, and then shyly directed her eyes towards me. In order to dispel her embarrassment, I adopted a breezy tone and asked what action her husband had taken. She replied that he had been strenuously warned off, which I took to mean that he had at the very least received a forceful boxing of his ears.

'Did you inform anyone about these activities?'

Mrs Murchison shook her head. 'We instructed our daughters not to associate with R——, and to inform us if he behaved improperly towards them.'

'And did he?'

'Not to my knowledge.'

'Did he persist in these visitations?' I asked.

'For a time,' she said, 'but they seem to have ceased some months ago. I suppose he outgrew such things.'

I expressed my admiration for Mrs Murchison's charitable characterisation of R—— M——'s behaviour, and again begged her pardon for obliging her to speak of such matters. We then thanked her for her hospitality and asked for the directions which had been the original motive for our call.

We left our ponies tethered outside the Murchison house and walked the remaining length of the village. The M— dwelling was by some distance the most poorly constructed in the township, resembling less a house than a smoking dung-heap. The land to the fore was ill-kempt and overgrown. The door was open and we peered into the chamber. To the left was what appeared to be a dilapidated byre. The stalls were empty of livestock, but the stench was nevertheless rank and few would have considered this a place fit for human habitation. No fire was lit and the chamber was cold and almost in darkness.

Mr Sinclair called out a greeting, to which there was no reply. He stepped into the room and repeated his salutation in Gaelic. A pair of hens, which had been pecking at the dirt, scuttled past our legs. Something stirred to our right and our eyes were drawn to a figure seated in a chair by the tiny aperture in the wall.

'Mr M—?' my companion enquired.

The figure got to his feet with some difficulty and took one or two steps towards us, leaning heavily on a gnarled stick. He spoke a few words in the language in which he had been addressed.

Mr Sinclair replied and the man approached us. I have rarely seen such a dismal specimen of the human race. Bent over as he was, he could barely have stood more than five feet tall. His beard and hair were thick and dishevelled, his clothing ragged. At my suggestion, Mr Sinclair asked him if we might step outside to converse for a few minutes. The homunculus looked at us with some suspicion and shook his head. He indicated that if we wished to speak to him we could sit at the table in the centre of the room. We seated ourselves on the benches around the table, the surface of which was speckled with droppings. As my eyes became accustomed to the gloom, I studied Mr M—. He had the same heavy brow and darting eyes as his son. His hands, which busied themselves filling his little pipe, were large, with long, crooked fingers, somewhat flattened at the ends. I wondered if perhaps he had been asleep when we entered, as now he appeared to have shaken off some of his initial confusion. Nonetheless, the expression on his face was one of distrust, if not outright hostility. He did not offer us any refreshments, not that I would have wished to consume the merest morsel in that filthy hovel.

Mr Sinclair asked if he was able to converse with us in English and we proceeded in that language. The advocate then explained the nature of our mission in elementary terms. I was struck by the fact that at no point did Mr M—— ask after the wellbeing of his son. Mr Sinclair began by enquiring about the welfare of the crofter's youngest offspring. He replied that they had been taken in by his wife's family in Toscaig.

Mr Sinclair then offered his condolences for the death of his daughter.

Mr M——'s eyes hardened. 'I have no daughter,' he said.

'I meant your daughter, Jetta,' Mr Sinclair said by way of explanation.

'There is no such person,' the crofter said through tight lips.

My associate's remarks, well-intentioned though they were, had done nothing to improve the atmosphere around the table.

'So you are quite alone then?' I said.

Mr M—— made no reply to this question, perhaps quite reasonably considering that the answer was self-evident. He lit his pipe and gave it a series of short puffs to get it going, his eyes flitting all the time between his two unwelcome guests.

'Mr M——,' I began, 'we have travelled some distance to speak to you and I hope you will be good enough to answer a few questions about your son. It is of some importance that we try to understand his state of mind when he committed the acts of which he is accused.'

Mr M——'s expression did not alter and I wondered whether he had understood anything of what I had said. I resolved to put my enquiries in the simplest possible terms. My expectations of hearing anything of interest were not high, but I had, at least, learned something from observing the lamentable conditions in which R—— M—— had dwelt.

'You recall, I am sure, the day the murders took place?' I paused here in anticipation of some sign of affirmation, but receiving none, I continued. 'Could you describe your son's state of mind on that morning?'

Mr M—— sucked noisily on the stem of his pipe.

'One man can no more see into the mind of another than he can see inside a stone,' he said eventually.

I decided to frame my question in a more direct way: 'Was your son generally of a happy disposition?' I asked. 'Was he a cheerful boy?'

The crofter shook his head, less, I construed, in disagreement, than to express that he had no opinion on the matter. Nevertheless, it did at least constitute some kind of response, and I took a little encouragement from it.

'Did your son tell you of his intention to kill Lachlan Mackenzie?' I said.

'He did not.'

'Did you have any inkling that he planned to do so?'

He shook his head.

'Is it true that there had been some disputes between yourself and Mr Mackenzie,' I persisted.

'I would not call them "disputes",' he replied.

'What would you call them?'

Mr M—— stared at me for a few moments. 'I would not call them anything.'

'But if you would not call them "disputes", you must by necessity call them something else?' I said.

'Why must I?' he said.

'Well,' I said, in a most affable tone, 'if you wish to speak of something, it is necessary that you give it a name.'

'But I do not wish to speak of it. It is you who wishes to speak of it,' he said.

I could not help but smile at his response. He was perhaps not as dim-witted as I had first supposed.

Mr Sinclair then made an attempt of his own to overcome the old man's obduracy.

'Would it be correct to say that Mr Mackenzie was waging some kind of vendetta against you?'

'That is a question you would need to be putting to Mr Mackenzie,' said the old man.

Mr Sinclair looked at me with a defeated expression.

Mr M—— then leant a little over the table towards us. 'Whatever my son has done cannot be undone. Nothing you or I might have to say about it is of any consequence.'

'But Mr M——, I'm afraid that you are quite mistaken,' said Mr Sinclair earnestly. He explained that his son's prospects of escaping the gallows depended to a very large degree on determining the state of his mind at the time he committed his crimes, and it was, accordingly, not out of idle curiosity that we had travelled from Inverness to put these questions to him.

The crofter looked at him for some moments. His pipe had gone out and he tapped the contents onto the table in front of him and began to fumble in his pouch for whatever dregs remained there. I took out my own pouch and pushed it into the middle of the table.

'Please …' I said with a gesture of invitation.

Mr M——'s eyes looked from me to the pouch and then back again, no doubt weighing the extent to which he would feel in my debt if he accepted the gift. He then placed his pipe on the table and said, 'I do not think I can be of any help to you, sir.'

I told him he had already been of great assistance and requested that I put a few questions to him about his son. As he did not object, I asked in turn whether his son had suffered from epilepsy; was given to violent swings of temper, or to raving or hallucinations; whether he was eccentric in his habits or behaviour; or if there was history of mental disorder in the family. To all these questions the crofter answered in the negative. I did not place a great deal of faith in his responses however, as despite the abject conditions in which he lived, he would have likely thought it shameful to admit to the existence of such propensities in his family.

As I could see no purpose in prolonging the interview, I stood up and thanked him for his hospitality. Mr M— stood up. He glanced down at the pouch of tobacco which remained on the table between us. His hand darted towards it and he secreted it in the pocket of his jacket. He then looked at us as if nothing had happened. We bade him good day and, with some relief, stepped out into the uncontaminated air of the village.

We neither of us spoke as we walked back towards our ponies. I was conscious that the route we were walking mimicked that of R—— M—— as he had set out two weeks before on his bloody project. And I wondered if there might have been some inadvertent truth in the crofter's remark about the difficulty of determining the contents of another man's mind. Naturally, if a man is in possession of his senses, one need merely ask him, and, assuming the truthfulness of his replies, accept his account of what he might have been thinking at such and such a moment. The problem begins when one is dealing with those who exist in the border-lands of lunacy, and who, by definition, do not have access to the contents of their own minds. It is in order to look inside the minds of such unfortunates that the discipline of psychiatry exists. I have no doubt that Mr Sinclair wished to know the contents of *my* mind, but not wishing to hasten to an injudicious opinion, for the time being I kept my counsel.

I reflected, as we walked the short distance to the junction of the village, that such a place would seem a kind of paradise to the denizens of our city slums, and, were it not for the sloth and ignorance of its inhabitants, it might be one.

When we reached our ponies, Mr Sinclair expressed the view that it might be beneficial to pay a visit to Mr Mackenzie's home, which was situated at the other extremity of the village. I could see no purpose in questioning the surviving members of the victims' family as I was concerned only with the perpetrator, but Mr Sinclair stated that it might aid him in the court-room to familiarise himself with the layout of the scene of the crime. The Mackenzie house was of reasonable construction and appeared well maintained. A stout woman was at the threshold, vigorously working a large churn. She looked up from her labour as we approached. She had a ruddy complexion and thick brown hair, tied up in a bun at the back of her head. Her forearms were rugged and muscular and her general gait and demeanour quite mannish. Nevertheless, she did not exhibit any discernible traits of low breeding and appeared to be a healthy, if unattractive, specimen of the race.

Mr Sinclair, having ascertained that she was the widow of the deceased, offered his condolences and I bowed my head to indicate that I endorsed these sentiments. He informed her that we were concerned with the investigation of her husband's murder (prudently avoiding mention of his precise role) and asked her if he might step inside for a moment, to 'acquaint himself with the geography of the house'. The lady indicated with a gesture of her hand that he was welcome to enter, but did not follow us inside. A fire burned at the far end of the room and the temperature was quite oppressive. I stood inside the doorway as Mr Sinclair made a cursory inspection of the premises. The house furnishings made no concession to fashion, but stood, nevertheless, in stark contrast to the hovel we had lately departed. Mr Sinclair's tour of the chamber took him around the large table where, no doubt, the family took their meals and I fancy he was attempting to reconstruct in his mind the gruesome events which had taken place there. It was only when he reached the far end of the table that his eyes were drawn to an old crone who, despite the heat, was bundled up in blankets in an armchair by the fire. The advocate at once excused himself for the intrusion, but the woman made no response. He repeated his apology in Gaelic, but her watery eyes remained fixed ahead of her and I concluded that she was in an advanced state of dementia.

I stepped outside the house and allowed my associate to complete his inspections in private. Mrs Mackenzie continued her churning, quite as if there was nothing remarkable about the appearance of two gentlemen in this remote shanty. I watched her for some minutes and reflected, as she went about her strenuous and repetitive labour, how little there was to distinguish her from a sheep at the cud. It is a shameful truth that the lower tribes of our country continue to exist in a state barely higher than livestock, deficient in the will to self-improvement which has brought progress to our southern regions.

Mr Sinclair emerged from the house, a light sweat having formed on his brow. He thanked the woman for allowing him to enter her home, then expressed his admiration for her ability to continue her toil in light of the events which had taken place. Mrs Mackenzie looked at him quite blankly.

'There are still mouths to feed and crops to be taken from the ground, sir,' she said.

Mr Sinclair nodded at the undeniable truth of this response and we took our leave, both from her and from Culduie, a place to which I shall be content never to return. The day being too far advanced to begin our journey back to Inverness, we returned to the inn at Applecross. I withdrew to my room to compile my notes and reflect on the findings of our excursion, while my associate took advantage of the hospitality below.

The Trial

The following account has been compiled from contemporary newspaper coverage and the volume A Complete Report of the Trial of Roderick John Macrae published by William Kay of Edinburgh in October 1869.

* * * * *

First day

The trial opened at the Circuit Court of Inverness on Monday the 6th of September 1869. At eight o'clock Roderick Macrae was conveyed to the court from his cell in Inverness gaol to a holding room in the basement of the building. He was transported in a windowless carriage, flanked by police horsemen, and the presence of this little convoy in the streets excited great passions among passers-by. According to John Murdoch, covering the case for the *Inverness Courier*, some who saw it 'called out offensive words, while others made missiles of whatever came to hand'. Such was the interest in the case that a crowd of several hundred people had gathered outside the court and enterprising vendors had set up stalls to provide for the throng. When the procession arrived, a great cheer went up and the out-riders were unable to prevent the crowd from surging forward and beating the sides of the cab. The carriage was brought to a halt and a number of men were injured as the police fought off the mob with batons. An elderly woman, Mary Patterson, was trampled underfoot and had to be attended by doctors. On subsequent days, barriers were erected and the police presence increased to ensure the safe passage of the convoy.

Special accommodation had been made in the court-room for the large number of reporters wishing to attend the trial and these were admitted by prior arrangement through a side entrance. Admittance to the public gallery was organised by the issue of special hand bills, which, it was later discovered, changed hands for considerable sums of money. By half past nine the public gallery had been filled and the Lord Justice-Clerk Lord Ardmillan and Lord Jerviswoode took their places on the bench. At the bar, the Crown was represented by the Solicitor-General Mr Gifford, a Mr William Crichton and assisted by Mr Gordon Frew, Crown-agent. For the defence, Andrew Sinclair was assisted by his colleague, Edward Smith. The Lord Justice-Clerk began by issuing a stern warning to those in the public gallery. No one would be permitted to enter or leave the court-room during evidence and any person disrupting the proceedings would be peremptorily ejected and their bill of admission confiscated.

The Lord Justice-Clerk then addressed counsel. He was aware, he said, of the existence of the 'so-called memoir' written by the prisoner. As the account had not been produced under the proper cautions and contained admissions which the prisoner might not wish to make in the course of his defence, 'neither the document nor any portion thereof' were admissible in evidence. He further sternly advised both sides against making any reference to the document in the course of their examination of the witnesses. The case would be decided on the basis of the evidence heard in court and this evidence only. Neither the Solicitor-General nor the defence raised any objection to this ruling, which was no doubt intended by the judge to pre-empt any later discussion in the presence of the jury.

At five minutes past ten, accompanied by a 'great uproar which the repeated striking of the Lord Justice-Clerk's gavel did nothing to quell', the prisoner was brought up to the dock. James Philby, reporting for *The Times*, described the moment:

Those awaiting the appearance of a monster were sorely disappointed. Once the initial tumult had died away, the most oft-heard remark was to the effect that the prisoner was no more than a boy. And, in truth, it was a most accurate observation. Roderick Macrae would be no one's idea of a murderer and certainly did not appear capable of the monstrous acts of which he is accused, being of small stature, though well-built around the shoulders and chest. His hair was unkempt and his complexion, no doubt on account of the weeks spent in his cell, pallid. On entering, his dark eyes surveyed the court-room from beneath his heavy brow, but he appeared quite in possession of his senses and made no reaction to the hullabaloo from the public gallery. His advocate, Mr Andrew Sinclair, stood by the dock and instructed him to take his seat there and this he did, adopting a respectful posture, with his hands resting in his lap and his head bowed. He generally remained in this attitude throughout the proceedings.

The Clerk of the Court then read the indictment:

Roderick John Macrae, now or lately a crofter of Culduie, Ross-shire, and now or lately prisoner in Inverness, you are indicted and accused at the instance of James Moncreiff, Esq., Her Majesty's Advocate for Her Majesty's interest: that albeit, by the laws of this and of every other well governed realm, murder is a crime of an heinous nature, and severely punishable: yet true it is, and of verity, that you, the said Roderick John Macrae, are guilty of the said crime, actor, or art and part: In so far as, (1.) On the morning of the 10th day of August 1869, within the dwelling-house of Lachlan Mackenzie in Culduie, Ross-shire, did wickedly and feloniously assault and attack the said Lachlan Mackenzie, and did, with a croman and flaughter, strike the said Lachlan Mackenzie several blows about the chest, face and head, and did fracture his skull, by all which, or part thereof, the said Lachlan Mackenzie was mortally injured and immediately died, and was thus murdered by you the said Roderick John Macrae.

The indictment went on to similarly detail the assaults on Flora and Donald Mackenzie.

The Lord Justice-Clerk then instructed the prisoner to rise and addressed him:

'Roderick John Macrae, you are charged under this indictment with the crime of murder. How say you: are you guilty or not guilty?'

Roddy stood with his hands at his sides, and after glancing towards his counsel replied in a clear, but quiet voice, 'Not guilty, my lord.'

He resumed his seat and Andrew Sinclair rose to submit the Special Defence of Insanity. This was read by the Clerk of the Court: 'The panel pleads generally not guilty. He further pleads specially that at the time at which the acts set forth in the indictment are alleged to have been committed he was labouring under insanity.'

Mr Philby wrote, 'For a young man who had never previously ventured more than a few miles from his village, he did not seem unduly unsettled by the array of learned faces which now scrutinised him from the bench. Whether this was due to the insanity claimed by the defence or merely spoke of a certain *sang-froid*, it was not at this point possible to venture an opinion.'

The jury of fifteen men was then empanelled. The Lord Justice-Clerk instructed the jurors to dismiss from their minds anything they might have read or heard about the case and reminded them of their obligation to consider only the evidence to be set forth in the court-room. He then asked the jurors if any of them had formed a settled opinion about the case or laboured under any prejudice about it. The jurors replied in turn that they had not, and, at half past ten, the case for the prosecution was opened.

The first witness to be called was Dr Charles MacLennan, who had carried out the post-mortem examination of the bodies. The practitioner was dressed in a tweed suit and yellow waistcoat, and boasted drooping moustaches, which leant him a suitably sombre air. It was unlikely that, as a rural doctor, he had ever been called upon to take part in such proceedings and he appeared nervous as he entered the witness box. As he began his evidence, wrote Mr Murdoch for the *Courier*, 'the festive atmosphere in the public gallery quickly dissipated and the gravity of the occasion overtook the room'.

To a hushed court-room, Mr Gifford led Dr MacLennan through a meticulous account, lasting some thirty minutes, of the injuries sustained by each of the three victims. At the conclusion of his testimony the doctor was shown Productions No. 1 and No. 2, a flaughter and a croman. The appearance of the murder weapons elicited gasps from the gallery. The blade of the flaughter was badly bent out of shape, testifying 'to great force with which it had been wielded'.

The Solicitor-General then asked the witness, 'Have you seen these items before?'

Dr MacLennan: 'No, sir.'

'Can you tell us what they are?'

'They are a flaughter and a croman.'

'And what would be their normal use?'

'They would be used for breaking ground or otherwise tending a croft.'

Mr Gifford, a tall and distinguished man, impeccably attired in a black suit, here paused to give full weight to the question he was about to ask.

'Now,' he said, 'in your professional opinion, and given your careful examination of the three victims in this case, would the injuries sustained be consistent with the use of these weapons?'

'Most certainly,' the doctor replied. 'If used with sufficient force.'

Mr Gifford nodded solemnly.

'If I might put one further question to you,' he said, 'how would you characterise the injuries to the deceased, I mean, in comparison with other cases you have examined?'

Dr MacLennan exhaled sharply, as if the answer was self-evident. 'They were without question the most brutal I have ever had the misfortune to encounter,' he said.

Mr Gifford then indicated that he had concluded his examination. If his intention had been to leave the jurymen in no doubt about the seriousness of the case before them, he certainly succeeded. Several of them, it was reported, looked quite ashen.

Mr Sinclair had no questions for the doctor and the witness was excused.

Roddy had listened to this evidence with some attention, but no show of emotion, 'quite as if,' wrote Mr Philby, 'he were no more than an interested spectator'.

The next witness was Carmina Murchison. She wore a green taffeta dress and would not, *The Scotsman* noted, 'have looked out of place in the salons of George Street'. Not a single newspaper omitted mention of Mrs Murchison's striking appearance and Mr Philby was even moved to note that 'no juryman with blood in his veins could doubt a word which emerged from such lips'.

Led by Mr Gifford, Mrs Murchison related how she had met Roderick Macrae on the morning of the 10th of August and exchanged a few words with him as he passed her house. A map of Culduie had been drawn up and was displayed on an easel in the court-room and Mrs Murchison indicated the position of her own house, that of the prisoner and that of Lachlan Mackenzie.

'Did you find,' Mr Gifford asked, 'the prisoner to be in a state of agitation?'

'No, sir.'

'He did not appear nervous or anxious?'

'No.'

'Did you believe him when he told you that he was going to break some ground at Mr Mackenzie's property?'

'I had no reason to disbelieve him.'

'And he was carrying some tools for this purpose?'

'Yes.'

Mrs Murchison was then shown the Productions. She covered her eyes at the sight of the weapons and they were swiftly removed.

The elegant Mr Gifford apologised with a little bow, before

asking, 'Were these the tools that the prisoner was carrying?'

Mrs Murchison: 'Yes.'

'And these would be the normal tools to carry out the work stated?'

'Yes.'

'But this was not the normal time of year to break ground, was it?'

'Not for the purpose of planting crops.'

'But this did not sound any alarm in your mind that this might not have been the prisoner's true purpose?'

'Roddy had lately been carrying out a good deal of work for Lachlan Broad.'

The Lord Justice-Clerk: 'Lachlan Broad is the name by which Mr Mackenzie was known in your community?'

'Yes, my lord.'

Mr Gifford: 'Why had the prisoner been carrying out work for the deceased?'

Mrs Murchison: 'It was in repayment of a debt owed to Mr Mackenzie by Roddy's father.'

'And what was the nature of this debt?'

'It was in compensation for a sheep which Roddy had killed.'

'A sheep belonging to Mr Mackenzie?'

'Yes.'

'What was the extent of this debt?'

'Thirty-five shillings.'

'And Mr Macrae – the prisoner's father – was unable to pay this sum?'

'I believe so.'

'So, in lieu of payment the prisoner was labouring for Mr Mackenzie?'

'Yes.'

'And, in view of this arrangement, there was nothing untoward in your exchange with the prisoner?'

'No.'

'Nothing which might have alerted you to what was about to occur?'

'Nothing whatsoever.'

Mrs Murchison then related how, some time later – she estimated half an hour – she saw Roderick Macrae walking back through the village, now covered from head to foot in blood. Thinking an accident had befallen him, she ran to help. When she asked what had occurred, he replied that he had killed Lachlan Mackenzie. He made no mention of the other victims. Mrs Murchison then described the general commotion in the village and how Roderick Macrae had been imprisoned in the Murchisons' outbuilding.

Mr Gifford: 'How would you describe the prisoner's demeanour at this time, Mrs Murchison?'

'He was quite calm.'

'Did he make any attempt to abscond?'

'No.'

'Did he not struggle with your husband or the other men who imprisoned him in the outbuilding?'

'No.'

'Did he express any remorse for what he had done?'

'No.'

Mr Gifford then turned to the matter of motive.

'How,' he asked, 'would you describe relations between the deceased, Mr Mackenzie, and the prisoner?'

'I could not say.'

'Were they friends?'

'I would not say so.'

'Enemies, then?'

Mrs Murchison made no answer to this question.

Mr Gifford expressed some surprise that in a village of a mere fifty-five souls the state of relations between two members of that community could be concealed.

Mrs Murchison: 'I never heard Roddy express any ill feeling towards Lachlan Broad.'

'You were not aware of any vendetta between Mr Mackenzie and the Macrae family?'

'I was aware that there had been some disputes between them.'

'What was the nature of these disputes?'

'There was the killing of the sheep.'

'Anything further?'

'There was the matter of the allocation of land in the village.'

Mr Gifford asked Mrs Murchison to elaborate.

'In his capacity as village constable, Mr Mackenzie allocated a portion of Mr Macrae's croft to his neighbour, Mr Gregor.'

'You are referring to Mr John Macrae, the father of the prisoner?'

'Yes.'

'On what grounds was this re-allocation made?'

'Mr Macrae's wife had died and Mr Mackenzie argued that as the household was reduced in number they needed less land.'

'And this was felt to be unjust?'

'Yes.'

'So there was the matter of the killing of the sheep and the matter of the re-allocation of farming land. Anything else?'

'It is difficult to express.'

'Difficult to express because it did not exist or because you cannot explain it?'

Mrs Murchison was silent for some time and had to be prompted to answer by the Lord Justice-Clerk.

'There was a general air of oppression,' she said eventually. 'Mr Mackenzie often acted in a high-handed manner and in particular towards Mr Macrae.'

'I see. Perhaps if you have difficulty explaining the relations between Mr Mackenzie and the prisoner, you could tell us your own opinion of the deceased?'

'I did not care for him.'

'Please tell us why you did not care for him.'

'He was a bully.'

'A bully?'

'Yes.'

'By which you mean what?'

'He took pleasure in wielding power over those around him

and especially over Mr Macrae and his family.'

'He tormented them?'

'I would say so, yes.'

Mr Gifford then concluded his questioning and Mr Sinclair rose for the defence, appearing, at first, quite flustered. 'It must,' wrote Mr Philby, 'be an unusual occurrence for a provincial pettifogger to be involved in a case of such notoriety, or perhaps he was merely bedazzled by the enchantress in the witness box.' In any case, after some obsequious enquiries about Mrs Murchison's comfort, he commenced his examination.

'For how long have you lived in Culduie, Mrs Murchison?'

'For eighteen years. Since my marriage.'

'So you have known the prisoner all his life?'

'Yes.'

'And how would you describe your relations with him?'

'They were quite normal.'

'You were on friendly terms?'

'Yes.'

'Before the acts for which he is here accused, have you ever known him to be violent?'

'No.'

'And you were on good terms with his family?'

'Generally, yes.'

'Generally?'

'Yes.'

'Could you elaborate?'

'I was very close to Una Macrae.'

'The prisoner's mother?'

'Yes.'

'And his father?'

'Less so.'

'Was there any reason for this?'

'We were not on bad terms, it is only that I had less to do with him and he with me.'

'But there was no particular reason for that?'

'No.'

'But you were on intimate terms with the prisoner's mother?'

'Yes. We were very close.'

'And her death occurred when?'

'In the spring of last year.'

'This must have been a quite traumatic event.'

'It was a terrible thing.'

'For you?'

'For me, and for her children.'

'How would describe the effect of her death on her children?

'They were quite changed.'

'How so?

'Jetta –'

'The prisoner's sister?'

'Yes. She became morose and terribly concerned with charms and otherworldly things.'

'Superstitious things?'

'Yes.'

'And the prisoner?'

'He seemed to withdraw into himself.'

'Could you explain what you mean?'

Mrs Murchison looked towards the bench, as if for some assistance. The Lord Justice-Clerk indicated with a gesture of his hand that she should continue.

'I am not sure I can properly explain it,' she said. 'Only that perhaps Roddy sometimes seemed quite separate from the world.'

'"Quite separate from the world",' Mr Sinclair repeated meaningfully. 'And this change,' he went on, 'took place after his mother's death?'

'I believe so.'

'Did you ever observe in the prisoner any signs of insanity?'

'I do not know if it is a sign of insanity, but I now and again saw him talking to himself.'

'In what manner?'

'Quite as if he was in conversation with himself or with an

unseen person.'

'When did you see this?'

'Often, when he was working on the croft or walking through the village.'

'And what was the substance of these conversations?'

'I could not say. If you drew near, he would cease.'

'Did you ever hear him raving or behaving as if under some delusion?'

'No.'

'Did you ever hear of him being restrained because he was a danger to himself or to others?'

'No.'

'You did not feel that he was a dangerous character?'

'No.'

'He was not thought in the village to be a dangerous character?'

'I don't believe so.'

'So it was a surprise to you when he carried out the acts which have brought us to this court-room today?'

'Oh mercy, yes, a terrible shock,' replied Mrs Murchison.

'So these acts were quite out of character?'

'I would say so, yes.'

Mr Sinclair then thanked the witness and concluded his questioning. Before Carmina Smoke could step down, the Solicitor-General rose for a second time.

'If I might clarify one point,' he began, 'on the morning of the murders, did you see the prisoner engaged in this mumbling to himself?'

'No, sir.'

'And when you conversed with him did he seem quite rational?'

'Perfectly rational, yes.'

'He did not – and this is a point of utmost importance – appear alienated from his reason?'

'I don't believe so.'

'It is not, if you will forgive me, a matter of "belief", Mrs Murchison. Either he did or he didn't.'

At this the Lord Justice-Clerk intervened, stating that the witness had answered the question in a satisfactory manner and it was not for the Crown to badger witnesses into providing the responses he desired. Mr Gifford begged the judge's pardon and Mrs Murchison was excused, 'with the gentlemen of the jury,' Mr Philby noted, 'closely observing her exit.'

The next witness to be called was Kenny Smoke. Led by Mr Gifford, Mr Murchison described the events of the morning of the 10th of August. He confirmed that the prisoner had been quite calm, had openly admitted to his deeds and had offered neither resistance nor made any attempt to flee.

Mr Gifford then asked him to describe the scene he had discovered in the home of Lachlan Mackenzie. At this point, according to Mr Murdoch, the court-room assumed a most sombre atmosphere: 'Mr Murchison, a most vigorous and hearty fellow, visibly struggled to describe the horrors to which he had been witness, and he is to be commended for the sober account with which he was able to provide the court.'

'Lachlan Mackenzie's body,' Mr Murchison testified, 'was face down on the floor somewhat to the left of the door. The back of his head was entirely shattered and pieces of skull had been strewn some distance from the body. His brains had spilled out to the side of his head. His face lay in a great pool of blood. I lifted his wrist to see if there was a pulse, but there was none.'

Mr Gifford: 'Was the body warm?'

'Quite warm, yes.'

'And then?'

'I stood up and then saw the boy lying on the floor between the door and the window. I went to him. I did not see any signs of injury, but he was dead.'

'The body was warm?'

'Yes.'

'And then?'

'I saw the body of Flora Mackenzie laid out on the table.'

'You say, "laid out". Was it your impression that the body had been placed there quite purposefully?'

'It did not appear that she had fallen there.'

'Why do you say that?'

Mr Murchison here hesitated for some moments. 'It was not a natural posture. Her feet did not reach the ground and I thought that she must have been lifted onto the table.'

'Please describe, if you can, what you saw.'

'There was a great deal of blood. Her skirts had been lifted up and the private parts had been mutilated. I examined her for signs of life, but she was quite dead. It was then that I noticed that the back of her head had been opened up. I pulled down her skirts to cover her decency.'

'What did you do then?'

'I went to the door, thinking to prevent anyone else from entering.'

Mr Murchison then described the arrangements made to remove the bodies to the outbuilding and how in the process of this, Catherine Mackenzie, the mother of the deceased, had been discovered in the gloom at the back of the room. She was taken to the Murchisons' house, 'quite gone in the head', and attended by his wife.

Mr Gifford then moved onto the motives for the murders. Kenneth Murchison described the meeting at which the com-pensation for the killing of Lachlan Mackenzie's sheep had been decided.

Mr Gifford: 'And this was in the amount of thirty-five shil-lings?'

Mr Murchison: 'Yes.'

'Why was this sum settled on?'

'It was the price that the animal would have fetched at market.'

'And was it the deceased, Mr Mackenzie, who demanded this sum?'

'The sum was proposed by Calum Finlayson, who was at that time serving as constable for our villages.'

'Did Mr Mackenzie agree to this sum?'

'He did.'

'And Mr Macrae, the prisoner's father, also agreed to this sum?'

'Yes.'

'And did Mr Mackenzie demand that this sum be paid immediately?'

'No.'

'What arrangements were made for the payment of this compensation?'

'It was agreed that the sum would be paid at a rate of one shilling per week.'

'This out of consideration for the straitened financial situation of the Macrae family?'

'Yes.'

'And did Mr Macrae fulfil his obligations with regard to these payments?'

'I believe he attempted to do so, but it may be that they were not made regularly.'

The Lord Justice-Clerk: 'Do you know if the payments were made or not?'

'I do not know, but I know that Mr Macrae did not have a great deal of income and that the payments would have been quite burdensome.'

Mr Gifford continued: 'But the arrangement was reached amicably?'

'I would not call it amicable.'

'But you have stated that both Mr Macrae and Mr Mackenzie accepted the proposal of the constable.'

'It was accepted, yes, but Lachlan Broad made it clear that he was not satisfied.'

'How so?'

'He thought that there should be some additional punishment of the boy.'

'The "boy" being the prisoner here?'

'Yes.'

'And did he propose what this punishment should consist of?'

'I cannot recall, but he made it clear that he would like to see the boy punished.'

'Even although the compensation agreed upon was acceptable to both sides?'

'Yes.'

Mr Gifford here paused and raised his eyebrows in a questioning manner, but the witness did not add anything.

'Would it be fair to say that Mr Mackenzie and Mr Macrae were not the best of friends?'

'It would be fair.'

'And this enmity between them, if I can put it in such a way, pre-dated this incident with the sheep?'

'Yes.'

'So how did this enmity arise?'

Mr Murchison held out his hands. 'I cannot say.' He puffed out his cheeks and let forth a 'baffled sigh'. 'Mr Macrae lived at his end of the village and Mr Mackenzie lived at his.'

Mr Gifford appeared content not to labour this point. 'Nevertheless, an agreement was reached which left Mr Macrae indebted to Mr Mackenzie?' he said.

'Yes.'

Mr Gifford then led the witness through the process of Lachlan Broad's election to the position of village constable.

Mr Gifford: 'Would it be fair to say that this role in your community was not a popular one?'

Mr Murchison: 'In what sense?'

'In the sense that it was not a position which members of your community sought out?'

'I would say so, yes.'

'Then you must have been pleased that Mr Mackenzie took it upon himself to shoulder this burden?'

Mr Murchison made no reply.

Mr Gifford: 'You were not pleased?'

'I was neither pleased nor not pleased.'

'But is it not true that you and some other members of your community made great efforts to find an alternative candidate to oppose Mr Mackenzie?'

'Some effort was made.'

'Why did you feel the need to do that?'

'It did not seem right that Mr Mackenzie should be elected unopposed.'

'That was the only reason?'

Kenny Smoke hesitated for a few moments, before responding, 'There was a perception that Mr Mackenzie might use his powers to advance his own interests.'

'You mean, the powers inherent in the role of village constable?'

'Yes.'

'And did he do so?'

'To some extent.'

'To what extent?'

'He enjoyed wielding power over the community.'

'Can you be more specific?'

'He instituted a scheme of works whereby the men of the community were obliged to give their labour for a certain number of days.'

'And what was the purpose of this scheme of works?'

'General improvements to the roads and drainage around the villages.'

'Were these schemes, as you put it, in advance of his own interests?'

'Not specifically.'

'Not specifically?'

Mr Murchison made no reply to this.

Mr Gifford continued: 'Were these improvements to the benefit of the community in general?'

'They were of benefit, yes.'

'So Mr Mackenzie instituted a scheme of improvements beneficial to the community and the men of the community contributed their labour towards this scheme?'

'Yes.'

'And this you describe as being in advance of Mr Mackenzie's own interests!' Mr Gifford at this point directed an expression of bewilderment towards the jury.

'Now,' he continued, 'if I can turn to another incident, would it be true to say that arable land is in short supply in your village?'

'It is not plentiful.'

'And how is the land allocated?'

'Each family has their rig.'

'"Each family has their rig",' he repeated. 'The rig being their portion of the available land?'

'Yes.'

'And is this land allocated on a yearly basis, for five years, or for how long?'

'In practice, each household farms the land which lies between their house and the Toscaig road.'

'That portion being regarded, to all intents and purposes, as their land?'

'Yes.'

'So, in effect, each strip of land belonged to the property to which it was adjacent?'

'In effect, yes.'

'Without regards to the population or make-up of the household?'

'Generally, yes.'

'Shortly after Mr Mackenzie's election to the position of village constable some of the arable land in Culduie was re-allocated, was it not?'

'Yes.'

'Could you describe that re-allocation?'

'A portion of Mr Macrae's land was given to his neighbour, Mr Gregor.'

'Why was that?'

'As there were more people in Mr Gregor's household than in Mr Macrae's, it was decreed that they required more land.'

'I see. And how many people were in Mr Macrae's household?'

'Five, including the two infants.'

'That would be Mr Macrae himself, the prisoner, his daughter and the two younger children, aged three years?'

'Yes.'

'And in Mr Gregor's household?'

'Eight.'

'And how was that household constituted?'

'Mr Gregor and his wife, Mr Gregor's mother and their five children.'

'So their need for land was greater than that of the Macrae household?'

'Yes, but –'

'Did Mr Mackenzie personally benefit from this distribution of land?'

'No.'

'So, it was quite fair to re-distribute this land in accordance with the greater need of the Gregor household?'

'You could say that it was fair.'

'I am asking if you would say it was fair, Mr Murchison.'

Before answering Mr Murchison drew his hand across his moustaches and surveyed the court-room.

'It was not right,' he said.

'But you have stated that the Gregor family's need for land was greater than that of the Macraes.'

'It might have been fair in law,' said Mr Murchison, clearly by now becoming aggravated, 'but it was not done. Crofts are not divided up in this way. Each family works their portion of land and it passes from one generation to the next.'

'I see. So Mr Mackenzie's action was unprecedented?'

'It was vindictive.'

'Ah!' said Mr Gifford, as if he had finally succeeded in reaching the nub of the matter. '"Vindictive" is a strong word, Mr Murchison. So rather than using his powers for the general good, Mr Mackenzie was perceived to be pursuing some kind of vendetta against Mr Macrae?'

'Correct.'

Mr Gifford directed a meaningful look to the jury, then thanked the witness and concluded his questioning. *The Scotsman* noted that

Mr Murchison 'seemed a fine fellow, but his baffling adherence to the idea that land should be allocated on the basis of tradition rather than utility was yet another example of how the intransigence of the Highland tribes is bringing about their own demise'.

Mr Sinclair then rose for the defence.

'For how long have you known the prisoner?'

Mr Murchison: 'All his life.'

'And how would you characterise your relationship with him?'

'I like him well enough.'

'Would you describe him as feeble-minded?'

'Feeble-minded? No.'

'Then how would you describe him?'

Mr Murchison puffed out his cheeks and looked towards Roddy, who looked back at him with a faint smile.

'Well, there's no doubting he's got a brain in his head. He's a clever lad, but –'

'Yes, Mr Murchison?'

The witness cast his eyes towards the ceiling as if searching for the right words. He shook his head and then said, 'He's daft.'

'"Daft"?' repeated Mr Sinclair. 'Could you explain what you mean?'

Again Mr Murchison seemed to struggle to express himself. 'He sometimes seemed like he was in a world of his own. He was always a solitary boy. I never saw him playing with other children. He could be sitting amongst folk, but, for all the world, it was like there was nobody else there. You never knew what was going on in his head.'

'And he was always like this?'

'I believe so.'

Mr Sinclair allowed some moments to pass before putting his next question. 'Did you ever observe the prisoner speaking to himself or appearing to be in conversation with another person who was not there?'

Mr Murchison nodded. 'Aye, now and again, I saw him muttering to himself.'

'Frequently?'

'Not infrequently.'

At this point the Lord Justice-Clerk intervened. 'How often do you mean by "not infrequently"?'

'Quite often.'

The Lord Justice-Clerk: 'Every day, every week or once a month?'

'Not every day, but certainly every week.'

'So it was quite normal for you to observe this behaviour?'

'Yes, my lord.'

Mr Sinclair: 'And did you ever overhear what he was saying to himself?'

'No.'

'Why was that?'

'He would cease whenever anyone came near him. And, in any case, it was more of a muttering, rather than a speaking out loud.'

'I see. And had the prisoner always behaved in this way?'

'I could not say.'

'Did you observe him talking to himself in this way when he was a child?'

'I don't believe so.'

'Can you remember when you first observed him behaving in this manner?'

Mr Murchison shook his head and was instructed to answer by the Lord Justice-Clerk.

'I cannot recall.'

'Was it ten years ago, five years ago, or one year ago?'

'More than one year ago.'

'But not five years ago?'

'No.'

'Did you ever see the prisoner behave in this way before his mother's death?'

'I could not say with any certainty.'

'In conclusion, would it be fair to say that you did not regard the prisoner as completely normal?'

'That would be fair.'

Mr Sinclair then concluded his questioning and Kenny Smoke was excused. The next witness to be called was Duncan Gregor. Mr Gifford began by questioning him about the morning of the murders, but the Lord Justice-Clerk intervened, putting it to him that since the events in question were not in dispute, there was no need to waste time going over ground that had already been established. Mr Sinclair did not demur and for the rest of the day, proceedings moved along at a more rapid pace. A pattern emerged whereby the Crown sought to establish rational motives for the murders, while Mr Sinclair attempted, with varying degrees of success, to portray the accused as not being in his right mind. Ironically, the defence's best moments were provided by the testimony of Aeneas Mackenzie. Mr Philby described him as, 'a porcine fellow [who] did not appear to grasp that his derogatory statements about the accused were in greater service of the defence than the Crown'.

When asked for his view of the prisoner's state of mind, he bluntly replied, 'He was a lunatic.'

'A lunatic?' Mr Sinclair repeated mildly. 'Could you explain to the court what you mean?'

'Just that. Everyone knew he was off his head.'

'"Everyone" being who?'

'Everyone in the parish.'

'You mean he had something of the status of "village idiot"?'

'Aye, that and more.'

'What more?'

'He had always a stupid grin on his face. He would always be sniggering about something when there was nothing to be sniggering about.'

'I see. So would you say that he was not of sound mind?'

'Aye, I most certainly would. There was many a time I'd have happily wiped the grin off his face and I'd do it now if I had the chance.'

When Mr Sinclair concluded his examination, it took Mr Mackenzie some moments to grasp that he was excused, and he left the stand 'mumbling to himself in a manner that suggested it was he whose sanity might be in question'.

The final witness of the day was the schoolmaster, Mr Gillies, whom Mr Philby, clearly by this time enjoying himself, described as having 'lady's hands and a face one would struggle to describe – or remember'. Mr Gifford elicited a glowing testimony to Roddy's abilities from the schoolmaster. He then questioned him about his visit to the prisoner's father to suggest that he continue his education.

'And what was the result of this visit?'

'Unfortunately, Roddy was required by his father to work on the family's croft.'

'Were you in the habit of making such proposals?'

'That is the only occasion I have done so.'

'And why did you single out the prisoner in this way?'

'He was without doubt the most gifted pupil I have taught.'

Mr Gifford then moved onto Roddy's general behaviour and demeanour. 'Was he an unruly pupil?'

'On the contrary, he was well-behaved and attentive.'

'You are aware, Mr Gillies, that my colleagues for the defence have lodged a plea of insanity in this case?'

'Yes.'

'Did you ever detect any signs of insanity in the prisoner?'

Mr Gillies appeared to give this question serious thought before replying that he had not.

'You never witnessed him raving or talking to himself?'

Mr Gillies shook his head. 'Never,' he said.

After a brief consultation with his team, Mr Gifford indicated that he had no more questions.

Mr Sinclair rose for the defence.

'Was the prisoner popular amongst his schoolmates?' he asked.

'Not especially.'

'What do you mean by "not especially"?'

'Simply that,' said Mr Gillies, looking somewhat bemused.

'Did he play or socialise with his fellows in the normal way?'

'I think he was a rather solitary boy, quite happy in his own company.'

'Somewhat aloof from his peers?'

'You could say that, but I saw nothing abnormal in it. Some children are naturally gregarious, others less so.'

Mr Sinclair seemed unsure whether to pursue his line of questioning, then decided that he had little to gain from providing a platform for a witness who seemed to have such high regard for his client.

As it was by then half past four, the proceedings were adjourned for the day. The Lord Justice-Clerk informed the jury that they would be accommodated in a hotel for the night and counselled that they should desist from discussing the particulars of the case or forming any opinion about it.

It had all, wrote Mr Philby, 'made for excellent entertainment and every word was closely followed by those fortunate enough to have gained admission. Indeed, as if to corroborate the worthy Aeneas Mackenzie's testimony, the only person who did not appear gripped by the spectacle was the prisoner himself.'

Second day

The trial resumed at half past nine the following morning. Roddy was brought in to cheers and catcalls from the public gallery, the occupants of which, wrote Mr Murdoch for the *Courier*, 'appeared to believe that they were in a theatre rather than a court of law, and that the unfortunate prisoner was no more than a pantomime villain, brought forth for their entertainment'. Roddy did not once glance towards his tormentors. Mr Sinclair greeted him with a friendly pat on the shoulder as he took his seat in the dock. The Lord Justice-Clerk allowed the din to continue for a few minutes, perhaps reckoning it prudent to allow the spectators to let off a little steam before bringing the court to order. And indeed when he finally struck his gavel, the court-room was rapidly hushed.

This respectful silence was short-lived, however, as Mr Gifford rose to call John Macrae as the first witness of the day. Mr Philby of *The Times* described Mr Macrae as a 'tiny, bent figure with the appearance of a man twice his forty-four years. He leaned heavily on a gnarled stick and stared out from the dock with an expression of bewilderment in his small, dark eyes. The prisoner kept his head bowed for the duration of his father's evidence and the crofter did not look at his son.' The judge then sternly warned those in the gallery to remain silent on pain of being taken below and held in contempt. It was agreed that, as he was more proficient in the 'ancient language of the Highlands', Mr Macrae's examination would be conducted in Gaelic and a translator was duly brought forth. Mr Gifford, in deference to the apparent infirmity of the witness, commenced his examination in a mild tone.

He began by asking about the witness's relationship with the deceased. Mr Macrae appeared confused by the questions put to him and there were murmurs of amusement in the gallery, which were quickly curbed by the bench. Mr Gifford then re-phrased his question, all this, on account of the translation process, taking a good deal of time: 'Were you and Mr Mackenzie on friendly terms?'

Mr Macrae: 'I know a good number of Mackenzies.'

Mr Gifford smiled patiently. 'I am referring to your neighbour, Lachlan Mackenzie, or Lachlan Broad, as he was known.'

'Ah, yes,' said Mr Macrae. This response brought a fresh outburst of laughter from the gallery. The judge then ordered that the macers eject one of the culprits, an act which, despite the disruption it caused, appeared to have the desired effect.

Mr Gifford then repeated his question.

'I would not say that we were friends,' replied Mr Macrae.

'Why was that?'

'I could not say.'

'Was there any reason that you and Lachlan Mackenzie were not friends?'

Mr Macrae made no reply. The Lord Justice-Clerk then asked, through the translator, if Mr Macrae was having difficulty understanding the advocate's questions. Then, having received assurance that he was not, reminded the witness that he was required to answer the questions put to him or be held in contempt.

Mr Gifford then asked Mr Macrae about the reduction of the croft. After a laborious series of questions regarding this incident, he asked, 'Did you feel aggrieved about this settlement?'

'No.'

'You were not aggrieved that a portion of your croft, from which you derived the food to feed your family, had been taken from you?'

'There were others who had greater need of the land.'

'Did your son feel aggrieved about this settlement?'

'You would have to ask him yourself.'

'Did he show any sign of being aggrieved about this settlement?'

No reply.

'Did you discuss this incident with your son?'

'No.'

Mr Gifford appear somewhat exasperated and appealed to the Lord Justice-Clerk to compel the witness to answer his questions more fully. The judge replied that it was for the gentlemen of the jury to decide whether the answers given were satisfactory.

The Solicitor-General then moved to an incident which had not yet been introduced.

'Do you recall,' he asked, 'a morning sometime in April or May this year when you were gathering sea-ware on the shore at Culduie?'

'I do.'

'Can you tell the court what occurred that morning?'

'It is as you say,' Mr Macrae replied, to stifled laughter from the gallery.

'You were gathering sea-ware?'

'Yes.'

'With your son?'

'Yes.'

'For what purpose were you gathering this sea-ware?'

'For the purpose of spreading on the croft.'

'Did you speak to Mr Mackenzie that morning?'

'He spoke to me.'

'And what did he say?'

'He told me to return the sea-ware we had gathered to the shore.'

'Did he give any reason for his instruction?'

'We had not the permission to remove it.'

'You require permission to remove sea-ware from the shore?'

'It seems so.'

'Whose permission did you require?'

'The permission of Lord Middleton, to whom the sea-ware belonged.'

'Lord Middleton being the laird of your district?'

'Yes.'

'Had you gathered sea-ware from the shore before?'

'Yes.'

'Frequently?'

'On a yearly basis.'

'And had you sought permission to do so on these previous occasions?'

'No.'

'But on this occasion Mr Mackenzie asked you to return the sea-ware you had gathered?'

'Yes.'

'Why do you think he did so?'

'It was his role to enforce the regulations.'

'And you accepted that?'

'Yes.'

'You did not feel aggrieved at Mr Mackenzie's actions?'

Mr Macrae made no answer.

'You were compelled to return a large quantity of sea-ware, which you had spent some hours harvesting, this in accordance with long-established practice, yet you did not feel aggrieved?'

The crofter looked at the advocate for a few moments, then

replied, 'I was not happy about it.'

Mr Gifford here exhaled theatrically, and was reprimanded by the Lord Justice-Clerk for doing so. He then excused himself, but was unable to resist a meaningful look towards the jury.

'And is it true,' he continued, 'that on the following day, the village in its entirety gathered sea-ware for the purpose of spreading on their crofts?'

'I do not know what their purpose was.'

'But they gathered sea-ware?'

'Yes.'

'And you did not?'

'No.'

'Can you say why they were allowed to gather sea-ware and you were not?'

'They had permission to do so.'

'And you did not seek permission to join them?'

'I did not wish to take what did not belong to me.'

There was some laughter in the gallery. Mr Macrae kept his eyes fixed on his left hand, which was gripping the edge of the witness box. Mr Gifford allowed a few moments to pass before proceeding.

'So, if I may summarise,' he said, 'your testimony is that you bore no grievance towards the deceased, a man who had reduced the size of your croft, who had ordered you to return sea-ware to the shore, and to whom, on account of the incident with the sheep, you were indebted a considerable amount?'

Mr Macrae made no answer.

Mr Gifford pressed him for an answer.

'It was not for me to hold a grievance towards Mr Mackenzie.'

The Lord Justice-Clerk at this point reminded Mr Gifford that it was not the witness that was on trial, and the question of whether he bore a grievance towards the deceased was immaterial. It was clearly important to the Crown's strategy, however, that in order to prove the defendant had acted rationally, it was necessary to establish the existence of a grievance against the victim. It was thus a visibly infuriated Mr Gifford that concluded his questioning. A gleeful sketch in the following day's *Inverness Courier* described how the 'Crown's finest legal mind had been bested by a simple crofter'.

Mr Sinclair rose for the defence and, addressing the witness in Gaelic, enquired whether he was quite comfortable.

'Now,' he said, 'I must ask you about your son, who is here accused of the most dreadful crimes. Prior to the events which have brought us to this court-room, did you ever know your son to be violent?'

Mr Macrae made no answer.

'Did your son ever strike you or threaten to strike you?'

Mr Macrae made no answer and was reminded by the Lord Justice-Clerk of his obligations.

'No.'

'Did he ever strike your wife or any of his siblings?'

'No.'

'Did he ever strike any of your neighbours?'

'No.'

'So you would not say that he was given to violence?'

'No.'

'So if he committed these acts of which he is here charged, you would say that it was out of character?'

Mr Macrae did not seem to understand this question.

Mr Sinclair: 'Would you describe your son as a violent person?'

'I have never had cause to describe him.'

Mr Sinclair smiled, in 'a clear attempt to conceal his growing irritation', and rephrased his question: 'If you were asked to describe your son, would you describe him as a violent person?'

'I don't believe so,' the witness replied.

'Were you ever violent towards your son?'

'I was not.'

'You never struck him?'

'I did strike him.'

'When did you have occasion to strike him?'

'When necessary.'

'I see. And could you give an example of when you found it necessary to strike him?'

'When he had disobeyed me or had caused some trouble.'

'"Caused trouble" – so your son sometimes caused trouble? Could you describe to the court an occasion when your son caused trouble and obliged you to beat him?'

Mr Macrae did not reply.

'We have heard testimony about an incident in which your son killed a sheep belonging to Mr Mackenzie. Did you strike your son on this occasion?'

'I did.'

'Can you tell the court why you did so?'

'He had caused trouble.'

'I see. And did you strike him once or repeatedly?'

'Repeatedly.'

'And with what did you strike him?'

'With my stick,' which he helpfully held up.

'And on which part or parts of his body?'

'On his back.'

'You struck him repeatedly on his back with your stick?'

'Yes.'

'And was this an isolated incident?'

Mr Macrae did not appear to understand this question.

'Were there other occasions on which you had cause to beat your son?'

'Some.'

'And did you always beat him with your stick?'

'Not always.'

'Did you strike him with your fists?'

'Yes.'

'And, when you struck him with your fists, where would you strike him?'

'Around the body.'

'On his head and face?'

'Likely there, too.'

'And this was a frequent occurrence?'

The Lord Justice-Clerk here asked Mr Sinclair to be more precise in his question.

'Did you beat your son on a daily basis, on a weekly basis, or less frequently than that?'

'On a weekly basis.'

'And you felt it necessary to do so?'

'The boy needed disciplining.'

'And did this discipline improve his behaviour?'

'It did not.'

Mr Sinclair then examined the papers in front of him and, after some consultation with his assistant, declined to ask any further questions.

At this point, Mr Gifford requested that an alteration to the scheduled order of witnesses be made. The Lord Justice-Clerk made no objection and Allan Cruikshank was called.

Mr Gifford commenced his examination of the witness. 'Please state your occupation, Mr Cruikshank.'

'I am factor to Lord Middleton of Applecross.'

'And the village of Culduie constitutes part of Lord Middleton's estate?'

'It does.'

'And, as such, you are responsible for the management of that village?'

'I am responsible for the management of the estate. I am not concerned with the day-to-day matters in the villages.'

'These would be matters for the village constable, would they?'

'Indeed.'

'And in the case of Culduie, this was Mr Lachlan Mackenzie?'

'That is correct. He acted as constable for Culduie, Camusterrach and Aird-Dubh.'

'These being the neighbouring villages?'

'Yes.'

'So in his capacity as constable to these communities you would have cause to meet with Mr Mackenzie and discuss their administration?'

'We did meet, but not frequently.'

'Did you direct him on the details of how the villages should be managed?'

'We discussed the running of the villages in general terms, but I did not concern myself with the minutiae.'

'"General terms" being what?'

'The general upkeep of the road and by-ways, ensuring that tenants did not fall into arrears in their rent, that sort of thing.'

'And did you find Mr Mackenzie to be competent?'

'Mr Mackenzie was unquestionably the best constable that has served the estate under my tenure.'

'You had confidence in his abilities?'

'Great confidence, yes.'

'Now, do you recall an occasion towards the end of July this year when Mr John Macrae and his son – the prisoner here – visited you?'

'I do.'

'Before this meeting, did you know Mr Macrae?'

'No.'

'Are you often visited by tenants from the estate?'

'I am not. It was most irregular.'

'Why is that?'

'If a tenant wishes to discuss some matter related to the management of their village they should do so with their constable.'

'In this case, Mr Mackenzie?'

'Correct.'

'Did you express this view to Mr Macrae?'

'I did.'

'And how did he respond?'

'He told me that Mr Mackenzie was the subject of his visit.'

'Could you elaborate?'

'It appeared there existed some ill feeling between the two men, or at least that Mr Macrae felt he had been ill-used by Mr Mackenzie.'

'Did you ask Mr Macrae why he felt this way?'

'I did. He related some trifling incidents, but I am afraid I cannot recall the details.'

'Nevertheless, it appeared to you that, rightly or wrongly, Mr Macrae harboured some grievance towards Mr Mackenzie?'

'It appeared so.'

'And what action did you take?'

'I did not take any action. It was a matter of no concern to me.'

'Did you inform Mr Mackenzie of what had occurred?'

'I cannot recall.'

'Did you see Mr Mackenzie between this meeting and the time of his death?'

'I did.'

'When did you see him?'

'I saw him on the day of the summer Gathering.'

'This was when?'

'I believe it was the 31st of July.'

'You spoke to him that day?'

'Yes. We drank an ale at the inn in Applecross.'

'I see. And can you recall if you mentioned this incident – the meeting with Mr Macrae and his son – to him?'

'I believe I did.'

'In what terms did you mention it?'

'It was an amusing incident.'

'Mr Mackenzie found it amusing?'

'He appeared to.'

Mr Gifford then concluded his questioning. The defence had no questions for this witness.

Mr Macrae was then recalled and the evidence of the factor was put to him.

'If, as you have testified, you felt no grievance towards the deceased,' Mr Gifford enquired, 'why did you feel the need to pay this visit to the factor and make these plaints against him?'

At this point, the occupants of the public gallery, some of whom, wrote Mr Murdoch, 'must have keenly felt the humiliation which was to be heaped on the crofter', were quite hushed. Mr Macrae's eyes darted about the court-room as though seeking some assistance. The Lord Justice-Clerk found it necessary to prompt him to answer.

'I wished only to know better the regulations under which we lived.'

'And you did not feel that this was a question you could direct to the deceased?'

'No.'

'Why was that?'

After some moments of silence, he replied, 'I was not on good terms with Mr Mackenzie.'

'And you felt that he had acted in a vindictive manner towards you?'

Mr Macrae made no response.

Mr Gifford presumably feeling that he had made his point, moved on. 'On Monday the 9th of August, the day before the murders took place, did you receive a letter?'

'I did.'

'Who was the letter from?'

'From the factor.'

'And what were the contents of the letter?'

'It was a notice of eviction.'

'You were to be put out of your house?'

'Yes.'

'How did you react to this letter?'

Mr Macrae made a vague gesture with the hand which was not gripping his stick.

Mr Gifford rephrased his question. 'What did you propose to do about this notice?'

'I did not propose to do anything.'

'Did you intend to comply with the notice?'

Mr Macrae looked at the advocate for some moments.

'It was not up to me whether I complied with the notice,' he said.

'Who was it up to?'

'The powers-that-be.'

'Did you discuss this state of affairs with your son?'

'I did not.'

'Did you ever express the view that you would be better off if Mr Mackenzie was dead?'

'No.'

'Did your son ever express the view that you would be better off if Mr Mackenzie was dead?'

'No.'

'Did you put it to your son that he should kill Mr Mackenzie?'

'No.'

'Are you sorry that Mr Mackenzie is dead?'

'It is no concern of mine.'

At the end of this exchange, there was a collective exhalation of breath in the court-room. Mr Macrae was released from the witness box for a second time and, it was reported, refused the room at an inn which was offered to him, preferring to spend the night at the railway station, waiting for the train by which he would begin his journey home.

Allan Cruikshank was then recalled. Mr Gifford asked him to remind the jury of his employment, before resuming his examination of the witness.

'We have heard,' he began, 'that you met the deceased, Lachlan Mackenzie, at the Applecross inn on the 31st of July and that in the course of your conversation you mentioned the visit paid to you by John Macrae and his son, the prisoner here.'

'That is correct.'

'Did you see the deceased on any other occasion after this time?'

'I did.'

'What were the circumstances?'

'Mr Mackenzie visited me at my home on the evening of the 7th of August.'

'Three days before his death?'

'Yes.'

'And what was the reason for his visit?'

'He petitioned me to order the eviction of John Macrae from his croft.'

'On what grounds?'

'There were a number of issues.'

'These being?'

'The Macrae family were greatly in arrears with their rent. They were further indebted to the estate on account of a number of fines raised against them –'

'These fines having been raised by Mr Mackenzie?'

'Yes.'

'Can you recall the reason for raising these fines?'

'I cannot. I believe they were large in number.'

'Were there other factors?'

'Mr Macrae had been negligent in his duty to properly maintain his dwelling and land. It was further felt that the Macraes' continued presence was not conducive to the happy management of the village.'

'In what way?'

Mr Cruikshank was unable to answer this question. After some moments he mumbled, 'They were felt to be a bad influence.'

'Did you take any steps to verify this?'

'I did not.'

'Why not?'

'I had every confidence in Mr Mackenzie's judgement.'

'Is it not the case that a large number of tenants on the estate are in arrears in their rents?'

'Regrettably, yes.'

'So why was Mr Macrae singled out in this way?'

'His debts were of such an amount that they had become unmanageable. There was no prospect of him meeting them.'

'The court has heard that in the previous year the extent of Mr Macrae's croft had been reduced. Might it have been the case that had he had more land, he might have been able to sell any excess crops in order to meet his debts?'

Mr Cruikshank replied, 'I was not aware of any such reduction, but,' he added, 'you would have to sell a great deal of potatoes, or whatever these people grow, to tackle such arrears.'

'You were not aware of the reduction in the size of Mr Macrae's croft?'

'No, sir.'

'So it was carried out without your consent?'

'Well, without my knowledge. I have no doubt Mr Mackenzie acted with the best motives.'

'Would you have expected to be consulted on such a matter?'

'As I say, I'm sure Mr Mackenzie acted out of the best motives.'

'That is not what I asked. I asked if you would expect to be consulted on such a matter.'

'I would expect to be consulted if it was to be a matter of a general re-allocation of land in the villages, but if this was a case of a small portion of a single croft, I'm sure it could be agreed between the villagers themselves. They are not children.'

'Did Mr Mackenzie report an incident to you in which Mr Macrae had taken sea-ware from the shore without the proper authorisation?'

Mr Cruikshank laughed at the suggestion and replied that he had not.

'Were you aware that Mr Macrae was also indebted personally to Mr Mackenzie on account of compensation for the sheep killed by the prisoner?'

'I was not.'

'Had you been aware of these things,' suggested Mr Gifford, 'might you have suspected that there was an element of malice in Mr Mackenzie's proposal to have Mr Macrae evicted?'

Mr Cruikshank weighed his answer for some moments before replying, 'I can only say that to my knowledge Mr Mackenzie carried out his duties as constable admirably. I had no reason to question his motives, and the evidence he presented supported his proposal.'

'So you agreed with Mr Mackenzie's assessment that he should be evicted?'

'I could not see any other course of action.'

'And you drew up the necessary papers?'

'Yes.'

'Immediately?'

'Out of respect to the Sabbath the letter was drawn up and delivered on the following Monday.'

'This being Monday the 9th of August, the day before Mr Mackenzie's death?'

'That is correct.'

Mr Gifford thanked the factor for his evidence and, as Mr Sinclair had no questions, he was excused.

The Reverend James Galbraith was then called. He was, Mr Murdoch reported, 'every inch the staunch man of God that inhabits the remoter parts of our country and presides over his flock with unbending will. He was attired in the plain garb of his ilk, and it was manifest from his dour visage that he was untroubled by worldly pleasure. He looked upon Mr Gifford with the disdain he might reserve for a metropolitan dandy, and even the renowned advocate appeared to tremble a little beneath his gaze.'

Mr Gifford: 'You are minister to the parish of Applecross?'

Mr Galbraith, with the 'air of a teacher correcting a backward pupil', replied, 'My parish encompasses the villages of Camusterrach, Culduie and Aird-Dubh.'

'And, as such, John Macrae and his family were among your parishioners?'

'Yes.'

'Indeed, John Macrae was an elder in your church?'

'He was.'

'Now, is it correct that Mr Macrae sent for you on the evening of the 9th of August?'

'He did. He sent his daughter to ask if I would call on him that evening.'

'And you did so?'

'I did.'

'And what was the reason for his request?'

'He had received a notice of eviction from the factor.'

'And how did you find Mr Macrae that evening?'

'He was distressed.'

'Did he ask for your help?'

'He asked if I would intervene on his behalf.'

'And did you agree to do so?'

'I did not.'

Mr Gifford affected an expression of surprise at this response. 'Could you tell the court why you did not do so?'

Mr Galbraith fixed the advocate with a withering stare. 'It was not a matter with which I could involve myself.'

'Surely the wellbeing of your parishioners is your concern?'

'My concern is with my parishioners' spiritual wellbeing. It is not for me to meddle in the management of the estate.'

'I see. Did you offer any guidance at all to Mr Macrae?'

'I reminded him that the tribulations of this life come to us in just payment for our sins and that he must accept them as such.'

'But you offered him no practical advice as to how to deal with the situation in which he found himself?'

'I led him in prayer.' This brought a ripple of laughter from the gallery, which was rapidly quelled by a stern look from the preacher.

Mr Gifford thanked the witness and resumed his seat.

Mr Sinclair then rose for the defence.

'Was the prisoner, Roderick Macrae, present during your visit?'

'He arrived home as I was leaving.'

'Did you converse with him?'

'In the briefest terms.'

'Did the prisoner attend your church?'

'He did not.'

'Had he ever attended your church?'

'When he was a child.'

'And he ceased attending when?'

'I could not say with any certainty.'

'One year ago or five years ago?'

'Closer to one or two years ago.'

'Would that be around the time of the death of his mother?'

'Around that time.'

'As you have stated that you are concerned with the spiritual wellbeing of your parishioners, can you tell the court what steps you took to persuade the prisoner to resume his attendance?'

'It is not my role to compel parishioners to attend. I am not a whipper-in.'*

'So you were not worried about his non-observance?'

'A shepherd must concern himself with the wellbeing of his flock as a whole. If the flock contains black sheep, they must be cast out.'

'And Roderick Macrae is a black sheep?'

'We would hardly be gathered in this court-room if that were not the case.'

The remark was, observed the wry Mr Philby, 'likely the closest the stern Presbyterian had ever come to making a joke'.

'Quite so,' replied Mr Sinclair. 'But if I may press you a little, what was it that so marked out Roderick Macrae?'

'The boy is a malevolent individual.'

'"Malevolent" is a strong word, Mr Galbraith.'

The minister made no reply to this observation. Mr Sinclair tried again: 'How did this malevolence manifest itself?'

'Even as a child, the boy had no respect for the Lord's House. He was shifty and inattentive to prayer. I once caught him relieving himself within the grounds of the church.'

The Lord Justice-Clerk here struck his gavel to subdue the laughter that emanated from the gallery.

'I see,' said Mr Sinclair. 'Would you say that you saw signs of madness in the prisoner?'

'I would say that I saw signs of wickedness in him.'

'What signs were these?'

---

* *A 'whipper-in' was an official who travelled round rural districts ensuring that children attended school.*

Mr Galbraith apparently did not think this question worthy of response. The judge instructed him to answer.

'One need only to observe him. If it is not apparent to you, I would suggest that you are as Godless as he is, sir,' he replied witheringly.

Mr Sinclair smiled thinly at the witness. 'I am only seeking your comments as an educated man about the temperament of the prisoner,' he said.

'My observation is that the boy is enslaved to the Devil, and if proof is required we need only look to the deeds he has committed.'

Mr Sinclair nodded wearily and the witness was excused.

The next witness could hardly have struck a greater contrast to the clergyman. Archibald Ross's appearance in the court-room caused a great deal of mirth in the gallery. He was dressed in the style of a country gentleman, in 'a suit of yellow tweeds, quite obviously procured for the occasion'. He wore highly polished shoes with large square buckles and, round his neck, a green silk cravat. He was, wrote Mr Philby, 'every inch the dandy, and his appearance might lead an observer to conclude that the far-flung village of Applecross, where he resides, must indeed be quite *à la mode*'.

After some preliminaries regarding Ross's place of birth and occupation, Mr Gifford asked how he had made the acquaintance of the prisoner. Ross then described how he had met Roddy in the courtyard outside the stables of Lord Middleton's house.

'And what was the prisoner's role that day?'

'To carry a coffer up the mountain.'

'And what did that coffer contain?'

'Refreshments for the shooting party.'

'And did the prisoner carry out this duty competently?'

'That part of his duty, yes.'

'After this day did you ever meet the prisoner again?'

'I did.'

'When did this meeting occur?'

'Some weeks ago on the day of the Gathering.'

'This was the 31st of July?'

'If you say so,' replied Ross with a grin.

'Please tell us what occurred.'

Ross described how he had met the prisoner outside the inn at Applecross and how they had gone inside and drunk a quantity of ale. They had then walked to the Big House to watch the shinty match between the villages.

'Were you inebriated?'

'Perhaps to a small degree.'

'Was the prisoner inebriated?'

'I would say so.'

'Did the prisoner divulge any intimacies to you?'

'He told me that he wanted to go to Glasgow to make his fortune, but that he was reluctant to do so as he had become attached to a local girl.'

'And who was this local girl?'

'Flora Mackenzie.'

'And this Flora Mackenzie was the daughter of the deceased Lachlan Mackenzie?'

'Yes.'

This revelation caused an uproar in the gallery, which it took repeated threats from the bench to subdue.

'And who is herself one of the victims of the crimes here charged?'

'Yes.'

'And did the prisoner tell you anything further concerning his relationship to the deceased Miss Mackenzie?'

'He told me that she had rejected him and that, in any case, there existed some bad blood between their two families and their parents would never consent to them being wed.'

This brought further exclamations from the gallery.

'You then watched the shinty match?'

'Yes.'

'Then what?'

'We drank some whisky and then Roddy spotted this girl –'

'Flora Mackenzie?'

'Yes. He spotted her walking in the grounds of the Big House with a friend.'

'And what did you do?'

'I expressed the view that he should openly convey his feelings to the girl so that he might properly know where he stood with her.'

'And did he agree?'

'Not exactly, but I insisted and we caught up with the girls and introduced ourselves.'

At this point, Mr Philby reported, the 'generally disinterested prisoner displayed some signs of agitation, hunching low over his knees, as if hoping that he might find a farthing on the floor of the dock'.

'Then what happened?'

'We walked a little way together.'

'Where did you walk?'

'To a small bridge among some trees.'

'A secluded spot?'

At this point Archibald Ross made a 'lewd wink' to counsel and replied, to much laughter, 'I construe that you are no stranger to such adventures.'

Mr Gifford ignored his remark.

'And what happened there?'

'In order that Roddy might be alone with the object of his affections [sic], I led Flora's companion onto the bridge and indicated to him that he should continue along the path.'

'Then what?'

'I made some conversation with the girl and then some time later, Flora Mackenzie came back along the path.'

'Was she walking or running?'

'She was running.'

'And she was alone?'

'Yes.'

'How much time had elapsed?'

'A matter of minutes.'

'And what did she do?'

'She took her friend by the arm and led her away.'

'In which direction?'

'Towards the Big House.'

'And did she appear distressed?'

'Perhaps. I could not say with any certainty.'

'Was she weeping?'

'I could not say.'

'Were her cheeks flushed?'

'Yes, but in my experience there are a good many reasons for a girl's cheeks to be flushed,' said Ross with a smirk.

The Lord Justice-Clerk at this point reminded the witness of the gravity of the proceedings and threatened to have him taken down if he made any more remarks of that nature. Ross made a low bow to the judge and offered an obsequious apology.

Mr Gifford continued his examination of the witness: 'So, Miss Mackenzie went into the woods with the prisoner and returned – running – some minutes later, and took her friend with her back towards the Big House?'

'Yes, sir.'

'And where was the prisoner at this time?'

'He was in the woods.'

'And did he reappear?'

'Yes.'

'How many minutes later?'

'Not many, one or two.'

'And what was his demeanour?'

'He seemed somewhat distressed.'

'How do you know this?'

'He was weeping.'

'Did he tell you what had occurred?'

'Yes, sir.'

'Would you be so kind as to share what he told you with the court?'

'He said only that his advances had been rejected and he was quite broken-hearted.'

'"His advances" – were those the words he used?'

'I cannot recall.'

'But you understood that he had made some "advances"?'

'Yes.'

'And did the prisoner display any other sign of distress?'

'His face was red on one side.'

'And what was the cause of this?'

'The girl had struck him.'

'Did you see the girl strike him?'

'No.'

'So how do you know she struck him?'

'Roddy told me.'

'Then what happened?'

'I tried to make light of what had occurred, but seeing that my friend was genuinely aggrieved, I proposed a glass of ale to cheer him up.'

'And did he agree?'

'He did.'

'And you returned to the inn?'

'Yes.'

'And you there took some more ale?'

'We did.'

'And how was your friend – the prisoner – at this time?'

'He was greatly revived in spirits.'

'Did anything else of note occur that day?'

'As we were enjoying a glass of ale, a great brute of a man set upon Roddy and gave him a fearful beating.'

'Why did this man set upon your friend?'

'For no reason that I could see.'

'Did you hear any words spoken between them?'

'No, sir.'

'And who was this "great brute of a man"?'

'I learned later that he was Lachlan Mackenzie.'

'The deceased Mr Lachlan Mackenzie?'

'Yes.'

'And what happened next?'

'I took Roddy outside and set him on the road back to his village.'

The Solicitor-General then concluded his questioning and Mr Sinclair rose for the defence. He explained that he wished the witness to cast his mind back to the day of the deer-stalking party.

'Was the hunt that day successful?'

'It certainly was not,' Ross replied with a laugh.

'Why was that?'

Archibald Ross then described how Roddy had 'swooped down upon the deer, waving his arms like a great bird and squawking like a banshee'.

'This in order to startle the deer?'

'Yes.'

'What did you make of this behaviour?'

To loud laughter from the gallery, Archibald Ross pulled a comic face and tapped the side of his forehead with his finger. He was sternly reprimanded by the Lord Justice-Clerk and instructed to confine himself to verbal replies.

Ross then said, 'I thought it was the most foolish thing I had ever seen.'

Mr Sinclair: 'And had the prisoner given any indication prior to this act of what he intended to do?'

'Not at all.'

'It was quite sudden?'

'Out of the blue.'

'And prior to this act, what had been your impression of the prisoner?'

'I had not formed any particular impression.'

'There was nothing strange in his behaviour?'

'No.'

'Or in his speech?'

'No.'

'He was quite rational?'

'Yes.'

'Right up until the moment he scared off the deer?'

'Yes.'

'Now, you have testified to Mr Gifford that after the incident in the woods with Flora Mackenzie the prisoner was quite distressed?'

'Yes.'

'He was or had been weeping?'

'Yes.'

'And yet only a short while later, you testified that ...' – he here consulted some written notes before him – '... he was "greatly revived in spirits"?'

'Yes.'

'What was the witness doing immediately before he was set upon by Mr Mackenzie?'

'He was dancing a jig to a fiddle.'

'Dancing a jig?'

'Yes.'

'And how much time had elapsed between the incident in the woods, which had apparently distressed the prisoner so much, and dancing this jig?'

Here Ross hesitated for some moments. 'Perhaps an hour.'

'More than an hour or less than hour?'

'Less than an hour.'

'And did it strike you as in any way strange that the prisoner might one minute be weeping and the next minute dancing a jig?'

'I merely thought that his spirits had been enlivened by a glass of ale.'

'You did not think that just as on the mountain when the prisoner was one moment entirely rational and the next doing the most foolish thing you had ever seen, that he was subject to quite extreme swings of behaviour?'

'I did not think about it,' said Ross. And with that Mr Sinclair concluded his questioning and Mr Ross was released from the witness box, not before, wrote Mr Philby, 'waving flamboyantly to the gallery, quite as if he was an actor concluding a theatrical performance, which in a sense he was'.

The Crown then called Ishbel Farquhar, a girl, described in *The Scotsman* as 'representing the best virtues of Highland woman-hood, being of modest appearance and with a rosy hue to her cheeks'. She was dressed in a dark pinafore and had her hair neatly arranged in plaits. Her appearance seemed to cause Roddy some anguish. His eyes began to dart around the court-room, 'alighting on everything besides the girl who then occupied the witness box'.

After some preliminaries, Mr Gifford asked, 'Can you tell the court how you came to make the acquaintance of Flora Mackenzie?'

'She came to work in the kitchens of the Big House.'

'Where you were also employed?'

'Yes, sir.'

'And you became friends?'

'Yes.'

Miss Farquhar answered in such a low voice that she was asked by the Lord Justice-Clerk to speak up so that the jurymen might hear her replies.

'And you were with Flora Mackenzie on the afternoon of the Gathering in Applecross on the 31st of July?'

'Yes, sir, I was.'

At the mention of her friend's name, Miss Farquhar began to weep and Mr Gifford gallantly produced a handkerchief from his pocket and passed it to her. When she had composed herself, the Solicitor-General apologised for distressing her.

'We are here, however, on the gravest business,' he continued, 'and it is necessary that you testify to those parts of the narrative which have a bearing on this case.'

'I'll do my best, sir,' replied Miss Farquhar.

'Did Flora ever speak to you about the prisoner?'

'Yes, sir, she did.'

'And what did she say?'

'She had once or twice walked out with him and that she liked him well enough, but that he had some queer ideas and sometimes said strange things.'

'What sort of queer ideas?'

'I do not know.'

'She did not tell you?'

'No.'

'Can you tell us what you were doing immediately before you met the prisoner and his friend, Archibald Ross, on the afternoon in question?'

'We were taking a turn around the grounds of the Big House.'

'And you were approached by Archibald Ross and the prisoner?'

'Yes.'

'And in what condition were they?'

'They were drunk.'

'Both of them?'

'Roddy more so.'

'How inebriated was he?'

'He had difficulty speaking and he walked unsteadily.'

'Nevertheless, you allowed them to accompany you?'

'Yes.'

'And you went with them into the woods near the burn?'

'Yes. There did not seem any harm in it.' The witness again began to weep.

'So you did not think of the prisoner as a dangerous character; as someone who might do harm to you or to Flora?'

'I did not know him.'

'Please tell the court what occurred in the woods.'

'When we reached the burn, Mr Ross took my arm and told me that he wanted to show me something and led me onto the bridge.'

'And did the prisoner and Flora Mackenzie accompany you onto the bridge?'

'They continued along the path by the burn.'

'What happened then?'

'Mr Ross leaned over the bridge and started talking about the trout and salmon in the river and pointed to the water, but I could not see any fish.'

'Yes?'

'Then he tried to kiss me.'

'Where did he try to kiss you?'

Miss Farquhar did not answer, but touched her neck with her hand.

'And did you let Mr Ross kiss you?'

'I did not.'

'What did you do?'

'I drew away from him, but he held my arm and would not release me and then he made ...'

'Please continue, Miss Farquhar.'

'He made an improper suggestion.'

'A suggestion of a sexual nature?'

'Yes, sir.'

'I see. And then?'

'I was frightened because he was gripping my arm. Then Flora came back along the path and he released me and we went away together.'

'Was she running or walking?'

'She was running.'

'And did Flora Mackenzie tell you what had occurred when she had been alone with the prisoner?'

'She told me that Roddy had said some coarse things to her and that he had put her hands upon her and that she had slapped him.'

Mr Gifford apologised for pressing her and then asked, 'Did she indicate where the prisoner had put his hands?'

At this point, reported Mr Philby, the prisoner 'became more agitated than at any previous point in the trial. His cheeks became quite crimson and he twisted his hands in his lap and seemed to shrink inside his own skin. If he admitted to no remorse for the murder of three people, he certainly appeared to feel some for the advances he had made towards the unfortunate Miss Mackenzie.'

The witness kept her eyes cast down and refused for some

moments to answer.

'Did Flora say, Miss Farquhar, that he had put her hands on the intimate parts of her body?'

She nodded and the Lord Justice-Clerk ordered that the record show that the witness had answered in the affirmative.

'Anything else?'

'No, sir.'

Mr Gifford then thanked her and concluded his questioning. Mr Sinclair declined to cross-examine the witness and she was excused.

The final witness called by the Crown was Hector Munro, MD, 'a small plump man with mutton chop whiskers and a ruddy complexion'. He gave every appearance, wrote the sly Mr Philby, of 'being a close acquaintance of a certain Mr J. Walker, esq.'.

Dr Munro gave his profession as general practitioner and stated that he was employed on a regular basis as medical officer to Inverness gaol.

Mr Gifford: 'And what are your duties in this employ?'

Dr Munro: 'To attend to the general health of the prisoners.'

'And in this capacity were you required to examine the current prisoner, Roderick Macrae?'

'I was.'

'And did you do so?'

'I did.'

'And did you examine the prisoner with a view only to assessing his physical condition?'

'No. I was requested by the Fiscal to assess the mental state of the prisoner.'

'In order to ascertain whether the prisoner was of a sound state of mind?'

'Yes.'

'Can you tell the court something about the physical condition of the prisoner?'

'I found him to be in generally good health, although suffering somewhat from scurvy, no doubt precipitated by poor diet.'

'But he was otherwise in sound health?'

'Yes. He was quite vigorous.'

'Now, as to his mental condition, can you tell us by what means you sought to assess this?'

'I conversed with the prisoner at some length.'

'About the crimes for which he is here indicted?'

'About these crimes, yes, and about his circumstances in general.'

'And did the prisoner converse with you in a civilised manner?'

'A most civilised manner, yes.'

'And what was your assessment of the mental condition of the prisoner?'

'I found him to be fully in possession of his reason.'

'"Fully in possession of reason",' Mr Gifford repeated, placing great emphasis on these words. 'And on what basis did you reach this conclusion?'

'The prisoner was aware of his surroundings and why he was there. He answered my questions in a clear and deliberate manner and exhibited no signs of delusion or disorder in his reasoning. I would go as far as saying that he is among the most articulate and intelligent prisoners I have encountered.'

'"Among the most articulate and intelligent prisoners you have encountered" – that is quite a statement, Dr Munro.'

'It is my truthful opinion.'

'And did you ask the prisoner specifically about the crimes with which he is charged?'

'I did.'

'And what was his response?'

'He freely admitted responsibility for them.'

'Might he have done this out of some desire to please you – because he might have believed that this was what you wanted to hear?'

'I cannot speak to the prisoner's motives, but, if I recall, I put the question to him in a quite neutral manner.'

'In what manner?'

'I told him that I heard about some crimes which had occurred in his village and asked him if he knew anything about them.'

'And what was his response?'

'He replied without hesitation that he was responsible.'

'And did you ask him why he had committed these crimes?'

'I did. He replied that he had committed these crimes in order to deliver his father from the tribulations which had been caused to him by the victim.'

'The victim, Lachlan Mackenzie?'

'Yes.'

'And those were his words: "to deliver his father from the tribulations which had been caused to him"?'

'I believe so, more or less.'

'And did you ask him about the other victims?'

'Not specifically.'

'And did you think him truthful in his responses?'

'I saw no reason to disbelieve him.'

'Did you ask the prisoner any further questions relating to these crimes?'

'I asked if he felt any remorse for what he had done.'

'And how did he reply?'

'He replied that he did not.'

'He felt no remorse for the murder of three people?'

'No, sir.'

'Did this not strike you as unusual? Perhaps even as a sign that he was not fully in possession of his reason.'

'In my experience, prisoners rarely express remorse for what they have done. Any feelings of regret they might feel are generally limited to the fact of their being apprehended.'

This last remark lightened the atmosphere in the court for a moment and the Lord Justice-Clerk allowed the ripple of laughter to subside of its own accord.

'This lack of remorse, then, is not, in your opinion as a medical man, a symptom of loss of reason?'

'Not in the least, sir.'

'You are aware that the prisoner has lodged a Special Defence of Insanity – that he was, at the time of committing these acts, alienated from his reason?'

'I am.'

'Did you find the prisoner to be labouring under a state of insanity?'

'I did not.'

'Is it possible that when he committed these acts, he was labouring under a state of insanity?'

'Given the account of his crimes he provided to me and the rational manner in which he spoke, I do not believe that he was insane at the time of these acts.'

Mr Gifford then thanked the witness and concluded his questioning. Mr Sinclair rose for the defence.

'How long,' he asked, 'have you been employed in the capacity of medical officer to Inverness gaol?'

'Some eight years.'

'You must have examined a great many prisoners in that time.'

'Indeed I have.'

'And what proportion of the prisoners you have examined would you consider to be insane?'

'I am not sure I could say with any certainty.'

'Half? More than half? Less than half?'

'A great deal less than half.'

'Could you be more specific?'

'A very small proportion.'

'Ten out of a hundred? Five out of hundred?'

'Perhaps one out of a hundred.'

'One out of a hundred! That is indeed a small proportion,' Mr Sinclair exclaimed. 'And the other ninety-nine men – what has brought them to your gaol?'

'They have committed some crime or other, or have been accused of doing so.'

'And why do these men – this ninety-nine per cent of men – commit their crimes?'

Dr Munro appeared somewhat bemused at this line of questioning. He looked towards the Lord Justice-Clerk, who merely indicated that he should answer the questions put to him.

'If I was pressed to venture an opinion, I would say that they are there because they are unable to control their baser instincts.'

'Their instincts to steal from or strike out at their fellows?'

'For example, yes.'

'But this inability to control their instincts is not, in your opinion, indicative of a loss of reason?'

'No, sir.'

'They are merely bad men.'

'If you wish to express it thus.'

'How would you express it?'

'I would say that they are criminals, sir.'

Mr Sinclair paused rather theatrically and, while facing the gentlemen of the jury, asked, 'So in ninety-nine per cent of the men you examine in your capacity as medical officer to the prison in this town, you find no signs of insanity.'

'That is correct.'

'Would it be correct to say, that in general, when you inspect the prisoners at the gaol, you are not looking for signs of insanity?'

'My examinations are generally limited to a physical examination of the prisoners, yes.'

'Do you consider yourself expert in the field of Criminal Anthropology?'

'To the extent that I have been examining prisoners for eight years, I would consider myself to have some expertise.'

'Would you consider yourself expert in the field of Criminal Psychology?'

'I would.'

'Could you explain to the court the meaning of the term "moral insanity"?'

'I am not familiar with that term.'

'Could you explain to the court the meaning of the term "mania without delirium"?'

Dr Munro shook his head.

'You are not familiar with that term either. Are you familiar with the works of Monsieur Philippe Pinel?"

'I am not.'

'Are you familiar with the work of Dr James Cowles Prichard?'

'I have heard of him.'

'Then you will have read his volume, *A Treatise on Insanity and Other Disorders Affecting the Mind*?'

'I cannot recall.'

'It is your testimony that you cannot recall whether you have read a work of the greatest significance in current thinking about the psychology of criminals; a field in which you profess expertise?'

'My expertise is based on my experience examining members of the criminal population.'

'A population which, by your own estimate, embraces only the minutest proportion of men labouring under mental disorders.'

'Yes.'

'Given that you have been called here today to provide testimony in the most solemn of proceedings, do you not think that as a professed expert it is your responsibility to acquaint yourself with the current thinking in that field?'

'I do not believe that any medical man, if called upon to examine the prisoner, would reach a different conclusion to the one I reached.'

'If you will forgive me, Dr Munro, that is not the question I put to you. The question I put to you is this: is it not your responsibility as a so-called professed expert in Criminal Psychology – the application of which is of crucial importance to this case – to fully apprise yourself of the thinking in this field?'

The good doctor was by this time, wrote Mr Philby, 'becoming rather flustered and glanced about as if hoping to find a whisky

---

* *Philippe Pinel (1745–1826) was a pioneer of criminal psychology. He coined the term* 'mania sans délire' *in his* Nosographie philosophique ou méthode de l'analyse appliquée à la médecine *(1798–1818).*

bottle secreted in the witness box'.

Mr Sinclair did not press him for an answer, no doubt calculating that his silence was more damning than anything he might actually say. Instead he took a more conciliatory tone: 'Perhaps I am being unreasonable,' he began. 'It might be more helpful if you could tell the jury what training or education you have received in the field of Criminal Psychology.'

Dr Munro looked beseechingly to the judge, who instructed him to answer with a gesture of his hand.

'I have received no such training.'

Mr Sinclair, who was clearly relishing this revival in the fortunes of his case, directed an expression of great astonishment towards the jurymen.

'Would it thus be more accurate to describe you as self-educated in this field?'

'That would be more accurate, yes,' replied the doctor.

'In that case, perhaps, since you have read neither the works of Dr Prichard nor of Monsieur Pinel, you could tell the jury some of the volumes with which you have educated yourself.'

Dr Munro appeared to give this question some thought, before replying that he could not, at that moment, recall any specific titles.

'You cannot recall a single volume which you have read on the subject in which, when asked earlier, you professed expertise?'

'No.'

'Are we then to understand, Dr Munro' – he here made a sweeping gesture towards the jury – 'that you are entirely unqualified to make any pronouncement on the state of mind of the prisoner?'

'I believe I am qualified.'

'But you have no qualifications!'

The witness did not appear to have the will to defend himself against the advocate's onslaught, and with a meaningful shake of his head, Mr Sinclair concluded his examination.

Dr Munro, clearly relieved that his ordeal was over, made to exit the witness box, but was reprimanded by the Lord Justice-Clerk, as he had not yet been excused. Mr Gifford then rose to re-examine the witness. He apologised for detaining the doctor further, before asking him to remind the court how long he had been engaged in practice at Inverness gaol. He then asked the doctor how many prisoners he had examined in the course of his employment.

Dr Munro, clearly appreciating that he was being given an opportunity to redeem himself, replied that while it was impossible to put an exact figure on it, it must run to 'many hundreds'.

'And in your long experience only a very small proportion of those who pass through your care might be termed insane?'

'That is my opinion, yes.'

'Your medical opinion?'

'Yes.'

'Do you recognise the signs, or symptoms, of insanity, Dr Munro?'

'I do.'

'Could you please enumerate those signs for us?'

'Firstly, a prisoner might be labouring under some delusion –'

Mr Gifford here apologised for interrupting the witness. 'Could you please explain what you mean by the term "delusion"?'

'I mean simply that the prisoner is suffering from some erroneous belief. Perhaps, he hears voices in his head, sees visions, or believes himself to be someone that he is not.'

'Thank you. Please continue.'

'A prisoner might be disordered in his thinking; that is, he speaks in an ostensibly reasonable manner, but one thought does not follow from another in the normal way. Likewise, his statements might simply bear no relation to reality.'

'Anything more?'

'I have encountered prisoners who spout incomprehensible gibberish; whose speech is nothing more than a stream of unintelligible, unconnected words, or is not even recognisable as language.* There are also prisoners who are unable to comprehend

---

* *A mischievous sketch in* The Scotsman *suggested that the prisoners to whom Dr Munro referred might merely have been speaking Gaelic.*

the simplest of statements put to them, or reply in an inappropri-ate or irrelevant way. Then there are those who might be termed as imbeciles, who are simply, for one reason or another, defective or childlike in their development.'

Mr Gifford encouraged the doctor to continue.

'In a small number of cases, there are those prisoners who do not respond at all to their surroundings, who sit or lie in the cor-ner of their cell and do not react to any stimuli, often muttering to themselves or repeating the same action *ad nauseam*.'

'That is a most comprehensive enumeration,' said Mr Gifford. 'And this knowledge of the various forms of insanity you have gleaned how?'

'From my experience in dealing with the prisoners at Inverness gaol.'

'But you must at some moments have encountered cases which presented you with difficulties in providing a diagnosis?'

'I have.'

'And what would you do in such instances?'

'I might confer with a colleague or consult some textbook or other.'

'I see. And would you say that this process of consultation and your long experience in dealing with criminals qualifies you to pronounce on the sanity or otherwise of any given individual?'

'I would.'

'Now, before you leave the witness box, I beg leave to put one further question to you. During your examination of the prisoner here, did he exhibit any of the signs of insanity or conform to any of the behaviours which you have just now described?'

'He did not.'

'He was not delusional?'

'No.'

'He was not disordered in his reasoning?'

'No.'

'He was cognisant of his surroundings and the circumstances which had brought him there?'

'He was.'

'And in your medical opinion, can he be considered to be insane or alienated from his reason?'

'No.'

Mr Gifford at this point offered a withering look towards the defence bench, and without any further theatrics, concluded his questioning. Dr Munro was now excused and, with a look of gratitude towards the Solicitor-General, 'scuttled away, no doubt in search of the refuge of the nearest hostelry'.

At the conclusion of the prosecution case, this being the custom under Scots Law at the time, the Prisoner's Declaration was read by the Clerk of the Court. This was the only statement permitted to the accused:

My name is Roderick John Macrae, aged seventeen years. I am native of Culduie in Ross-shire and reside at the northernmost dwelling in that village with my father, John Macrae, a crofter. And, the charge of having caused the death of Lachlan Mackenzie, aged thirty-eight years, Flora Mackenzie, aged fifteen years, and Donald Mackenzie, aged three years, by means of blows administered with a flaughter and croman in their home on the 10th day of August in this present year having been read over, Declares – I freely admit that I am responsible for the deaths of the persons named. On the morning in question I went to the house of Lachlan Mackenzie, armed with these weapons, with the intention of killing him. I killed Lachlan Mackenzie in repayment for the suffering he had caused to my father and to my family as a whole. It was not my intention to kill Flora Mackenzie or Donald Mackenzie. Their deaths were necessitated by their presence in the house and my wish to prevent them from raising the alarm. I believe that the success of my enterprise should be attributed to Providence, and I similarly accept whatever fate Providence dictates for me. I am of sound mind and make this statement freely and under no duress. All of which I declare to be truth.

[Signed]

Roderick John Macrae

The Trial

The prosecution rested. As it was by then around four o'clock, there followed a discussion at the bar about whether the proceedings should be adjourned for the day. Mr Sinclair, no doubt anxious that the jury should not spend the night with Roddy's declaration of his own sanity ringing in their ears, argued for a continuation. Mr Gifford contended that, as there was no possibility of the trial concluding that day, they should start afresh in the morning. The exchange, at least on Mr Sinclair's part, became quite heated, but after a brief, whispered consultation with his colleagues, the Lord Justice-Clerk declared the court adjourned. Mr Sinclair, *The Scotsman* reported, 'became quite red in the face and was heard to audibly mutter about a conspiracy against his client, a statement for which he was sternly reprimanded by the judge and for which he immediately apologised'.

Regardless of Mr Sinclair's feelings about the judge's perfectly reasonable ruling, such a display of petulance in the presence of the jury could hardly be said to be in his client's interests. The judge repeated the previous day's cautions to the jurymen and the court was emptied. Those in the public gallery left in an atmosphere, 'somewhat akin to schoolboys being discharged for summer'.

The evening editions of the newspapers carried colourful accounts of the exchanges between the advocates and Dr Munro, and the *Inverness Courier* reported that 'no other topic was discussed at the inns and street corners of the town. Those who had been fortunate enough to be present at the trial held court like great sages and arguments raged long into the night about whether the unfortunate prisoner was for the gibbet.'

Among the reporters, opinion appeared to be similarly divided. *The Scotsman*'s account of the day's proceedings concluded that 'the glimmer of hope provided by his advocate's masterful demolition of Dr Munro was immediately extinguished by the declaration, from the prisoner's own lips, that he was indeed of sound mind. It would now require a quite astonishing reversal to convince the jury that the wretched crofter is innocent of the crimes charged.'

For John Murdoch writing in the *Courier*, however, the case was not so clear cut: 'While there can be no questioning the skill with which Mr Gifford has presented the Crown's case, the jury will have heard enough along the way about the peculiar behaviour of the accused, to sow some seeds of doubt about his soundness of mind.'

In the following morning's edition of *The Times*, Mr Philby wrote:

> *It is a most irregular occurrence for the defence in such a case to rest on a single witness, but it must be admitted that the trial of Roderick Macrae is no ordinary event. What is at issue are not the facts of the case, but the contents of the perpetrator's mind and, thus far, this is something few, if any, could truthfully presume to know. The prisoner has at all times conducted himself in a respectful and modest manner, such that it is quite impossible to imagine him carrying out the brutal crimes with which he is charged. Yet carry them out he did, and that one capable of such a frenzy could then sit quietly as a mouse for two days, speaks, to this observer, of a kind of lunacy not enumerated by Dr Hector Munro. A great weight thus rests on the shoulders of the eminent James Bruce Thomson, in whose hands the fate of Roderick Macrae rests.*

Third day

Mr Philby was not alone in grasping the importance of Mr Thomson's evidence. His arrival in the court-room was anticipated with more excitement than any point since the first appearance of the prisoner himself. Mr Thomson, dressed in a tight-fitting black suit with the chain of a gold fob watch traversing his midriff, took his place in the witness box with an air of great solemnity. According to *The Times*' man, he 'cast a haughty gaze over the public gallery and then fixed, in turn, the judges, the Crown and defence with a no less arrogant air. The renowned alienist made it quite clear that he thought himself the principal player of this particular piece of theatre.'

The Lord Justice-Clerk brought the court to order and, once the formalities had been completed, Mr Sinclair commenced his examination by asking the witness to state his profession.

Mr Thomson: 'I am Resident Surgeon to the General Prison for Scotland at Perth.'

'And for how long have you held that position?'

'Some fourteen years.'

'And in that time how many prisoners have you examined?'

'Around six thousand.'

'And you have examined both the physical and mental condition of these prisoners?'

'I have.'

'And would it be correct to say that you have given particular attention to the psychological state of the prisoners under your care?'

'It would be correct.'

'And would you say that you have some expertise in the study of the mental condition of criminals?'

'Modesty aside, I would say so, yes.'

'On what basis would you claim this expertise?'

'In addition to my experience in examining prisoners, I have made an extensive study of the literature on this subject. I have been elected as a member of the Medico-Psychological Association and been invited by this body to read a paper on the psychological effects of prison on the inmate. My article on epilepsy among prisoners has been published in the *Edinburgh Monthly Journal* and I will shortly publish further works on the psychological and hereditary aspects of crime in the *Journal for Mental Science*.'

'That is most impressive, sir,' said Mr Sinclair. 'And would I also be correct in saying that those criminals found unfit to stand trial on the basis of insanity are accommodated in your institution?'

'That is correct.'

'So, as well your large experience with what might be termed the general prison population, you have had a good deal of contact with the criminally insane.'

'Indeed.'

'And would you draw any distinction between the general prison population and those deemed to be criminally insane?'

'There is a similarity in that criminals of both creeds to a great extent are without the moral sense. However, the habitual criminal is generally disposed towards crime by heredity, and is for the most part incurable. There now exists a criminal class which dwells in the over-crowded slums of our cities. These people are born into crime, reared, nurtured and instructed in it. It might thus be argued that such criminals cannot truly be held responsible for their actions, since they are born to them and are powerless to resist the tyranny of their circumstances.'

There was, observed Mr Murdoch, 'something of the incantatory quality of the Free Church preacher in the rhythm and intonation of the alienist's oration'.

'And is it possible,' asked Mr Sinclair, 'to identify members of this hereditary criminal class of which you speak?'

'Most assuredly.'

'How so?'

'Due to the filthy conditions in which these colonies breed and their lack of regard for the rules on consanguinity, there is often found among them abnormal states, such as spinal deformities, stammering, imperfect organs of speech, club feet, cleft-palates, hare-lips, deafness, congenital blindness, epilepsy, scrofula, and so on. All this usually accompanied by weakness of mind or imbecilism. Those born in crime are as distinct from an honest working man as a black-faced sheep is from the Cheviot breed."*

'Now, is it correct that you travelled to Inverness to examine the accused in the present case?'

'At your request, sir, I did.'

'And did you examine the prisoner?'

'I did.'

'And what were the results of this examination?'

'I found that in certain respects, he exhibited the low physical characteristics of the hereditary criminal class.'

---

* *The ideas expressed here by Thomson are more fully set out in his article 'The Hereditary Nature of Crime', published in the* Journal of Mental Science, *1870. They are an example of the then prevalent theory of 'degenerationism', a kind of reverse evolution.*

'In which respects?'

'He is of less than average height; his skull is misshapen; his ears are abnormally large and pendulous. The eyes are small and close-set, and, as any observer can see, his brow is heavy and protruding. The skin is pallid and unhealthy, although this I would attribute to a deficiency of diet, rather than to any hereditary factors.'

'And in your investigation into whether the prisoner should be regarded as a criminal through heredity, did you undertake any enquiries beyond this physical examination?'

'I did. In your company, I travelled to the prisoner's domicile in the village of Culduie in Ross-shire.'

'And why did you feel it necessary to carry out this journey?'

'As I believe I stated at the time, if one finds that one's glass of water is foul, one must check the well.'

The Lord Justice-Clerk here intervened to request that the psychiatrist explain what he meant by this figure of speech.

'I mean simply,' said Mr Thomson, 'that one cannot ascertain whether an individual's characteristics have been passed to him by heredity merely from a physical examination. One must also check the source from which he has issued.'

Mr Sinclair: 'And what were the findings of your visit to Culduie?'

'The inhabitants there are generally of low physical stock, small in stature and generally unattractive in appearance, this no doubt engendered by the prevalence of inter-breeding attested to by the high incidence of certain family names in the area. The living conditions of the prisoner and his family I found quite unfit for human habitation, their hovel – I would hesitate to call it a home – lacking ventilation or sanitation and being shared with livestock. The father, with whom I conversed for some minutes, I found to be dull-witted to the point of idiocy. The prisoner's mother died in childbirth, a likely indicator in our modern era of some congenital frailty. The prisoner's sister had committed suicide, which is suggestive of some infirmity of mind running in this unfortunate clan. I did not have the opportunity to examine the younger siblings of the accused, those having been taken away to be cared for elsewhere. In summation, I would say without hesitation that the prisoner is derived from substandard physical stock.'

'So you would conclude that he belongs to the hereditary criminal class which you previously described so eloquently?'

'I am quite conscious, given the defence which you are putting forward in this case, that you wish me to answer in the affirmative. However, while the prisoner bears a certain resemblance to the urban criminal brood and this is undoubtedly due to his low breeding, I would not classify him as a member of the criminal classes; that is those classes who are born into crime and over whom crime exerts an irresistible pull.'

At this point, Mr Sinclair 'gave every indication that the rug had been forcefully yanked from beneath his feet'. In a somewhat faltering fashion, he asked Mr Thomson to account for his conclusion.

'It is quite straightforward, Mr Sinclair. One must look for the causes of crime not only in the hereditary material of the criminal, but also in his environment. While to educated men like ourselves, the Highland settlement might seem a squalid shanty, it is a paradise compared to the slums inhabited by the urban villain. The air is clean and free-flowing and, while the population lives in poverty, the vast majority of people labour honestly on the land or in some other low work. Petty thievery and swindling is to a great degree unknown in these parts. Thus the individual, no matter how base in their physical make-up or limited their mental capacity, is not brought up or nurtured in an atmosphere of criminality. The prisoner here may have been born into a life which would make a civilised man baulk, but he was not born into crime.'

There was a pause in proceedings while Mr Sinclair consulted with his assistant. Mr Gifford, it was reported, 'leaned back in his seat, and, had it not been unseemly to do so, would likely have rested his feet on the table before him'. Those in the public gallery, perhaps not yet fully grasping the significance of the exchange, whispered among themselves. The Lord Justice-Clerk seemed content to allow a moment's hiatus, before he asked Mr Sinclair if he had concluded his examination of the witness.

The advocate indicated that he had not and hastily put his next question to the witness: 'We have heard the testimony of Dr Hector Munro, a general practitioner, who stated that the prisoner exhibits none of the normal outward markers of insanity or imbecility. Would you agree with this assessment?'

'I would.'

'But would you also agree that it is possible for a person who does not exhibit such signs to be regarded as insane?'

'I would, yes.'

'How could this be?'

'Over these last decades our understanding of the functioning – or dysfunctioning – of the mind has been greatly augmented by the labours of my continental and English colleagues, such that there is now a general acceptance in the field of Criminal Anthropology of the condition of moral insanity, or "mania without delirium" as it is sometimes termed.'

'Could you describe what is meant by this condition?'

'Briefly put, it consists of a morbid perversion of the affections without any concomitant impairment of the intellectual faculties. Thus an individual might appear to be fully cognisant of reality and entirely rational in his discourse, and yet be entirely without the moral sense. This is manifested by the habitual nature of the petty criminal who is quite powerless to refrain from thievery and, in the higher criminal – those guilty of murder, ravishment or infanticide – of a complete absence of remorse. The morally insane are entirely incapable of resisting their violent or criminal urges. These unfortunates are distinguished by the prevalence of malicious feelings, which often arise at the most trivial provocation. They see enmity where none exists and indulge themselves in great fantasies of revenge and mischief; fantasies which they are then powerless to resist acting upon.'

'Would you thus aver that such individuals are not responsible for the deeds which they commit?'

'I cannot speak to the legal point of view, but from the perspective of the student of Criminal Psychology, they cannot be regarded as responsible in the normal way, for such individuals are born – for whatever reason – without the moral sense. They do not have within their make-up the normal checks and balances of civilised men and women. As such they cannot be regarded as fully responsible for their actions. They are moral imbeciles and no more culpable for their condition than a cretin is for his.'

At this point, the Lord Justice-Clerk intervened to prompt Mr Sinclair to progress his examination of the witness from these 'no doubt fascinating' generalities to the present case. Mr Sinclair acquiesced, although not without first remarking on the necessity of acquainting the jurymen with current thinking in the field of Criminal Psychology.

'Now,' he continued, 'the court has been read a statement in which the prisoner freely declares himself to be of sound mind. In your long experience of dealing with the criminal population, is it possible that a person who might make such a statement could still be regarded as insane?'

'Quite possible, yes,' replied Mr Thomson.

'How could that be so?'

'If a prisoner is labouring under some delusion, that delusion is as real to him as this court-room is to us. If a person is insane, he is, by definition, unable to recognise himself as such.'

'I see,' said Mr Sinclair, pausing to allow the jury time to absorb this statement. 'With that in mind, what value would you place on the prisoner's own declaration about his state of mind?'

'None whatsoever.'

'"None whatsoever",' Mr Sinclair repeated with a meaningful look to the jury.

The Lord Justice-Clerk here intervened: 'For the sake of clarity, Mr Thomson, is it your evidence, that the prisoner is insane?'

'My evidence is merely that if the prisoner *were* insane, he would not be aware of the fact. Indeed, were he to express the idea that he was insane, it would imply the opposite, since such a view would imply a degree of self-knowledge entirely absent from those not in possession of their reason.'

The Lord Justice-Clerk conferred for a moment with Lord Jerviswoode and then indicated that Mr Sinclair should proceed with his examination. He thanked him and continued. 'Now, Mr Thomson, you have examined the prisoner with a view to ascertaining the state of his mind, have you not?'

'I have.'

'And what form did this examination take?'

'I conversed with him at length on the subject of his crimes.'

'And what were your findings?'

'The prisoner is certainly of reasonable intelligence and he displayed a grasp of language exceeding what would be expected of one of such low breeding. To a large extent he conversed freely with me and without apparent discomfort. In common with the higher rank of criminal I have described, he showed no remorse for his acts; indeed, I would venture to say that he displayed a perverse pride in admitting them.'

'And would you say that this is characteristic of those individuals suffering from the condition of moral insanity?'

'This behaviour is indeed common to the moral imbecile, but it does not in itself signify moral insanity.'

'In your answer to my previous question, you described the morally insane as ...' – he here read from a note handed to him by his assistants – '... harbouring "malicious feelings, which often arise at the most trivial provocation".'

'Yes.'

'Now, we have heard here in evidence testimony describing the provocations caused to the prisoner and his family by the deceased Mr Mackenzie.'

'Indeed.'

'Whether one regards these provocations as trivial or otherwise, would you regard the prisoner's desire to avenge himself against Mr Mackenzie as indicative of this condition of moral insanity?'

'If one was to accept the prisoner's own version of events, then one could reasonably conclude that he was labouring under this condition, yes.'

This 'being a point of utmost significance', the Lord Justice-Clerk asked the witness to clarify his answer.

Addressing himself directly to the judge, Mr Thomson continued. 'It is quite commonplace in many disciplines, my own included, for ideas to become accepted as fact merely by virtue of being oft-repeated. In the present case, I fear that a certain narrative – namely, that the prisoner committed these acts in order to deliver his father from what he perceived to be the oppressive acts of Mr Mackenzie – has, through force of repetition, been unthinkingly accepted by the court and various witnesses. And yet this story is entirely dependent on the statements of a solitary witness: the prisoner himself. I, myself, see no particular reason to accept that version of events, or at least not to subject it to thorough scrutiny.'

The Lord Justice-Clerk: 'And have you subjected it to such scrutiny?'

'I have.'

'And what is your opinion?'

'My opinion is that there is no reason to believe the words of an individual who, by his own admission, has committed the most sanguinary deeds. And furthermore, that an alternative explanation provides a more plausible account of his actions.'

Mr Sinclair was by this time unable to conceal his anxiety. He moved to interrupt the judge's line of questioning, but was immediately silenced.

The Lord Justice-Clerk: 'And do you have such an explanation?'

'I do,' said Mr Thomson.

'Then I would ask you to share it with the court.'

'My view is based on inconsistencies and omissions in the account the prisoner repeated both to Mr Sinclair and to myself. Specifically, these inconsistencies regard the injuries inflicted on Flora Mackenzie, which, to my mind, speak of an altogether different motive for the crimes committed. It would be my contention that when the prisoner embarked on his bloody project, his true purpose was not to avenge himself on Mr Mackenzie, but on this gentleman's daughter, who, as we have heard, rejected his lewd advances towards her. In this account, Roderick Macrae was driven not by a quasi-noble desire to protect his father, but by his sexual urges towards Miss Mackenzie. I would thus contend that the prisoner set out in full knowledge that Mr Mackenzie was not at home and proceeded to violate his daughter in the most depraved way. Then, disturbed in his actions, a struggle ensued resulting in Mr Mackenzie's death.'

There were a few moments of silence, followed by an outbreak of whispered commentary from the gallery. The judge struck his gavel repeatedly to restore order. Mr Sinclair appeared quite lost.

The Lord Justice-Clerk: 'And why should one believe this version of events over the one previously given?'

'Clearly I was not present when these deeds were committed,' Mr Thomson continued, 'but the injuries inflicted on Miss Mackenzie are entirely inconsistent with the motive described by the prisoner. Furthermore, when I questioned the prisoner in his cell, it was only at the mention of these injuries that he exhibited any sign of anxiety. A fissure appeared in the persona he had presented to the world.'

The Lord Justice-Clerk then looked to the crestfallen Mr Sinclair to continue his examination. The judge, no doubt conscious of the gravity of the witness's statements, allowed him some moments to gather his thoughts. After some consultation with his associate, Mr Sinclair continued.

'Were we to accept such a version of events, would it not speak even more profoundly of a loss of reason than the version that has previously been put forward?'

Mr Thomson gave the advocate a thin smile, aware that he was endeavouring to salvage his case from the implications of his testimony. 'It may be that in a straightforward case of a sexually motivated attack, one may or may not deem the offender, in his inability to control his base urges, not to be fully responsible for his actions. This case, however, is distinguished not by the nature of the crime itself, but by the dissembling nature of the perpetrator's statements after the fact. Had he admitted outright to the motives for his attack, he might, as you say, be deemed morally insane, as he would not have known that the acts he had committed were wrong. However, in fabricating an alternative explanation – an explanation which seeks to cloak his actions in a guise of righteousness – the perpetrator betrays his knowledge of the shameful nature of his real objective. It is the concealment of his true motives for these murders which reveals his knowledge that what he did was wrong. Those unfortunate persons who labour under the condition of moral insanity, are entirely unable to distinguish right from wrong. They sincerely believe whatever foul deeds they commit to be justified. In the present case, however, the motive claimed by the accused speaks not only of a desire to obscure the true purpose of his attack, but of an ability to deceive and dissemble which is not present in those whom one would deem insane.'

'If, however,' said Mr Sinclair, in a valiant attempt to rescue his case, 'the version of events given by the accused, in the immediate aftermath of the assault, was accurate, you would judge him to be insane?'

'I would.'

'And since neither you nor any other witness was present at the attack, you cannot say with any certainty that the prisoner's account is any less true than the one you have put forward.'

'You are quite correct, sir, to point out that I was not present. However, the version of events I have presented accords more accurately with the physical evidence of the case. Had the defendant's motives been as he has claimed, there would have been no reason to inflict such dreadful injuries on the unfortunate Miss Mackenzie. Even if he had felt the need to subdue her before lying in wait for her father to return, a blow to the head to render her unconscious would have been sufficient. Instead, he chose to wickedly defile her. I do not see any relation in this action to his professed desire to deliver his father from the tribulations he had supposedly endured at the hands of Mr Mackenzie.'

'But you must admit that another interpretation of the

prisoner's actions is possible?'

'Other interpretations may be possible, but they do not properly account for the facts of the case.'

At this point Mr Sinclair resumed his seat and it was necessary for the Lord Justice-Clerk to ask if he had concluded his questioning. The Crown declined the opportunity to examine the witness and Mr Thomson was excused. The court was adjourned until the afternoon, when the closing statements would be put to the jury.

The Crown summation did not last more than an hour and was delivered by Mr Gifford with 'an air of complacency, which some jury members might have felt quite alienating'. The Solicitor-General asked that the jury attend only to the facts of the case. Roderick Macrae had carried out his acts in a pre-meditated manner – evidenced by the fact that he had gone armed to the Mackenzie home – and killed three blameless individuals in a 'frenzied act of the utmost brutality'.

'Mr Sinclair will try to pull the wool over your eyes,' he said. 'He will attempt to portray his client as an imbecile, given to talking to himself and hearing voices in his head.' He reminded them that 'while the prisoner might occasionally have been given to eccentric behaviour, not a single witness – excepting Aeneas Mackenzie – has been willing to testify that he was insane. And Mr Mackenzie's opinion, for what it was worth, appeared to be based on no more than an understandable dislike of the prisoner and the fact that he sometimes laughed inappropriately. I would put it to you, gentlemen, that if that were all that was required as a diagnosis of insanity, we would all be in the asylum. Instead, I would suggest that far greater weight be placed on the evidence of Mrs Carmina Murchison, who testified that when she conversed with Roderick Macrae only minutes before he committed his crime, he was, in her words, "perfectly rational".'

'We have listened,' he continued, 'to an entertaining dialogue between Mr Thomson and Mr Sinclair regarding the motives for these crimes and their implications as to the state of mind of the accused. Nonetheless, fascinating as their discussion undoubtedly was, they are dancing on the head of a pin.'

He then re-counted the various incidents which had occurred between Mr Mackenzie and the prisoner's father, culminating in the eviction of the Macrae family from their home. 'It was this that provided the motive for the defendant's actions; the motive but not the justification. We have heard also that the defendant harboured some romantic feelings towards Flora Mackenzie, feelings he expressed in the grossest manner, and perhaps his rejection by her contributed to the enmity he felt towards the Mackenzie family. It may be true that we do not know – that we cannot know – the true motives for this attack, but, gentlemen, it matters not.'

Mr Gifford then took pause before delivering his final remarks. 'I would remind you of the facts: Roderick Macrae went forearmed to the house of Mr Mackenzie with the intention to kill, and kill he did. The prisoner himself, as we have heard from numerous witnesses, has made no attempt to exonerate himself from blame and nor should you. And if you harbour any doubts as to his sanity, we have heard from not one but two experienced specialists, both far more qualified than you or I to pass judgement on this matter. We heard first from Dr Hector Munro, a man of great experience in dealing with the criminal population and with demonstrable knowledge of the signs of insanity. His verdict: not only is Roderick Macrae fully in possession of his reason, he is "among the most articulate and intelligent prisoners" the doctor has examined.

'We have been privileged to hear also from Mr James Bruce Thomson, who you must bear in mind was the defence's own witness; a man whose expertise in this field is indisputable. And his conclusion? That Roderick Macrae is fully in possession of his reason and no more than a wicked and dissembling individual.

'Finally, we have the declaration of the prisoner himself, offered under no duress: "I am of sound mind." Gentlemen, the only person in this court-room who believes – or professes to believe – the prisoner to be insane is my colleague, Mr Sinclair. But this belief flies in the face of the evidence presented to the court.'

The jury, Mr Gifford concluded, would be derelict in their duty if they returned any verdict other than guilty of each of three charges before them.

When Mr Sinclair rose to make his closing remarks to the jury, it was not with the air of a beaten man. He had, wrote Mr Philby, 'rallied commendably from his humiliation at the hands of his own witness, and if there is an award for those who most zealously defend lost causes it should be awarded to the doughty advocate'.

'Gentlemen, as my learned colleague has stated, the facts of this tragic case are not in question,' he began, resting his hand on the partition of the jurymen's benches. 'The defence does not dispute that the unfortunate victims died at the hand of the prisoner. What is at issue here are not the bare facts of the case, but the contents of a man's mind. I would aver that there are not three victims in this case, but four; the fourth being the wretched individual who has sat before you these three days. And who is this individual? A young man of a mere seventeen years; a hard-working crofter with a deep attachment and loyalty to his family. We have heard how deeply changed he was by the tragic death of his beloved mother, and how since that time his family have existed under a cloak of gloom. We have heard from the prisoner's own father, the father to whom he is so devoted, that he regularly beat him with his fists. We have heard from his neighbours, Carmina and Kenneth Murchison, that he was in the habit of conducting animated conversations with himself, conversations which ceased whenever a third party drew near, a fact which perhaps speaks of the disturbing nature of the thoughts to which he was giving voice. Mr Murchison testified that the prisoner appeared to "exist in a world of his own". Mr Aeneas Mackenzie was more forthright. Roderick Macrae, he testified, was regarded as the village idiot; an imbecile; an individual whose behaviour was often incongruous with his surroundings. I suspect that if other witnesses have been more reluctant to brand the prisoner insane, this is due only to the tolerance and good nature of the residents of Culduie. Mr Mackenzie in his blunt way was only giving voice to what everyone thought. We have heard too how

Roderick Macrae was given to violent swings of mood and eccentric behaviour. By any measure, he was not of sound mind. And when Lachlan Mackenzie, in his newly acquired role of village constable, took to abusing his power to persecute – for there can be no other word to describe his actions – to *persecute* Roderick's family, this disturbed young man was pushed beyond the edge of reason. At the very end of his tether, Roderick set out to kill Lachlan Mackenzie and in carrying out this terrible project, claimed the lives of two innocent bystanders.

'These were dreadful acts, of that there is no question. But it is what happened in the aftermath of these acts which speaks to the state of Roderick Macrae's mind. Did he behave as you or I would behave? As any sane person would? Did he attempt to flee, or to deny responsibility for the acts he had committed? He did not. He quite calmly gave himself up to capture and openly admitted what he had done. He expressed no remorse. And at no point since has he wavered from this stance.

'Gentlemen, you must ask yourselves why he behaved in this way. The answer can only be that in his own mind he did not believe – he *does* not believe – he had done anything wrong. In the mind of Roderick Macrae the acts he committed were a just and unavoidable reaction to the harassment of his family. Of course, in this he is wrong. Every man and woman in this court,' – he here gestured grandly around the room – 'can see that what he did was wrong. But Roderick Macrae cannot. And herein lies the crux of the case. Roderick Macrae no longer knew right from wrong. In order for a crime to be committed there must be a physical act – which is not here in dispute – but there must also be a mental act. The perpetrator of the act must know that what he was doing was wrong. And Roderick Macrae did not know.

'Now, you will have listened intently, as you should, to the evidence of the learned Mr Thomson. He speculated – I shall not shy away from it – that the true object of Roderick Macrae's assault was not Lachlan Mackenzie, but his daughter, Flora. But I would put it to you, I would put it to you strongly, that Mr Thomson's

opinion of this detail of the case is nothing more than speculation. What would it entail to believe that he is correct? It would
require us to believe that in the immediate aftermath of his assault
– in the very moments after the commission of three bloody murders – Roderick was able to fabricate a falsified explanation for
what he had done. It is inconceivable that any sane person could
have the self-possession to do such a thing.'

Mr Sinclair paused, placing a finger to his lips and casting his
eyes towards the ceiling, as if he was himself in the process of
thinking this question through, before continuing.

'One might contend that the accused had concocted this
story in advance of his actions, that he went to the Mackenzie
home to kill Flora, but intended afterwards to claim that he had
gone there with the purpose of killing her father. But there is
a fatal flaw in this narrative: Roderick did not know and could
not know that Lachlan Mackenzie would return home and disturb
him in his actions. To give credence to Mr Thomson's version of
events requires the most convoluted thinking, and, I would aver,
a complete disregard for logic. Instead, all the evidence presented
here in court points to the fact that the prisoner intended to kill
Lachlan Mackenzie, an act which, in his own disturbed mind, was
just and righteous. The fact that in the commission of this deed,
he also took the lives of Flora Mackenzie and Donald Mackenzie,
a mere child, speaks eloquently of the alienation of reason he
experienced. Mr Thomson quite correctly drew your attention to
the horrible injuries inflicted on the person of Flora Mackenzie,
but I would ask you, are these the actions of an individual in possession of his reason? Quite clearly, gentlemen, they are not. And
if one accepts the view – the view to which all the evidence points
– that Roderick Macrae killed Lachlan Mackenzie out of an irresistible urge to avenge himself for the ills done to his family, then
you must agree with Mr Thomson that Roderick Macrae was not
in possession of his reason, that he was suffering from "mania
without delirium" or "moral insanity" and thus cannot be deemed
to be responsible in law for his actions.

'It is for this reason that I ask you to return a verdict of not guilty in this case. There is an onerous responsibility on your shoulders. But you must act in accordance with the law and not be swayed by any reasonable and human feelings of revulsion towards these dreadful acts. At the time of the commission of these crimes Roderick Macrae was suffering from an absolute alienation of reason and, for this reason, he must be acquitted.'

It was, wrote Mr Philby, 'a bravura performance, delivered with great aplomb. No one present could doubt that the prisoner had received the ablest and most rigorous defence and that the finest spirit of justice is thriving beyond the boundaries of Scotland's metropolitan hubs.' As he resumed his seat, Mr Sinclair dabbed his brow with a handkerchief and received a clap on the shoulder from his assistant. From across the aisle, Mr Gifford offered a low bow of his head intended to convey his professional appreciation.

The Lord Justice-Clerk allowed a few moments of hubbub, before he brought the court to order. He commenced to charge the jury at three o'clock and spoke for some two hours. 'His summation,' wrote Mr Philby, 'was a model of even-handedness and a credit to the Scotch legal system.' After the customary introductory remarks and praising counsel for the manner in which they had conducted the case, he explained to the jury that 'in order to return a verdict of guilty, in regard to any of the three charges contained in this indictment, there are four things of which you must be satisfied upon the evidence. In the first place, that the deceased died by the blows and injuries described; in the second place, that these blows were wilfully administered for the purpose of destroying life; third, that it was the prisoner in the dock who so administered these blows; and, if you are satisfied on these points, in the fourth place, that the prisoner was in possession of his reason at the time when he committed these acts. If the evidence is defective in any one of these particulars, the prisoner is entitled to an acquittal; but if, on the other hand, you are satisfied of these four things, there remains nothing for you but the stern and painful duty of conviction.'

There was, of course, little dispute over the first three points, but as was his duty in law, the Lord Justice-Clerk proceeded to recount over the next hour or so, the evidence first of the medical witnesses, then of those villagers who had seen or spoken to the accused in the aftermath of the crimes.

He then turned to the Special Defence of Insanity. 'The test you must apply,' he said, 'is that a person may be found to be insane, if at the time of the act, or acts, he was labouring under such a defect of reason or from a disease of the mind, that he did not know the nature and quality of the acts he was committing, or that he did not know what he was doing was wrong. It is not for you, or for I, gentlemen, to question the validity or not of these guidelines. These are the rules in law and this is the assessment which you must make in this case.'*

'We have heard in the course of this trial from a number of witnesses who have known the prisoner for his whole life, and their accounts of his character are entitled to form part of your consideration. In particular, we heard evidence from Mrs Carmina Murchison and her husband, Kenneth Murchison. Both of these witnesses are to be commended for the clear and sober accounts of the most distressing aspects of this case. And both of these witnesses testified to the prisoner's habit of appearing to converse with himself in an unusual manner. We do not, however, know the contents of these conversations, and while this behaviour can rightly be seen as eccentric, it is not adequate, in itself, to regard the prisoner as deprived of his reason. On the other hand, you may regard this behaviour as a fragment – though no more than that – in a larger picture which might, in totality, add up to a picture of insanity. We have also heard the testimony of the victims' relative, Mr Aeneas Mackenzie, who was forthright in his view that the prisoner was not of sound mind. However, you are entitled to ask yourselves whether his evidence might be tainted by the understandable feelings of anger he clearly felt towards

---

* *This is a summary of the M'Naghten Rules, which had been the accepted test of insanity for criminal cases in both English and Scottish courts since 1843.*

the prisoner. You must also consider the intemperate manner in which his evidence was given, and pay heed to the fact that Mr Mackenzie is in no way qualified to pass judgement on the sanity or otherwise of the prisoner. As such, Mr Mackenzie's statements should be treated with caution. However, as with the evidence of the other residents of Culduie, it is for you to decide what, if any, importance should be placed on his testimony.'

The Lord Justice-Clerk then moved on to consider the evidence of the prisoner behaving in an unpredictable or eccentric manner. He summarised the incidents that took place during the deerstalking party and with Flora Mackenzie on the day of the Gathering. He was dismissive of both. The first, he said, 'cannot be regarded as more than an act of silliness on the part of an immature young man, aged a mere fifteen years at this time.' In the second, he continued, 'the dual roles of youthful attachment and the effects of alcohol – to which the prisoner was unaccustomed – should not be overlooked.' It was a matter for the jury to evaluate the importance of these incidents, but the judge cautioned against giving them undue weight in their deliberations.

He then turned to the evidence of the two expert witnesses. 'Both sides in this case,' he began, 'have called witnesses who are experts in their field, either through study or through experience, and both these witnesses have passed judgement on the critical matter of the sanity or otherwise of the prisoner. You are obliged to give full weight to the opinions of both of these witnesses, but you are not required to agree with them. If you choose to disregard the evidence of one or either of these witnesses, you should do so only after the fullest consideration and with good reason.

'Dr Hector Munro, called by the Crown, is a medical doctor of long experience both in general practice and at Inverness gaol, where by his own reckoning he has examined many hundreds of prisoners. Dr Munro conversed at length with the prisoner and found him to be "one of the most intelligent and articulate prisoners" he had examined. He enumerated various indicators of insanity and stated that he found none of these present in the prisoner. In view of his experience in dealing with the criminal population and his demonstrable knowledge of diseases of the mind, Dr Munro's opinion deserves to be treated with proper consideration.'

The Lord Justice-Clerk then turned to the evidence of Mr Thomson, 'a man of the highest standing in the field of Criminal Psychology. It was also the opinion of Mr Thomson that the prisoner was not insane and was cognisant of the wrongful nature of the actions which he committed. Now, while this opinion must, like that of his colleague Dr Munro, be afforded the fullest weight in your deliberations, it is my duty to evaluate his reasons for reaching this conclusion. This is of particular consequence because Mr Thomson's opinion rests on a distinct interpretation of the facts of the case, an interpretation distinct from that put forward by the Crown. Mr Thomson contended that the prisoner went to the Mackenzie household not with the goal of murdering Lachlan Mackenzie, but with the intention of harming his daughter, Flora, for whom, we have heard, the prisoner had a strong attachment. Mr Thomson supported this view with reference to the obscene injuries inflicted on Miss Mackenzie's person, injuries which, in his view, would not have been inflicted had Miss Mackenzie merely been an incidental victim in this crime. Moreover, what convinced Mr Thomson that the prisoner was not labouring under what we have heard called "moral insanity" was evidenced by the fact that in various statements the prisoner asserted that his motive had been to kill Lachlan Mackenzie. This disingenuous stance, Mr Thomson insisted, illustrated that the prisoner knew what he had done was wrong and can thus not be regarded as morally insane.

'Gentlemen, these are complex issues about which you must reach your own conclusions. But I must introduce a note of caution. Mr Thomson's opinion rests on a single piece of evidence – the nature of the injuries suffered by Miss Mackenzie – and his interpretation of the motives for inflicting these injuries. But this interpretation is no more than that. It is not fact. Mr Thomson was not a witness to the crimes and you are entitled to consider other interpretations of the evidence you have heard; in particular those parts of the evidence which suggest that the actions of Mr Mackenzie provided the prisoner with the motive for his assault. If you choose to disagree with Mr Thomson's interpretation, you are entitled to consider his view that, if the true target of the prisoner's assault was indeed Mr Mackenzie, he may, in view of his subsequent behaviour, be regarded as suffering from an alienation of reason.'

The Lord Justice-Clerk here gave pause as if to allow the jurymen to digest this complex section of his summation.

'However,' he continued, 'even were you to disagree with Mr Thomson's view, this must be set against the totality of the evidence that has been put before you. It is not enough for you to think that no man could commit such heinous acts and be deemed to be of sound mind. Sane men can and do commit such crimes, and the mere fact of committing such an act does not, in itself, place an individual outside the boundaries of reason. Regardless of your feelings in this matter, that is not the test in law. Your verdict must be reached solely through a dispassionate assessment of the evidence which has been presented to you in this court.'

The Lord Justice-Clerk concluded by reminding the jury of the solemnity of their task. 'The charges before this court are of the very gravest nature and a guilty verdict will result in a capital sentence.' He then thanked the jurymen for their close attention throughout the trial and charged them with delivering a verdict only after solemn consideration of the evidence.

The verdict

As it was by then after four o'clock, the Lord Justice-Clerk instructed the jury that if they had not reached their verdict by seven o'clock, they would be returned to the inn for the night and would resume their deliberations in the morning. He cautioned them that this constraint of time must form no part of their consideration and reminded them once more of the solemn nature of the task with which they were charged.

Roddy was taken downstairs and the court officials vacated the chamber. Not wishing to risk missing the climactic moment of the trial, those in the public gallery remained in their places, arguing among themselves with newly acquired legal expertise about the niceties of the case. The more worldly reporters retired *en masse* to the appropriately named Gallows Inn on Gordon Terrace, having first pressed shillings into the hands of waiting boys to fetch them if the bell was rung. Great quantities of wine and ale were ordered and drunk with alacrity, the presumption being that the jury would not be long in returning its verdict. The consensus was that, despite the valiant efforts of his advocate, Mr Thomson's evidence had condemned the unfortunate prisoner to the gibbet. Only John Murdoch departed from the notion that the verdict was a foregone conclusion. His southern colleagues, he explained, overlooked the empathy the jurymen might feel towards an ill-used crofter. The resentment caused by centuries of ill treatment of the Highlander was keenly felt, and in Roderick Macrae, they might see an individual who had revolted against the vindictiveness of the powers-that-be. Mr Philby listened with interest to the Nairnshireman's opinions, but argued that the jury could not allow such sentiments, no matter how valid, to colour their thinking. Others merely derided Murdoch, arguing that his radical views had blinded him to the facts of the case.

As the clock on the wall of the inn moved towards half past six, the mood altered, however. Clearly the members of the jury had found something to discuss. Then at ten to seven, the boy-messengers burst in: the bell had been rung. The reporters scrambled for the door, throwing coins on the table as they went. They received an admonishing stare from the Lord Justice-Clerk as they were admitted to the press box. The court-room was in any case already in a tumult of anticipation. After silencing the room, the judge warned in the sternest terms against any disruptions to proceedings. Roddy was then brought up, his demeanour, wrote Mr Philby, 'barely altered from his first appearance, although his head perhaps sat more heavily on his shoulders'. The jury was then brought in and the foreman, a tanner named Malcolm Chisholm, rose.

The Clerk of the Court asked if they had reached a verdict.

'We have not,' replied Mr Chisholm.

This statement was greeted with as great an uproar as an acquittal, and it required the macers' expulsion of two individuals from the gallery for order to be restored.

The Lord Justice-Clerk commended the jury for the earnestness with which they were treating their task and instructed them to re-convene in the jury-room at ten o'clock the following morning, adding that they should refrain from any dialogue about the case until that time.

The newspapermen once again decamped to the Gallows Inn, where the wine flowed 'like the River Ness in spate'. Mr Philby later reflected that 'the verdict which would only a short time before have seemed the most astonishing reversal, now seemed a great deal more likely'. If the jury had seeds of doubt in their minds, his logic went, these could only germinate overnight. He spent much of the evening in discussion with John Murdoch, who despite his previous statements, did not expect the verdict to be in the defendant's favour. 'Up here, we are too used to cowering before the authorities to go against the Crown,' he told Mr Philby. In any case, even if the prisoner were to 'jouk the gibbet', a lifetime's confinement in the General Prison under the supervision of Mr Thomson would be a dubious reward.

The evening degenerated into carousing, and Mr Philby confessed that he had 'too freely taken advantage of the Highland hospitality', so much so, that when roused by his landlady the following morning, he had no need to even re-tie his boots.

The public gallery was opened at ten o'clock. The fact that there was no more evidence to be heard had done nothing to diminish the numbers that gathered. Those who failed to gain entry remained outside the court building, wishing to be among the first to hear news of the verdict. Mr Philby and his colleagues loitered in the corridors of the court, nursing their hangovers with hipflasks. In the event, they did not have long to wait. At quarter past eleven, the bell was rung for the second time. Before the arrival of the jury, the Lord Justice-Clerk warned that he would not hesitate to empty the court-room if necessary, and, as if in deference to the solemnity of the moment, Roddy's arrival was accompanied by an eerie hush. He was quite pale and his eyes were ringed with dark circles. Mr Sinclair, who looked similarly ashen, shook his hand. The jurymen then filed in. Roddy observed them, as if some interest in the proceedings had finally stirred in him. The men had a doleful air about them, as if taking their pews at a funeral. Not one of them met the prisoner's eye. The Clerk of the Court rose and asked if they had reached a verdict. Mr Chisholm replied that they had.

The Lord Justice-Clerk put the question to them:

'How say you, gentlemen, do you find the prisoner guilty or not guilty?'

Mr Sinclair bowed his head.

The foreman replied, 'My lords, in respect of the first count, the jury finds the panel Guilty. In respect of the second count, we find the panel Guilty; and in respect of the third count we find the panel Guilty.'

The court-room remained silent for some moments. Then the Lord Justice-Clerk asked, 'Are your verdicts unanimous?'

'They are by a majority,' the foreman replied, 'of thirteen to two.'

Mr Sinclair placed his head in his hands, then turned to look at his client. Roddy remained motionless in the dock. Nothing happened for a few seconds. There was no reaction from the gallery, as if it was only now the spectators grasped that what they had been watching was no mere pantomime.

The Lord Justice-Clerk thanked the jurors for their diligent attention throughout the proceedings. 'You must,' he said, 'feel no compunction about the verdict you have delivered as it is in accordance with the evidence you have heard. All responsibility lies with the prisoner, whose acts have brought us to this place and the consequences of your judgement are a matter for the Law and the Law alone.'

The Trial

The verdicts were then signed by the judges. Roddy was instructed to stand and the judge donned the black cap.

'Roderick John Macrae, you have been found guilty by the verdict of the jury of the murders charged against you, a verdict which proceeds upon evidence which could leave no disinterested observer in any doubt. You have killed three people, one a small child, another an innocent girl in the flush of youth, and you have inflicted injuries on their persons of the most shocking nature. We have heard, as we should, a great deal of discussion of the motives for these wicked crimes, but having been pronounced guilty, these motives are of no consequence, and there is but a single sentence that can be pronounced. You are condemned to suffer the last penalty of the law. I hope that you will use the short time left to you to repent your actions and make use of the ministers of religion available to you, but I fear, from what I have heard in these proceedings, that you will not do so.'

He then formally pronounced that the prisoner would be executed at Inverness Castle between the hours of eight and ten o'clock on the morning of the 24th of September. He then removed the black cap and added, 'May God have mercy on your soul.'

Epilogue

THE TRIAL OF RODERICK MACRAE ended on Thursday the 9th of September. The following morning Mr Sinclair sought out John Murdoch and presented him with Roddy's manuscript. There was at this time no formal mechanism for appeal in Scots Law and the advocate hoped to enlist Murdoch's assistance in mounting a campaign for the commutation of Roddy's sentence. His logic appears to have been that the publication of Roddy's memoir would lead to a wave of popular support for the condemned man.[*]

Mr Murdoch was sceptical, though not unsympathetic to the advocate's plan, and agreed to read the manuscript and approach the editor of the *Inverness Courier* with a view to printing a series of extracts in the newspaper or a 'Special Edition'. Mr Sinclair left the matter in his hands and spent the weekend drafting a petition to the Lord Advocate, Lord Moncrieff, the highest legal authority in the land.

In his letter, Mr Sinclair made no attempt to claim that his client's conviction was unsafe, or that there was anything improper in the conduct of the trial. Instead, his appeal for clemency was made on openly compassionate grounds. After a perfunctory summary of the particulars of the case, he made his plea:

As both the evidence heard at trial and the prisoner's account attest, Roderick Macrae was driven to the acts of which he has been found guilty by the purposeful and determined persecution of the individual who was to become his principal victim. Sufficient evidence was heard at trial of the eccentric behaviour and mental defects of the accused, for the jury to deliberate into a second day; and the verdict, when it came was by majority, this in itself evidence that it is within the bounds of rationality for a reasonable

---

[*] *Forty years later, albeit in very different circumstances, a petition signed by 20,000 people was instrumental in the overturning of Oscar Slater's death sentence.*

man to take the view that the accused was not of sound mind. And this in the face of the repeated and self-damaging pronouncements made by the prisoner himself; pronouncements, I might add, which do not speak of a rational mind. For what sane man would freely make statements which, if accepted at face value, would consign him to the gallows? That such reasonable doubts about the sanity of my client exist in the minds of the jurymen surely militates against the imposition of the severest penalty of the Law.

During his incarceration, my client applied himself diligently to the production of an account of the events leading up to the crimes (a copy of which I submit for your consideration). In so doing he has demonstrated abilities and an intellectual capacity far in excess of what might be expected of an individual of his education and background. Mr J. Bruce Thomson, Resident Surgeon to the General Prison in Perth, stated in evidence that in his many years' experience of dealing with convicts and madmen, he has never encountered a single prisoner capable of producing any work of literary merit, a judgement which underscores the exceptional nature of Mr Macrae's memoir. To put to death an individual with the sensibility and intelligence to produce an extended literary work, would, I strongly aver, be a cruel and uncivilised act.

In addition, the prisoner's age – a mere seventeen years – and his otherwise unstained character, may also be offered in mitigation. The acts for which Mr Macrae has been found guilty were quite out of character and there is every reason to suppose that, given his exceptional gifts, after a period of incarceration he might live a productive and fruitful life.

If we measure our society by the compassion we extend to all its members, then it must be admitted that in extending such compassion to the most wretched amongst us, we demonstrate our fidelity to the most civilised Christian values. It is in this spirit that I petition your Lordship to extend clemency to the person of Roderick John Macrae.

May it therefore please the Lord Advocate to take this Memorial into his most favourable consideration, and thereafter to advise Her Most Gracious Majesty to exercise her royal prerogative to the effect of commuting the sentence passed upon the prisoner.

> [Signed] Mr Andrew Sinclair esq.
> Solicitor to the prisoner.

Epilogue

The petition was submitted on Monday the 13th of September and on the same day, the *Inverness Courier* printed John Murdoch's article, 'What we have learned from this case'. Murdoch began by reflecting on his experience in the court-room, describing Roddy as 'a forlorn individual, whom to look at one would suppose had no connection to the proceedings around him. Whether this was due to a callous indifference or an alienation of the mind; or whether this attitude was affected or real, I am not qualified to say. But neither am I convinced that entrusting the task of resolving this question to fifteen honest, but equally unqualified, jurors is the most prudent means to serve justice in a case of this character.' Murdoch went on to discuss Roddy's memoir. His account was, he wrote, 'by turns both shocking and affecting, and certainly does not appear to have been written with a view to winning the prisoner's release. Nevertheless, the eloquence and intellect it displays stand in stark contrast to the bloody deeds it ultimately describes; and if nothing else, there seems a madness in this.' Murdoch fell short of directly appealing for the commutation of Roddy's sentence, instead expressing in a general way that the law as it stood was 'inadequate to deal with proceedings of this nature. Our highest legal minds should, with alacrity, reconsider our procedures in relation to cases which hinge on the sanity or otherwise of the accused, and until such a review can be conducted,' he wrote, 'it would be unseemly to send a man to the gallows.'

Mr Murdoch also wrote the same day to Lord Moncrieff and, although the letter has been lost, it is reasonable to assume that it expressed similar sentiments.

On receipt of Mr Sinclair's appeal, the Lord Advocate would have been obliged to communicate with the trial judges and with the General Registrar for Scotland, William Pitt Dundas, but whatever the contents of their correspondence, events quickly took over.

John Murdoch had lodged Roddy's manuscript with a local printer, Alexander Clarke. What appeared, however, was not a complete printing of the 50,000-word document, but a twenty-four-page chapbook comprising the most gruesome and sensational passages. Within days, scores of other, greatly bastardised, versions were printed up and down the country. The most notorious of these was entitled *HIS BLOODY PROJECT: the RAVINGS of a MURDERER*, printed by William Grieve of Glasgow. *His Bloody Project* ran to a mere sixteen pages and consisted of little more than Roddy's description of the murders; his killing of Lachlan Mackenzie's sheep (followed by the line, 'It was at this moment I discovered my taste for cracking skulls, and resolved that I would not be long in indulging it again.'); together with a wholly fictional passage in which Roddy 'wickedly defiled' a twelve-year-old Flora Broad. The pamphlet sold tens of thousands of copies in a matter of days. Various gruesome cartoons, etchings and ballads (most notably *On This Fine Morning, I Killed Three* by Thomas Porter) followed, and rather than becoming a cause célèbre, Roddy became a national bogeyman. The irony that all these productions portrayed Roddy as being quite out of his mind must have been entirely lost on those who devoured them.

In all likelihood, Mr Sinclair's scheme never had any chance of success. There were no legal failings to which he could point, nor could he reasonably argue that the conviction was unsafe in evidence. His hope that the publication of Roddy's memoir would lead to a surge of popular support for his petition was, it must be said, hopelessly naïve. Nonetheless, there was no other course of action open to him and it speaks well of him that he supposed that the public would embrace Roddy as he had.

In any case, the following week, Mr Sinclair received a courteous, but perfunctory reply from Lord Moncrieff stating that 'there being nothing amiss either in evidence or in the conduct of the trial', he was under no obligation to consider an appeal for clemency. 'Such talents that you claim for the accused, whether real or not, can play no part in the consideration of the Law.' And, thus, the capital sentence was confirmed.

Mr Sinclair continued to visit Roddy on a daily basis. He found him in a general state of torpor, with 'no appetite either for food or conversation'. At no point did Roddy bemoan his situation or express any fear about his approaching fate. Nor did he accept the ministrations of the prison chaplain, who entreated him to use the time left to him to reconcile himself to his creator. Despite having the necessary materials available to him, Roddy wrote nothing else, save the following brief letter to his father:

Dear Father,

I am writing in the hope that this letter will find your situation improved. I myself have but a brief time left and do not crave longer in this world than that which is allotted to me. The walls of my cell make for a dreary vista and though I would dearly love to see Culduie once more, if I could hasten my execution I would gladly do so. For the time being, however, I am quite comfortable and you must not concern yourself about my wellbeing, nor lament my passing.

I wish to say that I am sorry for the trouble I have caused, and that I earnestly wish you might have been blessed with a more worthy son.

[Signed]
Roderick John Macrae

The letter was delivered to Culduie on the afternoon of the 22nd of September, but John Macrae never read it, having been found that morning dead in his chair by Carmina Smoke. He was interred next to his wife in the burial ground at Camusterrach. The house and its outbuildings were allowed to fall into a state of disrepair and the land was distributed among the remaining residents of the village. The role of constable was assumed by Peter Mackenzie.

On the 24th of September, the morning of his execution, Roddy's only request was that he might take a turn around the prison yard. This was allowed to him, and, according to Mr Sinclair, he completed his circuits 'quite as if he was entirely elsewhere'. He was then accompanied from his cell by his advocate, a minister of the Church of Scotland and two gaolers. As the party approached the chamber where the execution was to take place,

Epilogue

Roddy's legs gave way beneath him and he had to be dragged the remaining yards by the warders. All necessary preparations had been made and, aside from the hangman, Dr Hector Munro and the Prison Governor were also present. As the hood was pulled over his head, tears streamed from Roddy's eyes. Mr Sinclair hid his face in his hands. Roderick Macrae was pronounced dead at twenty-four minutes past eight o'clock. 'The hanging,' stated the doctor's report, 'was conducted in an exemplary fashion, and no undue suffering was caused to the prisoner.'

Historical Notes and Acknowledgements

In terms of research and inspiration, I owe my greatest debt to five volumes: *Highland Folk Ways* (Routledge, 1961) by I.F. Grant, an entirely indispensible guide to the way of life and traditions of the Scottish Highlands; *The Making of the Crofting Community* (John Donald, 1976) by James Hunter, which is the best book on the historical development of the Highlands I have come across; *Children of the Black House* (Birlinn, 2003) by Calum Ferguson, which offers a more anecdotal history; *The Origins of Criminology: A Reader* (Routledge, 2009) by Nicola Rafter, which introduced me to the writings of J. Bruce Thomson and other pioneers in this field; and finally *I, Pierre Rivière, having slaughtered my mother, my sister and my brother* (Bison Books, 1982), edited by Michel Foucault.

I am also grateful to Applecross historian Iain MacLennan, both for the wealth of information contained in his book, *Applecross and Its Hinterland: A Historical Miscellany* (Applecross Historical Society, 2010) and for his generous responses to my emails. Gordon Cameron, curator of the Applecross Heritage Centre, has been similarly generous with his time and provided me with the text of the song 'Coille Mhùiridh', composed in the 1820s by Donald MacRae. The English translation is, I believe, by Roy Wentworth. The translation of 'Càrn nan Uaighean' was suggested to me by Francis and Kevin MacNeil.

I should also note a debt to the *Sermons* of Reverend Angus Galbraith (1837–1909), which inspired the funeral oration of his namesake in this book. James Galbraith's 'police statement' also paraphrases the words of the Reverend John Mackenzie of the Parish of Lochcarron, who wrote in his 'Statistical Account' of 1840: 'Not farther back than the middle of the last century, the inhabitants of this district were involved in the most dissolute barbarity. The records of presbytery, which commence in 1724, are stained with an account of black and bloody crimes, exhibiting a picture of wildness, ferocity and gross indulgence, consistent only with a state of savagism.'

James Bruce Thomson (1810–1873) was a real person and the articles mentioned in the text can be found online. The theories propounded by Mr Thomson in the novel are closely based on these articles, but his personality and character are the products of my imagination, as is his memoir. The character of John Murdoch is likewise loosely based on the radical reformer (1818–1903) of that name.

In 2013 I won a Scottish Book Trust New Writers Award and I am greatly indebted to this organisation for the fantastic support and encouragement they have given me during the writing of this book. I would also like to thank the always helpful staff of the Mitchell Library in Glasgow and the National Archive of Scotland in Edinburgh.

Despite all the help and advice I have received, I do not claim to be an expert either on the period in which this book is set or on the Highland way of life in general. This is a novel and as such I have taken some liberties with historical fact and, at some points, as novelists do, made stuff up. Needless to say, any inaccuracies, whether by design or error, are entirely my own responsibility.

I am deeply grateful to my publisher, Sara Hunt, for her wonderful enthusiasm, generosity and support throughout the writing of this book. Also to Craig Hillsley for his meticulous and sensitive editing.

On a personal note, this book would not have come into being were it not for the frequent visits I made to Wester Ross both in my childhood and as an adult, and for this gift I am hugely grateful to my parents, Gilmour and Primrose Burnet. I must also thank my great friend and sounding-board-in-chief, Victoria Evans, who is always generous with her time and whose notes are always pertinent and astute.

Finally, to Jen: thank you for your patience, encouragement and for putting up with my sulks. Like Una Macrae, you are the sunlight that nurtures the crops.